R.L. BYRD

Black Coffee

R.L. Byrd PUBLISHING

Published by
R.L. Byrd Publishing, a brand of R.L. Byrd, LLC
PO Box 98334
Atlanta, GA 30359-2034
www.richardleonbyrd.com

Cover Design by WINC Atlanta

The publisher does not have any control over, endorses, or assumes any responsibility for third-party websites or their content.

ISBN: 978-0-9905577-2-2 (PB)
      978-0-9905577-3-9 (HC)
      978-0-9905577-4-6 (EB)

Printed in the United States of America | First Trade Book Edition: June 2012

Reissued: July 2014

Black Coffee

the sequel to

Looking for Sweet Love

www.RichardLeonByrd.com

Acknowledgments

Robert J. Ackerman
Author of *Silent Sons*. I too am a silent son. Thank you for your insight, wisdom, and words. What an eye-opener.

WINC Atlanta and contributing companies
I would like to thank WINC Atlanta (and its support team) for the vision and design of the book cover, book trailer and promotional photographs, and videos for this book: Thank you, Dereck Wallace and DeMarques Coleman (Project Facilitators), Thierry Jones (Photographer/Graphic Designer), Nieshia Deas (Videographer), and Nicole Manley (Makeup Artist). With special thanks to the Boy Next Door (Wardrobe Supplier), Engine 11 Firehouse Tavern (Photo shoot Location), and The Epicurean (Project Caterer).

Dorothea (www.dorotheaonline.com)
"Boy, you're a writer and you need to write," is what she said to me. And true to her words, writing has been the most fulfilling part of my life. Ironic, how, no words can express my deepest gratitude for her insight.

Black Coffee Models
I would like to express my sincere thanks and unending gratitude to the following *Black Coffee* models for their participation in making the *Black Coffee* cover, trailer, and video interview possible:

Davius Billingslea

Chaos

DeMarques Coleman

Thomas Flowers

DeShaun Johnson

Ramon McElrathbey

Willie Melton

Reico Walker

Noted Songwriters and Music Publishers

Dedication

This book is dedicated to all the brothers who have made me who I am today. First and foremost, to Richard Warren Walker, who, like so many fathers, gave me life, and yet was also absent from that life. To my maternal grandfather, Joe L. Byrd, who stepped in and provided that fatherly figure, I needed, until his passing in 1988. And to Roosevelt Blackburn Sr., my stepdad, who took over and embraced me and welcomed me into his world and taught me responsibility, humility, dedication, and unending determination and drive—I miss you man (RIP).

To our neighbors Mr. Ike Kenty and Mr. Henry Reynolds, God bless their resting souls, who beat my behind when I did wrong and sent me home to get another beating for the same wrongdoing. Little did I know, at the time, that they were instilling in me integrity and character. To John Beckham for the free haircuts—from my first, when I was barely a year old, to the last, many, many years later—and the lessons behind them: It's always good to help out your fellowman and neighbor; and it's a good thing to cut your girlfriend's son's hair for free, too.

And to the late Andrew Moses, the uncle who gave me hell growing up. But then that was his way of toughening up all his boys. And I would be remiss if I didn't mention all the countless uncles, cousins, neighbors, schoolteachers, and fraternal brothers (A-Phi-A) who have influenced me along the way.

Last, but definitely not the least, to the ultimate father—my Heavenly Father—for blessing me with not just one, or two, but a multitude of fathers who provided me all the valuable life lessons that have aided me in my journey through life. And with this, I can truly say that I'm a walking testament, that it really was a village, of brothers, that raised a child. May God bless each and every one of you. You're definitely not forgotten.

Contents

1 | Restless, Remembering, Rebirth   1

2 | Bailey's   3

3 | The Road We Travel   14
DK's Journey

4 | My Soul Must Move On   23

5 | The Vessels Emerge   28

6 | DK's Blue Letter   34

7 | The Brothers' Retreat   40
Day 1: Why Are You Here?

8 | The Brothers' Retreat   49
Day 1: Donnell's Breakdown

9 | The Brothers' Retreat   56
Day 1: First Impressions

10 | The Brothers' Retreat   70
Day 2: We Are Silent Sons

11 | Laying It All Out   86

12 | The Brothers' Retreat   90
Day 3: Jessie's Conference Call

13 | **The Brothers' Retreat**   94
     Day 3: Listen, My Dick's Talking

14 | **The Brothers' Retreat**   111
     Day 4: Am I My Brother's Keeper?

15 | **K103.5—*The Brotherhood* Goes on Air**   118

16 | **Sweet V's**   126

17 | **K103.5 ICON Awards**   135

18 | **Get Right Church and Let's Go Home**   142
     Greater Antioch

19 | **The Battle**   147
     The Divas vs. the Brothers

20 | **The Debriefing**   160

21 | **The Plagues**   167

22 | **Brass to Gold**   177

23 | **Miguel's Bachelor Party**   186

24 | **Jessie's Birthday**   192
     You Gonna Make Me Love Somebody Else

25 | **Creep, Creep, Creep**   206

26 | **Something's Got a Hold of Me**   216

27 | ***The Love Forum:* A Special Edition**   226
     Chile! Whatchu Talkin' 'Bout

28 | A Sunday Kinda Love   235

29 | A New Year's Resolution   241

30 | The Final *Brotherhood*   248
Being the Best Men We Can Be

31 | Quentin's Birthday   259

32 | Drama at the House   267

33 | The Drive Home   270

34 | Say You Love Me   277

The Brotherhood

DK "Love" Niles

Michael Todd Crawley

Malcolm Crawley

Dr. Xavier "X" Houston

Quentin "Q" Blakely

Pastor Richard Levine

Kirk "Magic" Wonder

Donnell Carter

Miguel de Souza

Brasselton "Brass" Minyard

We've come a long way but still have miles and miles to go. To all the Michaels, Malcolms, Xs, Pastor Levines, Dr. Houstons, Magics, Quentins, Donnells, Miguels, and Brasses in the world: *Keep the faith, my brothers, and keep forging up that rough side of the mountain.*

We'll get to the mountaintop someday.

Restless, Remembering, Rebirth

Somehow, the things that die, or end within the fall or winter seasons of our lives, are miraculously reborn.

May 16, 2009
Dallas, Texas

*F*our days before spring. Four days before life began to renew itself from the dormancy and dead of winter. DK sat in bed thinking, *DK, what in the world will this day bring?* You know how you just have that funny, if not queasy, feeling about something? Well, Saturday was that day, and strangely enough, he began to notice everything about it. Like the slight overcast that partially stopped the moon's light from shining into his bedroom; or the sixty-six-degree temperature that was good and right for a quiet night's sleep (with the windows open that is), problem was, he just couldn't take his ass to sleep; or how the rain started coming down and splashed onto the windowsill about four-thirty AM or so; or even the Johnny Gill and Stacy Lattisaw cut "Where Do We Go from Here" that played in the background, which made him think about the life and death of his homegirl Melissa Morgan. And although two months and three days had passed since her death, he was still going out of his mind trying to deal with her passing and just didn't know (as Johnny and Stacy's song reminded him) where to go from there. Not only had he lost his partner in crime at K103.5 (and the radio station will never be the same), he also lost the one person who gave him that one-on-one advice about life's little issues. And that laugh. Man, did it bring a smile to his face just thinking about it, and he quietly said to himself, "HA! Boy am I missing that."

But something else was ailling him; throwing him *for a loop*; causing him to get this gut wrenching feeling that something wickedly, terrible, was blowing his way. Something he probably wouldn't be able to get away from (or walk away from) if his stressed-out, depressing, and empty life depended on it. And with his stomach churning and tied in knots, all he could do was sit there, glued to the bed, wringing his hands, thinking—better yet, hoping. *DK . . . man . . . I sure as hell hope all this worrying turns out to be for nothing. And, God, please don't let this have anything to do with my lunch date with Jessie later on today.*

Not only did Jess call him up last Tuesday night, frantic as all hell, with all her screaming, crying and yelling, but she also said that she had something to give him—something about a blue envelope.

"From MELISSA!!?" he asked her repeatedly, trying to make sure he had heard her right.

"Yes, DK—MELISSA!" she confirmed, annoyed all in her voice.

And with the acknowledgement of Melissa's name in his ear—aside from Jessie mentioning the mysterious envelope that she needed to give to him—the second he ended the call, he was nothing more than a zoned-out zombie; walking around for days not able to eat, sleep, or do anything but shake his head and repeat over-and-over-again, "Damn! On top of everything else, this is all I effin' need."

Armed with nothing more than the information Jessie gave him (*Melissa's name*, the *blue envelope*, and meeting her for lunch later in the week) he tortured himself, conjuring up all kinds of crazy shit in his head—not good shit either. His mind was consumed with craziness like: *What in the hell is Melissa writing me for? And most importantly . . . when did dead folk start writing letters? Crazy as that sounds!*

Suddenly, for some reason, he glanced over at the TV as a scene from the movie *The Color Purple* came on. You know the scene where Shug Avery's momma, Momma Avery, is sitting in church—while Shug is at the juke joint—and she, very emphatically, tells the choir to sing "God's Trying to Tell You Something." And as he watched the scene play out, almost to the point of being mesmerized by it (not that he hadn't seen this movie one hundred and one times already), he quietly sat there . . . staring at the TV, wondering: *Is he? Is God trying to tell me something?*

Chapter 2

Bailey's (DK's POV)

*A*fter a full night of worrying my ass off, ill-at-ease and a whole lot of sleepy, I finally dragged my ass out of bed, washed up (hittin' all the hot spots), threw on one of my good old sweat suits (that would be the blue one, that shows that D-thang swinging in them boxers), and started the thirty-mile drive—in a light rain, I might add—to meet Jessie at Bailey's. Damn! Bailey's. It was the first time that I'd been back since Melissa died. I can remember the first time she told me about it, and I can't help but laugh. That crazy girl ran into my office, with her hands on her stomach, all hunched over, talking 'bout, "Ungh-ungh, boo-boo, got your message, and boy, I am not trying to go to Big Jim's Rib Shack today, and definitely not for the third time this week! Ungh . . . UNGH! Not even trying to go there with you, boo. And boy, if I have to shit out one more rib, it is not going to be pleasant up in here! You heard?"

Damn! One thing that I loved about my girl was that she didn't hold anything back. Nada! She told me that a good friend of hers had just opened up a small, but trendy joint, a few blocks down from the radio station (some sort of small-time chef breaking out on his own) and she wanted to go check him out, give him a little support. I looked at her crazy butt, laughing, and said, "Aiight, Lis, we can go check your lil', small-time friend out," although, those ribs were calling my name. *DK, come get us!* But when she said the magic words, "My treat, boy," I was like, *Oh hell, yeah! That's what I'm talking 'bout.* And never giving up a free meal—especially when a sista is paying (now, how often is that?)—we ventured off and pulled up to what had to be, damn near, the busiest place I've been for lunch (especially in Dallas) in quite a while. Hell, just to get into the parking lot alone, we waited damn near ten minutes. (And doesn't it make you mad when you have to pay to park just to get something to eat?) Man, oh man, there were people and cars everywhere, and as soon as we made it into the parking lot and found a place to park (and I put my hard-earned money into that damn pay box), I started noticing that most of the K103.5 crew were either walking out of, or going into Bailey's. That girl! I guess she told everybody about Bailey's grand opening, and if you knew Melissa, you knew that she had the gift of gab and a knack for persuasion. Not only could the girl talk you to death, but she could get you to do just about damn near, anything, for her crazy ass;

3

although I gotta give, my girl, her props on this one. This shit right here, this joint, was just effin' unbelievable!

We made our way through all the madness (walked right up to the front door, skipping all the people waiting in line) and rushed inside where we met this character by the name of Chef Luda (*Luda* was his first name, *Bailey* his last). He stood at the front door, greeting people, talking about some "comment ça va, Lissie," and I looked at him, all frowned up, and said, "Huh? Excuse me. What did you just say?"

Melissa saw the look on my face and threw her hands up as if to say, *Come on, DK, get it together.* She sounded out "Coam-on-sah-vah" and said, "It means, how am I doing, silly." She put her hands on her hips, flashed one of those big-ass smiles (which meant she was up to something), and gave me one of those looks that said, *Watch me work this.*

I smiled and looked in another direction, shaking my head and saying to myself, *Oh Lord, here we go.* All I could do was stand there, with this stupid grin on my face, and watch her do her thing.

"Well, I'm doing just fabulous, Luda. And, boy, you're talking to me like I'm used to that Cajun tongue of yours. That would be a big NOT! But rather than how am I doing, I think the *tea* is, or should be, *how-you-doing?*" Lis turned around and gave me a big wink as she wrapped her arms around Chef Luda's waist and looked up at him with those big puppy-dog eyes.

"You sure you're doing okay, boo-boo?" she asked.

Chef Luda returned the intimate gesture and wrapped his arm around Lis's shoulders and answered, "Well, baby gul, I's doing mighty, mighty fine. 'Bout as fine as dis old man can expect, under da circumstances."

"Oooh! That's good news, Luda. Good news! Lord knows, I'm so happy to hear you're doing fine. And what you talkin' about you being old? PUH-LEASE!"

Chef Luda laughed at Melissa, and she gave him one of those *Don't even try it* looks of hers. "Now, Luda . . . WHEW! You got it smelling too good up in here, and your girl, and my boy here, are starving! By the way, you do know I'm eating for two, don't cha? Yes, yes, your girl is expecting. So get the purse ready, baby. You gone have to loosen up the purse-strings, for sure, for this one. You're paying for three today, boo, and did I mention, WE . . . ARE . . . STARVING? Oooh, what we gots to eat?"

Chef Luda shook his head and grabbed Melissa's crazy butt, engulfing her in a big bear hug, while I stood there looking at them (like an idiot), thinking, *Damn, I'ma have to tune out everything and listen real hard just to understand what this brother is talking about.* As soon as those thoughts cleared my head, Chef Luda answered Melissa, or Lissie as he called her, in that unforgettable Cajun drawl. "Well, I do believe I can fix dat eatin' part. Don't know much 'bout da oda stuff going on in dat belly of yo's, but it sho' is good to see ya! And who's dis here friend you done brought wit cha?" Chef Luda let out a hearty chuckle and extended his hand for me to shake while introducing himself.

"I'm Chef Luda, and yous be?"

"I'm DK Niles, better known as DK Love. Me and Melissa work—"

"Yah. Yah. Da DK from da *DK and Melissa Morning Show*. Boy, you knows, yous a fool on dat there radio. Have me's a-cracking up. Mmm-huh! And you sho' do look familiar too—you sho' do. Humph!" Chef Luda scratched his head and stared at me real hard. "So, Mr. DK—and you too, Ms. Lissie—wha' y'all critters think 'bout da place?"

I said to myself, *Critters! Well, I be damned. First, the nigga interrupts me. And now he has the nerve to be calling somebody—hell, anybody for that matter—a critter.* Up in here looking like the last damn critter, his own damn self. Like the last Spike Lee reject—balding something terrible on top of that. I mean terrible as in patches, yo. Guess he didn't get the memo that sometimes you just gotta let that shit go. And if the Spike Lee–reject look and the balding didn't beat all, dude was blown up a good two hundred pounds or so (hell, we definitely could see where the food was going). Can you believe that shit? My boy Spike would not be pleased! Not pleased at all. I just looked at him (sizing him up, you know how we black people do), shook his hand, and gave him one of those quick and dirty smiles (fake as it was) as he and Melissa started chatting again. While they chatted, I took a quick look around and thought, *Damn, this Negro ain't no effin' joke* (despite that damn critter comment). I asked myself, *What is Melissa talking about? This definitely ain't no small-time chef* (no pun intended). I'm telling you, this place was absolutely *the* shit! And by this time, I was a-scratching and a-itching to get a peek at—and a little taste of—what Bailey's had to offer. And for the first time ever, I forgot all about Big Jim's Rib Shack and those meat-be-falling-off-the-bone ribs.

For starters, on the outside, Bailey's kinda reminded me of New Orleans a little (go figure, right?). The building put you right smack-dab in the middle of the French Quarters with its bright yellow stucco walls and big ole white-trimmed doors and windows. But what really stood out were the full-length shutters, painted a deep green, that were attached to every single window and door of the building. The look definitely said, *Buyer beware! There are no five-dollar lunches being served up in this camp.* And nothing said *Hey, this is a small piece of New Orleans in the big ole heart of Texas* more than Bailey's covered balcony. Man, when your eyes traveled up, they went straight to these red, white, and blue streamers hanging on the blades of at least twenty white ceiling fans—just slowly twirling in the air. I stood there in awe and couldn't help but say "WOW!" because they hung from the bluest ceiling there was; a blue that matched the cloudless Dallas sky perfectly. The balcony's railing (thank God for that), which stopped all the crazies and drunks from falling down to the street below, was made out of this white decorative ironwork that added just the right touch of sophistication and class to the joint. And all of this was topped off by huge—I mean huge—hanging flower baskets, which added that Southern flava. Or as Melissa put it, "That Southern charm, darling. You know, the South just ain't the South without having some sort of flower baskets hanging outside."

And let's not even talk about the location. I was like, "DAAAMMMNNN!" What could be better than being positioned right in the middle of a nice, artsy, mixed-use neighborhood with its blocks and blocks of apartments, shops, bars, and eateries? And if that didn't make your eyes tear up from just being proud of the brother, get this: Bailey's sat right at the end of a V-shaped corner (yes, man, the building was shaped like an effin' *V*), sandwiched between two well-traveled streets appropriately named Biscayne and Bayou. Can you believe that shit? Talk about two stories of prime real estate!

On the inside, Bailey's had a nostalgic feel. We stood behind these huge green wood doors, on a raised wood floor, that had four beautiful inlaid marble steps leading down to the main dining area. The exposed ceiling and ductwork was painted black, the floors were heart pine wood, and the walls were an antique brick. (Gotta give me and the family our props for the architectural background, you feelin' me?)

"DK? . . . DK! Melissa to DK, are you in there? Come back to Momma, baby. Come back to Momma!"

I laughed, trying to play off some of the embarrassment, and jokingly said, "Sorry, Lis—or should I say *critter*? Or maybe even *creaster* from the big ole black pregnant lagoon?" I laughed out loud, which pissed her off, and I attempted to clean it up. "Just kidding, baby girl. You know I *loves* you. All kidding aside, though, I kinda got a little distracted . . . just checking things out, you know?"

"Mmm . . . huh. Not too much, Mr. Distracted—especially on the critter and creaster comments, baby. And word to the wise: You might want to leave the jokes alone. You know I'm from the hood. Alley as I want to be—when I need to be, that is. Don't make this a hood moment, boo. Anywho, speaking of checking things out, Chef Luda is ready to seat us. So get it together, Mr. Niles, and make sure you pay attention, 'cause he's going to give us the fifty-cent tour of the place while taking us to our table. And—"

Before Melissa could finish running that mouth of hers, Chef Luda popped back up and said, "Critters, y'all ready?" This dude with this critter mess! I'm telling you man, I felt the need to get with this cat (after I had eaten, that is) and let him know about the incorrectness of his statements. What's more, I just couldn't stand anybody calling me a critter—that one word just brought up too many bad memories. Anyway, as he walked us to our table, he proudly pointed out the bar to the right, noting its historical value, as it came from one of the great Chitlin' Circuit juke joints (he wouldn't tell us which), and I have to admit, it did give the place a kind of nostalgic feel. As we walked by the bar, Chef Luda pointed out the numerous pictures—all of them autographed—hanging on the walls, which he had collected during his lifetime. I quickly noticed some of the greats, like Lena Horne, Cab Calloway, Eartha Kitt, and Muhammad Ali. I said to myself, *Damn, boy! Go 'head on, with your bad self.* Chef Luda seated us at a table for two, right in front of a small stage at the front of the joint, where there was this sharp female singing R&B and jazz in between the band playing that god-awful Louisiana Zydeco music. He pulled up a chair, motioned to the waitress to come over, and told us what was good on the menu.

"Naw, y'all gotta have some of dat good ole boudin and cracklin' cornbread for sho'. Then we's got the best damn crawfish etoufee west of Lousana, and I got that cinnamon-raisin bread puddin' with dat warm rum sauce fo y'all too."

Melissa said, "Oooooh! No, you don't, Chef Luda." And she started stomping her feet. "No you don't! Oomph, that sho' does sound good, boy."

Lord have mercy, that girl! I couldn't do anything but just shake my head and laugh. Hell, she couldn't help but laugh at her own damn self. While she was laughing and showing all the pearly whites, my girl placed her hands over that big protruding belly of hers and rubbed it round and round—as if to let Chef Luda know that she was good and ready for that free lunch. Then from out of nowhere, we heard an all-too-familiar voice.

"DK Niles and Melissa Morgan? Say it ain't so."

"Judge Hoffanstanter?" questioned Melissa. "Oh my god! It *is* you! Boo-boo, it's so good to see ya, and you looking good enough to eat. Did you hear that Chef Luda . . . hint, hint?"

I shook my head at Melissa and echoed, as I got up to shake his hand, "Judge, how you doing, man? You do look good these days."

"DK, couldn't be better. Oh man, sit back down, no need to get up on my account. And Melissa, look at you. I see you're as feisty as you ever want to be. And just glowing, I might add. As a mother-to-be should, I suppose." Hoffanstanter leaned toward the table, which prompted Melissa to kick me underneath it; lowered his voice; and said, "You know, you two . . . I gotta tell ya, y'all should be real proud of yourselves, because that morning show of yours is doing Dallas real, real good. And, Ms. Melissa, you definitely got something on your hands with *The Love Forum*. Ten o'clock this Sunday night, right?"

"You got it, Judge. And, honey, the *Quiet Storm* Sundays haven't been the same since. Tell him, DK."

"Yep, she's right, Judge . . . haven't been the same since," I said in agreement.

"And, boo, you definitely don't want to miss this week's *Forum*. It's going to be a treat. Don't miss it, Judge."

The Judge laughed at her crazy behind and told her, "You don't have to worry about that, Melissa. I'll definitely be tuning in. And kudos to you, because

I don't know where or how you came up with the idea, but discussing love and relationships on the radio is BRILLIANT. Tell you the truth"—the judge came in a little closer, scratched the back of his head a couple of times, and whispered to her—"that *Love Forum* of yours has even given me a couple of pointers, and a few ideas for me and the little missus' relationship." Then he laughed out loud. "Whew-hoo! Yes, it did, Melissa. Yes, it did. Thank you, my sister, and a job well done."

"Oh, Judge, you're so welcome." Melissa drew her hand back and playfully hit him. "You and the little missus. You know you need to stop, Judge. Ooooh, you need to stop it."

"Now—and this is just a suggestion, Melissa—what you really need to do is a forum with the brothers. Get our point of view out there. Not that I don't mind listening to the *Love Forum* divas discuss relationships, but there's a voice missing—a male voice. For instance, do you know how many brothers I've counseled in my chambers and the fascinating, if not troubled, life and relationship stories they have? I don't see how they can be overlooked, if not told. And if there's one thing I've taken from your show, it's a comment by one of the divas—that 'we can all learn from someone else's story.' And I've learned throughout my years in the judicial system, and as a mentor, that we all fit in someone's life story somehow—whether directly or indirectly. Just think about how many listeners would tune in to hear us brothers talk about *our* world, which happens to be a world that has been silent for way too long."

Melissa's brows furrowed as she nodded to the idea. "Hmm, Judge, you do bring up an interesting point. One that, sad to say, I've heard too many times before. And, boo, I guess since I've heard it so many times, it must hold some truth. I never realized that so many brothers think that no one is telling their side of the story. It just never occurred to me."

"Yep!" I agreed. "Even my favorite movie, *The Color Purple*, didn't portray us black men in a positive light—and remember the backlash from when it came out? Speaking of movies and black men, tell me this, you two: Can you honestly name a movie, that's not a comedy, that has positive images of black men, where we aren't selling or doing drugs, killing somebody, or all pimped out?"

Melissa and the judge looked at each other with balled-up faces. After a while, they said in unison, "Not really."

"My point exactly. You better listen to the man, Lis. Listen to him, baby girl. You just might want to add some male voices to that forum of yours."

The judge nodded his head in agreement. "DK, I believe you hit the nail right on the head, my man." Then he pushed away from the table, glancing down at his watch. "Well, not to seem like I'm running, but I have to get out of here for a one thirty meeting. Gonna be cutting it real close, I see. Before I go, I need to mention that I'm truly grateful to the both of you for recommending

Pat Carter for that administrative assistant position. Let me tell you, and hear me when I tell you this, the office hasn't been the same since she started. That little lady—oh, my god—that little lady is a gold mine. She's keeping me and the office well organized."

The Judge grimaced as he closed his eyes and shook his head. "Hmph, yes, she is. Yes she is." And snapped back when he heard his phone ring. "Matter of fact, that's probably her texting me right now to remind me about my one thirty across town."

I was starting to get a real good feeling about hooking Pat up with that job—although I had my reservations. If you knew Pat, you would know exactly what I mean—just as cranky as she wanted to be—but Melissa convinced me that it was a good thing. Hmph. That good feeling went to hell and a handbasket when I noticed the judge's facial expression abruptly change from delight to . . . well, pissed. He pursed his lips, squinted, and just stared at us before saying, "Although . . . Pat, can be a little emotional at times—if not downright mean. Is everything all right with her at home?"

Melissa, coming to the defense of her longtime girlfriend, threw her head back, raised her eyebrows, and questioned the judge, "Oh really? You think she's having problems at home, Judge? Oh my god, how do you figure?" And although she already knew the answer, I guess she wanted to hear it for herself—straight from the horse's mouth. My girl waited calmly for the judge to respond, and I could tell it was killing her. It kinda tickled me to see her trying to hold it all in and not give anything away or give him something, with her body language, to get alarmed about.

Finally, the judge broke the silence. "Oh, don't get me wrong, Melissa. She's doing an outstanding job, and boy, is she organized." He looked at us with a bit of skepticism, before sarcastically telling us, "I guess what I'm trying to say is that . . . I owe you big-time for this one, I guess."

With all the rigmarole going on between Lis and the judge, I thought to myself, *Pat, a little emotional at times? Bruh-man, if only you knew the half of it! Get ready, because it's going to be on, before you know it, and you're going to be right in the middle of all the craziness.* Pat was going through a tough separation with her husband, Donnell—well, hell, let's be for real, a bitter breakup headed for an equally bitter divorce. Lis, being the good friend that she was, convinced Pat to get out of the house and take the job with the judge. All from the advice of a good friend, she called Ms. Doretha (yah, the psychic). Knowing that Pat was going to need some good connections in the legal system to fight Donnell in court, especially for custody of the kids, she begged me to help Pat land that job, and now, I was racking my brains wondering if I had made the right decision in helping her.

As I pondered the situation, I heard crazy-ass Melissa say, "You *guess?* You better recognize, Judge. You better recognize! You know you owe us, honey—

and don't forget about the election, which we helped you win by the way." And then she leaned into the table, gave him one of those infamous looks of hers, and whispered, "Now, don't forget where you came from. You hear?"

Judge Hoffanstanter laughed and gave Melissa one of those devilish—if not devious—smiles, walked around the table, and stood right behind us. (I could smell the crab cakes on his breath; he was just that damn close.) He grabbed my shoulder, which prompted me to turn my head, and I noticed he had placed his hands on both my and Lis's shoulders. Not soon after, he was squeezing it hard.

"I haven't forgotten, Ms. Melissa Morgan, and you too, Mr. DK Niles. So whatever you need—I mean, whatever—just let me know, and I'll make sure it happens. Well, hold on, let me throw in a little caveat for some clarity." The judge squeezed our shoulders even harder this time and said, "Within the confines of the law, that is."

Lord, I could see Melissa looking at me from the corner of her eyes, her facial expression saying, *I know he better recognize.* But not soon after Melissa gave him that look—hell, he must have felt the vibe in the air, although I don't see how he could have missed it, as it was thick enough to choke the shit out of him—he quickly said, "Well, my good folks, I don't want to overstay my welcome. It's been real good seeing y'all, and you two enjoy that lunch, you hear? I'm sure it's going to be well worth the wait."

Me and Lis said our thank-yous and good-byes and watched the judge walk over to Chef Luda. "And, Chef Luda, man, I gotta tell you, that lunch sure was on point and well worth the wait, 'cause those crab cakes, oh, my brother, they were nothing to joke about. Man, you put your foot, crusty and all, in them jokers." Judge Hoffanstanter, laughing and coughing at the same time, fanned his face, shook his head, and repeated, "Nothing to joke about at all, I tell you." He reached down and grabbed Chef Luda by the arm in a gesture that said, loud and clear, *Negro, get your big ass up and walk with me.*

Chef Luda, who was taken aback a little, responded by saying, "What? Oh . . . okay . . . I feel ya." And he quickly got up, gave me and Lis a big wink, and told us he'd be back in a few. As the two of them walked off, me and Lis quietly looked at each other. I broke out in a smile, and she turned her head to the side, tilted it up a little, and rolled her eyes as if to say, *Hmm-huh, I saw it too.* You know how some things make you uneasy but you laugh at the situation anyway? Well, me and Lis shared a good laugh, and at how in sync we were, and then talked about Judge Hoffanstanter and what our next move was going to be against his shady ass.

That Judge Hoffanstanter, I tell you, what a character! He was a political long shot that we worked hard and tirelessly to get elected into office. We needed someone in the judicial process who had our—as in the black people's—best interest at heart, and he fit the bill perfectly. He was easily electable: Light-skinned, green-eyed, tall and athletic, and well spoken, not to mention with a last name like *Hoffanstanter*—let's be real—who would have thought, with a name like *Earl Hoffanstanter*, he would turn out to be a brother?

Elected chief judge of the District Court of Appeals, Hoffanstanter was in charge of the judicial process for the Fifth District, and he never let me or Lis forget about how indebted he was to us for helping him land such a powerful and prestigious position. As a matter of fact, he immediately started returning the favor by becoming a regular guest on the *DK and Melissa Morning Show*—we called it the "Talk to the Judge" segment. This was where he answered all the radio listeners' calls and questions, crazy or not, and gave good, honest feedback and advice concerning their legal problems, and my brother was damn good at it. Seeing him triggered an alarm in my mind, and I had a hunch—deep down in my guts—that I needed to hurry up and cash in on that favor. As I, and everyone else for that matter, knew that getting him elected wasn't the issue—remember, *Earl Hoffanstanter* was not one of our typical cultural names—keeping him in office was going to be the problem, especially when everyone found out that he was not who they thought they had voted for; and I knew that I had only a little over a year left to cash in the favor he owed us. Before I knew it, the hot boudin and cracklin' cornbread was on its way to the table—with Chef Luda right behind.

"So yaw gotta tell me what yaw thank 'bout dat good ole boudin. Yaws won't find no better sausage, stuffed with dat rice and pork, with good ole cracklin' cornbread to boot, nowhere else in Texas. Uhm-huh, I said it!" Chef Luda laughed and danced around the table (he's a fool) as he helped the waitress serve up our food and drinks.

"Luda, Luda, Luda. Hmph! I know that's right. Nowhere else," Melissa said in agreement. "Oomph! Boy, you know you threw down with this here cornbread. Hmph! Scrump-deli-i-cious, Luda. Scrump-deli-i-cious! Now you got to tell us, 'cause you know I need to know. You know how your girl flows. So despite everything looking and tasting so good and running so wonderfully, what has been your biggest challenge or disappointment with opening up Bailey's?"

Without hesitation, Chef Luda replied, "Lissie, if yaws can help me find someone who's as passionate 'bout dis here food as I am, I would bless you, ma child, 'cause I can't find nan one soul. Nan one, I tell you. Either everyone is in here for dat paycheck or trying to get at my recipes, or God forbids both." Laughing a little, but serious as all get-out, Chef Luda let us know that getting good help was his biggest challenge, and I started looking around the room at the wait staff. I wondered if the cute waitress serving the food next to us was stealing the recipes. *Hmm, Ms. Bee, she looks shady.* Or what about the waiter over there, or even the bartender at that old Chitlin bar? Just that quick, Chef Luda broke my train of thought by saying, "Like I said, Lissie—and you too, DK—if

11

yaws know of somebody, anybody, let ya boy know. I'm looking for dat someone who's as energetic and passionate 'bout dat food and da business as I am." We all looked at each other, shared a slight smile, and I thought, *Passionate about food as he is? If going on looks alone, 'cause he's a big one, hell, nobody can be that damn passionate.* But then again, I saw this as another opportunity—and shit, ain't nothing wrong with that. Fit in where you can get in, is what I always say. And as soon as I said those words, the lightbulb went off: *Hell, I do believe I can get my eat-on, for free, if I can find somebody that fits the bill.* And I wondered, *Who on God's green earth could that be?* As I pondered these, Chef Luda said his good-byes, leaving us to eat, and started going from table to table, greeting people and saying his Cajun-flavored "hellos," "how's the food?" and "y'all come back to see us, you hear?" Bailey's. Damn. Definitely brought back memories for sure and, hands down, some of the best damn Cajun food in and around Dallas and west of Louisiana, for sure. And the person I shared it with—my homegirl Melissa Morgan (rest in peace, Lis)—made it that much more tasty and special.

◆ ◆ ◆

Hell, my mind was so full of thoughts of Bailey's and Melissa I didn't even remember pulling into the parking lot, let alone recall how I even got there. As usual, Bailey's was packed, and this Saturday was no exception, even with the rain. Matter of fact, I drove around a good two or three times, trying to find a parking space, grumbling, "Goddamn you, Jessie Harris." When I finally found one, I quickly glanced across the lot to make sure I had not missed Jessie's car, and I'd be damned, no effin' car—and my weakness was waiting for people. As I waited, I slumped down in the seat, slid a Seal CD in the player, and turned up the stereo volume. Instinctively, I went straight to his cover of "A Change Is Gonna Come" by Sam Cooke—man, what a song.

My career as a DJ goes back some twenty-something years to the days of doing house parties and club scenes at the young age of fifteen, and you can guess that I take great pride in being a disc jockey; and as a result, I know the music industry very, very well. And just putting it out there. I'm familiar with all types of music, as well as with a wide variety of musicians and performers—from present-day artists such as Usher, Beyoncé, and the Black Eyed Peas to such great artists of the yesteryears as Marvin Gaye, Marion Williams, and Donny Hathaway. However, I couldn't recall a more appropriate, soothing, and I-need-to-hear-this-song-at-this-moment jam, which at this point exemplified my life to a tee, than Sam Cooke's "A Change Is Gonna Come." And I'm telling you, my boy Seal put it down and did it good justice. As I sat there in the parking lot with the melody swirling in my head, I started thinking about my life—which was definitely at a crossroads—and I slowly drifted off to sleep.

Soon I found myself back in 1980s Albany, Georgia, walking down this red-clay dirt road. Damn. I could not get over how vivid and crystal clear everything appeared. It was so real I think I even uttered "Hmph" as I slept. Hell—I swear—I could even smell the pine trees and hear 'em a-swishing and a-swooshing in those strong Georgia gusts of wind that seemed to never die down. And despite the wind burrowing down that road like a hurricane, it was still somewhat of a nice, warm spring day, which, when I think about it now, was quite unusual for that time of the year. And as I trekked home with those heavy walls of wind almost knocking me over at times, I could not think of what was worse, the actual wind or the sound it made—which was effin' unbelievable, and unforgettable, for that matter. It was as though a freakin' freight train was coming to a screeching halt as metal wheels scraped against the metal tracks in a tight, narrow tunnel. And that high-pitched screeching noise set my eardrums on fire. My ears were ringing and burning as the wind whipped around my small nine-year-old frame and engulfed me in a barrage of swirling red clouds, leaving my hair, face, clothes, and my brand-new white Converse tennis shoes (damn, I loved those shoes) completely covered in red dirt. I was coughing and gagging from a mouthful, throatful, and lungful of sand, and I could feel my eyes swell up with dirty tears; and boy, did it sting something awful. I couldn't believe it. After all these years, I still had not forgotten even one minute of the ordeal—and how could I? Who could forget the strange sensation—it was almost fear—of walking, seemingly pushing and fighting, one's way home, down an unfamiliar road, through a blinding sandstorm? But what happened next—truly unforgettable—was the beginning of a string of events that would eventually shape me as a person. A string of events so powerful that I found myself a-tossing and a-turning in the car seat. Hell—I hate to admit it—I even teared-up a little as I began reliving each and every one of them.

Chapter 3

The Road We Travel: DK's Journey
(DK's POV)

As I relived walking down that old dusty road on that warm spring day—and what a day it was!—I clearly recalled how my dirt-filled eyes stung like crazy. It was a pain that, once experienced, one would surely never forget. I tell you, this would be one of the effin' memories I would continue to relive throughout life: walking down a strange road, partially blinded, and coping with a pain words could not even begin to describe. Somehow, I gradually made my way down that road, on a short prayer, with an eerie feeling that something just wasn't quite right. Oh, don't get me wrong. I knew I wasn't supposed to be there in the first place; and a woman's voice—that would be my mom's, a voice that I had tuned out so many times in my life—kept reminding me with each and every step. All I could hear was her telling me, over and over, "Dicky, don't let me catch you going down that dirt road. You stay on the paved streets in the neighborhood, you hear me?" I said, "Yah, Ma." Of course, her reaction was, "Boy, what did you say to me?" I corrected myself: "Yes, Mam." But I knew I wasn't going to pay any attention to what she just said. Why couldn't I go down that road? I wanted to know where it led and, most importantly, what was down there.

I guess I can find some kind of humor in it now, because there I was, walking down the same road she told me not to go down. Coughing, gagging, tearing up, and thinking, *Why didn't I listen? She told me not to come down this road. Why am I down this road?* And with those thoughts pounding relentlessly in my head, I started walking so fast I was damn near running, and at some point, I probably was— hell, no probably about it, I *was*. I ran right out of that windstorm and landed right in front of this old rundown place with about a dozen or so wrecked and beat-up cars scattered around the yard, some even lying on top of another. The place sat on the right-hand side of the road (funny how you remember shit like that) and was isolated from everything. It was just there, as if somebody had carved a place out of a bunch of trees and plopped it right in the middle of nowhere. This rusty old truck, which I could tell had been painted red at one time, was parked in the middle of the yard—which was nothing but a sea of red dirt, not a patch of green grass or weeds anywhere. A little boy of about four or

14

five years old ran out from the side of the yard in a pair of dingy old overalls, without a shirt or shoes on, playfully kicking up dirt and waving a stick in the air as if he was fighting a bunch of invisible villains around him; which, I must say, kinda amused me. I passed by the tail end of the truck, and my eyes picked up every detail. I read the numbers on the tag, 021 APR; noticed that the door to the bed of the truck was gone; and caught a glimpse of a long gun—maybe a rifle or even a shotgun—hanging across its back window, which was caked in red mud. As I walked along the side of the truck, I noticed that the roof was kinda smashed in above the driver's door and the hood—well, hell, there was none. When I had finally passed it altogether, I could see the house (I guess that was what it was) in back, and it made me frown. Don't ask me why, but I instinctively said, "Eew . . . Damn!" I don't know, it kinda reminded me of the house in that movie *Sounder*, or one of those sharecropper houses I had just seen a few nights before in the movie *The Autobiography of Miss Jane Pittman*—you know, the small clapboard houses built with wood, which you could see straight through to the backyard, with the rusty tin roof; and I don't know why, but it intrigued me. Probably because I had never seen anything like it before—not in real life at least—and I couldn't help but stare. And those long stares made me wonder why it sat so close to the road when all the houses and apartment buildings in the neighborhood sat a ways back, and I tried to figure out why it did not have a lick of paint on it—just a few coats and smears here and there. Then all of a sudden, I heard loud *pop*s, which scared the shit out of me. They came from up on the porch, where this huge red flag (with a big blue X with tiny white stars on it) occasionally did a *pop, pop, pop* as it flapped in the wind. Not quite sure why, but I was drawn to the house—looking, staring, just being noisy, I guess. And as I walked by, this kinda mangy, but frightful-looking, huge dog bolted from underneath the house and lunged right at me. I yelled, "Shit!" (Yah, I cursed back then) and jumped back, but then quickly noticed it was held back by a long, metal chain that was wrapped around one of the concrete blocks holding the house up off the ground. And when that dog came up from underneath that house, man, my effin' heart dropped. The dog started running, barking and growling and pulling on the chain, as if, the chain was not even there, and all I could see was a big round head and two rows of big, sharp-ass teeth. I tell you, that dog pulled on the chain so hard I thought he was either gonna break the chain, or bust straight through that concrete block. Now, my moms didn't raise no fool, so I picked up my pace and started to run but then remembered what she had told me so many times before: "Dicky, never run from a dog, son, be it a real one or a man acting like one. Just keep your eyes on 'em and try to walk away, but walk away slowly, baby. Don't let him see you're scared." I did as she said, for once, and kept my eye on the dog as he growled at me and clawed the red dirt, sending it flying everywhere, and pulled on the chain with all its might.

He was pulling so hard he started choking, and coughing, and slobbering at the mouth. But he kept pulling, pulling, and pulling. I took one step forward and took one look at the dog; two steps forward, one look at the dog; three steps forward, one look at the damn dog—hell, I started running all while looking at that effin' dog. I didn't know what Moms was talking 'bout when she told me never to run from a dog.

"Daddy, Daddy, look . . . look . . . there's a black nigger!"

I stopped dead in my tracks as the screen door swung open and this white man, in a shirt just like the flag on the porch, came out and shouted, "Nigger boy, get your black ass out of here! Hey! You hear me there, nigger? Hey boy! Get you black ass out of here before I shoot you!"

The little boy ran to the edge of the yard, hurled his stick at me, and yelled over and over, "Get the nigger, Daddy! Sic King on 'im. Sic the dog on that nigger!"

If I had any pee in my bladder, I probably would have pissed all over myself. But I just stood there, in shock maybe, questioning what I had just heard: *What! Did that little boy just call me a nigger? A nigger? I just know that little white boy did not just call me a nigger, and a nasty one at that (LOL!).*

Although at the time, the incident was not anything to laugh at, I have long since realized that sometimes you have to laugh at what causes you pain; and although my recollection of what happened next on that dirt road is somewhat blurred, I remember the white man running down the porch steps to his car, saying, "Turn 'em loose, boy!" Just that quick, I saw the dog running towards me, and I took off! As I ran down the road, I heard a couple more *pop*s; and this time, it didn't sound like that damn flag, flapping in the wind. I didn't know if they were running after me, shooting at me, or what. It was as though my mind had blanked out everything, except, dodging the dog that was right on my ass. With nowhere to run but straight down the road, I had no other option than the ditches that ran alongside it. Both of them were filled with dirty red water and, just my luck, were too wide to jump over. Then you had to climb up a steep hill to get to the other side. I did not want to, but with the dog closing in, I curved to the right and jumped right in the ditch feet first. Water, leaves, and garbage flew up everywhere. I waded knee-deep through muddy water, which—oh my god—had this unbelievable stench to it, and tried to climb up the hill. I fell back down in the ditch a couple of times, hoping and praying I would make it up and over before the white man got to me. I finally got it right and made my way down the hill, to the other side, while the dog stood at the edge of the ditch, barking, growling, and clawing up red dirt.

Covered in red mud from my hair all the way down to my feet, with my new tennis shoes ruined, I hightailed it through the woods. You talk about somebody running. I ran through those woods like somebody had set my ass on fire. Man,

I ran and ran and ran and never looked back, nor did I ever go back down that dirt road again, just as I was told not to. Huffing and puffing, heart pounding a mile a minute, I stopped in familiar territory. I bent over, with my hands on my knees, and thanked God for letting me make it home safely. But instead of jumping up and down in joy or doing a congratulatory dance, I said, "Shit!" because now I had a much bigger problem. It was as if I was thrown from one hellish circumstance, right into another. There I stood at the door of our house, soaking and dripping wet, clothes stained with red mud and God knows what else, smelling god-awful, and my new tennis shoes, which I had begged Moms to buy, ruined. There I stood, trying to figure out what lie I was going to tell this crazy woman on the other side of the door, because I sure as hell could not tell her I was down that dirt road. So I just stood there, trying to come up with something; and I thought about it, and thought about it, and thought about it, until seconds turned into minutes and minutes turned into damn near an hour. Finally, I got up enough courage to finally take my key out of my pocket. But instead of inserting it into the keyhole, I just stood there, with the key in my hand, aimed right at the keyhole. It was like a scene from a horror movie being played out in extra-slow motion, and I was the star, eyes darting all over the place. I was shaking my head, mumbling, "Dicky, get ready for that whipping, boy."

As I tossed and turned in the car seat, I remembered moving to Albany, Georgia. My moms got a job at Albany State University, and we moved into a predominantly white neighborhood after I had spent most of my nine years of life growing up in a predominantly black one. Not that there was anything wrong with our black neighborhood. But you know how it goes. We always want what's best for our family, right? And I don't fault my moms. As a single parent, she did what she considered to be the best thing to do, and she probably did not give my circumstance much thought—a black male trying to fit into a white world, since we did live in one. And at that point, I was uprooted from a world where I was accepted and got along with everyone, and thrust into a world where I was hated, feared, resented, and mostly, misunderstood. But despite this, I was determined to fit in. And as the years rolled by, I learned to adapt to my environment. My speech changed, and I could switch from speaking perfect English to speaking Ebonics with ease. Ain't it funny how we can talk one way to fit in the white situation and then revert to talking the black way without giving it a second thought? My body language changed too. I seemed to have lost that swagger—you have to admit, black men have a walk that cannot be imitated—but the lost swagger turned into a walk of self-assuredness and determination. And my style of dress changed to fit in with the popular culture—that would be with my white friends. And I can't even begin to talk about the countless visits to my white friends' houses, where, when I met their parents, I would hear the same comment about me being a nigger. After a while, it soon became a game to me to see how long, after I walked in the door, I would hear, "Oh, you got a nigger friend." Or "You didn't tell us he was a nigger."

So there I was. I didn't fit into the white world; however, I was damn good at navigating within it. And unfortunately, I felt so uncomfortable, always questioning myself, in the black one. And as far as dating went, I had dated white women (the looks and stares I attracted were unreal) and black women (who did not think I was black enough or did not have that "swagga" that they liked or were used to). Hell, I even had one sister tell me, "Oh my god, are you for real? You grew up around white people, didn't you?"

Hell, my first erection and very first sexual experience was with a white girl. We were in this field in back of the school—a place where the neighborhood kids either rode bikes down the hill or just tumbled down the hill—and just playing around like normal kids did. We tumbled down that hill, bodies intertwined, and that was how and where I got my first erection. I didn't know what was going on, but I guess she did; and as we landed at the bottom of the hill, she stuck my hand in her pants, with her fast ass, and then in her panties. As my hand went in, I felt hair, which was soft, and then I noticed my hand was at the split between her legs, which was warm and kinda moist. She took one of my fingers and rubbed it around a hole, and then I felt something like a bump, which she made my finger circle around. Then she stuck my finger in the hole underneath the bump, which was warm and wet. She kept rubbing my fingers in it, and then she put another finger in, and then another; and my shit, hard as a rock, was rubbing against her leg, and it felt so good. She pulled down her pants and pulled her panties off and undid my belt. Then she unzipped my pants and grabbed my dick and put it between her legs. I didn't think about my folks always telling me, "Dicky, leave those white girls alone. We don't want nobody knocking at our door telling us you're dead." But all I could feel was my dick going in that hole, and I guess, by instinct, I began to fuck. This white girl and me, at the bottom of the hill, fucking. We were down there for a while, me on top of her just humping. I could smell her hair, her breath; and all these senses that I never knew I had started taking over. I was experiencing things I had never felt before with this white girl—who belonged with the very people I did not trust and seemingly detested. Soon I felt this powerful urge, a kind of rush; and I could feel that something was wrong. I pulled out, jumped up, and looked down at my dick as nut started spurting out of the head. I was scared as shit because I did not know what was going on. The only thing I could think of was, *Fuck! This white girl done did it to me. She done broke my shit!* And it was not like I could tell anybody that this white girl and I were getting it on at the bottom of the hill. I couldn't ask my moms—imagine the embarrassment of that—and I could not ask my pops as he was somewhere doing his own thing. So there

I was, becoming my own man, learning as I went along, finding my own way, discovering my attraction to white girls. But then again, was it really attraction?

A couple of tears fell down my face as I continued my journey down memory lane, and I quietly let out a small, but heavy sigh, as I thought about my memorable thirty-something years of life. And although I have had some significant struggles with not fitting into the white world, or the black one for that matter—and we won't even talk about the scars left from both—nothing from these would compare to the struggles and scarring left from my relationship with my pops (Mr. Doing His Own Thing). You know, I read somewhere that over 70 percent of black kids are raised in single-parent households. I don't know if that's true or not, but if it is, well, I was one of them; and sad to say, if we all have similar stories to tell, then a lot of us are walking around with some serious issues. Unfortunately, it took me most of my adult life to work through mine, and I'm still working through them. And as the years rolled by and I worked through those issues, and on myself, I realized why that old clapboard house on that ole clay road in Albany, Georgia, held so much power over my life. The realization came to me while I was watching a documentary about absentee fathers. As I watched, mesmerized, an image came on the screen that almost shut me down: I saw a house, similar to the one I saw on the side of that Georgia clay road, and it took me back to a similar house in rural Louisiana, and the connection was crystal clear. And so was the realization that the paintless wood clapboard house, I was watching, with the rusty tin roof, was the link to so many of my childhood memories. One particular memory, much more painful than that windy spring day on that Georgia clay road, involved my pops.

It was summer, and although I always looked at the summer months as a time to relax and enjoy myself without the hassles of school, this summer was special. My pops, seemingly out of the blue, sent me a plane ticket to come see him. As a kid, I did't find it strange that a man, whom I had only occasionally seen or heard from, was sending for me. I was just happy, happy, happy, with no questions to ask. Not only was it the first time that I'd seen him in years, this was also my first airplane ride, and I was looking forward to both. However, no matter how hard I try, I can't, for the life of me, remember what city I flew into, where I stayed, or even how Pops looked. The only thing I do remember is visiting his moms, my grandmother. It was strange because I knew only one grandma, my mother's mother, whom I loved to death; and I felt as if I was betraying her by calling this new woman grandma. Nevertheless, I remember driving down the highway with Pops, with the windows down, just a-sweating; and that Louisiana humidity did not help at all. To pass the time, I played a little game of counting the minutes it took before the next directional sign. I remember the last sign on the highway read, "Shreveport, 72 miles." But before we got there, we turned off the highway and took some pretty strange back roads, which my grandma—my mother's mom—called the Klan roads, because she could just see the Klan traveling down 'em. In less than a hop, skip, and a jump, we were there. Hell, I couldn't believe it. It took my breath away. I looked out the car window, and it was as if I was back in front of that clapboard shack on that old clay road in Georgia. My pops said in his country voice, "We're here, boy." And although it was not the same house, the same eerie and worrisome feeling came rushing back to me. And even though I was there with my pops in front of a house filled with his family—hence I should have felt safe—I could only think of that hateful and hurtful place.

As I made my way up the porch steps, my pops proudly introduced me to everyone as his son, and I felt good. When we finally made it onto the porch, the screen door flew open, and this stout, white-haired woman rushed out and gave my pops a great big hug, almost lifting him up off the porch, and said, "Oooh! Lordy have mercy . . . would you look-a here!" She looked down at me, somewhat strangely, and I'll never forget what came out of her mouth next.

"Dick"—that was my dad's name—"whose yard did you get this here boy from?" She looked at me, shaking her head. "Lord, always picking up strays. If it ain't a stray dog, it's a stray cat. If it ain't a cat, it's somebody's hungry behind child."

He scratched his head, squinted his eyes a bit—a look I was all too familiar with, one of those *What lie am I going to tell this woman?* looks—pursed his lips, and told her, "Momma, dis here lil' critter is Dicky, my son."

She proceeded to look me up and down and said, "Lord, I didn't even know you had a son. Don't look much like you, but Lord, he show is the spittin' image of yo' daddy at that age. Now don't think you gone leave him here like one of those strays for me to take care of now. You hear me?"

My pops said, "Yes, mam, sho don't have to worry 'bout dat." And I just stood there, looking at her, thinking, WOW! *A stray? Didn't know? Lady, I'm like ten years old. What do you mean you didn't know?* I mean, what do you say? Or what can you say after that? I was nonexistent, insignificant to them and to my pops, for most of my ten-year-old life. All I could think about was what my moms always said when she heard some unbelievably dumb shit or when she was just through with someone or something; and as my grandma kept up her tirade about strays, I guess I had had enough, and I heard the same words come out of my mouth: "Well, I do say. I can't believe this shit! I'm just too, out, DONE!"

To tell you the truth, I can't remember anything else about that trip after that—no special places, no special moments, nothing out of the ordinary, just what my pops' mother said and the whispers and stares from everyone. And I could not help but think, *I don't fit in. I'm not what they expected. Am I not acting black enough? Is that why they're looking at me, treating me differently?*

That pretty much summed up the trip, as well as the relationship between my pops and me. I got a couple of cards here and there after that, but soon they stopped coming altogether, and the years soon flew by without so much as a well-wish or a simple hello. I was the kid who existed but no one knew of or acknowledged—not even my pops. And although there was no red flag with the white *X* hanging on the porch, or a faded red truck in the yard, or red dirt (it was now black), or a dog (instead there were chickens and hogs), the same feelings came rushing back to me, and all I wanted to do was go home. I figured it was much better to be hated or not wanted by people who didn't know me than by people who did or, at the very least, should.

♦ ♦ ♦

"DK! DK! Are you all right? Boy, I've been calling you on your cell phone for the last fifteen minutes," Jessie asked as she stuck her hand through the window and gave my head a slight push.

I yawned out loud and told her, "Hey, Jess . . . sorry, baby girl," all while stretching my arms out and shaking my head, trying to knock out the sleep. "I didn't get much sleep last night. You hungry?"

"Boy, what are you talking 'bout? I'm starving! And by the way, we may need to get you a strong one because, DK, boy, do I have news for you!"

As Jess and I dashed inside Bailey's and shook off the rain, which had started to pour down again, the hostess greeted us at the door and started asking us a series of questions. Honestly, I didn't hear a thing she said. I saw her lips moving, but as I'd done so many times in my life, I simply tuned her out. As I retreated into my own little world, I somberly looked around the place, almost as if I was looking for a familiar face; and the feeling I had was like when someone walks into the front door of their house, after they've suffered a major loss, knowing that the love of their life was never going to walk through the same door again and share the space the two of them called home. So yah, I knew that coming back to Bailey's was going to be hard, but I never imagined it was going to be this damn hard.

When I came back to the present from my unhappy place, I heard Jess ask for an intimate table for two. The hostess found a nice table at the front of the restaurant, in a cozy corner in front of a large window, which was directly across from the stage. She made sure we had everything we needed and then left us with a couple of menus, telling us our waitress would be with us shortly. Not that I had anything against my girl, but my focus went straight to the stage, where this young cat was singing Maxwell's "Lifetime." Damn, did it sound good. Homeboy was singing the song almost better than Maxwell himself, and his band was hellified off the chain. But as good as the performance was, it made my already-low spirits sink a little lower. I quietly withdrew, and looked out the window watching the rain bounce off the cars passing by; their headlights doing a little dance on our table. For some reason, I closed my eyes; and as I listened to "Lifetime," I knew I was indeed letting life pass me by. I had given up—on people, on love, on my career. I was simply living day by day, existing in a confusing and hurtful world.

"Hi, hon, can I get you something to drink?" asked the waitress. "My name is Bee, and I'll be your waitress today."

Looking down at the menu, I answered, "Yah. I guess I'll have a screwdriver—matter of fact, bring me two." I raised my eyes over the menu's top and looked up at Jessie, who was still studying hers, and hesitantly, but sarcastically, said, "Hell, bring me three. I feel I'm gonna need something hard, if not have a little buzz, to get me through this one right here."

Bee looked at me looking over the menu at Jessie, let out a slight giggle, and said, "Okay, hon, I know exactly what you mean, trust and believe I do." She winked and smiled. "I'll make sure you get the hookup. The bartender's my brother, you know. He'll do you real good, and I guarantee you'll get that buzz. I'll be right back to take your orders."

As soon as Bee had left, Jessie reached across the table, grabbed both my hands, and closed her eyes. She shook her head, took a deep breath and let out a small but heavy sigh. "DK, it was surreal! I got out of the car and started walking . . . a little confused, a little excited, and a whole lot of worried. Baby boy, what I'm about to tell you . . . is just . . . well, words can't even begin to describe it."

Chapter 4

My Soul Must Move On
(DK's POV)

A wreck! That's exactly what Jessie was—one helluva mess. She kept reaching across the table and grabbing my hands—for about the fifth or sixth time—only to pull her hands back and place them over her heart. I could see her heart jumping right through her chest—in and out, in and out—as if it was going to explode or something; and for a split second, I thought it would. She reached across the table again, and this time, I grabbed both of her hands and held those bitches down. This shit was starting to get on my effin' nerves.

I asked, "Jess, what is it, baby girl? Tell me, what's got you so upset?"

"OH MY GOD! I'm so, so sorry, DK. Okay, okay, okay." She let out a big heap of air that had a shrill to it. Just hearing it sent chills through me. But the shrill didn't even compare to the look on her face: It was wrenched with so much pain—or maybe guilt? I felt real bad for her; even as I quietly worried about my own damn self, thinking, *What in hell is she about to tell me?*

Trembling something awful, Jessie drew up one side of her lips—in a forced attempt at a smile—and began recounting her ordeal.

◆　◆　◆

"Oh my god, DK"—Jessie shook her head and took a couple of deep breaths—"it had been almost two months since Melissa passed away, and my soul was restless. Boy . . . oh my god . . . you just don't know how restless my soul was. I needed answers but didn't know where to turn. And for some reason, my mind kept going back to Ms. Doretha, the psychic. Lord, I couldn't believe that I was actually walking down her driveway that day. But there I was, fifteen minutes late for my two o'clock appointment. And as I approached her door, I stopped . . . and just stood there, as if to collect my thoughts. And as I stood there, I threw back my head, shut my eyes, and quietly reassured myself that I had made the right decision to come. I took a deep breath, regained my composure, opened my eyes, and reached for the doorbell. The chiming music was both beautiful and soothing. It kind of relaxed me. Soon afterward, I heard Ms. Doretha's voice come over the intercom. "Dear, come in, the door is open. I've been expecting your late arrival."

◆ ◆ ◆

Ms. Doretha greeted Jessie with a big hug. Jessie hugged her back, tightly, and they stood there hugging and consoling one another. Then they walked into the kitchen, and she sat down at the kitchen table. That was when she noticed a stack of blue envelopes. The top one had her name scribbled on it. Before she could ask Ms. Doretha what the envelopes were, and most importantly, who they were from, the psychic asked, "Dear, can I get you some green tea?"

She answered, "No, Ms. Doretha, I'm fine." And although green tea was her favorite, she was more interested in those blue envelopes than any tea. And as she continued to stare at the envelopes with puzzled eyes, she thought, *Jessie, do you really want to know?*

"Well, go ahead, dear. They're for you."

"Ms. Doretha, what are they?"

"My Melissa—that sweet, sweet child—wrote them before she passed. She wanted me to give them to you when you were ready. I think you're ready, dear."

Jessie turned around to face Ms. Doretha straight on. "I'm sorry, I . . . I'm not understanding what's going on here. Ms. Doretha, what are these envelopes, and what do they have to do with me?"

"Well, dear . . ." Ms. Doretha paused and shook her head. "I went to see Melissa the day before she passed—well, depending on how you look at it, the day before the accident. Sweet child, I just had to see my beautiful, sweet darling before she left this earth. Plus, I knew she had some unfinished matters to address." Ms. Doretha picked up the stack of letters and placed them in Jessie's hand. She squeezed Jessie's hand tight and closed her eyes as if she was performing some sort of reading. Not saying a word, not even looking at Jessie, she turned around and headed toward the stove. Out of nowhere—in a cracked and hurt voice—she told Jessie that Melissa was with them. Startled, Jessie asked, "Ms. Doretha . . . here . . . *now?*"

"No, dear." The psychic walked back to the table, placing a cup of green tea in front of Jessie. "She's within our hearts. I know you need to know that she's all right and in a better place—and she is—but you also need to know that her earthly work is not finished. Dear, you're the vessel. Yes, Jessie, you're the vessel she will need to make her work complete."

"Ms. Doretha, I don't understand . . . what are you saying?"

"Dear, read the letter addressed to you. All the answers—for now—are within the letter."

24

Jessie looked at Ms. Doretha, slyly, as she slowly opened the letter. For some reason, she needed to see it with her own eyes. She needed to figure out what Melissa was thinking, where she was coming from. And hell, make sure Ms. Doretha didn't write the letters. As she looked down, she felt chills all throughout her body. It definitely was Melissa's handwriting; she could recognize that chicken scratch anywhere. She stared at the letter for a while—a stare that was too long—and then she heard Ms. Doretha say, "Well, what does it say, dear?"

Jessie looked up at Ms. Doretha and was met with a slight smile and a short nod. Visibly shaking—this was all beginning to be a little too much—she looked back down and started to read:

Dear Jessie,

If you're reading this letter, it means that you've seen Doretha. Girl, I told you, she's the truth! You probably have a thousand-and-one questions on your mind so I'll start by saying that Jessie . . . you have been a true sista, soror, diva and friend. I have truly cherished our friendship and girl, I love you so much. Jess, I truly believe that God puts us on this Earth for a reason and our steps or journey in life are already ordered. I guess my journey was to one, come into the Divas lives and show y'all—and Dallas—the paths to love; (Girl, I'm smiling ear to ear as I put the pen on this paper to write the next few words), as well as two, bring that beautiful girl, Meli, into the world. Jessie, I hope that she's a bundle of joy!

Well, you're probably wondering what in the world is going on. Girl, Doretha came by the house today—what a surprise that was!—and I knew. I knew the time was near. I don't have time to write everything I want to say to you because I've written eight other letters—yours was the last. In the stack, there should be a letter for Quentin, DK, Magic, V, Pat, DeDe, Britt and Darlene. Yes girl, I was a writing fool today. Doretha sat with me and guided me through what life has to offer each of the Divas. I also have insight for DK, Quentin, Magic and my precious little Meli. Jessie, there is so much I want to accomplish and now I don't know if I have a couple of minutes, hours, days or what—that's one thing I didn't want Doretha to tell me. But I'm at peace. Jess, I need you now more than ever. Please help your sista out by delivering the letters to everyone. If asked what the letters are for, just say that enclosed, are my parting words and wishes for each of them.

Jessie, DK should receive his letter first. He should (and will) continue The Love Forum with Magic—it should have a twist though. We've heard about all the Divas' relationship woes but what about the brothas. What were they thinking and feeling? What was going on in their heads? What are their views about relationships? Maybe it's time we started listening to what our brothas have to say—if we do, maybe the state of our black relationships can improve. Deliver the letter to DK. He has all the information he will need. I must tell you though; you'll experience great pain because of the new Love Forum—prepare yourself diva! Three men, your past (Michael Crawley), your present (Dr. Houston) and your future (by now your heart is telling you yes, but your mind is saying no) will play out a drama that will rock K103.5, Dallas and each of your lives—but all of you (according to Doretha) will find happiness in the end.

Well girl, I gotta go. Just know that through life, there are going to be joys, sorrows, laughter, and heartache. And yes, I know your heart is aching and the Divas' lives have changed tremendously, but keep the faith girl, you're going to have to press on day by day to reach your final destination. I'm not saying that it's going to be easy. But Jessie, on my short life on earth, I realized that finding love, whether true or not, takes you down many roads. Some roads may take you for the ultimate thrill ride—remember Marvin, girl. Others may just lazily wind you through the country-scape called life. A few may slowly lead you back to where you began—that would be Marcus (I know you're smiling). While others, without notice, abruptly end.

The Divas were blessed to travel down the same road for many years. Amazingly, we ended up in different directions in life. Relationships formed and relationships ended; marriages began and marriages died; love ones faded into memory and children sprung out of the midst. But most importantly, Jessie, in our own ways, we began to quench our desire for sweet, sweet love. Good-bye diva. I love you beyond words.

Melissa

♦ ♦ ♦

I looked at Jess and said, "Wow, baby girl, that's some heavy shit. I . . . I . . . I just don't know what to say. I'm effin' speechless."

"DK, that's exactly what I said. I was . . . boy, I was simply speechless. All I could do was look up and stare at Ms. Doretha, straight into those dark eyes of hers, and Lord, my heart—oh my god, my heart just sunk. I could see and feel the sadness in her eyes—the sadness she had at losing Melissa, I guess—and . . . and . . . I just broke down in tears."

"Naw. Come on, you didn't start bawling in front of the lady, Jess. Oh shit, did you?"

"I know, I know. I'm so embarrassed. I just couldn't help it. It was like something just overtook me, and before I knew it, I started choking up and trying my damndest to keep the tears from falling, but they came down anyway. I was crying for a good while, and as the minutes rolled by, Ms. Doretha gave me a moment to cry it all out. She quietly sat there, just looking at me with a caring, but distraught look on her face, until I slowly pulled myself together."

"So what happened next, Jess? You said she gave you some blue envelopes to give to the rest of us. So where are they? Where's mine?"

"I have it right here." Jessie reached in her purse and pulled out my envelope. I could see my name scribbled on top of it. But before she handed it to me, she looked at me with one of those *I have to tell you this, but I really don't want to* looks (which I really hate) and said, "DK, first, I gotta tell you"—she took a deep breath and then let it out—"after I had a chance to pull myself together, Ms. Doretha said she had some important news and directives to give me concerning all of us (which brought up all sorts of thoughts, fears, and oh-my-gods in my already-fragile state of mind)—"

"Oh shit, *come on*! Jess . . . Lis is dead. She's not effin' coming back—although, wouldn't that be some shit." I smirked. "What more can that damn psychic—HUMPH! Ms. Do-re-tha—tell us that we haven't already figured out? Lis is dead. HELLO? Not coming back. Can we say 'need to move on with our lives'? . . . Oh hell . . . enough of this shit. All I need to know is, *does this have anything to do with my blue envelope?*"

"Boy, no . . . HERE, take the envelope, but you need to listen to me. I'm telling you, you need to hear this."

"Okay, damn it! All this effin' drama. Aiight, Jess, so what did the witch say?"

"Ooooh no, you didn't just call her a witch. Boy, you need to pray. Anywho, as I got myself together, I sat real, real still. I could feel myself gripping the arms of the chair, mortified, my ears zooming in on every word coming from her mouth as she reached over the table and grabbed my hands. She told me, 'Jessie, dear, as I've told you before, you're the vessel. Yes, Jessie, you're the vessel that will be used to make Melissa's work complete. And what I'm about to tell you, your destiny, will place you on a road that will not only lead you to a fulfilling professional life, but will also lead you to the love of your life.' Oh my god, DK, when she uttered those words, my jaw just dropped! I just sat there dumbfounded. I can't even put it into words . . . describe how I felt . . . or even tell you what was going through my mind. All I could do was just sit there. And I looked at Ms. Doretha as if I could see inside her . . . peer into her soul . . . read her mind. DK, all I could think of, all that kept going through my mind was *My god, what is this woman about to tell me?*"

Chapter 5

The Vessels Emerge
(DK's POV)

*A*s I sat there at Bailey's and looked at Jessie's pretty ass, I could not help but wonder why she had such a hard time finding a good man—because the girl was effin' gorgeous! Hell, even Lis kept trying to feel me out for a possible connection; but at that time, I was not even trying to hear that shit, or entertain the notion, or give it one bit of thought. If you really want to know the truth, I just felt that she was a little too power hungry for me. Not that she probably was, but that was my perception; and you know what they say—perception is not too far from the truth. And like my moms always told me, "Dicky, go with your gut feeling, baby; it'll never steer you wrong. And don't forget to listen to the signs God gives you." But what really turned me away from something between the two of us was that I didn't think my ego could take dating a woman who was more successful than me. I know, pretty shallow thinking on my part, but Jessie was just plain out of my league. Clearly! She was a big-time marketing director at one of Dallas's big marketing firms. And what did the Bible say about finding someone equally yoked—if you take that stuff seriously—and hell, we were far from being equally anything.

I mean, when I looked at Jessie, I saw a beautiful sister who would get up early in the morning; put on expensive clothes (shoes costing more than my whole gear); drive downtown to one of Dallas's impressive high-rises; walk into one of those big corner offices; and sit back at a huge desk to perform one of those high-power jobs. She would walk into a corporate boardroom, demanding attention, and make decisions and land deals that most of us could only dream of—decisions that would impact the wealth of the company and the jobs of its everyday employees. And after a full day of wheeling and dealing and scrutinizing every choice concerning the company's bottom line, or somebody's livelihood, she would come home (late in the evening) and *wouldn't* be able to turn that shit off. If you were her man, she would treat you as if you were one of the employees. Now, don't get me wrong, some sistas will tell you in a heartbeat that they can bring home the bacon, fry it up in the skillet, and never let you forget yous the man; but hell, I have yet to see one do it. Been there, done that. I'm not even going to try to figure that one out anymore. I'm staying as far away from that effin' drama as I can, because you know, that's all it's going to be—drama with an effin' capital *D*. And when the shit hits the fan—and trust me, it will—you can almost guarantee that a brother will hear, and you can ask anybody on this one: "Negro, if you was any type of a man, maybe you could afford to . . . . Or if you was any type of man, maybe you could handle your business. Or if you was any type of man, I wouldn't have to do what I do."

When I floated back to reality, Jessie was still holding my hands and moving her lips, but she wasn't saying a word. I admit, I was not paying much attention to a thing she was saying (I really have to do something about my habit of tuning people out). She had probably been talking a good one to two minutes before I tuned in, which was when Bee came back to take our orders.

"Sorry about the time, hon. Whew! We're just swamped today. Not enough people to wait on all these tables. Lord, how y'all doing? Y'all okay?"

Me and Jess looked at each other but didn't say a word. This didn't faze Bee though; she didn't skip a beat. "Here are those three screwdrivers, hon. Sorry it took so long. And I told the bartender to use Grey Goose. Hmm-huh, I see you smiling. I thought you'd like that. He gave you a double shot too. Oh, and I used freshly squeezed orange juice. Gotta treat you right, right?" Bee gave me a wink. "Take a sip. Tell me how you like it."

I took a huge sip from one, closed my eyes, and just released a big "MMMMM."

Bee said, "Glad you like it. Are we ready to order?"

Me and Jess both ordered the crab cakes. And after Bee had left to place our orders, Jess smiled, finally, and said, "DK, you have to read the letter Melissa wrote you. Basically, in a nutshell, I think she'll be letting you know that she would like for you to continue *The Love Forum* on her behalf, and there may be a strange piece about me in there as well."

I scratched the back of my head and said, "Oh yah, what's the strange piece?"

"Uhm . . . well . . . she may tell you that I'll be there holding your hand, guiding and leading you through each step along the way."

Hell, that snapped my ass clear back to reality. Next thing I knew, I pulled my hands straight from her grip and said, "What? What did you just say, Jess? What are you talking about, and what's this shit about *The Love Forum* and holding my hand, leading me every step along the way?"

"Well, DK . . . that's just the thing. As I sat with Ms. Doretha—"

"Oh hell, here we go with this Ms. Doretha shit again!"

"Boy, will you stop and let me finish? Stop now! Oh my god, Lis didn't lie. You are a mess. Anyway, boy, Ms. Doretha told me about *The Love Forum* continuing in Melissa's name, and that you would be the driver but would probably need some help . . . someone to help you with the directions, that is."

I shrugged, took another sip of my drink, and said, "What are you talking about? I don't recall agreeing to do anything, let alone a new *Love Forum* with you and your crazy diva girlfriends. Trust, I got things to do in my life, and doing *The Love Forum* is not one of them."

"Okay," she said. "I see you're going to test my patience, and I'm gonna have to get street up in here with you." Jessie took off her earrings as if she was about to throw down or something, and said, "Negro, that's just the thing. It's NOT with the divas—well, one show may be—it's with the men of the divas. Our boyfriends, lovers, and husbands. Just like Melissa said in my letter. Weren't you listening?"

I sat there looking at Jess, thinking, *Not too much street now, girl.* But I couldn't get mad. I knew I wasn't wholeheartedly listening to her explanation, but I did pick up bits and pieces. I wasn't quite sure what she was babbling about or really trying to say, so I asked, "Say that again, Jess. What now?"

Jess pushed her chair up to the table and leaned over, as if that was going to make me hear her any better, and said, "Think back to the time when you and Lis were talking with Judge Hoffanstanter about a male voice on the forum. Yah, I heard about it. She told me."

"Yah, I remember, but that was over a year ago."

"Lord, how time flies, huh?"

"Uh-huh. And your point?"

"Well, baby boy, the time for that voice has come, and the moment is now. More importantly, you're the man to make it happen."

I rolled my eyes. "How do you figure? And if I do it, what's in it for me?"

Jess laughed and shook her head. "Well, Mr. What's-in-it-for-me, Lis always said you would be a fantastic program director, and that it's always been a dream of yours—"

"Yah, it has been a longtime dream."

"But you're torn. You and everyone else knows that you're the best damn DJ in Dallas—hell, probably in the South—and although you're the voice Dallas prefers to hear on that weekday morning commute, Lis knew that you would rather be behind the scenes, running the show. So she thought, what better way to get DK's feet wet and prove to K103.5—and yourself—that you can do it, than by you taking on *The Love Forum*? It'll be your baby—with a little help, of course."

"Hmm, I'm still not sure about this, Jess, but you got my attention, baby girl. You do have my attention, FULLY! Go 'head, keep talking."

"Well, I'm glad I have your attention—finally!" She was shaking her head as if to say, *Boy, I don't know what I'm going to do with you.* "As I said, I sat with Ms. Doretha, and she laid out Melissa's vision. And, DK, it's a beautiful vision. She also told me that I would receive a phone call on this past Thursday (and I did) and would be invited to meet with Sharon and Demetrius Williams—"

"The two W's? Demetrius and Sharon? You mean Demetrius as in the vice president of K103.5 and Sharon as in K103.5's program director? My boss! His wife!" By this time, I was getting a little frustrated and had already downed my first two screwdrivers and was working hard on the third, looking for Bee to get me a couple more. For some reason, I was overwhelmed with this uneasy feeling; and suddenly, I didn't trust Jessie, and I started wondering why she was telling me any of this, for one. And two, what did any of it really have to do with me? And I was sure the look on my face mirrored what I was thinking, so I just plain out asked, "Aiight, let's cut all the bullshit. Come straight with me. Why would you be meeting with the two W's, especially Sharon? What's really going on?"

Jessie paused, and her lips curled for a brief moment. I kept looking at her, wondering, *What is she doing up at K103.5 meeting with my boss?*

After that brief awkward moment, she broke the silence. "Well, it appears Melissa knew that I would be leaving DataComm International . . . branching out on my own, starting up my own company. She kinda brought up my name and credentials to the top brass at K103.5, although they already knew who I was from me working with them on previous projects. So long story short, they called me in. We met, discussed their programming and marketing objectives; talked strategy; went over financial baselines, timelines, and obligations; and they hired me (on the spot) as *The Love Forum*'s executive producer and the marketing consultant for K103.5."

For a brief moment, my mind snapped back to seeing Jess as a power-hungry manipulator; but I chilled and listened to my mom's voice going off in the back of my head saying, *Never judge a book by its cover, baby.* So I decided to listen to what else she had to say.

"DK, Melissa wanted so much for the station to continue with *The Love Forum* but wanted me to steer it in the direction she thought would be beneficial not only to men but to women as well. Once we set the show's format and get it up and going, you won't need any direction from me." Jessie grabbed her glass of water and took a couple of sips. "Now, Ms. Doretha—and just hear me out—said that you would need a little guidance and some help getting it off the ground in so little time. But once it's off the ground and on solid footing, baby boy, it's all you. And the reason I keep mentioning Ms. Doretha is that Melissa left the majority of the details with her. Go figure, right?"

I wasn't even trying to answer any questions. All I kept thinking about was her being up at K103.5. I just couldn't let that shit go, so I said what I was thinking, "So, you're up at K103.5? No! No! You gotta be effin' shitting me!" I shook my head, made a sound that seemed like a long hiss, and said, "Now this shit makes sense. I knew something was up when you called." And I said in my mind, *I knew it! I knew something was up. I could just feel it.* I guess my moms was right when she told me to listen to the signs God gives you. Flustered, I said, "Damn, I don't believe this effin' shit. So the station knows too, huh? Am I the last one to effin' know? When were they going to tell me, Jess? When? And why is this coming from you? Shouldn't this be coming from *them*?"

"Well . . . now that I'm a part of *them* . . . I guess we're telling you now, Mr. Nasty Mouth." She laughed.

"Say what? What did you just say?" And I thought, *Oh yah, I got your Mr. Nasty Mouth, baby. Heehee, hawhaw, back atcha.* I looked at her as if to say, *You, my girl, and everything, we're cool and shit. But, trick, what the hell are you talking 'bout?*

Jessie gave me one of those looks and said, "I'm *scared* of you! Don't get mad at me. I'm just the messenger, honey. I know I'm—maybe we're catching you off guard, but everyone has your best interest at heart. We thought it would be best if all of this came from a close friend of Melissa's, since it's so close after her death, and everyone knows what you're still going through. And to tell you the truth, I do consider myself to be a close friend of yours too." Jess leaned over the table. "Well, I guess you can consider this as our first *Love Forum* business meeting." She reached out to shake my hand, but ended up caressing it instead. "Of course, lunch is on the station—the first *Love Forum* business expense—and, boy, don't play. You know you love a free lunch. Anyway, I have all the details for the new *Love Forum* right here." She pulled out a red folder from her bag; took out a pair of old women's glasses, plopping them almost at the tip of her noise; smiled; and said, "Okay, baby boy, you ready?"

Before I could say "yay," "nay," or "I guess so," Bee was back with our food, and suddenly, I wasn't hungry anymore, though I managed to eat a few bites anyway. Jessie went through the plans for the new *Love Forum*, and we began discussing them, starting out with her letting me know that I needed to rename *The Love Forum* with something that would appeal to both men and women.

Without much thought, I said, "Well, it has to be something catchy. How 'bout *The Brotherhood: The Brothas Speak*?"

Jess smiled, nodded her head, flashed a thumbs-up, and said, "DK, boy, I think we have a winner, and I believe the blue letter sitting in front of you has all the details you need for *The Brotherhood*. Well then, I've taken care of everything here, including the bill. Just read the letter. Everything you need to know is in it." Jess got up, gathered her belongings, and scooted around the table. She stood behind my chair, gave me a big hug along with an equally big kiss on the side of my head, and whispered, "You may be surprised at what you'll find in the letter. And what you've been looking for, the answers you so desperately want to hear, what you've been longing for all your life—I guarantee you, you'll find them while doing the forum. But you won't be able to find out unless you do."

I let out a big sigh, wondering what answers she was talking about. Then I heard her voice change. Now it had more inflection and power as she said,

"DK, unless you do the forum, the love Ms. Doretha speaks of, the love of my life, will never be as well. And, baby boy, I need you to come through for me with this one here. I want that love so bad, so I'm counting on you, DK. As a matter of fact, a whole lot of people are counting on you. Melissa's counting on you. Dallas is counting on you. And the eight brothers in your letter—including Magic—are counting on you."

I said, "Eight brothers? What!" I thought, *Damn! That's a whole lot of niggas with a whole lot of issues to be dealing with.* I turned my head to look at Jessie, to try to get a good vibe off of her, to try to figure out where she was coming from, what was going on in that head of hers—hell, could she be trusted? But damn, nothing. She just gave me one of those big beautiful smiles, kissed me on the head again, and said, "Okay, I'm going to leave you to read your letter. You probably need some privacy. Give me a call if I need to cancel the room reservations. You'll see what I'm talking about in the letter. If I don't hear from you, which I have a feeling I won't, I'll take it as a sign that you're going to go through with the new forum; and I'll see you bright and early Monday morning." She clutched her chest, shook a little, and said, "Oooh, boy, I'm so excited! First, we're going to start promoting *The Brotherhood* on the *DK and Magic Morning Show* starting this Monday. After that, we'll start working on the rest of the show's details—the meat and potatoes, that is." Jessie did her sighs, "whews," and "oh my gods" as she could not contain her excitement and blurted out, "Boy, it's going to be a crazy week of phone calls, meetings, and promoting, promoting, promoting. We don't have much time either. Your retreat is five weeks away from this coming Tuesday. So get ready. It's happening June, the twenty-third, baby boy. June the twenty-third."

Jessie gave me a big hug good-bye, and I watched her fine ass walk away—walk, girl, walk—and suddenly my stomach started to turn and knot up. I was cramping something terrible as I thought about the whole thing. *Five weeks from this Tuesday? Damn! How the hell am I going to pull this off? Shit! I don't even know those effin' cats, other than my sidekick Magic—and hell, I don't even know him that well.* Not that I was punking out or anything like that, but I had not felt this way in a long, long time; and I just sat there as if my ass was glued to the effin' chair, sweat beading up on my forehead and my right leg going up and down about a mile a minute underneath the table. I couldn't think straight. My mind was going in a hundred different directions; I didn't know what was expected of me or what I was going to do about this forum mess. With a quick grunt, I picked up the envelope and slowly opened it. I took out the matching blue paper, unfolded the top part, and the first thing that caught my eye was "DK, letter one of three." I took a quick look back inside the envelope, but there was nothing more in it; and I thought, *Fuck! What kind of game are these crazy bitches playing on me?*

Chapter 6

DK's Blue Letter
(DK's POV)

*A*s I sat at Bailey's, I began to blank out everything around me. Soon, everything was either lost in blackness or a complete and total blur. I even tuned out the music, along with all the noise coming from the patrons chit-chatting, clinking glasses, and banging silverware against china at about fifty or so tables—oblivious to any and everything. In my own little world, I slumped down in my chair and held the last screwdriver in my hand, slowly swirling around the last few swallows of melted ice, liquor, and OJ. I was racking my brain, trying to figure out the last time I felt this nervous about the unknown—if there ever was a time. But today, all this unknown shit at every turn was kicking my black ass; and for the life of me, I just couldn't muster up the strength, or the courage, to reach down for that effin' blue letter. I found myself just staring—seemingly for hours, but I know it wasn't the case—my gaze drifting from it, to the near-empty glass in my hand, and the only thing I could do was ask myself, *Where the hell is that damn Bee?*

"Sorry, hon, are you okay? Do you need a refill?"

"Yah, Bee, I'm down to the last drops. Well, on second thought, naw. I'm good."

"Well, maybe some dessert? We have the best darn bread pudding topped off with the sweetest rum sauce you'll ever want to taste."

"I think I'm good, Bee."

"You sure, hon? You're starting to sweat something awful over here. Look a little peaked too, and I'm not liking that look at all. Maybe I can get you a tall glass of cold water?"

I wasn't trying to be rude, but my mind was elsewhere—on that effin' letter. It got so bad that I got to the point where although I was looking at it, I couldn't see a thing. If there were words on the page, I didn't see them. Even if I did, they would be effin' Greek to me at this point. My mind was so messed up that I didn't even notice that Bee had left, but before I knew it, she had returned with a great big pitcher of iced water. She poured me a glass and, to my surprise, sat down and put the glass right in my hand and made me take a couple of swallows.

"Hon, you've been sitting here staring at that piece of paper for quite a while. Now I'm not one to get in anybody's business, but it just looks like you need a good friend right about now. Does any of this have to do with that pretty little thang that just left?"

I shook my head but then admitted, "Yah. Matter of fact, it does, Bee." I took a big gulp of the ice water and, in amazement—what was it about this woman?—let my guard down and handed the letter to her. "Do you mind reading it to me? I'm just not in my right mind right now, if it's not too much trouble."

"Sure, hon. No trouble at all." Bee motioned over to the bar, and the bartender did a double thumbs-up. "I just told him I was going on break and to have one of the other girls cover my tables." Bee got up, pulled her chair over beside mine, and put the letter down on the table in front of us. She pointed at the first line, as if to get me to follow along as she read; placed her other hand on my shoulder; and looked at me with these pretty, big, dark eyes, which I never noticed until then, and asked, "Are you ready?"

"Ready as I'll ever be, I suppose."

Bee let out a big sigh, pointed to and tapped at the first couple of words, and said, "Well, hon, here we go." And she started to read:

Dear DK (Letter one of three),

Boy! Right off the bat I have to tell you that you . . . are . . . a . . . shitty mess (LOL)! But I love you so much boo-boo and I know you'll miss me as much as I'll miss you and everyone there at my beloved K103.5. By now you and Jessie have had your little discussion—what a conversation that must have been? Whew! Honey, if I could have been a fly on the wall (child what you talking 'bout (LOL!)). Well . . . you've received your letter, and by now, you've discovered that this is the first letter of three; and you must be figuring that Ms. Doretha has the others. Guess what? You're right! Each letter (with Ms. Doretha's foresight) should guide you through hosting the Love Forum, *as well as, guide everyone on their journey to reaching their true fulfillment in life—some will be pleased and others will be hurt and disappointed, but it is their journey . . . their lot in life.*

First and foremost . . . well hell, boo . . . can we talk? Let's see, I think I've known you for a little over six years now (and they've been the best years of my life by the way) and I've watched you patiently wait for your chance to spread your wings: Well, boo-boo, here's your chance. You're the master of your own destiny now. And with you doing the "Love Forum," you'll find out that not only are you good at producing a show, it will also open up a brand new world for you; one that you've wanted for a very long time. But you'll need some help doing it and that's where Jessie comes into the picture. Un-huh, boy, you don't think I know you by now? You're probably sitting there, reading this letter, with all these thoughts and crazy reservations (silly as they may be) going through your mind but listen to me, DK, you can't do it alone. Jessie will be able to pitch and sale the show (the way you envision it) to K103.5's top brass and more importantly, she's going to do what I couldn't—open up the market to where you'll be heard (over the internet) in major cities like Miami, Atlanta, DC, New York, Chi-town and LA. You're going to arrive baby boy . . . this is your moment . . . your calling . . . your blessing.

Now that all that mushy stuff is over and done with (EWW!), let's talk about the love forum men (YAY! And I know that's right). I'm here to tell you, boo, you're going to have your work cut out for you! Getting all our men (especially my Quentin) to participate is going to be one helluva chore. You're going to have to be very creative and do some serious back room deal-cutting and major ass-kissing to get all of them to participate (pucker up); but once you do, all of you will love the experience and come into your own—also, the divas will find out some things as well (some good, some troubling and some just outright bad). One of the first things you need to do is make contact with Dr. Franklin Mayweather; he'll be the group's psychotherapist and instrumental in getting you brothers to really act, think and care for each other as brothers (that's what's lacking in our black men right now). Next, you'll need to start rounding up the following husbands, lovers and boyfriends and I've left a little comment with their names (take the comments to heart, boo):

Brass (Britt's boyfriend). Make sure you line up Brass to be a part of the Forum 'cause this one is going to take the cake (talk about drama). Brass (according to Ms. Doretha) will be instrumental in starting the group off on the right road—he's going to be your ice breaker—and this thug will grow with the show (to everyone's disbelief) and eventually evolve into his own.

Dr. Xavier Houston (Jessie's current beau). Xavier (or X as you guys will call him) will find out and confirm that Jessie is the love of his life. He's never felt like this about any woman and will fight for her love and attention until the end—be there for him.

Michael Todd (Jessie's old flame). Michael will have some revelations about him and Jessie's relationship and may try to get back in the house (don't let him). Ms. Doretha says that his stay will be short but it will be a stay the listeners will not soon forget. The Love Forum discussion (or session as you will call them), after this one leaves, will not be planned but will be the one with the highest ratings and most drama. And hear this, sparks will fly between the co-hosts of this session and someone you're all too familiar with and know personally.

Malcolm (Michael's brother and Tracy's husband). Malcolm (according to Ms. Doretha) will find his way (finally) and him and Tracy will do some self-discovering of their own and some serious conversations will follow. You'll have an interesting forum around this brother; it will leave the sisters and brothers talking about it in the offices, on the chat-lines, and in all the social networking scenes for weeks, if not months.

Miguel (Darlene's fiancé). Miguel and Darlene will find happiness (I do wish I could be there for their wedding). Miguel and you will be instrumental in helping out one of the brothers. Your help will turn his life around and put his feet on the foundation he will need for new beginnings.

Pastor Richard Levine (Pat's man). Pastor Levine will be torn: Torn between doing what's right morally and ethically or doing what's right for the church. He will also have to make a hard choice—his happiness or the happiness of the one he loves.

Quentin (the love of my life). Ms. Doretha finally told me what held Quentin back from marrying me; and I think that a lot of brothers probably experience this (and some of us sisters too). He will eventually come head to head with his demon and will find happiness in the end (I'm so happy for him and the woman that he will share his life with. She'll be good for him and our precious little daughter, Meli).

Last, but definitely not by any way or by any means the least, is my boy. Yes honey, YOU! All I have to say is that the Forum is just what you need. It will open up so many doors: The door to all your fears; the door to love (the third try is the charm, boo-boo); the door to happiness; and the door to the answer you so desperately need and want to know. And when you find this answer, the forum that you will host after finding it will be . . . well . . . a shocker to the K103.5 listening audience.

Oh, and our boy Magic (he can definitely spin those hits can't he?) well, what can I say, he's Magic. Contact him first so that he can help you get the other brothers on board. So, that sums up the brothers that you need to get on the show. It will be therapeutic for all involved and you will need to start by getting all the brothers on a plane and heading to the snow cap mountains of Alaska for a four day, three night retreat. Jessie should be working out all the details. June twenty-third, baby boy . . . June, twenty-third is the day everything begins. Good Luck, DK! I'll be looking down on all of you from heaven—'cause I know it better not be hell. Okay! Make me proud boo, and remember, I'll always love you and will always be with you.

Melissa

PS: You'll know, in your heart, when you'll need to contact Ms. Doretha (Jessie has the number) as she holds your other letters and has the insight you'll need to continue on your journey. She'll be waiting for your call.

Bee folded up the letter and slid it up underneath my hand. She had one of those inquisitive looks on her face, and after listening to a few of her "uhms" and "whews," I asked, "Well, what do you think? I mean, do you think it's a good idea? Would you listen in?"

Bee reached for the pitcher and filled my glass up with more iced water. "I think it's a wonderful idea! I mean, what would be better than eight brothers talking about their personal struggles and their thoughts about love, marriage, fatherhood, and everything else going on in the life of a black man? And best of all, it will be on the radio, for others to hear and learn from. And who doesn't have a radio?"

"You really think it's a good idea? You not shitting me, right?"

"Hon, it's a great idea! And no, I'm not shitting you!" She laughed. "I love it. And I loved tuning in every Sunday to hear Melissa Morgan's *Love Forum*, with the *Love Forum* divas, when it was airing last year. I'll especially be tuning in to hear you brothers talk, and maybe the discussions will even help out my situation a little."

"Oh yah," I said. "What situation is that?"

"Well, my father is getting his life in order." Bee sighed a little, brushed her hair back, and cradled her face in her hand, looking at me with those beautiful big eyes. "We got some devastating news about his health sometime ago—a fatal illness—and it's been rough."

"Oh my god, Bee, I'm sorry to hear that."

"Don't be. The doctors said he only had a year and a half to live. That was two years ago, and he's been preparing for the end ever since. Getting his life in order. Making amends and doing things he's always wanted to do. Living out his dreams, if you will." Bee paused, closed her eyes, shook her head a couple of times, and let out a hurt-filled "Hmph!" She looked at me, her lips curling up, trying to hold back the tears, and said, "I'm sorry. Like I said, it's been rough. The family's been standing by his side, encouraging and helping him every step of the way, though. We're even helping him fulfill those dreams of his. Opening up this restaurant was one of them."

"What!" What the hell did she just say? I started choking on the water I was drinking but somehow got out, "You"—I coughed up some water—"talking about Chef Luda?" I couldn't effin' believe it! And she did not look anything like his ass.

"Yes, hon . . . yes." Bee smiled and laughed a little. "That's my daddy . . . uh-huh, all of him." She let out another little laugh and then said, "I wouldn't trade him in for anyone else, though." And she poured herself a glass of water and picked up a napkin to dab away the tears about to fall out the corner of her eyes. "I'm his oldest, and the bartender over there is my baby brother."

"Well, I be damned. I would have never guessed."

"Yah, not too many people know, and if it's all right with you, I'd like to keep it that way. We're cool, right? And are you okay?"

Still coughing, I answered, "Oh yah, no problem. Yah, yah, we're cool, and I'm okay." I tried to look serious and sound somewhat concerned. "Yah, yah, your secret is safe with me. No doubt about that."

"Good, and thank you, hon. So . . . as far as the forum is concerned, I say do it. Life's too short." She tapped me on the shoulder. "And maybe this will help you decide. I'll share another secret with you." She smiled and looked over at the bar, where Chef Luda was now standing. "If I could fulfill this one wish for my daddy, it would make me, and him, so happy."

"Oh yah? What wish is that?"

"He wants, with all his heart, to leave this world knowing that I'm with a man that I love and one who truly loves me for me. I was hoping that I would even be able to have him walk me down the aisle, but I know that's unlikely now, as time has slipped away, so I guess I'll have to settle for him just knowing that I found love. Maybe your show can help me, and all the sisters out there who are like me, find a good man, or at least know how to weed out the bad ones."

As I sat there listening to Bee, my apprehensions about doing the forum fell away. I didn't think about it anymore. I just knew I had some work to do— phone calls to make, houses to visit, and backroom deals to put together; if that was what it was going to take to get the fellas to buy in and participate. And just as Melissa said I would, I called Magic first and got him on board. Now I just had to convince the other seven to take the bait.

Chapter 7

The Brothers' Retreat
Day 1: Why Are You Here?

Tuesday, June 23, 2009

*D*K, Magic and Dr. Mayweather sat in one of the private dining rooms of the Westmark Baranof Hotel in Juneau, Alaska, and waited for Jessie and Sharon Williams to phone in for the first day's conference call—a call to debrief and exchange information about the retreat, and in the back of everyone's mind, the drama unfolding amongst the brothers. As they waited, DK, leaning back on the hind legs of one of the dining room chairs, checked out the room, which was nicely decorated in muted tones of beige, red and gold. He tilted his chair forward, sat upright, and began tapping his fingers on the long dining table, which was strategically placed and lavishly set for twelve in the middle of the room. In front of him was a large flat-screen monitor hanging above the bar with the words "Welcome to the 2009 Brotherhood" scrolling across the screen. And although he had grown impatient with waiting, tapping his fingers louder and louder with every passing minute, he stared at the scrolling letters and could not have been more proud of this accomplishment. He smiled and thought, *Damn, I can't believe this shit. We're finally here. This shit's finally happening.*

Looking around the room, his eyes rested on the room's sitting area—a cozy alcove, next to the entrance, with a small gold metal and glass coffee table and semicircular brown leather loveseat. DK looked at Magic as he laid on the loveseat, with one foot on the coffee table and the other dangling over its arm. Amusing himself, Magic playfully switched between humming and whistling Old Dixie as he fiddled around with the speaker phone at the edge of the coffee table, occasionally picking up the receiver, checking to see if anyone was on the other line. Dr. Mayweather, who was wearing down the carpet with his pacing back and forth, felt the anxiety in the room and tried to release some of it by starting up a conversation.

"DK, how you feelin', man?"

"I'm good, Doc. How you feelin'?"

"Brother, can you believe this here? I mean, really. Man, who would have thought that ten brothers would be getting together to form a support group like this. Brothers discussing the world we live in. Our lives. Our struggles. Our joys and our sorrows. And best of all, all of it being broadcast to hundreds of thousands, if not millions, of radio listeners."

"Yah, Doc, I'm feelin' you on that but, you got to admit, we got our work cut out for us, though." DK cocked his head to the side and gave the Doc a funny look. "Dealing with ten brothers? I mean, I'm thinking this ain't gonna be nothing but effin' drama and headaches—the headache of dealing with all the bullshit ten brothers gone bring to this here table."

Dr. Mayweather paused from his pacing and said, "Could be, but I don't think so. Nine to ten brothers is the ideal number for a support group. Small enough to function with everyone present and large enough to continue as a group, if one, two, or even three of the brothers become M-I-A."

"M-I-A?"

Magic jumped in. "Missing in action, playa. . . . Damn, nigga, you slow! With yo bougie ass."

Dr. Mayweather got a kick out of that and said, "Well, DK, I think this is probably the perfect time to tell you thank you, my brother."

"Thank you for what?"

"I'm just glad you picked the ole doc, here, to be a part of the retreat and the new *Love Forum*. I can't tell you how excited I was when I got your call. Man, I . . . I just can't put enough words together to convey my deep appreciation for you, Jessie, Sharon, and everyone up at K103.5."

"I hear you, Doc, but it wasn't me, trust. So tell me, what room are you in?"

"Room 1421, I believe."

"Okay, I hear ya. I'm right next door—1419." DK stopped his finger tapping and got up to fix himself a drink, but not before asking Magic, "What about you, playa?"

"Man, I'm in 1418, and you talking about a phat-ass view. Damn! Ma girl Jessie hooked this shit up, didn't she? Hey man, fix me one too. You fixin' a screwdriver, right?"

DK, a little annoyed, answered, "Yah, man, one screwdriver coming up. And yah, our girl hooked us up." He was getting pissed that Jessie had not called and looked at the phone hanging above the bar, just as a red light started glowing and blinking. Without a second thought, he snatched the handset off the hook.

"Hello? Jessie? Is this you? It's about effin' time!"

"Hello? DK?"

"Yah, this is DK. Who is this?"

"DK, it's Valerie. Is Donnell there?"

"Donnell? Naw. Donnell should be up in his room. Have you tried calling up there? You okay, Val?"

"I tried his room and his cell phone. The front desk put me through to you. And no, everything's not okay. I really need to talk to him. Please tell him to call home."

"Okay. Anything I can help you with?"

"DK, PLEASE, just tell him to call home. It just got really crazy around here with Pat. Please tell him to call home ASAP."

"Okay! Calm down. I'll tell him."

There was a sigh of relief, followed by a somewhat worried voice. "Thank you, DK. You have a good night—you hear?"

DK assured her that he would relay the message and then hung up the phone.

Magic said, "Man, ain't that some shit. Donnell got his ho calling up here at the hotel. Where's his wife? Where's Pat? What kinda crazy shit they got going on now?"

DK shook his head. "Yah, ain't that some shit? I don't know about them two, man, but let's get off that subject. As I was saying, all the brothers must be on the same floor, huh, Doc?"

Dr. Mayweather had a puzzled yet concerned look on his face. "I think that's the plan, DK. We have connecting rooms for a reason, I suspect. What about the lady that just called?"

"You talking about Val? Valerie?"

"Yes, who is she? Don told me that he was married."

"Not for long, Doc. Val is Donnell's new lady. Pat's old news."

Magic laughed; coughing, spitting, and raising his legs off the floor, waving his hands all around. "DK, what you talking 'bout? That's his ho. That's the new Ms. Thang. And, Doc, she's fine as hell. A couple years away from jailbait. I ain't lying."

"Don't listen to him, Doc." DK looked at Magic and started laughing with him. "Valerie's Donnell's new lady friend. Him and his wife Pat are in the process of getting a divorce, and man, they've been fighting like some hood rats in the middle of a hot ass street since day one. And dude will not let those kids go."

"Yah. That shit's getting ridiculous, yo. Every time we turn around, Jess is on the phone with Pat talking about some drama that just unfolded and what she's going to do to get them kids back 'cause—what did she say DK? . . . Ain't no trick gone be living up in her house, laying on her shit—take that as you please—and raising her kids. Hell, I ain't mad at her, though. I need to snap my fingers and wave them bitches in the air for that shit," Magic said, laughing and bouncing up and down on the loveseat.

"Hey, Doc? I'm curious. How do you know Jessie and Melissa? 'Cause the two of them made, damn well sure, I snatched your $150-an-hour ass up, big-time, for this here gig—and honestly, I can't effin' figure out why. Can you help a brother out?" DK asked as he walked across the room to give Magic his drink.

Dr. Mayweather, who had started pacing again, stopped dead in his tracks and looked at DK. He was wearing one helluva expression—face all scrunched up, eyebrows coming together, and mouth hanging open. The Doc shook his head, pulled back a chair, and sat down from the shock of it all, all the while looking at DK in disbelief. It took him a good minute before he could find the words to answer.

"A jokester, huh? Well, it's kind of funny that you should mention that. I was surprised as all get-out when I got your call as well. Not to mention being equally surprised when Jessie and Sharon called shortly thereafter with the nuts and bolts of the project. It was all somewhat strange, though—how it all came down, that is—because for once, my calendar was wide open. Perfect timing, I guess; and I didn't have one excuse not to accept. Tell you the truth, I only accepted because of Melissa Morgan. I made a promise. And I don't break promises."

"Oh yah? What was the promise, Doc?"

"To continue reaching out into the community with our outreach work."

"Outreach work?" DK asked as he frowned all up and held his hands out to his side, "Man, why are you effin' here? What's the purpose of you being here, man?"

"Aw shit! Aiight! I do believe we need some kinda excitement in this joint. Get him, playa! Tap that ass!" Magic yelled as he jumped up off the loveseat and started swinging his arms in the air like a little bitch. "Go windmill on his ass, DK. Go windmill on 'em!"

"Ah, Magic, shut the hell up, man. Sit the fuck down!" DK yelled. "I'm trying to figure out why they wanted this nigga so effin' bad. I mean no disrespect, Doc. Forgive me if you feel that way. I know you're a psychotherapist and what not, but why you, bruh? What makes you so effin' special? Help a brotha out. PLEASE!"

Dr. Mayweather got up from his chair and walked right up on DK. He could feel and smell the Doc's breath on his face. "Well, for starters, always do your research, brother. And thanks for being so forward." Dr. Mayweather gave DK a soft jab to the chest with one arm and grabbed him by the neck with the other. "But to answer your question, for one, there are not that many black male psychotherapists out here—not ones that can get down with the get-down, at least. Two, me and Melissa got acquainted by working with several outreach programs. One in particular was a male support group for economically and socially challenged Latino and black males. As for Jessie Harris, I officially met her and Sharon Williams, face-to-face, a couple of days ago upon my return from speaking at a world conference, about support groups, in Shanghai, China. Three, I'm damn good at what I do and don't take no shit from nobody. Don't let these clothes fool you. You feeling me, man?"

DK said, "Oh . . . okay, Doc, I'm feelin' ya. I ain't mad at you, man." He shook himself free from the Doc's grip and walked over and grabbed Magic's empty glass. As he headed back over to the bar, the Doc told him, "As a matter of fact, DK, while we're on support groups, you may be interested to know that I've started hundreds of groups in and around Dallas, as well as throughout Texas—teenage groups, singles' groups, couples' groups, drug abuse groups, and men's groups—which is my focus and specialty, by the way. Most of them have been so successful, that they've been going on for years, with new members reaching out for their help each and every day."

DK, noticeably irritated (and it showed) said, "Okay, I hear you, Doc. One more question: How does all of this support group stuff fit in with the new *Love Forum*?"

Magic, who had sat back down and was feeling the screwdrivers, looked up at DK as Dr. Mayweather made his way over to the bar (heading straight for DK) and thought, *Oh shit, this nigga's about to go off, again. Let me get my ass up.* So Magic got up and walked over, wedging his way in between DK and Dr. Mayweather, "Yah, Doc, I'm curious too. What's this support group all about?"

The Doc stepped back from the escalating tenseness between him and DK, looked at Magic, then back at DK, and answered, "Well, brothers, as I discussed with the K103.5 management team, the original *Love Forum*—although it provided some support for the divas, mostly camaraderie—didn't go that extra mile and provide that true support group for the ladies that participated. Melissa, knowing this, wanted to make sure the brothers had a strong foundation for the journey we're all about to embark on; and according to her psychic friend—Ms. Doretha, I believe—what a journey we're about to take . . . starting with tonight's dinner. Jessie, Sharon, and I mapped it all out when we met a couple of days ago and wanted it to be a surprise for everyone—including you and Magic. After tonight, it's going to be just you and me, DK. And you too, Magic. Brothers, we need to get along and make this work."

Magic, confident that everything was cool, grabbed the drink DK had fixed him and headed back over to the loveseat. Then the phone began to rang, again. "Hey, quiet, you two. Area code 214 is coming through. Gotta be our girls Jess and Sharon. Let's see if I can make this shit work." He hit a couple of buttons on the speaker phone and told DK, "Say something, playa."

DK ran over to the phone and said, "Hello? Jessie? Hey, baby girl, are you there?"

"Yes, I'm here. You guys made it. Good! How's everything?"

"Hey guys, this is Sharon too. How you doing? Is it cold up there?"

"Sharon, my girl—"

"Hey, Magic!" Laughing. "You behaving yourself?"

"I'm always behaving myself, girl. That's what playas do, ain't it? Although, I'm not the one you should be asking that question." Magic laughed out loud and clapped his hands while looking at DK and Dr. Mayweather. "WHEW! Yawl's a mess. And naw, Sharon, it's not as cold as I thought it would be. It's about fifty-one degrees, and it's been raining on and off since the three of us arrived this morning. And what is it about Jessie and DK always bringing rain? Y'all some gloomy cats, yo."

"What? I can barely hear you. Hold on. Sharon, can you hear them?"

"Oh, girl, look at us. The volume button is set on Low. I got it, girl. Go ahead and do your thing. I'ma let you talk. I'll just listen and jot stuff down."

"Okay. Thanks, Sharon. DK, can you hear me?"

"I hear you, Jess," He assured her.

"Good. I'm happy that I can, finally, say that I'm calling with the latest update for tonight. Our Mr. Quentin—Mr. Procrastinator, I see—is the last of you fellas to arrive. Spoke with him about five minutes ago, and he's en route to the hotel. The other brothers are already there. Have you seen anyone?"

"Naw. Not yet, baby girl. It's just me, Magic, and Doc Mayweather." DK called out to Magic, "Hey, Magic, what time is it?"

Magic, up fixing another drink, looked at the wall clock. "'Bout six twenty, playa."

"Thanks, man. . . . Jess, they should be coming down in a few since dinner starts at seven, and it's around six twenty now. By the way, you guys are twenty minutes late."

Jessie let out a long sigh. "Well . . . if you haven't figured it out by now, you guys will be staying in Juneau for the night. Sorry, I couldn't get the lodge to charter your plane today. Your arrival schedules, every last one of them, threw everything off. Your plane to Angoon leaves tomorrow morning."

Magic, with a sour look on his face, asked, "My girl, Jessie. This the playa. How long is that plane ride to Angoon? Better yet, what's there? 'Cause with a name like *Angoon*, can't be too much, not even some tight little snow bunnies. Hey, question for ya: Why can't we just stay in Juneau? 'Cause this hotel is the shit, girl."

"You like that, Magic, huh? I knew you would. And, boy, forget the snow bunnies. That's not why you're there in the first place—"

"Magic is too much, girl," Sharon piped up.

"Ain't he, though, Sharon? And, Magic, boy, you know the station doesn't have that kind of money to keep y'all up in that joint. And besides, I've scheduled some pretty interesting days for you guys in Angoon. For starters, you guys will do your meet and greet at the hotel tonight with Dr. Mayweather. Tomorrow morning, you're off to Angoon, where you'll be staying at an all-inclusive lodge."

"I got my own room right, Jess?" Magic asked.

"Yes, Magic," she replied, laughing. "Everyone has their own room."

"Hey, baby girl?"

"Yes, DK?"

"So how are we going to work this? Are you guys going to call us each morning to go over the itinerary and find out what happened the night before?"

"Yes, that's the idea, although it's going to be an early start for me and Sharon. You guys are three hours ahead of Dallas. Did you get the updated itinerary I sent over about an hour ago?"

"Yah, got it. It's the one that has us getting on the bus tomorrow at eight o'clock in the morning and then going to the airport to take the chartered plane to Angoon at nine, arriving there 'bout tenish, right?"

"That's the one."

"Anything we need to know before then, Jess?"

"No, I think everything is covered in your new itinerary. You're set for the trip to Angoon. When you arrive, the lodge staff will pick you up from the airport and check you in. There will be a light brunch waiting for you. They'll purchase everyone's fishing licenses and take you on a tour of the area. I think you'll even enjoy some whale watching. And then you're back at the lodge to enjoy a wonderful dinner prepared by a culinary chef—so they tell me—using nothing but fresh Alaskan seafood and local fruits and vegetables. And I'm so glad that none of you have any food allergies or special diets. Lord, wouldn't that be a mess."

"My girl?"

Jessie broke out laughing with Sharon. "Yes, Magic?"

"I don't know about these playas here, but your boy's diet consists of scrimps and grits in the morning—every morning. So I know they gone have some scrimps, girl. If not, the playa's packing it up and taking it to the house."

"Ooh, girl, no, he didn't," Sharon said.

"Sharon!" Jessie exclaimed. "Yes, he did. Girl, you know he ain't right."

It took Jessie a while to finally calm down. Then she said, "Lord, Magic, I don't know about you sometimes. Anyway, okay, you three. We want to save the station a little bit of money, so we need to keep these calls within thirty minutes—under twenty if we can—let's plan to conference in about six o'clock every morning, Alaska time. You have the 800 number on the new itinerary and the code, which I forgot to put on it—is *42169*."

We faintly heard Sharon in the background say, "Girl! Three o'clock in the morning, Dallas time! Uh-huh."

Jessie muted the phone and told Sharon, "It'll be okay, girl. I'll call you first and conference you in with me, before we dial in. Aren't you up at that time coming into the station for the *DK and Magic Morning Show* anyway? And it's only for four days, girl."

"Four days? Uh-huh. Jessie, I can't do three o'clock—definitely not for four days. Do you have us on speaker?"

"No, I muted the phone. What's the problem? Do you need for us to change the time?"

"Girl, I'm so sorry. I just can't do early mornings. I can't be under any stress right now. Me and my husband have been trying to have a baby for over a year now, and I'm trying to follow my doctor's instructions to increase my fertility. Girl, I need to be in a deep, deep sleep at three o'clock and really shouldn't be coming out of it—not even for this, girl."

"Oh my god, Sharon. I didn't know!"

"Yah . . . I know, and it's okay. This is why we hired you as the *Forum*'s program consultant. I need you to help me manage the process. I'm fully aware that this is going to be a crazy and stressful year for you—one that I surely can't handle alone, not right now, at least. I really need to manage the intimate details of the show. Hell, use the brothers to help you out. As a matter of fact, they should be the ones managing the day-to-day business anyway. They just need a little help, a little guidance in the right direction. You're the marketing guru. You know what's going to be best for the station and, most importantly, drive up that one word we'll be judging you—and paying you—by. *Ratings*, remember?"

Jessie looked over at Sharon, who was just about in tears, and thought about DK. She asked herself, *Is this what Melissa and Ms. Doretha were talking about? Is DK going to be the new program director? Is Sharon going to leave?* Jessie told Sharon, "Yes, I remember. If that's what you want. The brothers and I will definitely make that happen. Just tell me—well, us—what you need from us, and it's done." Jessie said in her mind, *I got to come with it if DK is going to be the next program director.* Jessie knew that this was one of the things Ms. Doretha had predicted to come true, and she knew that it wouldn't be long before all the rest would start to unfold—including her finding and experiencing true love. She just didn't know when, where, or how.

"I tell you what, Jessie. You just brief me at the station later in the morning— all four mornings, if you don't mind." Sharon pushed out a dry laugh, which had so much hurt in it, and said, "I'll call you into the office, and we'll go over all the details and challenges, if any."

Jessie said, "You got it." Then she unmuted the phone and told the brothers, "Okay, guys. I'm sorry about that. Me and Sharon had to have a little sidebar discussion. So . . . where was I? Okay, as I was saying, to make sure y'all take advantage of your first night in Alaska, I've arranged for you guys to have a boy talk session with Dr. Mayweather so that he can get familiar with all of you, and you guys can get familiar with each other. Should be interesting, and I can't wait to hear about it tomorrow morning. Good night, DK . . . Magic . . . Dr. Mayweather. I'll talk to you guys in the morning."

Jessie and Sharon wished the brothers well, said their good-byes and hung-up, leaving the brothers to prepare for dinner and their first Brotherhood session with Dr. Mayweather.

Chapter 8

The Brothers' Retreat
Day 1: Donnell's Breakdown

Seven o'clock had finally come and gone. A couple of hours had passed by now. DK, Magic, Dr. Mayweather, and all the brothers sat around the table with stomachs full of food and drinks, talking trash; telling tales, if not tall ones; cutting up; and just plain having a damn good ole time—a good ole ass-kicking time. The room resonated with laughter—jokes about being part of the Brotherhood, oohs and aahs about the hotel, and conjured-up stories about what Angoon would be like and what would happen when they all finally got there. Magic, in charge of music, did his thing by spinning out *old-school* hits; one after the other; hit, after hit, after hit—until he had the brothers so hyped up that they were singing, clapping, snapping their fingers, and bouncing up and down in their seats; getting down in every which way imaginable, especially when Earth, Wind & Fire's classic "On Your Face" started booming in the room. DK, who was swaying from side to side and double-clapping while waving his hands in the air, yelled out, "Damn, Magic! Listen to that *bass*, boy. Ahhh, shit now! You got it pumping real good up in here. We waking up every effin' body in this hotel with this shit!" DK was amazed, if not amused, by the brothers, and just stopped and proudly sat and stared at them, occasionally pointing out and laughing at their antics. He couldn't believe it. It was finally happening, finally going down. They were in Alaska, singing and jamming to Magic's grooves—having a hellified of a good time—and only minutes away from the first Brotherhood discussion with Dr. Mayweather.

Pleased and elated, he could not get over how he had manned up and mustered up enough courage, let alone business savvy, to slam-dunk this deal and get the brothers to buy into the Brotherhood. He patted himself on the back, smiling. *You go, boy. You finally put those business skills God gave you to work.* He was proud, but that proud moment took a sharp, dark turn when he started thinking about how this triumphant moment would eventually end for some of the brothers, and he asked himself, *Did Melissa's letter hold any truth? I mean, what about Dr. Houston over there? Will I have to be there for this cat? And what about Michael? Will he leave the Brotherhood? And why? What about his brother Malcolm? Look at him acting a plumb fool? What's going to be the big deal with him? And the million-dollar question everybody's been asking since day one, since the first* Love Forum *aired: What really kept that quiet nigga—uh-huh, that Quentin—over there from marrying my girl Melissa?* He kept on and on until all the unanswered questions, rambling through his head, started to get the best of him; and suddenly, he knew. He knew he had to consult a higher power. He closed his eyes and consciously blocked out all the other brothers' hoopla, hollering, and what-have-you. He said a quick prayer in his mind: *Lord, I look to you for guidance as I make this journey. Guide me, Heavenly Father, and show me the path you want me to take—*

"Aye, playa, heeeey! How you feelin' ova there?" Before DK could respond, Magic started singing to "On Your Face" and blurting out to the beat, "DK's in the house (DK's in the house) . . . DK's in the house (DK's in the house) . . . my nigga's 'bout to show 'em what the hell it's (hey! hey!) . . . all about. Heeeeyyyy! Keep the smile on your face. Keep the smile on your face."

DK quickly snapped back from his prayer, laughed at Magic's ass with the rest of the brothers, and grabbed everyone's attention by standing up, raising his water glass, and tapping it repeatedly with his spoon. "That's my man, Magic, spinning out those *old-school* hits for us and keeping us entertained. Let's give our brother a good round of applause for keeping the music flowing and keeping us in good spirits."

Everybody started clapping and doing their own comically flavored Heys! and Okay's! Some started chanting, "Go, Magic, go Magic, go Magic, get your grove on, get down now."

Magic broke out dancing doing the robot, then the snake; and after a while, he just started to shake, which made all the brothers break out in gut-wrenching laughter.

"Brothas, welcome. I'm DK Niles from K103.5, and y'all know my sidekick over here—crazy as he wanna be—as none other than the music maestro himself, Mr. Kirk 'Magic' Wonder."

Magic jumped up and said, "Yep! Yep! Bask in all this *wonder*, y'all. Bask in all this chocolate *wonder*, my niggas!"

DK laughed as he grabbed Magic's shoulder and pushed him down in his chair. He told his audience, "Let's give this fool another round of applause. . . . Aiight! Aiight!" DK said as the brothers started settling down. "I gotta tell you, when I was asked to restart *The Love Forum*, I was a little hesitant. But as this new journey unfolds each and every day, I can tell you, brothers, I definitely can see the good." DK nodded and broke out smiling as he looked around the room. "Man! Can I see the good. All right, y'all. First, on behalf of K103.5, I'd like to thank each of you for consenting to be a part of this journey. Although, some of you drove a nigga crazy, trying to get y'all on board and sign those consent and waiver forms. But it's all good, though, 'cause we're all here and most def, having a damn good time.

"Now, although the retreat will be run by Dr. Mayweather—the brother sitting at the other end of the table—I'll be in the background planning and making sure everything goes well. If you have any questions or problems—with anything, brothers—please don't hesitate to call or come and talk to me or Magic. I'm in room 1419. Magic's across the hall in 1418. I promise you, we'll make sure that we get you the answers you need, or at least try to resolve your problem or point you in the right direction. So with that being said, I'm gonna turn it over to Dr. Mayweather. By the way, he's in room 1421, in case some of you brothers want to get your psychotherapy on later. Doc?"

"Thanks, DK, and good evening, my brothers. It's good to see all of you again." Dr. Mayweather stood up, maneuvered away from the table, and started pacing around the room. "Brotherhood, first and foremost, I want to thank each of you for taking time out of your busy schedules last week to come into the office so we could talk and perform your initial assessment. I understand that K103.5 has received all of your consent, waiver, and confidentiality forms; and I want to reiterate, before we begin, that I take your privacy very seriously. I hope each of you will take everyone else's privacy equally seriously. So let's get this straight. What's discussed and revealed among the group is for the betterment of the group and should not be shared or discussed outside of the group. What happens in the Brotherhood stays in the Brotherhood. Now that I've said all that, I must tell you: There are four reasons why I would need to break our privacy and confidentiality trust and reveal details of the Brotherhood. Those four reasons are as follows: One, danger to yourself; two, suspected child abuse; three, suspected abuse of an elderly person; and four, physical danger or threat to another individual—that's physical danger inside or outside of the group, brothers. Other than those four reasons, your privacy will be held in absolute confidence—only to be released with a signed affidavit by you, or with a court order."

Malcolm said, "Well, let's hope that none of us go off the deep end—get caught up in some crazy shit with our baby's mamas or some old bitty. Or even break off in somebody's ass up in this camp." He laughed and then asked, "Wouldn't that be some shit?"

"Yah," said Donnell, "let's not give our crazy-ass women any ideas—especially my bitch. This better be strictly confidential, Doc Mayweather. I'm holding you to your mothafucking word on this one, man."

The mention of crazy women made DK yell out, "OH SHIT. Donnell, man, I totally forgot! Val called up earlier. Said she needs you to call home ASAP. Something about Pat and some effin' crazy shit that was going down at the house. Bro, she's been calling you all night. You need to call home."

On hearing this, Dr. Mayweather stopped the session and told the brothers, "Let's take a ten-minute break. Donnell, you can use the house phone over on the coffee table if you'd like. I believe you can charge the call to your room, or you can use a credit or debit card."

Donnell acknowledged Dr. Mayweather's suggestion and headed over to the sitting area while the other brothers filed, one by one, out the room. Dr. Mayweather, DK, and Pastor Levine stayed behind. Pastor Levine, having Pat's best interest at heart, kept Donnell in his peripheral vision and tuned in to his phone conversation. Seeing this, DK and Dr. Mayweather tried to pull the pastor into their conversation, but they only received an occasional "yes" and nod of the head. Pastor Levine was intent on listening in on Donnell's phone call.

"Val? Hey, baby, it's me. What's going on?" Donnell listened to Val's response and completely went off the deep end. He started cursing and walking back and forth and then stopped and kicked the coffee table, hard, flipping it over and sending the glass top flying through the air and shattering against the wall. "WHAT! I TOLD YOU NOT TO LET THAT CRAZY BITCH IN MY HOUSE! WHY DID YOU, FUCKIN' DO THAT! What? Naw! I'm the one that has custody of the kids until the divorce. She only picks them up on the weekends. That's the mothafucking agreement. THE MOTHAFUCKIN' LAW! Who told her to get my kids? GODDAMMIT! That crazy bitch knew I was coming on this retreat—she was just a waiting. What did she say, Val? What did she fuckin' say?" Donnell tried to listen but kept his eyes on Pastor Levine. The pastor, noticing this and feeling a little uncomfortable, got up to walk outside and took his cell phone out to call Pat. Before he could make it to the door, Donnell yelled out, "Hold on, Val! HEY, NIGGA! HEY, NIGGA! HEEY!" The pastor turned around with a question mark on his face. "Yah, I'm talking to you. If you about to call Pat, you better tell that bitch I want my fucking kids back in my goddamn house before the sun rises— on my fucking front door, in the morning, you got that?"

DK and Dr. Mayweather rushed to get up and said, "Whoa, Donnell! Whoa, man!"

Donnell didn't pay them any mind. He dropped the phone and started walking over toward Pastor Levine. DK ran over and grabbed Donnell by the arm. "Don, what's wrong with you, man? You gone talk to a preacher like that? Don . . . come on . . . you gone rush up on a man of god like that?"

"A man of god? Nigga, what you talking about?" Donnell's face was squinched up as if it was on the verge of exploding. His eyes, dark and big, made him look like a deranged man—almost psychotic. He snatched his arm from DK's grip and pointed both his hands, immitating pistols, at Pastor Levine's head. "Like I said, nigga, you tell that crazy bitch she better have my kids back at my mothafucking house, in the mothafucking morning. The sun betta not catch her black ass. If it do . . . I'm calling the mothafucking law—and I mean that shit. If my kids aren't in my house—so Val can get them ready for school tomorrow—you gone be ministering and singing to her black ass in jail. You got that, my nigga?"

Dr. Mayweather stood in front of the pastor with both arms out—trying to block him from moving toward Donnell—but he couldn't hold the pastor back. "I'm telling you, brother Donnell, you gone make me lose my religion up in here! You gone make me LOSE IT, Negro!"

Dr. Mayweather turned and grabbed the pastor and started pushing him toward the door. Donnell, without notice, rushed over and bum-rushed Pastor Levine, making DK yell out, "Oh HELL, no! Hell no! I know this nigga's not fighting the pastor up in here! Get the pastor out of here, Doc. Get him out!" Donnell was still trying to rush the pastor and was eventually able to tackle and pin him up against the wall, jacking him up by his shirt. "Like I said, nigga. You tell your sister Pat to have my fucking kids in my goddamn house by morning."

Pastor Levine, knocked Donnell's hands off of him and then decided to drop his arms to his side, with the palm of his hands facing out, as if to say, *I'm not going there with you, brother.* He calmly told Donnell, "Brother, get a hold of yourself . . . calm down. Don't do this . . . don't do this here, brother. We can work this out." He held up his hands. "I tell you what, I'm going to walk outside. You just try to calm yourself down. I'm going to call sister Pat and see what's going on. I'm pretty sure there's a simple, if not logical, explanation for everything."

Donnell said, "Yah! You call sister Pat, or whatever you want to call that crazy bitch of a wife of mines. By the way, is that what you so-called men of god call the women you're fucking nowdays, sister this or sister that—or in your case, I guess it's sister Pat, huh?"

Pastor Levine just shook his head in disbelief. Dr. Mayweather, taking control of the situation, pushed the pastor out of the room and then quickly came back inside to talk to Donnell. He told DK to join the other brothers outside and keep them there until he came back out to get them. He walked DK to the door, patting him on the back along the way, and assured him everything was going to be okay. Then he closed the door, walked over to the phone to tell Valerie good-bye, hung up, and then sat Donnell down for a tough, frank, man-to-man conversation.

The two just sat on the sofa, silent and motionless for quite some time. The calm was meant to allow Donnell to *recalibrate.* A technique the Doc used on his clients when they were upset or needed some time to pull themselves together, to readjust. While Donnell recalibrated, Dr. Mayweather watched his breathing get slower, and slower, and slower—until he was relaxed and noticeably at ease. Dr. Mayweather told Donnell, "You know, Don, sometimes we react in certain ways to certain things—out of fear, intimidation, misunderstanding of the unknown. Let's talk about that phone call."

Donnell, looking straight ahead, rolled his eyes and shook his head. "Naw, man. I don't have nothing to talk about. Everything's good on my end. Everything's good at the house. I'm telling you, nothing's going on for you to be concerned about. You let me handle my business, and you keep up with yours."

"Don, come on now. What did we talk about last week? It's apparent that something's causing you some strife in your life. No one reacts the way that you did if everything is good at the house and there's nothing to be concerned about. For you to react in such an aggressive manner—almost to the point of becoming violent—it raises a whole lot of red flags with me. You and I both know that all's not well at the house. I want to talk to you about it."

"What are you trying to say, Doc? What the fuck are you getting at? Just come on with it, man."

Dr. Mayweather slid closer to Donnell and held his head down in an attempt to make contact with Don's eyes. "I want to help you, man. As a matter of fact, that's why I'm here. This is what this brotherhood is all about—brothers helping brothers."

"I don't need any help. At least not from you. Come on now, a shrink? Who do you think I am? I don't think so, man."

"Okay, the term would be *psychotherapist*; but anyway, are you saying that you don't want my help or you just don't want to talk about it right now?"

Donnell raised his head, stared straight ahead, and answered in a dry voice, "Don't need your help, didn't ask for it, and don't want to talk about it now, tomorrow, or ever!"

Dr. Mayweather shook his head and asked, "What's with so many of us men, especially us black men, where we'll never talk about or discuss what's really bothering us? *Hmm. Hmm. Hmm.* My Lord. We'd rather suffer alone—in silence—and let it eat us alive than reveal what's really going on with us. I'm telling you, Don, it's not healthy. Let's put the cards on the table, shall we? I was in the room. I heard you on the phone. I saw what happened."

Don turned his head to look at the Doc, somewhat annoyed.

"Yah, you can give me that look if you want, my brother. I've seen it oh so many times before—too many times before. Now, listen to me."

Don just sucked his teeth and turned away from the Doc, shaking his head.

"Don? Don! Come on, brother, listen to me now. I see you as one of those men walking through life silently, in pain. The type of man a fellow doctor in the field—Dr. Robert J. Ackerman, I believe—called silent sons. He coined the term sometime ago."

"Silent sons?"

"Yes. *Silent sons* . . . Although Dr. Ackerman used the term to describe men who were dealing with issues as adults—issues that were more or less triggered by experiences in their childhood—I just simply use it as a term to describe men, including myself, who quietly and silently walk through life in pain. Donnell, listen here, man . . . you already know I'm a straightforward and to-the-point kinda brother, so my question to you is, *are you walking through life in pain?*"

Donnell scratched and shook his head, as if he was irritated by the question, and kept quiet. "Okay, I have another question for you. What if you lost the one thing you're so aggressively trying to protect, your kids? What if Pat was given physical and legal custody and you were excluded because of your explosive behavior?"

Donnell jumped up and said, "You try it, nigga. You just fuckin' try it! I'll fuck you up and anybody else who tries to take away my goddamn kids."

"That's good! That's the reaction I thought I would get from you. Why is that, Donnell? Why do you need to be the caretaker? You don't think Pat, their mother, can take care of the kids. Hasn't she done that, and probably very well, for the past six to seven years?"

"Yah. So fuckin' what! And I really don't give a shit. Like I said, nobody is going to take my fuckin' kids. I'm gone be there for them, man. I'm gone be there. I made a promise on my dead pappy's grave that I'll be the man that he wasn't. So I'm gone be there for my kids, man. I'm gone make damn well sure they see my face every fuckin' day of their lives. Something I never had the opportunity to see of mine." Donnell sat back down, grew quiet, and dropped his head back down in his hands. "I don't know, Doc. I don't know. I can't lose my kids, man. They need to be with me. I need to be with them. I'm going to make sure they know what having a father in the house is like."

Dr. Mayweather sat back down and reached over and put his arm around Donnell's shoulder. "No one, to the best of my knowledge, is doing, or going to do, anything to take your kids from you. But, and just listen to me, I want you to think about what it would be like for the kids to grow up in a house without their mother. Put yourself in Pat's shoes. Try to imagine what she's going through. How all of this may be tearing her up. When you think about it, and I trust that you will, and you want to talk about it some more (and we'll do it when you're ready), I'll be here. Don? Look at me. Don't be a silent son, my brother. Talk. Are we good?"

"Yah, Doc, we're good."

Dr. Mayweather got up and pulled Donnell up with him, "Okay then, now let's get those brothers back in here." He gave Donnell a big hug, which lasted a while, and headed over to the door.

Chapter 9

The Brothers' Retreat
Day 1: First Impressions

*A*fter being left out in the hallway for over thirty or so minutes, the brothers walked right back into the room, one by one, and headed over to their respective seats—all except Pastor Levine, who asked Magic to switch places with him so he wouldn't have to look at Donnell's face across the table. Seeing this, the brothers knew something really bad had gone down; and since the pastor did not say much in the hall, they anxiously waited for the session to continue so they could get the scoop, if not just bits and pieces, of what went down between Donell and the pastor.

As they waited, each brother occasionally looked around the room to see if he could get a good read on how the other brothers were doing; and it was obvious—everyone was a-twitching and a-turning in their seats, growing impatient, moment after passing moment. The Doc, taking his sweet-ass time, kept shuffling through and rearranging his notes, which started to piss the brothers off. It was pissing them off so bad they soon forgot about him and his papers and started watching the clock on the wall behind him—watching and listening to every *click, click, click* of the second hand as the seconds slowly ticked by. They waited and waited and waited, alternating between looking at the Doc, at each other, and up at the clock. No one said a word. The only sound in the room came from either the Doc's shuffling of his papers, or the clock's ticking, or the brothers' tapping of either fingers, knuckles, or glassware against the table. They waited and waited and waited, until DK asked, "Is this a game? What's going on, Doc?" But his questions fell on deaf ears, and he thought, as he looked at the Doc, all evil, W*ell, hell, maybe this is part of the Doc's game plan—a test to see who would eventually snap, speak out first . . . or maybe even get us to start worrying. Hell, if that's his plan, he's doing a damn good job. It's working—we're worried!*

The mood was solemn, uneasy; and the brothers' frustration, which increased with every passing *click* of the clock, was starting to show. The tension in the room was getting worse, simply overwhelming the brothers. They started feeling apprehensive about what was coming, what was actually waiting down the road the Doc had paved for them, and they were all wondering the same damn thing: *What kind of craziness is gonna happen up in here next?* An "Uh-hum" came from the head of the table, and all of them turned and stared straight at the Doc—hard. Everyone's eyes fixed on him. They tuned their ears in to him like hawks, zooming in and picking up every word spewing from his mouth.

"All right, brothers. I see we're all back and patiently"—he looked around the room and saw the looks on the brothers' faces: they were letting him have it—"well, I see, maybe we're all impatiently sitting around the table. So I guess we need to hurry up and get back to business. Hopefully, you've all had enough time to check those e-mails, answer those voice messages, and make those much-needed phone calls home. But before we start, let's refill our drinks, grab some chips and dip or whatever you need from the bar, and get comfortable. We have a good ways to go before the night's over." The Doc continued talking as the brothers got up and refilled their drinks and grabbed some snacks. "Now, I know most of you are aware—because I've noticed y'all are some gossiping brothers—that we've had our first issue, which is no big deal, by the way. Issues are expected and welcome. That's right! *Welcomed.*

"In order for a group to grow and have longevity, there must be some conflict. If we don't have conflict, we're not going to get to the point where we can truly get to know each other and, most importantly, develop trust. To sum it all up—and give you some insight on what's happened—I'll just say that Pastor Levine told Donnell that he would make a phone call to find out what was going on back in Dallas. And the pastor did, and the issue has been resolved. Am I correct, Donnell? Pastor?"

Donnell answered, "Yah, Doc, everything is cool for now."

"Forgive and forget. Words I always try to live by, Doc," answered Pastor Levine.

Dr. Mayweather clapped his hands and held them together, as if he was about to pray, and let out a big "WHEW!"

"Okay, good. Let's get down to business. Now, most of you are wondering—and probably have been wondering for a while now—what's really the purpose of this retreat. Well, I'd like to talk about that. There is an objective—actually three. The first objective is for each man to experience personal growth. Objective two is to establish a closer relationship with each brother—forming a true brotherhood. And objective three is for each of you to have a better understanding of yourself as a man. So we have growth, brotherhood, and understanding—growing together, bonding as brothers and understanding each other and ourselves. Hopefully, over the next three days (before we leave), each of you will experience at least one of them—if not all three. So brothers, are you ready to get started? Are you ready for our first exercise?" The brothers, almost in unison, said a combination of unenergetic *yah's, I guess so's, and mm-huh's,* and watched Dr. Mayweather push back his chair, cross his legs, and lean to one side (laughing as he looked down at his notes). He looked back at the clock—it was five-after-ten—and said, "Okay, let's start this, brothers.

"For the past couple of hours, we've been having a pretty good time (for the most part) and *joking around* with each other. I want to continue that *joking around* with an exercise. What's the exercise, you ask? Well, what I want you to do is describe the brother sitting next to you. Tell us what your first impression of him was when you first met. All right! Y'all are looking at me like, *what*. Trust me brothers, there's always a rhyme and reason why I do everything that I do; just know, in the end, you'll see and know why. Now, let's get back to that exercise. I know we're still getting to know each other, so, if you don't know a brother's name, just look down at his name-tag. Sounds good? All right, let's go."

Magic, who was sitting across from Donnell, grabbed his butter knife and waved it in the air, "Oh shit, Donnell, we fixing to cut your ass up all kinda ways, drama-causing nigga."

Dr. Mayweather stepped in and said, "No, brother! Just describe the brother's physical attributes. Maybe his mannerisms, as you see them, in a good way. All of your first impressions should be told in a good light. We don't want any negativity. All your comments should be positive and, most of all, honest. The purpose of this exercise is to let the brother you're describing see how people may view him for the first time. Remember, my brothers, it only takes a person a few seconds to form an opinion about you—based on your appearance, dress, how you conduct yourself as well as speak. It's almost impossible to reverse or undo that opinion once it is formed. DK, let's start off with you, since you're at the head of the table. I want you to start with the brother on your right. Say his name, describe him, and tell us what your first impression of him was and why. Go ahead, DK."

DK looked to his right, and his eyes drifted up and down, as if he was gathering his information for the first time. He started smiling and nodding his head. "All right, most of y'all know the brother to my right as Michael. Michael, do you go by *Michael* or *Mike*—maybe *Todd?*"

Michael turned and gave DK a kinda weird look, almost tensed up. "*Michael* or *Mike*, doesn't matter, man. I'm cool with both." Mike picked up his drink, took a big swallow, and slouched down in his chair, thinking, *Todd? What does this nigga know? What's he trying to say, and why is he coming for me like this for?*

"Aiight, cool. *Mike* it is. Mike is one of those model-type-looking niggas with the cocoa butter–colored skin and waves popping in his head. You can tell he got his gym going on inside the polo shirt—showing the muscles and shit. I would say this is the nigga pulling all the honeys." DK put his hand to his mouth and coughed. "One thing's for sure, I definitely wouldn't leave him alone with my girl—pretty-ass nigga!" All the brothers smiled, and some laughed out loud.

"He's the brother that probably gets everything just on looks alone. But hey, I gotta give credit where credit is due. By the conversation I've had with him, the brother's definitely intelligent and has a good, sound head on his shoulders."

Dr. Mayweather, oblivious to the snide remark, said, "Excellent. That's what we're looking for. Let's keep it going. Next."

Michael coughed and said, "Good looking out, man. I guess it's my turn, then." Michael turned to his right, his lip curling up, and said, "My first impression of Donnell was—hell, here we go! Another six-foot-two, 330-pound out-of-shape football player with no contract, constantly talking about those woulda-coulda-shoulda, long-gone football days; and for some reason, my intuition kicked in—kicked in strong, fellas—and told me something ain't quite right with this cat. He's shady. Shady, I tell you. Watch your back, fellas."

Dr. Mayweather cleared his throat. "Positive comments, brothers, positive. And, Mike, man, was that really your first impression?"

Mike turned to the left and then to the right, looking at all the brothers, and said, "What? You said be honest, Doc, so I'm being honest."

Dr. Mayweather raised his eyebrows and pushed out his lips. "Okay, let's keep it going."

Mike, in acknowledgement, scratched behind his ear and continued. "My bad, Don. No disrespect intended, just my observation. On the real, though, Don appears to have his shit together. He has the nice Cartier watch on—I know he didn't get that from no street vendor. He's sportin' the Polo pullover and sportin' some nice loafers—Johnston & Murphy, right? Okay. No response. I see how it is. I guess I'm done. Doc?"

Donnell, not even acknowledging Mike, turned to his right and said, "Well, the brother sitting next to me is Malcolm. Mike's older brother, right, man?"

"Yah, that's right," answered Malcolm.

"You didn't have to answer. You can tell, man. Anyway, Malcolm's tall, sporting the shiny bald head, trimmed mustache, and long goatee—long enough to braid that shit. Guess that's the new style or something. He's an okay-looking dude. Even though it's kinda cold as shit up here—Alaska ain't no joke. What is it? 'Bout forty-nine degrees outside? And he done broke out in the silk, lime green at that. Silk pants and matching silk shirt. A walking advertisement for somebody's hoodwear shop. I ain't mad at you, bruh-man. But you sportin' some bad-ass shoes, though—what's those? Green crocodile print?" Everybody busted out laughing and started looking underneath the table and saying,

"What?"

"Let me check those bad boys out."

Donnell, who was just a smiling, said, "No disrespect to you either, man. Just telling it like it is." He looked at Mike and said, "Ain't that right, Mike? Oh, and, Malcolm, about my first impression: It was like, oh shit, a true playa's in the house. This nigga's even sportin' a big-ass gold chain with an equally big-ass cross hanging down from it."

All the brothers—except for Mike, who you could tell by the look on his face was fuming—looked at Malcolm's neck and either smiled or started cracking up.

"And from what I've heard from Pat, that's my soon-to-be ex-wife in case y'all don't know"—Donnell turned and looked at all the brothers—"she said you ain't nothing but the devil in disguise—if not the devil himself."

"Nigga! What you talking about?" Malcolm asked as he sat up and looked Donnell dead in his face.

"I'm just telling you what I heard. Plus, what all she and her crazy, diva girlfriends said about you—well, hell, it helped me form my opinion . . . sorry, I mean my first impression about you. Your business—which is all over the streets, man—hit me before you did. If you really want to know what I'm talking about, you need to ask Pat and her girl Jessie, 'cause they were talking about you like you was a dog in the streets. Whatever it was, it was big and had something to do with that gospel singer DeDe and that wife of yours. What's her name?"

Mike said, "Tracy."

"Yah, Tracy. Had those cackling bitches up all night talking about it. Pissed me the hell off 'cause I couldn't go to sleep with all that cursing and laughing they were doing."

"Nigga," said Malcolm, "you just foul. Shady. Just like Mike said, shady-ass nigga! Man, don't let me have to use this knife on your ass, for real. Listen here, partner. I ain't no punk-ass bitch. You gone get fucked up playing with me—"

Dr. Mayweather was quick to jump up and interrupted the two. "Okay, brothers, let's keep it moving. Let's keep it moving, now! Malcolm? Let's just calm down. Your turn."

Malcolm let out a big breath of air and took it down a level. "Aiight. Aiight. Thanks, Donnell, guess you keeping it real. And thanks for the tip, brother!" And then he mumbled *Bitch-ass, drama queen* under his breath. He looked around the table and said, "Bros, how y'all feeling? Yah. Y'all probably recognize my name from my wife calling up to the station. I guess that's what Donnell is *trying* to refer to, but I'm gonna let that go and introduce y'all to my man Brass here. I'm telling you, when I first met this cat, I knew he was a true playa—holding on, with a firm grip, to that platinum playa's card for life. And just like me, his girl aired all of his dirty laundry on the radio. Ain't that a bitch, Brass? But we not gone get into that—hear that, Donnell?

Malcolm didn't even look down at Donnell, he just focused in on Brass. "Now my brother Brass here is funny as hell. On the plane, he kept me cracking up with those off-the-wall jokes of his. I mean, come on, man, where do you get that shit from?" Malcolm started laughing. "Let's just say I felt real comfortable with the cat . . . from the first moment he opened up those reefer-stained lips of his—yah, they black man. You know you smoking that shit. My boy's definitely a people person, and as y'all can see, the brother is dark complected—not as dark as those lips, though—with a close-shaved bald head and sportin' that perfectly lined mustache and goatee. Man, what barbershop you going to? I need to check 'em out. Look at that shit! That line is perfect!"

Malcolm started laughing and shook Brass's shoulders a couple of times. "The brother is definitely putting us to shame with his pump on from the gym too. Man, why you got to wear the muscle shirt showing the six-pack? Why?" Malcolm started play-jabbing at Brass and, in one of those snide voices, said, "Conceited-ass nigga. Hell . . . I thought my brother, Mike, took the cake, but boy, you're really on that look-at-my-fine-ass trip tip. Both of y'all sitting over here like yawl's dicks dipped in chocolate." Malcolm laughed. "I'm just kiddin', man. Oh! Before I forget, my man is loaded down with tattoos, all up and down him too. Stop at the neck, my brother, stop at the neck. Don't do the tattoos on your face. That would be too much." All the brothers laughed and started nodding in agreement. "I guess that's all I got to say. It was a mouthful, huh? Did I miss anything, Brass?"

"Naw, you got everything, homey, except I'm probably the youngest cat in the room. Twenty-nine, y'all, and don't be hating on a brother, 'cause y'all know once you cats leave the twenties, y'all be hating on a brother for real, though. I guess it's my turn, huh?"

"Yah, it's your turn, brother Brass," said the Doc as he got ready for a colorful description of himself.

"Well, I gots da pleasure of introducing da next brother—da headman himself." Brass stood up, took a bow, and lifted up his shirt and showed off his tattoos. "Hey, Doc, ain't this da way you suppose to do this. You 'spose to stand up when you talking. Tease the crowd a little. See da tats, cats. Demand attention." Brass started laughing.

Magic looked at him, frowning, and told him, "Nigga, sit your ass down!"

"Aiight, Magic. Aiight. I got you, my nigga. Enough of da silly stuff. I'm stealing your spotlight, huh, bruh? On the real, though. The Doc is about five ten, 'bout 190 pounds, or something like dat. He's a medium brown complexion and sportin' that low 1970s 'fro, with that connecting beard and goatee." Brass started laughing. "But it's tight, Doc, it's tight. One thing I do like about da Doc is dat he looks professional. Like, take his clothes, for example. Look at 'em—da ironed long-sleeve blue shirt with da white collar and cuffs, da pearl cuff links that match dose white teeth of his. Yah, the Doc definitely gives you that *about it, 'bout it*—even if he ain't. But I know he is, trust. The Doc is all about business. He even walks like he's about business—with authority. I likes dat. He knows how to handle his self. You go, Doc!"

"Well, thank you, brother Brass, I think." Dr. Mayweather looked at Brass and shook his head as he looked at him with his shirt halfway up, showing his ripped abs and tattoos, and couldn't hold in his laughter. "Brass, man, you're one of a kind, my brother. One of a kind." Dr. Mayweather stood up and walked over behind Quentin. "Now, this brother right here is someone special to the Brotherhood. Some of y'all know him as K103.5's first gentleman—well, that's what his lady used to call him, at least. Yep, this is Melissa Morgan's beau, Quentin."

Magic said, "Aaaah, shucks now! Look at you, my nigga. You got titles and shit—the first gentleman—all right now. We got royalty up in this mug."

Dr. Mayweather looked down at Magic and slowly inched his way down to him and continued talking while he did. "As I was saying, Quentin was Melissa's longtime beau. You brothers probably know of him because of his on-the-air relationship with the former K103.5 diva—God rest her soul—Melissa Morgan, the other half of *The DK and Melissa Morning Show.*

"Now if you brothers haven't already noticed, Quentin is somewhat of a medium dark-toned brother with a low-cut fade and smooth waves at the top. He has connecting well-trimmed sideburns and goatee, with some serious, serious dark, penetrating eyes. I mean dark *and* penetrating. My mother called those types of eyes, hurt eyes, because they looked like they were hiding a lot of pain inside. Anyway, not to get off track, he dresses conservatively. And by the way he carries himself, I got the feeling that he's a no-nonsense type of brother—no-nonsense, indeed."

Magic couldn't help but cut in. "Almost like the flip side of Mike over here—hurtful eyes, muscles, and all that."

Dr. Mayweather put his hand on Magic's shoulder, his way of getting him to stop cutting up, and said, "Okay. Yah, you got a point. He does kinda have that similar flavor of Michael, just reversed." He looked down the table at Quentin and over to Mike and put his hand over his mouth. "Wow . . . Magic . . . I didn't notice that until now. Interesting. Very interesting. Quentin? Your turn, brother."

Quentin cleared his throat and put his hand on Xavier's shoulder. "This is my boy X—Dr. Xavier Houston. We've been sitting here talking and getting to know each other since we last spoke at the hospital three . . . four months ago. He's a real cool dude.

"In case you guys didn't know, Xavier, or X as I'm calling him 'cause we already got one doctor in the room, is dating the ultimate diva herself—our girl Jessie Harris. You guys probably know her by either listening to her on the radio with DK and Magic, or you've talked to her already. She's the one that's been working out all the details of your trip—arranging for you to fly here to Alaska, making your hotel accommodations, and planning your daily activities. She's also the godmother of my three-month-old daughter, Meli—yah, it's short for Melissa—and she takes care of her when I'm in a jamb, which is about most of the time—"

Dr. Mayweather jumped in. "What about X? What was your first impression of him when you two met at the hospital for the first time?"

Magic said, "Uh-huh. I know that's right, Doc. I was beginning to think I was listening to an infomercial for our girl, like she was in the room . . . with all that Jess this and Jess that, worship and praise coming out of Quent. Like you feigning for her, playa."

Quentin told Magic, "Ah, man, hush. Y'all probably wish she was up in here, considering all the commotion that's been going on—and on our first day at it, at that." He laughed and pointed down to Donnell and the pastor and then turned and looked at the Doc, letting him know, "As far as X is concerned, the first time we met was at Dallas Memorial, after Melissa had the car wreck. He was in that doctor's coat—what do you call that coat, X?"

"It's called a white coat, man."

"Yah. He was in his white coat and talking to us about Melissa's condition. He was just like he is now. Kinda quiet, maybe even a little shy; cool demeanor; intelligent looking, with those round spectacles on; and, as far as the physical, a tall and lean brother. What are you, X, six one, six two?"

"Six one, man."

"Yah, six one. Back then, he had the fresh bald fade. Now he's sportin' those low twists like that singer—um, what's that singer's name, Magic, that hooked up with Halle Berry?

"Eric Benét?"

"Yah, Eric Benét. Looks different from when me, Jess, and the rest of the divas were at the hospital in bad shape. Damn, were we in bad shape! It was so bad I couldn't even think straight, fellas. But X made it better. He just came in and started talking to us, explaining Melissa's condition to us. It was real bad. She was comatose. X broke everything down for us. He seemed to really care, and we listened to him . . . trusted him." Quentin kinda laughed and jokingly said, "Yah, at the time, I just thought he was a nice doctor, working in the Trauma Center, with good bedside manners. One of those doctors that cared about his patients' friends and family in their time of difficulty. Little did I know, he had other intentions, because he hooked up with our girl Jessie not too shortly afterwards."

DK said, "wow! That's right. We got two of Jessie's men up in this camp. This shit's about to get scandalous—for real!"

"Ahhhh, shit!" said Magic.

"Naw. It's not going to be any of that, my brother. No scandals when it comes to my girl." X was adamant about this and leaned forward and pointed down the table to DK and over to Magic. "What me and Jessie do is our business. What she and Mike did is theirs. Mike, I think you're feeling the same way. Right?"

Mike looked down at X and gave him an *I don't care, whateva, nigga* nod, before saying, "Yah. You right about that."

DK turned around in his seat, leaned over Pastor Levine, crossed his legs, and mumbled to Magic, "Hell, I already know half the story. Somebody's in need of some prayer up in here. Sitting up here perpetrating."

"What? What you saying, playa?" whispered Magic.

X got up and walked down to DK. "Maybe I didn't make myself clear. It's not going to be any of that, man. A little bit more respect for the woman that got all of us up here, the woman working in the background for you, my man. Now did I make myself clear? You know where I stand, right?"

One could hear a pin drop, or maybe just the ticking of the clock. The room was that quiet. No one said anything, not one iota of a word. They just looked at X and DK as if to ask, *What the fuck?* And X went on talking as if nothing was even going down.

"Sorry, brothers, Doc . . . probably should get back on track with my first impression. I got Miguel, and like some of the other brothers here, we knew each other before the retreat too. When we first met, he was talking to his fiancée, Darlene, in Spanish. Just a-talking . . . and smooth with it too. I tell you, the brother is smooth with it, fellas. Jessie told me where he was from, but I guess I wasn't paying too much attention. I just figured it wasn't Mexico because he looked like he was mixed with us—half black. Miguel? Where you from, again?"

"Brazil, X. Brazil. São Paulo."

"São Paulo, how 'bout that—the big city. A city boy! You can tell, man, you can tell. Now when we first met, he had long curly hair, like a white boy, but now it's a close bald fade. And he looks just like one of us: a light-skinned black with light-colored eyes, kind of greenish brown in color—the old folks call 'em bedroom eyes."

The brothers looked at Miguel, trying to check his eyes out, and Magic started singing, and pointing at his own eyes: *You wish you had these ebony eyes.*

X said, "All right, Magic, we got ya, my brother. And Brass started singing the chorus from Club Nouveau's song "Jealousy," at Magic, which made the brothers laugh and start to cut up.

DK joined in and started singing the chorus to Club Nouveau's "Why You Treat Me So Bad," and all the brothers joined in, asking Magic, Why you treat us so bad? Magic? Why you treatin' us so bad?"

Magic, trying to be a good sport about it, told the brothers, "Ahh, niggas, ain't nobody jealous, and who's treating y'all bad?" For good measure, he looked for the songs on his laptop and played it low as X continued talking.

"When Miguel saw me, he came up and introduced himself in English. He had a bit of an accent, which took me a while to get used to; but once I did, we started talking and hit it off. He wasn't all the way one of us, but you can tell that he had that flava to him, like us, with the swagger to match.

"My first impression of him was he was polite, well mannered, and probably in his early, if not, late thirties." X started to laugh out loud. "And those clothes! Colorful, man, co-lor-ful! The bruh really wears the colors, or at least he did that day. I just assumed—and, Lord, I hoped—that it was something Darlene had picked out and bought for him to wear; although he toned it down today, not so colorful."

Miguel started laughing and asked, "What's wrong with a little color, man? I'm from Brazil. We love color."

Magic said, "Uh-huh. We know you love color, man . . . and that blackberry juice. You and that fine-ass Darlene Brookes. Boy, you done struck black gold, drinking up some good ole Texas tea. I'm still trying to figure that one out. Ms. Darlene Brookes? Miss Black Texas back in the day? Fine as she is, and she ended up with your high yella—I mean, white ass!"

Miguel said, "That's right. She fine, ain't she, Magic?" He started laughing and giving Magic some dab and started telling the brothers what his first impression of Magic was when they met over a year ago. "This brother right here—the Music Maestro himself, es fantastico. Es uno de los tipos a un amigo verdadero. He is really one of a kind—a true friend that'll have your back when you need him.

"So, let's see. I first met this brother at one of those K103.5, Old School Stepper parties. He came down from the DJ's booth, shirt drenched with sweat. He had on this big cowboy hat, tight Wrangler jeans, and big cowboy boots with these big shiny spurs spinning on the back. I tell you, in all of my years here in Dallas, I've never seen a brother—I mean, a black brother—wear Wranglers and cowboy boots. It amazed the hell out of me. I asked Darlene who—well, what was he all about? She elbowed me, said I was talking too loud, and told me that was Kirk, the DJ for the party and one of the DJs for K103.5, that he worked with Melissa and DK."

Miguel stopped and smiled and then broke out laughing. "I didn't know what to think. She introduced us, and there was an instant connection. He opened his mouth and started cracking us up with all of his jokes. I took to him right away."

Magic said, "I know that's right, Miguel. And hell! I'm from West Texas, where we represent—clothes and all."

"Just because you from Texas don't mean you have to look like it. A nigga in Wrangler jeans, boots, and a mothafuckin' cowboy hat. You look a mess," Donnell joked.

Everybody started laughing, and Brass came to Magic's defense. "Hey, let my brother be. Magic, do you, man. Do you."

Magic said, "At least somebody got a nigga's back. Y'all other niggas can kiss my mothafuckin' ass. Playa-hating niggas. Hate the game, niggas, don't hate the playa." Magic turned and looked back at the pastor, who had pulled up a chair at the bar and was trying to fix one of those Shirley Temple drinks, and asked, "Pastor? You hear 'em. How they gone come at me like that? You know you need to put one of those healings, or blessings, or whatever you got on these here fools."

The pastor laughed and asked Magic, what about him? What were his first thoughts of him when they met? And was Greater Antioch his church home?

Magic thought about it. He truly did not want to be disrespectful, nor was it his intention to judge, but his emotions got the best of him. And as he always said what he thought and meant what he said, he told the pastor exactly what was on his mind.

"You sure you want to know, Pastor?"

"Yes, brother Magic. I'd like to know what kind of first impression I'm leaving—good or bad."

"BAM! Okay then. Check this. Just like Malcolm and Brass, your history precedes you too, Pastor. Who don't know about the great leader of Greater Antioch Baptist? And no, I'm not a member, playa. Don't go there neither. I gets my religion in when I need it."

"So you're not a true saint of God," said the pastor.

The brothers felt a storm brewing and started butting in to change the direction of the conversation, but Magic overtalked them. "See, that's where you're wrong. I don't need to sit up in church with all the ritual churchgoers."

"What do you mean, brother Magic?"

"I mean, most black folk go to church because they've been doing it for so long, since childhood. They don't know nothing else. They go because it's expected. Kinda like getting ready for work or school every morning. You have a ritual you go through to get ready. Church and going to eat afterwards is the ritual for black folk on Sunday. We're the most spiritually adept people in the world, but just as morally corrupt as we want to be. We'll talk about and stab each other in the back in a minute, even before walking out the front doors of the church, and say hallelujah while doing it."

Everybody looked at each other, not knowing what to say. Finally, DK spoke up. "Come on, Magic, man. Don't be disrespectful, man."

"I'm not being disrespectful. I'm just telling the truth, and y'all know it. Anyway, back to you, Preacher. Let's just say that when you walked in the room, I was like, Damn! Look at him. Strolling in here looking like the last model on the cover of *GQ* magazine, and ain't got *not* one damn bit of religion in him."

Donnell shouted, "WELL!"

The pastor started coughing and choking on his drink. "WHAT! Why would you say that about me, brother Magic?"

"'Cause."

"Because of what?"

"'Cause ain't no pastor concerned about doing the Lord's work gone be messing 'round with somebody else's wife, and they ain't even divorced. She ain't even good and out the house yet. Ain't that right, Donnell?"

Donnell answered, "Uh-huh, got a point, man. You got a point. But it doesn't matter. Pat and the pastor can do whatever they want. Do what you do, Pastor. Can I get an *Amen* in here?"

Some of the brothers said *Amen*, and they all perked up in their chairs—thinking, *It's about to be on*—and started turning around, looking at the pastor, and then at Magic when he said, "Aiight. Aiight. But come on, Pastor. I need to knock you down a peg or two. Knock you on them knees. Make you pray. 'Cause you human just like the rest of us, so don't act like you all high and mighty and innocent ova there. And you know you want some liquor in that there drink. Look at ya. Strolling in here looking like the last *GQ* magazine cover model—beard and mustache perfectly lined with the tight fade haircut with a few waves popping. And we not gone even go there with you on those threads you got on, which leads me to my next question. Now, I know it ain't true that you *don't* wear the same suit twice, is it? 'Cause that's what they say."

"Brother, where is all this coming from? If you must know, I meet with presidents of corporations and countries. I have one of the most successful churches in Dallas. There is an image that needs to be projected."

"Well, I may not go to church, but I reads the Bible too, and I don't recall nothing about the Lord projecting an image to meet with kings, queens, and statesmen back in the day. He came and met them as he was."

"Brother, that was back in the day. Times have changed. Do you really think I would get in the door by coming as I was? I tell you what, you take that street, goodwill talk—'cause it's just talk—and see how far you go. Probably want make it to the end of the block."

"Don't get mad, playa. That was my first impression. You gave off this feeling that it's all about the pastor. Albeit you'll probably sell your momma, or even feed one of your church members—better yet, the first lady—to the lions to save your own self or soul. Take it as it comes, playa." Magic looked around the room at the brothers. "Fellas, am I the only one that peeped that?"

Nobody said anything. There were just a lot of coughing, "uh-huhs," and uh-hmms.

The pastor looked at Magic and said, "I'll do that, my brother—take it as it comes, that is." He touched Magic on the shoulder with one hand and extended his other to shake Magic's hand. "Thanks for sharing your impression with me. I didn't think of myself in the way you portrayed." The pastor turned to his right and looked at DK. "Well, brother DK, you're the last brother, and I know all the brothers are ready to get out of here, so I'll try to keep it short."

"Brother DK is a member of Greater Antioch, and I've been trying to get him to be more active in the church. When I first met him—how long ago was that brother DK?"

"About nine or ten years."

"Lord, has it been that long?"

"Yah, Pastor."

"Umph! How time flies. Yes, Lord. Anyway, brother DK had just moved to Dallas from Georgia, and he was looking for a church home. Back then, Greater Antioch was small—about eight hundred members, not the twenty thousand we have today. So I was able to meet with every soul looking for a church home or give counsel to those seeking salvation. Brother DK walked up to the front of the church—we were back there in a small church on Elm Street back then—in a nice suit. It was a blue pinstripe, right, brother DK?"

"Yah, I think so, Pastor."

"He was much scrawnier than he is today. I'll say about 160 pounds back then—looks about 190 today—five ten, five eleven, and had cornrows. IN THE HOUSE OF THE LORD! Lord, have mercy. Just like he does today. It was men's day that day, so we had dinner waiting in the dining hall. I invited brother DK to be my guest, and as we sat, broke bread, and talked, I think the most important thing that struck me about this brother was that he was quiet, somewhat shy, but I sensed he was searching for something." Pastor stared into space and started shaking his head. "Hmph! Searching for something. Back then I thought he was searching for God; but after all these years—nine to ten long years, to be exact—I still sense he's searching for that something." Pastor Levine raised his hands in the air and said, "My god! Just like the children of Israel, wandering through the vast wilderness, searching for the Promised Land."

Dr. Mayweather, noticing the clock had just struck one, grimaced at Pastor Levine's comments, got up, started clapping, and told the brothers they had had a very successful first session; that he was pleased with the outcome. DK got up as well. He started going around the table, shaking each brother's hand and thanking them for their participation. He asked everybody to do him a favor for an experiment the Doc was going to conduct on their last day and told everyone to read and fill out the card by their plate and to put two names down. Everything was coded, and no one would know who they were. He told everyone that they would meet in the hotel lobby in the morning, promptly at seven, as the bus was leaving at seven fifteen to take them to the airport for their flight to Angoon. Dr. Mayweather said his good nights to each brother at the door, and as the brothers were leaving, no one knew what to make of the first night's activities. Each one felt something powerful move through him, but just did not know if it was a good thing. They just walked back to their rooms, thinking the same thing: *Time will definitely tell.*

Chapter 10

The Brothers' Retreat
Day 2: We Are Silent Sons

Wednesday, June 24, 2009

*I*t was day 2, and the brothers had checked out of the hotel, loaded the bus, and were on their way to the airport. Destination: Favorite Bay Lodge in Angoon, Alaska. The Doc, DK, and Magic sat huddled together, with intentions of hashing out their strategy for the second session with the brothers later on that night, and to briefly go over the conference call they had just had with Jessie; but Magic and the Doc fell asleep—fell asleep just as soon as their butts hit the fabric on their seats. DK, who was also sleepy as all get-out, put off sleeping and started replaying the conference call in his mind. A call that left him curious, if not somewhat worried, about the strange, troubling questions that he walked away from it with.

He started replaying the events, and they flashed in his mind like pages turning in a book. He remembered the alarm clock going off at six, hitting the speakerphone button, and sitting on the edge of the bed as he dialed the 1-800 conference line number that ended in *421*—which he thought was odd but seemed all too familiar. The Doc, Magic, and Jessie were already on the call; and once he joined in, he found himself doing most, if not all, of the talking. He filled Jessie in on the prior night's activities, the good and the bad—if the brothers were actually participating and who needed that extra push to get them to join in and talk. She briefed him on their room assignments—everyone had their own room—and started to explain what to expect when they arrived in Angoon.

First, she said they would arrive at the Angoon airport around 9:00 AM; then they would travel to the lodge, check in, and get situated in their rooms. Not more than thirty minutes after check-in, they would be getting all of their fishing equipment and gear together for a boating excursion at 11:00 AM. Then they were off—off on a private boat for a day of saltwater fishing, with a little whale watching along the way. Jessie told them that a gourmet boxed lunch, prepared by the resort's chef, would be waiting on the boat and would be served at noon.

She let them know that as part of their trip's inclusive package, their catch of the day would be processed, packaged, and ready for them to take back to Dallas when they checked out on Friday afternoon.

Jessie said, "WHEW! I'm so excited! Aren't y'all excited? Come on now! You guys are going fishing on your own private boat. And get this: You'll have your own Coast Guard–certified fishing guide. So there should be no reason you guys won't have fun and catch a whole bunch of fish while you're at it. Bring me some fish back now. And please! Please don't show yawls color up there. Make sure you tip the guide, at least ten dollars each, before stepping one foot off of that boat when it's all over, you hear?" She laughed. "I'm just kiddin', just a little bit." Before ending the call, Jessie told DK that Judge Hoffanstanter had been desperately trying to reach him.

"Judge Hoffanstanter? What does he want, Jess?"

"I'm not sure. He called yesterday, talking about he needed your cell phone number—like, right, I was going to give it to him." She chuckled. "He don't know us, huh, DK?"

"That's right, baby girl. We don't be giving our numbers out like that."

"I know that's right, boy. He kept calling and calling, talking 'bout he needed to get in contact with you . . . get some sort of information, I think. Said he had some important info that you really needed to hear—from, or about, one of his close clients. A client you're supposed to know quite well."

"A client I'm supposed to know?"

Jessie answered, "Yes, DK." She was starting to sound as though she was getting aggravated by his questions. "I'm pretty sure that's what he said. *A client you know.* That's all he would tell me—or could tell me, I imagine."

"Huh? That's weird. That's it? That's all he said?"

"That's it . . . I did tell him that you were in Alaska, though, on important business, but not where. And I only told him that because he kept calling the station all day long. My god, he was getting on my damn nerves. Anyway, whatever it is, it's important. Something's going on he wants you to know about. And don't forget he needs to get that information from you too. Hmph! Whatever *that* is."

DK didn't know what to think. *What could it be? What was the judge calling him for?* He thought about it, and thought about it, and thought about it, and then asked, "Hey, Jess? Pat's still working for the judge, right?"

"I believe so. She hasn't told me anything different, and I just talked to her last night."

"Did she say anything?"

"Like what?"

"Anything about Donnell? Maybe about what went down with Pat and Valerie yesterday?"

"Boy! OH MY GOD! Whatchu talkin' 'bout. That's all we talked about—for a good three to four hours at that."

"Hmm. Okay. Three to four hours, huh?"

"Boy! At least."

"Well . . . uhm . . . its 6:20. We're done, right, Jess?"

"That's all I have. Magic? Dr. Mayweather? I know you guys must be sleepy, if not asleep. You haven't said a word the entire twenty minutes we've been on the call. Listen, I'm not going to keep you guys. I know you have to get ready to get on the bus and head to the airport. Just have a safe flight and enjoy the fishing and whale watching today. I'll talk to you in the morning. Bye now."

They hung up, and DK thought long and hard about why Judge Hoffanstanter was trying to reach him. He asked himself, *What type of information does the judge need? And why does he need it? And what exactly does he need to know?* He thought, *Damn! Melissa said Pat would need the judge's help. I wonder if he's trying to get at me about Donnell? Damn! Lord, why me? Why not one of the other brothers? I sure as hell hope he don't think he's gonna use me to get information about my man Donnell. Even if I don't like his ass, I'm not going to betray him like that. I made a promise: What goes down in the Brotherhood stays in the Brotherhood.*

And with those thoughts, DK made up his mind. He was *not* going to return the judge's calls. He felt that if Pat needed something to get Donnell with, she was going to have to get it from somebody else.

♦ ♦ ♦

The brothers had just finished a unique Alaskan dinner of pan-roasted French elk loin, braised spiced red cabbage, and Yukon Gold mashed potatoes after a long day of fishing and whale watching. They had been on the boat all day long, for over six hours, and had caught so much fish, that they made damn well sure word got back to the resort that the last thing they wanted to see, was a fish on a dinner plate. As they sat around the dinner table, they threw in their two cents' worth on what the elk tasted like. Most said it tasted like a sweeter version of beef. Then they continued debating well after they had finished eating it and were waiting for dessert.

The chef came out and apologized about dessert being late and proceeded to go around the table, meeting and talking with all the brothers. He asked them how they enjoyed the meal, and if anyone had any special requests for the remainder of their stay.

To everyone's surprise, Malcolm blurted out, "Yah. Yah, I have a request, Chef. Hey man, I saw that you have culinary classes for the guests. Classes to show peoples how to make some of those Alaskan meals pictured on all the walls."

"Yes, yes, as a matter of fact, I do. Are you interested in learning how to prepare some of our Alaskan cuisine? Or maybe you'd like to help me prepare dinner for your group tomorrow?"

Without batting an eye, Malcolm said, "That I would, Chef. That I would." He looked at the brothers. "You know, that's what I used to do back in the day." And then he told the chef, "Count me in, Chef. What time should I be in the kitchen?"

With an astonished look on his face, the chef did a thumbs-up and let out a hearty chuckle. "I see someone's passionate about cooking. Dude, you just light up talking about it—sort of like I used to do when I started out. Tell you what, meet me in the demonstration kitchen at 3:00 PM. I'll have your apron and hairnet ready and waiting for you."

Malcolm was now very excited. "That's a bet, Chef. I'll be there."

The chef walked over to Malcolm, shook his hand, and gave him one of his business cards. Then he apologized again for dessert being late. He said that the sorbet still needed some time to chill, but not to fret, as it would be ready in a few minutes. He told the brothers to continue enjoying their night and then left to go back into the kitchen.

Noticing it was about to hit 8:00 PM, the Doc stood up, cleared his throat, and knocked on the table a couple of times to get everyone's attention. "Well, brothas, while we wait for dessert, let's start today's Brotherhood discussion."

"First. Brothers, wasn't those some good ole vittles? Yah. Yah. You know it was good. I didn't see a piece of food left on anybody's plate. Uh-huh, every one of them plates, just clean. I think some of you may have even licked them a couple of times." The Doc laughed at his own attempt at a joke as he sat back down at the corner of the dining table, grinning, looking at all the brothers. "All right, all right. All joking aside, time to get back to business. I want to share with the group what I've learned from Bill Kauth, who wrote the original manual for men's support groups. One thing I found successful in my many years of conducting group sessions is to begin every meeting, as Mr. Kauth suggested, with what he calls rounds, or as I like to call them, *bouts*, like in boxing, because for each bout accomplished, *that's* one step, or fight, forward to wholeness.

"The bouts are where we'll have the opportunity to update the group on what's been happening in our lives since our last meeting, or maybe what's on our minds at the moment, or what we may expect to get from the day's session. But hold on, there's a couple of twists."

"Brass said, "Aw, hell. I knew it. I knew something was coming. Here we go with some bullshit, fellas."

"Naw. Naw. *Now*. It's not bad, brother Brass. The first twist involves an optional wild card for each bout, which can be used to ask a specific question. For instance, say you want to focus on a specific topic for the session. Let's say you want to know from the other brothers what makes a brother appealing to a woman. You want to know what the brothers think. You just let us know you're going to use your wild card, and just ask your question."

"Okay . . . okay . . . I feel you, Doc," said Brass.

"Now, Brass, and brothers, the second twist piggybacks off the first one. Twist two centers around each meeting being led by a different brother, and that brother, the leader, will have the option of letting the brothers talk about anything or use his wild card to steer the discussion in the direction of his choosing. I'll be the leader for today. And yes, I'm going to use the wild card. For tomorrow, let's go ahead and pick the leader. Any volunteers? Any takers?"

Malcolm raised his hand. "I'll do it, and I'm gonna use the wild card too."

"Okay, brother Malcolm. Want to tell us what your topic is going to be, or do you want to wait, till tomorrow, and surprise us?"

"Naw, we don't have to wait. I'm not gone leave y'all hanging in suspense. I can tell you today. Now, fellas, think about this: Think about when you first met yours, or the current lady you're with. What jumped first? The dick or the brain?" Malcolm got a good laugh looking at the brothers' reaction. "Doc? My topic for tomorrow is 'Listen, My Dick's Talking.'"

"All right now," the Doc said, and the rest of the brothers didn't know how to react. They either looked at each other, laughing; shook their heads in disbelief; or let out big sighs, as if to say, *Come on, Malcolm, you're kidding us, right?*

The Doc said, "Okay, brother Malcolm. That's what it is, then. Brothers, all I have to say is"—his mouth curved into an almost-smirk—"I think we better come up with some pretty damn good material for tomorrow night. I don't know why, but I have a feeling tomorrow's session is going to be a wild one.

"Getting back to today's session, my wild card question is: What was it like for you growing up? Give it some thought. And since most of you brothers are wondering exactly who I am—yah, I heard the gossip—I'm going to start us off by giving you a brief version of my bio, and then spin off into telling you what it was like for me growing up. Let's do this, brothers. And let's try to keep it under five minutes. Magic? You're the timekeeper. I'll keep your time when you're up."

Dr. Mayweather pushed his chair back from the table and leaned it against the wall, propping his head against it. He started telling the brothers, "All right, my name is Franklin Mayweather—you can call me Frank, Doc, or whatever you want—and I'm a clinical psychotherapist with my own practice. My office is located in downtown Dallas, and my specialty is working with groups. I have a bachelor's degree in social clinical psychology, a master's degree in psychology, and a doctorate in psychology as well. In 1992, I passed the National Professional Practice Examination in—yah, you guessed it—psychology. I became a licensed psychotherapist in our great state of Texas in 1993, and since then, I've been practicing full-time as a counselor slash licensed psychotherapist, for almost sixteen years now. I'm a native Dallasonian, married for fourteen years, and have two daughters, ages seven and nine. Let's see, what was it like for me growing up?"

Dr. Mayweather hesitated a little and then grabbed a glass of water, drinking half the contents, before saying, "I'm number six of seven children, and one of two of the seven that's still alive. All are dead except for my middle sister. My family's been plagued by one disaster after another. Guess that's why I wanted to become a counselor and help people. I tell you, brothers, life hasn't always been a bed of roses. My family wasn't rich, but not dirt poor either; and my mother did all she knew how to do to raise us alone. To make things worse, I lost my father at an early age, around three or four, and my mother passed away before I made it out of high school; but by the grace of God, I made it. I'm a survivor, a living testimony. And all of you sitting around this table—just because you're sitting around this table, are survivors too. Now, who's next? I want a volunteer survivor."

Brass started to moan. Then he grunted a little and pushed his chair back from the table. He threw his head back and moved both his hands from his forehead to the back of his head, over and over, in a torturous gesture. "Damn, Doc, I've been sitting here listening to you, trying to remember something about my childhood, what it was like growing up, but, Doc, I can't. It's like blank, man. I can't remember a damn thang. Nothing."

Dr. Mayweather asked Brass if he would consider doing a form of hypnosis called regression—a trip in time to an earlier period in his life. Brass scrunched his face up and said, "Huh? What you talkin' 'bout, Doc?"

"Well, remember our initial consultation before the retreat when we discussed blocking out what we don't want to remember or what causes us pain?"

"Yah. Yah, I remember."

"I asked you if I could get you to a place where you could remember what causes you pain . . . would you want to? And what did you say?"

"Yah. I remember, man. I guess I said yah, huh?"

The Doc got up, walked over to Brass, put his hand on the man's head, and told him, "I believe you're aware of your past, Brass. How do I know? You told me. I asked you the questions, and you told me what *you* wanted me to know, or could remember—in bits and pieces, that is." The Doc grabbed an empty chair and pulled it next to Brass's. He sat down and said, "You just need a jolt, some kind of a kick, something to push those experiences to the forefront. I can walk you through those experiences, Brass. Get to those memories you're trying to block out."

Brass shook his head. "I don't know, Doc."

"Yah, Doc. What you're proposing . . . I mean . . . can't that shit backfire and be kinda traumatic for Brass if it don't go down right?" asked DK.

The rest of the brothers nodded their heads.

The Doc answered, "It can, with someone who's not a trained psychiatrist, psychologist, or medical doctor. But I assure you, he's in good hands. And if he's willing, I want him to come face-to-face with his demons, face-to-face with whatever's holding him back, face-to-face with whatever may be preventing him from moving forward in his life.

"It's up to you, brother Brass. If you're ready, I'll ask the brothers to leave the room. I believe this is your time, brother. Your time to be a true survivor. And if I recall, you said you wanted to know what kept you doing the things that you do, why you can't seem to fly right. From your profile, I believe this may be the key—the key to answering some of those questions that plague you."

"Naw, naw, naw." Brass paused and shook his head. "I don't think so, Doc. I don't want nobody playing with my head. Plus, how I know you gone be on the up-and-up? Naw. I think I'm gonna pass, bruh-man."

"Brother Brass, listen to me. Hypnosis is not what you see on TV or in the movies. Trust me. I won't be able to make you say or do anything you wouldn't say or do while you're not under hypnosis. You'll be completely aware of everything that's happening. You'll remember everything afterwards too."

"I don't know, Doc. I got a funny feeling about dis here." Brass held his head down in his hands and mumbled, "I must be crazy, man. What the hell. I'm gonna do it, man."

The Doc clapped his hands and said, "Hot damn." Then he told the brothers to exit the room and he would come and get them when it was time, but Brass stopped him.

"If it's okay with you, Doc, I'm not too crazy about being alone in here with you doing dis here. Not dat I don't trust you or nothing. I just got dis picture in my head 'bout being on dis here table, ass out with one of dem apples stuffed in my mouth—like the brotha in that movie *Pulp Fiction*, or some of that crazy bullshit in dat movie *Deliverance*."

Brass laughed a bit, and the rest of the brothers did too. He said, "With all due respect, Doc, I'd rather have the brothers in here to make sure everything is legit and goes down like you say it will." He threw his head back and let out a couple of heavy sighs. Then he pressed the palm of his hands against his thighs and got ready.

"Okay," the Doc said, and silence fell over the room. There was only the sound of the wall clock ticking. A couple of minutes later, the doc said, "Remember the confidentiality agreement, brothers." Then he asked Brass to watch the clock on the wall and concentrate on the second hand going around and around and to listen and concentrate on the clicking of the clock. He watched Brass watch the clock and kept telling him that he was getting heavy, weighted down. "Brass, you're now tied down to the chair," the Doc told Brass and then asked him to get up and walk across the room.

Brass wiggled in the chair awhile, trying to get up, but he couldn't; and the Doc knew he was under—hypnotized—and started the regression.

"Now, Brass, I want you to relax. I want you to relax and release all of your worries, all of your fears. The weight of the world is being blown off your shoulders. There's a continuous stream of wind blowing on you, Brass. The wind is blowing all your worries and fears away. The wind is warm and soothing. You can feel it on your skin. It feels good to you. You can smell it. Springtime fresh, like lilac, jasmine, or wisteria. It's clean, kind of refreshing. The wind is bringing all this warm and fresh air all over your body. You can feel that warm breeze and springtime aroma engulfing you, blowing those worries away. Can you feel it, brother Brass? Can you feel it? Can you smell it?"

"Yah, Doc, I feel it. It's warm—real warm. It smells good too . . . nice . . . I like it."

"Good." The Doc noticed that Brass was breathing slower and that his body was relaxed. He lowered his voice, "You're relaxed now, brother Brass. Your worries and fears have blown away. The weight of the world is no more. Now I want you to listen to me, Brass. I'm going to count backwards from ten to one. Each of the backward counts will make you more and more relaxed. When I reach one, you'll be on a plane flying in a beautiful, clear blue sky with the sun beaming in your window. Nod if you're ready."

Brass gave a couple of quick nods, and the Doc began to count.

"Ten . . . nine . . . eight . . . seven . . . six . . . five . . . four . . . three . . . two . . . one. You're now sitting on that plane looking out the window, but you don't see the window or plane around you. You're outside the plane, outside in that beautiful, clear, blue sky. Take a moment to take it all in. You're watching the plane traveling to your left. Turn your head to the left, Brass." Brass turned his head to the left. "The plane is traveling into your future. Now turn your head to the right." Brass turned his head to the right. "This is your past. Look. There are some dark clouds in front of you. In a moment, we're going to turn that plane around and fly back into those dark clouds. We're going to fly into your past."

The Doc got up and moved to the other side of the room and said in a low voice, "You'll always be able to hear my voice and follow my instructions and hear the questions I'll ask you, and I'll be able to hear you talk as you travel back into those dark clouds, back your past. I'll be able to hear you regardless of how far you fly back into those clouds.

"You're approaching the edge of the dark clouds, Brass. You're flying into them. You're now in those dark clouds. It's stormy, but you're okay. In a moment, I'm gonna count backwards from ten to one. Each number will take you farther and farther back into your past. When I say one, you'll be out of the storm and in a previous life experience. This experience will have had a direct impact on your current life. You'll relive that experience as if you're watching

TV or a movie. It will play out right in front of you. And just like watching TV or a movie, you'll experience pain, sorrow, loss, love, and happiness; but you'll not experience it physically. When you hear me say *breathe*, you will no longer be looking at the TV or movie. You'll be far away from that experience, in a calm, peaceful place. Do you understand, Brass?"

"Yah," said Brass. "I understand, man"

"Okay, good. Now when I say breathe, what does that mean?"

"It means that I'll no longer be in that place . . . the movie will be over."

"Good. I'm going to start counting backwards from ten to one. Each number will take you farther and farther back into your past: Ten . . . nine . . . eight . . . seven . . . six . . . five . . . four . . . three . . . two . . . one. Brass, you're watching your movie. You're the star. Look familiar? Tell us what you see."

Brass was actually turning his head as if he was looking around, but his eyes were closed. All the brothers were either looking dead at Brass or looking around the room for some sort of acknowledgment that everything was all right, and this was a good thing. DK kept thinking, *God, don't let nothing go wrong here. Melissa, if you're looking down on this, intervene if you see something go wrong. God, please don't let nothing go wrong.*

Dr. Mayweather asked again, "*Brasselton?* Can you hear me?"

"I can hear you, man."

"What do you see?"

"I see my moms."

"Where is she?"

"In da castle."

"In the castle? What's the castle like, Brass? Is it nice? Where's the castle? Are you at an amusement park? Six Flags maybe? Disney World?

"Naw. Da castle is where my moms works. Da castle is like da neighborhood kitchen. I'm sitting watching TV with da rest of da kids. I can see Moms bringing in more plastic bags."

"Plastic bags? What are the plastic bags for?"

"For da rocks, man. Everyone's round da table putting white rocks in the bags. Man, don't you know nothing? Da castle is where they make crack from coke—cocaine, dat is—and put it in da bags to sell on da street."

"Hmm . . . how old are you, Brass?"

"'Bout eight . . . maybe nine."

"*Breathe.* Brass, that experience will disappear. I'm going to count to three and clap my hands. You're going to fly forwards a couple of years—two years later. And one . . . two . . . three. Where are you now?"

"I'm in da bunk bed with my cousin."

Dr. Mayweather sighed in relief. "Oh good! Are you sleeping over, or is your cousin at your house?"

"I'm staying at my aunt's. My lil' sister is with my grandma. This is my new home now. I don't like heights, plus Bobby don't like no one sleeping with him on da top bunk, so I'm sleeping with Cynthia."

"Okay, how old are Bobby and Cynthia?"

"Don't know. Bobby is in high school. He plays basketball, and Cynthia is a couple of years behind Bobby . . . I think."

"Brass? Why are you here? Why are you back in this place?"

"'Cause I'm thirsty."

"Why are you thirsty, Brass?"

"They won't give me nothing to drink. They scared I might piss the bed, but Cynthia said I could have some milk."

"Okay, Brass, just let the movie play out. Are you getting your milk?"

"I'm trying, but it won't come out. I keep licking, but it won't come out!"

"Brass, listen to me. Describe what you're doing. Where is everybody? Where's Bobby? Cynthia? Where's your aunt?"

"Auntie's in the other room watching TV. Bobby's in the top bunk."

"Where's Cynthia?"

"Laying down."

"What is she doing?"

"Moaning."

"Brass? Where did you say Bobby is?"

"I told you, man. He's in the top bunk. He's looking down and telling us to be quiet and hurry up. Cynthia's moaning and making all these noises and keeps asking me if it's coming out."

"What's coming out, Brass?"

"Da milk, man! She tells me if I lick her pussy dat da milk will come out. She tells me this is where milk comes from . . . I'm thirsty . . . she tells me to lick the bump harder . . . harder . . . so da milk will come out. She asks me if the milk is coming, and I say no. She tells me to keep licking and stick my tongue in the hole—that will make the milk come out quicker. She keeps asking, 'Is it coming out yet? I feel it coming out. You taste it?' I'm telling her, 'No, I don't taste no milk. It's not coming out.' It's hard to keep licking 'cause da hairs keep tickling my noise, and it smells funny; but I'm doing like she told me 'cause she's older and knows where milk comes from. And I'm thirsty. I'm so thirsty."

"Brass, listen to me, you know where milk comes from now, don't you? Did you ever get any milk this way?"

"Naw, but some white stuff is coming out. It don't taste like no milk I'm used to."

"*Breathe.* Brass, relax. You're far away from that experience. That movie is over. I want you to go back. Go back to the time where you moved into your aunt's house. What happened for you to get there? Why didn't you go to your grandma's house with your sister?"

79

Brass started to speak, but whatever he tried to say came out slurred, jumbled, unintelligible. He tried again, but the same thing happened, which caused him to drop his head and shake it from side to side, over and over.

The brothers, as if they were sitting on pins and needles, twitched and turned in their seats, staring at Brass, not one saying a word. They felt as if this was beginning to turn into another tense, if not intense, session with the Doc; and it showed all over their faces, which were either crinkled in a frown, tensed up, misery ridden, or just contorted in some shape, form, or fashion. And it got worse as they watched the events unfold with Brass, their newfound brother, as he squirmed in his seat and stammered, "I . . . I . . . I . . . I wanted to go . . . I wanted to go to Grandma and Grandpap's house."

The Doc asked, "Why didn't you go, Brass? How did you end up at your aunt's? Where's your mother and sister?"

Brass blew out a huge load of air and took a moment to get himself together. DK, concerned about what was going on, started to speak up; but before he could get the words past his lips, the Doc held up his hand, stopping him.

"Tell us about it, brother Brass. Tell us about that time."

Brass, still shaking his head, began rubbing the palm of his hands against his thighs. His face started to tense up, and he thrust out his lips as if he was getting angry. He kept shaking his head and rubbing his thighs.

The Doc asked, "What's on the screen, Brass? What are you looking at, brother?" Brass whispered something in a way that let everybody know he was disgusted.

"WHAT DID YOU JUST SAY?" asked the Doc.

"A crack-ho. I'm looking at a crack-ho."

"Who's a crack-whore?"

Brass looked down, avoiding eye contact with everyone, and answered, "My moms, Doc. She just got threw tricking for a rock—a fucking dime bag. This cat's pulling up his pants, tucking his lil'-ass dick back in 'em. Moms is crawling around the floor, butt-ass naked, looking for the rock he just tossed on the floor as he walked out. I SEE IT!" Brass continued yelling. "IT'S UNDERNEATH YOUR JEANS, MOMMA!" He raised his hand and pointed in the air. "It's right there! Underneath your jeans. Don't you see it?" He put his hand down and told the Doc, "She keeps crawling, picking, looking for it."

The Doc reassured Brass that he was doing good and said, "Keep watching the movie, brother Brass. Where are you?"

"I'm stooped down in the closet, looking through the slats. This is where me and Margie, my lil' sis, go to hide when my moms does what she do to get money or dat rock. She always tells us before a trick comes to go in there and don't make no noise. Don't come out till she tell us to. She said she don't want nobody knowing we're in there 'cause their likin' to rape both me and Margie then climb on top of her sayin' they fucked the whole family."

"How old is Margie, Brass?"

"'Bout four . . . hmm, maybe close to five 'cause I think she has a birthday coming up soon."

"Brass? I thought you said your moms worked in the castle?"

"Used to. She went from packaging da rocks, to running da rocks through da hood, to using da rocks. Didn't take long for her to start using," Brass told the Doc. "This 'bout da fourth or fifth place we done had to move to too. My gramps said it was better than having Moms stay with them. It kept her from selling everything in their house dat wasn't bolted down, glued down, prayed down, or held down by da grace of God. Gramps gets us out of one place, or problem, depending on how you look at it, and into another. He would pay da first couple of months, and we'd be kicked out or on the verge of being kicked out after da third. She could never keep a job. Not even down at Gramps's church."

Brass sat up in his chair and looked the Doc in the eyes. "I'm remembering now, Doc. I did dis. I 'caused all of dis to happen. I'm da one dat called Gramps to da house. All because I was mad dat Moms had been gone for days. When she came back, she ate up what little was in da house, shitted and pissed where she laid down at, went to sleep for a couple more days, and woke up itching real bad. She needed another hit. Yelling at me for money."

"Tell us about that, Brass."

"Doc, it was bad, man. It got so bad dis time we couldn't walk up to the apartment without seeing rent-due and eviction notices plastered on da door. There was no food in da cabinets, and none in the fridge either—not even a jug of water. We didn't have no clean clothes, or even toilet paper to wipe our asses with. We used old newspaper I found in da trash. My moms had smoked up everything we had. Even sold da pictures Margie had made dat were hanging up on da refrigerator. I couldn't think she would get much for 'em, which led me to believe maybe she was thinking about selling her too."

"Hmm . . . who took care of you and your sister, Brass? You said there was no food. How did you two eat?"

"I took care of Margie. I did what I had to do to get food. Sometimes I did errands for peoples around da hood. Sometimes I collected money for Mrs. Wilson upstairs when people played the numbers. She always gave me a dollar or two and some cookies or cake, for both me and Margie, when I came back with da numbers and da money. Sometimes I just stole what I needed from da store round da block. Whatever I had to do, whatever hustle I had to run, I made sure me and Margie always had something to eat, even if it was only a bag of chips or a pack of Now and Laters, Margie's favorite. We learned quick. We knew to eat first and hide da rest of da food, if there was any, for later. Hide it from Moms and da line of tricks coming in and out da house."

"You're doing real good, Brass. You're fine. I want you to keep watching the movie. Keep telling us what you see."

"Like I was saying, Doc, we ain't have no money. Moms tricked for da lil' bit of money or crack she could get and used da couple of dollars she did get to buy more crack. DAMN! I can't believe I'm back here. It's a bad scene, man. It's a fucking messed-up scene up in here."

"Brass? Earlier you said you caused all of this. Why? Why would say you 'caused all of this? Where are your grandparents?"

Brass said in a low voice, "I caused it, Doc. I know I caused it because I called them. I called Grams and Gramps ova to da house. They came and . . . and—"

"And what, Brass? Is the movie still playing? What do you see? What can you remember?"

"I'm watching my moms laying on a dirty, shitty, bloodstained mattress dat's on da floor, up against da living room wall. There's piles of dirty clothes all ova da place—on da mattress, on da floor, even on da kitchen counter—EVERY-FUCKIN'-WHERE! A crack pipe's laying on da bed by my mom's head, and my grams is trying hard to get Moms up. She's calling out her name. 'Betty! Betty! Please get up, Betty. Please get up, baby.' She's crying and hollering and carrying on, shaking da shit out of Moms, trying to get her up, but Moms is barely coming round."

"What's happening now, Brass?"

"Grams is running to da window, shouting down for Gramps to get out da car and come upstairs and help her."

"What happened when he got upstairs? What are you and Margie doing? Why haven't you guys called 9-1-1?"

"Man, the police ain't 'bout to come up to da projects. Not that late at night. Plus, how it's going to look for da good, reverend doctor to be caught with his crack-ho daughter laid out on a shitty mattress, butt-ass naked? Come on, Doc! Get real, man."

"Okay, Brass. Okay. Take a couple of deep breaths. Where is Margie, while all this is going on?"

"Me and Margie . . . we're . . . we're standing in the kitchen . . . watching. I mean, we've seen dis shit, time and time again."

"Okay. Has your gramps made it up to the apartment?"

"Yah. He's trying to get Moms up. She's coming 'round, but she don't know where she is. I don't think she recognizes him either."

"What is your grandmother doing?"

"Grams is packing up Margie's stuff in some grocery bags. She's hollering at me. Telling me to stop standing 'round like I'm stupid. Telling me to get some more bags, put what I need in 'em 'cause we was going with her and

Gramps." Brass suddenly grew quiet. He started breathing heavily. He inhaled, then exhaled, then inhaled again, then exhaled—heavily.

The Doc said, "You're okay, Brass. You're okay. Just keep breathing . . . slowly . . . slowly . . . slowly. What's going on now? What do you see?"

"I'm looking at my moms. I don't think she knows what da hell is going on. She's toast, man."

"What is she doing? Brass? Brass? Brass, remember you can hear me. You're okay. Tell me what's happening. What's playing out on the screen?"

"She's up . . . scratching everywhere. My gramps is trying to help her. He's beside da bed trying to pull Moms up off of it—probably 'cause it's nasty. He's calling her name out and telling her, 'It's Daddy. Betty, baby, it's Daddy. Daddy's gonna help you. I'm going to get you some help.'"

"You're okay, Brass. You're okay. Remember, it's just a movie. Tell us, what's happening now?"

"Damn, man!" Brass yelled as he began to choke up.

"What is it, Brass?"

"Doc, I don't . . . you sure you want to know?"

"I believe the question is, do you want us to know? Will talking about it help you? Is what you're watching . . . what you're about to tell us . . . is this what you believe you caused? If so, you'll never be able to tackle it if you don't confront it."

Brass started rubbing the back of his hands on his thighs, shaking his head. His eyes welled up with tears, and his voice began to crack and tremble as he resumed telling the brothers his story. "She's reaching between my gramps's legs, feeling him up, telling him she can make him feel real good—real good. She's telling him what she can do for a dime, and if he didn't have no dime-size crack rock, she told him what she would do for twenty dollars—she would rock his world . . . love him a long, long time.

"Doc, it sent my gramps to his knees. He had a heart attack right there—collapsed in da middle of praying; passed away on his knees, hands clutched in prayer . . . died just like dat. Dead on the spot.

"From that moment on, Grams was through with my moms. She took Margie with her and sent me over to my aunt's." Brass faked a smile. "I guess I was bad news. Grams told me I was just like my momma, bad news. I looked like her and acted like her. She said she didn't want no part of me. She didn't want to be reminded of dat devil woman dat killed her husband. He was a good pastor, a good father, and a damn good man, she said.

"Six months later, Grams was dead too. Folks say it was from a broken and grieving heart. That's when Margie went to live with my uncle and his wife over in Virginia, close to DC. She was better off there. She's doing real good for herself now—a teacher. Married too. With a kid. They left me with Auntie—a drunk on welfare who didn't care 'bout nothing—not even her own damn kids. So you know she didn't give a shit about me."

"Where is your moms, Brass? What happened to her?"

"She's gone, man. She went downhill fast after that—never was da same. We lost her. Da last, good thing I remember 'bout my moms was the advice she gave me. She told me, 'Brass, you got to do what you have to do to survive. Remember, it's a cruel, cruel world out there, baby. Nobody's gonna give you shit . . . and nobody's gonna care shit about you—not even family sometimes. You have to use whatever you have to use to get by. That includes even selling what God gave you—and you know what I mean—'cause you's a good-looking boy, yo momma's boy, for sure. Listen here, don't give a shit 'bout nobody, 'cause nobody's gonna give a shit about you.'"

"Brass? I want you to *breathe*. Breathe, Brass. I'm going to count forwards from one to ten. When I get to ten, you'll be back in the plane, looking out the window, looking at the clear blue sky again. One . . . two . . . three . . . four . . . five . . . six . . . seven . . . eight . . . nine . . . ten. Okay, Brass, I'm going to clap my hands, and you'll be back with us. You'll remember everything that happened."

The brothers looked at each other in shock. DK yelled out, "DAMN!"

Malcolm thought he needed to add something. "It's all right, Brass, man. We've all gone through some shit growing up. How you come out of it, man, is the main thing."

Magic and some of the other brothers even had tears in their eyes as they listened to Brass describe the sad and troubled road he had been traveling.

A couple of knocks on the kitchen door interrupted the session. It was the chef and one of his helpers. They rolled in a cart, and the meal was a welcome relief to the heaviness that had pervaded the room. "Gentlemen, I have bananas Foster for dessert," the chef announced as he set up the cart. His helper took out two large skillets and gave one to him. He told the brothers, "Bananas Foster is one of my favorite desserts. It's a sensual combination of cold and hot on your palate. Here, we have bananas sautéed in butter, brown sugar, and cinnamon over a medium low heat. I'm adding two flavorings now. Malcolm? Do you know what they are?"

"It better be a dark rum and some banana liqueur!"

"That's *right!* Dude, you do know your stuff." The chef took a small torch and ignited the rum and liqueur to a small flaming fire. After the flames subsided, he served the bananas with the warm sauce and topped it off with the long-awaited vanilla sorbet.

The brothers ate while the Doc and Brass left the room to talk. Brass's eyes were red and filled with tears. He was trembling a little as well, but he manned up, held back his tears, and held on to his composure for dear life. He had no intention of letting the brothers see him punk out; and as he and the Doc walked past the brothers, they either looked at him with well-wishing eyes or touched his arm, as if to say, *It's okay, man. It's okay.*

DK, who was sitting at the end of the table, got up before they reached him. He shook the Doc's hand and gave Brass a big helping of brotherly love. It was a breakthrough night, with Brass being able to constructively relive what he had so desperately tried to confine within the deepest, darkest recesses of his mind, and realize there was a way to free himself from the guilt and the nightmare. And Malcolm, basking in his element and happily joking around and talking with the chef, stumbled upon and found a lost piece of himself. Something had been awakened; a fire, if not a passion, had been rekindled. Both brothers found, or confronted, *something* that had been dead, if not buried, within them for a long, long time—*something* that let them become less of a silent son.

Chapter 11

Laying It All Out

Thursday, June 25, 2009
Dallas, Texas

*I*t was late—or was it early?— in the morning, and Jessie was up and at it, hard at work. Her nose was to the grindstone and she was brainstorming and coming up with all kinds of ideas for the Brotherhood project. Although K103.5 was not her only client, by far, they were the largest; and she found herself putting more and more of her time, effort, and energy into ensuring that the Brotherhood was a success. Every night she found herself planning, drawing up schedules, and laying out the details for the brothers' return to Dallas in two days, and going over the programming information that DK had put together for the first Brotherhood broadcast, which would air in just a little over a week. But this night was different. This night, Jessie found herself pacing back and forth, trying to figure out how to reintroduce the divas to the Dallas listeners; but she kept drawing a blank. She knew she needed to give the listeners the lowdown on where the divas were in their lives and relationships, because they kept calling and e-mailing the radio station, asking, "Wassup with the divas? Where are they? What are they doing now? Are they still with . . . ?"

Jessie thought about it, and thought about it, and knew having the brothers and divas do a show together was a way of answering all those questions, and a sure way of getting—and keeping—the show's ratings up, just as Sharon said she needed to. She needed to keep the listeners engaged and tuning in week after week to hear all about the divas' and the brothers' drama-filled lives—including her own—and she spent most of the night bouncing idea, after idea, after idea, off the walls of her small but nicely appointed condo.

However it was going to go down, Jessie knew that the reunion needed to be scandalous; and she said out loud to herself, "Lord, please help me. What do I need to do to make this thing right, Lord? And most importantly, what in the world have I gotten myself into?"

She stopped her pacing and walked over and stood in front of ten sheets of paper she had plastered on one side of her living room wall—each labeled with a number, *1* to *10*. She crossed out the one with the number *10* on it. "Lord, Lord, Lord . . . today starts the countdown. Nine days to go before the premier of the Brotherhood." She let out a big sigh and then calmly repeated to herself, "July 5th . . . July 5th . . . July 5th. What a Sunday that's going to be. Lord, give me strength."

She turned away from the sheets of paper on the wall and carefully navigated her way partway across her living room floor—over a minefield of note cards, Post-it notes, and pieces of paper—and sat cross-legged in the middle of it all. With a box of pizza and a glass of wine in front of her, she sifted through the papers and noticed her cell phone vibrating across the pizza box. She looked down at the number: It was Sharon. "Damn! What does she want? And I thought that heifer needed her rest?" Jessie checked the time—12:30 AM. She picked up the phone, but before answering, she asked herself, *Was this trick lying to me? It sure don't look like she's doing too much resting.* She rolled her eyes toward the ceiling *Oh well . . . whatever,* and answered the phone.

"Jessie Harris speaking."

"Jessie? Girl, this is Sharon. How are you tonight?"

"Girl, I'm good. I've been up, going over your account."

"Oh good. Then I won't feel bad about calling you at this godawful hour."

"What is it, Sharon? You okay?"

"Yes . . . well, no, I'm not okay. I just got off of the phone with the ICON Awards team. WHEW! That was a long conference call, girl. We started at 9:00 PM, and just finished—three hours of absolutely nothing. Not a goddamn thing accomplished. Girl, three hours of talking about nothing but nonsense and craziness."

Jessie listened as Sharon went on and on about the conference call, although she already knew what was up with the project. The ICON Awards, one of K103.5's biggest community recognition events, recognized local and national talents from all walks of life; and this year marked the first time that Melissa was not at the helm. The word was out that it was a mess, a shitty mess at that; and everyone who was approached by K103.5's executive team and asked to spearhead the project knew exactly what was up, and turned down every one of the radio station's offers.

Jessie said, "That doesn't sound too good, girl. Hmm. How is the ICON project really coming along—apart from all the craziness going on?"

Sharon wheezed out some air. "Whooo, girl, not so good. What's today?"

"Thursday. The twenty-fifth of June," answered Jessie.

"Hmm. How about that? It's the end of June, and the ICON Awards is in the first week of August, less than two months away, and everything is just falling apart right before my eyes. Girl, I'm telling you, I'm getting too old for this shit. Get this: The executive producer *just* quit."

"Ooh, Sharon, girl, NOOOO! Oh my god, what are you going to do?"

"I know, like, eew! Can it get *any* worse? Girl, anyway, the heifer just up and quit on me, with not an iota of a warning. I'm gone sue her ass, for sure—if she don't already know—just as sure as my name's Sharon Williams! Breaking my contract like that. HMPH! I don't think so. Anyway—and thanks for listening to me vent, girl—the reason I'm calling is . . . well . . . I'm calling to see if you'd like to take on this newly available role. K103.5 knows you love a challenge, and I was thinking we could even work in a plug for the Brotherhood and incorporate them into the show as well."

"Well, Sharon . . . I don't know," Jessie said.

"You don't have to answer right now, Jess, although we don't have too much time with this. All I'm asking is for you to just think about it. And about the money aspect, which is negotiable—we'll add another 30K to your contract with a performance bonus of another 10K if it's successful, granted you hit the mark with the sponsorship and funding we're looking for. It's going to be televised too, so we need to ensure that we get the appropriate sponsors and advertisers on board as well. To tell you the truth, right now—and I hate to say it—there's very little interest in the whole thing. You're going to have to drum up the interest—cold turkey. We know you have the connections to do it. Just think about it."

There was a brief pause on the phone, and then Sharon said, "HELL! I'm just gone beg, girl. Point-blank. I need somebody I can trust and rely on, somebody I know who's going to pull through and get the job done. I need a leader that can go in there and clean up all this shit and make this the best ICON Awards show ever—a show Melissa Morgan will be truly proud of."

"I'll have complete control?" asked Jessie.

"Complete control, girl."

It didn't take long for Jessie to make up her mind. Confidently, she told Sharon, "Okay. Although I may be biting off more than I can chew, which I doubt . . . for some reason, I'm going to say yes. . . . Something just popped in my head. I think I can make this work, including having the Brotherhood on the show and a special guest star, I have in mind, which will tie all of it together. Can you send me the ICON file? Send it to my home e-mail account."

Sharon laughed. "Girl, it was there when you picked up the phone."

"Aren't we sure of ourselves?" asked Jessie as she started laughing with Sharon.

"Girl, you got to be. You won't make it in this business, or in life, if you're not."

The two continued talking for a while. Later, after they said good-bye, Jessie immediately logged in to her e-mail. She felt an adrenaline rush as she opened the file and started pulling together her ideas—jotting them down and laying them all out. A couple of hours later, she was making all kinds of ruckus as she jumped up and down—doing a little cabbage patch dance in the process—and yelled out, "YES! YES! YES!" She had figured out how to get the divas and the brothers together and couldn't wait to tell DK, Magic, and the Doc about every last detail. She was worried, though. She wasn't sure if they would buy into the idea.

Chapter 12

The Brothers' Retreat
Day 3: Jessie's Conference Call

Thursday, June 25, 2009
Angoon, Alaska

DK, Magic, and the Doc got up for an early breakfast and were conferenced in with Jessie, who was overjoyed and simply beside herself. She just couldn't contain her excitement.

"Oh my god! Malcolm? Tracy's husband? And Britt's man, Brass? A breakthrough night? Now, you know, I would love to hear all about that one, but I know you guys aren't going to tell me; so I'll just leave it at that."

They could hear Jessie on the phone saying, "WHEW!" and then let loose with a whole bunch of adjectives before she told the Doc, "You said it was going to be healing, Doc Mayweather, but I had no idea it was going to be like this. Oh my god, I'm just so happy about all of this. I know Melissa would be too—just happy, bless her resting soul." She laughed and then said, "Hey, listen. I have a lot to tell you, guys—"

"Jess?"

"Hey, Magic."

"How's my girl Sharon doing, and how's everybody at the station? Y'all holding it down? Doing the thang right?"

"BOY, PLEASE! You know we are, and I talked to Sharon earlier this morning. She's good. And speaking of doing the right thing—hey, DK? I think I already know the answer to this, but I'm going to ask anyway: Did you have a chance to call the judge? Because he's still calling me like crazy."

Although DK knew he wasn't going to call, he answered, "Naw, baby girl. Not yet. Tell him I'll give him a call once I get back in town tomorrow."

Jessie, trying to process and get a good feel of what DK just said, and how he said it, told him, "That doesn't sound too promising. Well, anyway, that's between you and him." And although she sensed something was wrong, she couldn't help but wonder if it had anything to do with Pat or, better yet, the Brotherhood; and although she was concerned, she decided to leave it alone—she definitely didn't want to overstep her boundaries. All she knew was that she had a lot to tell the guys, a lot to run by them for their approval; and not knowing where to start, she, unexpectedly, started spewing out gibberish into the phone. The Doc, realizing something was wrong, interjected and got the conversation ball rolling.

"Jessie?"

"Doc Mayweather? Is that you? Ooooh, I almost forgot how you sound. You've been so quiet these past few days."

"I know. Hard to believe, right? Me, quiet."

Jessie said, "I know that's right. It is hard to believe, Mr. Chatterbox."

The Doc let out a quick, dry chuckle. "I apologize for not being more talkative, Jessie; but for the Brotherhood project, I thought I needed to sit back, observe, and soak it all in before I threw in my two cents' worth. And now that I've taken it all in, I do have a question for you."

"Oh lord. What is it?" she asked.

The Doc pushed his glass of water aside and slid the speakerphone closer to him. "Jess? DK, Magic, and I were talking before you conferenced in; and I think we need to have a session with the divas, get some of their feedback, especially as to what they like and dislike about their men, and vice versa."

Jessie, caught off guard, started coughing right into the phone.

"Baby girl? You okay over there?" asked DK.

Jessie cleared her throat. "Yah . . . I'm . . . okay." She quickly regained her composure and expected an argument, if not a long discussion, about the plan she was about to unveil to the fellas. "Doc Mayweather, funny you should mention that."

Magic said, "Oh lawd, that don't sound too good. I ain't liking the tone in that there voice of yours, Jess. What's going on?"

"Well, I think it's a good thing . . . but hey, you tell me."

"Okay, baby girl, we're hooked. You got us. So start reeling us hungry fish in—whatcha got to tell us?" asked DK.

Jessie yelled out, "WE'RE DOING THE ICON AWARDS!"

"What!" exclaimed Doc Mayweather.

"You're effin' kidding me!" yelled DK.

"Aiight, aiight." Magic said.

She told them, "I talked to Sharon this morning, and there's a new direction with the ICONs, which I won't get into, by the way. But to answer your question, DK, we're going to honor our Melissa with an award, and who better to present it than the divas and the brothers together?"

"Say what?" asked DK.

"I know! I know! Can you believe it? The show's less than two months away. Mark it on your calendar—it's Saturday, August 8th."

The brothers, sitting on the edge of their seats, could hear papers rustling on Jessie's end of the line, and they all leaned into the table, waiting, not wanting to miss a word she had to tell them.

"Now here's the plan," she said. "On Friday, DeDe, our songstress, will be flying in from LA. I've already called her and made arrangements for her and her agent. Brass's old flame, Britt, is flying in from Atlanta later in the day, so you tell him this is his time to make it right between them—if he wants her back. Saturday afternoon, the brothers and us divas will do a pre-ICON airing at V's shop—Sweet V's Beauty Shop, if you don't know—and the brothers will get complimentary haircuts and do a meet and greet with the customers—kind of a get-you-guys-out-into-the-public-eye event. Saturday night, we'll do the ICON Awards honoring our girl Melissa, and Sunday—well, Sunday will be the day."

"Sunday? What are you talking about, baby girl?" asked DK. "Sundays are the Brotherhood show's nights. We air on Sundays, remember?"

"Yes, I know. This is going to be a special Brotherhood show. So let's talk about it." Jessie could hear Magic whisper in the background, "I don't know, man. I smell some bullshit coming on." She pretended not to hear him and told them, "First, the divas and the brothers will attend Pastor Levine's church, Greater Antioch, for Sunday-morning worship; and later that night, on the *Quiet Storm*, all of us—the divas and the brothers—will be on the air talking about love and relationships. Because you and I both know, DK, that everybody wants to hear about"—Jessie paused and let out a soft but audible sigh—*what really went down in the divas' relationships—especially from the male point of view. So, DK?"

"Yah, baby girl."

"I'll leave the show's format up to you, Magic, and Doc Mayweather. So tell me, now that you've heard the game plan—what do you guys think?"

As Jessie waited for the brothers to answer, they sat and stared at each other with a *What did she just say?* look on their faces.

The Doc eventually broke the awkward silence by telling Jessie, "Well, that's not exactly what we had in mind. We were actually thinking more of a private couple's session, if not a group session, off the air."

DK and Magic looked at each other and shook their heads in agreement, but didn't say anything.

Jessie, sensing some hesitation, if not resistance, told the guys that she was in a dilemma and needed a way to market the ICON Awards and plug the Brotherhood at the same time. As far as she knew, this was the best way to do it. She also knew it was the exact kind of drama she needed to bring in the ratings, even if it came at her own expense. She knew that for ratings to soar, there needed to be, one, some type of mess or drama, and, two, a reaction to that drama; and she realized that her dirty laundry would be fair game to be aired to Dallas as well—which could get *really* ugly. She grimaced at the possibility, but soon discounted her apprehensions—because she *needed* and *wanted* this to work more than anything. She convinced herself that this was a risk she would have to take.

DK, unsure about the divas being on the Brotherhood, told Jessie, "Hey, Jess, I tell you what, let me do this, since we have that mountain hiking trip today, and Malcolm's leading our Brotherhood session tonight. Let me figure out a way to slide it in and run it by the brothers, get their opinion." As soon as he said it, he thought, *There's no way in hell they're gonna go for this shit*; and he told Jessie, "Mmm. A brotherhood with the brothers' past and present lovers, and their wives?" He frowned. "HMPH. Honestly, baby girl, I got a feeling that's not gonna go over too well. I mean, I can probably sell anything, but having the divas on the show? Probably not gonna be able to sell that." He let out a slew of *whews*, *whoahs*, and *damns* before asking again, "Bringing the divas into the mix, Jess? You sure about that? 'Cause you know, it's not going to be anything nice. Nothing but effin' drama in the studio booth—messy-ass drama at that. I can see it now."

Jessie, a little worried that her plans were falling apart and not wanting a deep discussion about it either, said, "Okay. Talk to the brothers, DK. I'll have my fingers crossed. Listen, you guys. Enjoy your day of hiking, and I hope you'll have another breakthrough session, just like you had last night. Guess that's it for me, guys. You have the itinerary for tomorrow, so, I guess I'll talk to you when you get back in town. BYE!" She hung up and said a little prayer that DK would realize how important it was to have the divas on the show. She thought about calling him on his cell phone to tell him in private, but she changed her mind. She just sat there and quietly told herself, "If it's God's will, everything will work out the way it's supposed to. God, I'm just hoping for the best."

Chapter 13

The Brothers' Retreat
Day 3: Listen, My Dick's Talking

The hint of night was upon the brothers, and it held off casting blackness across the roof, walls, and steps of the lodge. DK was in his own little world, sitting quietly with the brothers, peering out the window and thinking, *It's too damn light outside for this time of day*. Not used to the Alaskan sunsets, he felt it was kind of eerie to watch the sun shimmer across the lodge's lake at eight thirty. As he turned his attention back to the moment, he looked around the room and noticed that the brothers didn't seem to mind. They just looked tired and worn down from their long day of hiking through the Tongass National Forest; and by the look on their faces, everyone appeared to be glad they were out of the woods and back on familiar ground—back sitting around the infamous dining room table, which overlooked the lodge's sparkling and soothing blue Alaskan waterway.

The atmosphere, although somewhat jovial, was filled with a heavy air of melancholy; and everyone in the room noticed and felt it. Although the brothers had made it through another day of bonding, each of them sat contemplating their last night in Angoon with mixed emotions: They were happy they were going home, but sad the brotherhood and camaraderie they had shared for the last couple of days was about to end. Hungry, if not starving, they waited for the kitchen door to swing open so they could start tasting—and rag on, if need be—the special meal that Malcolm and the chef had prepared for their last night.

Magic's cutting up, as usual, helped hurry the hours along, easing the brothers' wait. He also worked his laptop, putting out nothing but hit, after hit, of oldies but goodies, which had the brothers yelling out "HEY!" and "Work that shit, boy!" and "Nigga, that's the jam!" He put on "We Are One" by Frankie Beverly and Maze. DK was acting a fool—dancing a la James Brown and belting out Frankie and the Maze's lyrics in his own flavorful way, repeating over and over, "We are one brothers, we are one, y'all." In the middle of the song, he stopped singing, or whatever you want to call it, hummed a little and cleared his throat. "Augh-ummm!" And then he told the brothers, "I'd like to propose a toast."

The brothers turned to look at him, crazy like, and raised their glasses of cognac, vodka, gin, and bourbon, and one orange juice, high up in the air.

DK told them, "By the end of the night—before we're all drunk and wasted, that is—I'd like for everyone to give a toast. I want you to toast to whatever this retreat has meant to you. Feel free to do it whenever you're ready. Doesn't matter when or how you do it—just as long as you do it. We got all night too, fellas."

As "We Are One" was winding down, DK said, "Okay, brothers, I'm gonna start this toasting thing off by telling you what it's meant for me." He stood up, all while keeping his glass raised above his head, and said, "Brothers, I'm truly blessed—blessed to be in the company of some good, good men. Not only have I learned a few *new* things about myself . . . well, I've learned a few new things about you too—eye opening things." He turned halfway back to the kitchen and pointed at the kitchen door. "Including that Negro in there, helping with the food."

The brothers laughed, and he told them, "Yah, the Doc's been slowly peeling back the layers of us silent sons, hasn't he?"

The brothers didn't answer; they just nodded at him. "All right, fellas. A toast. I just want to say thank you to Doc Mayweather. This has really been something, man."

The brothers nodded their heads, started clapping, and said, "Hear, hear."

The Doc smiled and raised his glass to DK, saying, "Thank you, brother DK. "You haven't seen nothing yet." He gave DK a quick nod and then looked at the brothers both to his left and his right, and said, "Brothers, just to let you know, I've been working with Malcolm on tonight's Brotherhood session, and if all goes as planned, I promise you, we're going to have some interesting conversations up in here tonight."

Pastor Levine, a little worried, asked, "What type of conversations, Doc? Do I need to pray on this before we begin?"

"You might need to, Pastor. We're going to talk about our women tonight— dick talking, as brother Malcolm puts it." The Doc, realizing what he just said, shook his head—as if he couldn't believe he just said "dick talking"—and told the brothers, "To tell you the truth, I'm kinda looking forward to it. It's going to be a wild one, I assure you. It's probably just the therapy we all need to open us silent sons up—especially these quiet ones over here: Quentin, Xavier, Miguel . . . and you too, Pastor."

DK, who already knew what was up, smiled and winked at the Doc. He told the brothers, "Fellas, this is our last night in Alaska, and our last dinner session—so we gotta make this shit count. We got one more session after this one, at breakfast tomorrow; so meet me down here at 7:00 AM, sharp. Don't be late, fellas. The Doc's gonna break us into groups, and before you even ask, he'll tell you the reason why, then. Let's just see if his theory or predictions about us—he's gonna tell us about that tomorrow too—comes to fruition."

Donnell said, "Groups! More fucking group shit. Man, I don't do well in groups—"

"Hmph! Ain't that the truth," said Mike. "We all know that. Tell us something we don't know, nigga!" And he threw up his hands, flipping his wrists in the process, giving Donnell the brush-off.

Donnell couldn't let that go. Half joking and half serious, he said, "Aw, shut up, nigga, with your punk-bitch ass."

DK, rushing to the rescue, told them, "Fellas! Come on. Can't we move past this bickering? Damn." He let out a long, heavy grunt and gave Mike and Donnell an evil look before sitting back down and picking up his drink. He took a couple of swallows and said, "Okay, brothers, as I was saying, the Doc's gonna get into the group stuff tomorrow at breakfast. For tonight, we're going to turn it over to our man Malcolm, who, as you know, is gonna be our session leader." He looked back through the kitchen door and yelled out, "What in the hell is he and the chef doing in there? DAMN!"

As soon as he did, the kitchen doors flew open, and Malcolm pimp-walked out in a pair of black-and-white-striped pants, a white chef's coat, and a fluffy white hat, with the similarly attired chef right behind him.

"My boys, dinner's ready. And don't your boy look the part?" Malcolm asked as he continued his walk toward the table.

Before the brothers could compose themselves and refrain from bursting out in laughter, the chef butted in and told Malcolm that he did an excellent job assisting with dinner, and that he might just have a bright, if not exciting, future in the culinary arts. The chef also told Malcolm that he was a natural at it, and that his passion should not go to waste. The chef kept going on and on about Malcolm and told him he never would have thought about preparing a dinner such as this, but that he understood Malcolm's intentions. The chef was just blown away by Malcolm's skills and was equally impressed by the combination of spices and liqueurs that Malcolm used in everything. "It just made the meal work," he said. He then asked Malcolm whether he would like to help serve dinner or join the group instead.

"I think I'll join the brothers, Chef, if that's okay with you."

The chef said it was and asked Malcolm to help him out by telling the brothers what they had prepared and, more importantly, why he suggested the dessert.

Malcolm raised his hand and gave the chef a big salute. Then he told the brothers, "Okay, fellas, today, we've prepared some dishes that's gonna blow your freakin' minds. We have a five-course meal ready for ya, and Davey here— he's the chef's assistant—is bringing out a cold shrimp bisque with a splash of brandy. We gone get y'all drunk tonight, fellas."

Brass said, "Aw, shit now. I'm ready, playa; and you got it smellin' good up in here too? Hell yah. Bring that shit on, boy-ee."

Pastor Levine shook his head and said, "Now, fellas, you know I don't drink. I'm doing just fine with this here OJ. I see y'all gone test me tonight, huh, brothers?"

Everybody started laughing because the pastor's right leg kept hitting the table, as it bounced up and down a mile a minute. Malcolm told him, "You drinkin' tonight, partna, or hell, you ain't 'bout to eat. Everything's cooked or flavored with liqueur, playa. And just like I said, we gone get y'all drunk tonight." Pastor Levine shook his head and fixed Malcolm with an *Is he a fool?* look, but Malcolm didn't pay him any mind and just kept on talking.

"After the bisque, we're serving up an appetizer." Malcolm started beating the table with both of his hands. "An appetizer that's going to rock your world— deviled crab, playas, deviled crabs. Brothers, you haven't had deviled crabs until you've had this recipe—my grandmama's. We even put the deviled crab back in the original crabshells—original, huh? Now, that's a true deviled crab, my niggas."

The brothers looked around the table in disbelief, asking themselves, "Is this the same Malcolm that came up with us? The same playa with the gold chain, big-ass cross, and lime green, silk pantsuit?"

Malcolm said, "Next, we'll serve a light mandarin orange salad—with real mandarin oranges, fellas—with a light honey Dijon dressing; and for the entrée, we've prepared a drunken Tennessee steak: a grilled choice-cut piece of meat marinated in nothing but the best Tennessee whiskey. That would be that Jack Daniel's, playas. And we're serving it up with prosciutto-wrapped asparagus— y'all don't know nothing 'bout that." He laughed. "Asparagus wrapped in bacon, niggas, which I slightly basted in virgin olive oil."

Quentin yelled out, "Damn, Malcolm! Go 'head on, boy!"

"For sure," said *X*. "HUMPH! I'm . . . speechless, man."

"Right. Right. All right fellas, I saved the best for last. Now for dessert, what goes better with a steak than an all-time American favorite? A classic with a twist. WE'RE HAVING CHOCOLATE SHAKES, BABY! A chocolate shake made with that Alchemy chocolate vodka, Godiva Dark Chocolate liqueur, and that good ole chocolate Blue Bell ice-cream, the ice cream of Texas. We didn't have time to make it from scratch—remember our first night, y'all?"

As the black of night cast its dark shadow over the lodge, the chef and Davey served the brothers, who ate—more like tore into—the bisque, then the deviled crab, then the salad (you could hear all the *oohs* and *awws* in the room), and then the entrée. Finally, the dessert was served, and the room was once again filled with the brothers' *oohs* and *awws*, which were louder this time. The brothers, almost at the same time, said, "Damn, Malcolm!" as they stared down at an over-the-top, liquored down, extravagantly decorated milkshake and started complimenting the chef on dinner and praising Malcolm's cooking skills, which lifted Malcolm's spirit to a place he could never have imagined, dreamed of, or even knew existed. In his thirty-plus-years of living, he had never experienced a feeling so great. It was as though he was floating away from the body of the Malcolm he'd known for so many years to something great; and unbeknownst to him, he was: He was floating toward a new beginning, a new life. The world he knew—the world he felt trapped within for so many years—was about to end.

Strangely enough, while Malcolm was floating, DK was sinking—sinking into a dilemma of *What do I do?* A dilemma that caused him to block out the brothers' rants and raves about Malcolm's dinner and travel back in time to a conversation he had with Melissa and Chef Luda—a conversation about helping Luda find someone who was just as passionate about *food* as he was. It was though a bolt of lightning had hit DK and energized his brain. He had found *that* someone who was not only passionate about food, but was damn good at making it do what it do; but for now, none of that mattered because DK was at war with his spirit, and it kept telling him, *Don't even go down that road, man.*

He asked himself, *Why should I help Malcolm? Hell, we all know he and Mike ain't right. And what's gonna be in it for me?* He looked at Malcolm, who was beaming from ear to ear—enjoying the brothers' praises, and smiled and joined the brothers in congratulating Malcolm. He said to himself, *Damn. I just don't know. Can I count on this Negro to do the right thing? 'Cause God knows he's not doing right by his wife—if Jessie's on point about that.*

DK sat there, at odds with himself. He didn't want to make the same mistake he believed he'd made with Pat and the judge; and he didn't want to put Malcolm's issues on the laps of Chef Luda and Bee, whom he thought were good people. He sat and thought about it and grew leery about recommending someone he knew little about.

Malcolm shook him out of his reverie. "What's wrong, playa? You don't like it? You're not drinking. Wassup?"

DK winced and quickly put Chef Luda, Bee, and Bailey's out of his mind. He told Malcolm, "No, it's good, man. I was just thinking about our session." And he asked the brothers to adjourn to the great room so they could begin.

Before they did, the brothers got refills of the dessert drink, adding a little extra of this and a little extra of that, and drunkenly gathered around the great room's sunken fireplace. DK, Magic, Malcolm, and the Doc sat at the base of the fireplace, facing the brothers, and noticed that the combination of liquor-infused meal and the dessert drink was working on the brothers. They were buzzed, if not already lit—dancing, singing, and freely talking about their life's issues with each other.

Malcolm told the Doc, "Guess my idea's working, huh, Doc?"

The Doc grinned at Malcolm. "It's a little unorthodox, but—and I hate to admit it—I guess so." He patted Malcolm on the back. "Let's see what the night's going to bring. Let's see if the brothers really open up like you say they will."

Malcolm returned the Doc's grin and started the session off by telling the brothers that they were in for a hell of a ride. He started asking the brother's a series of questions; but the last one, although expected, threw everyone off— including the Doc. No one expected Malcolm's session to start off the way it did; and Magic, with DK's help, seized the opportunity and deepened the experience, as only he could—which opened the door for some heavy discussions, just as Malcolm knew it would.

"All right, brothers," said Malcolm as he stood up in front of the fireplace, rubbing his hands together as though he was cold. "I'm going to kick this session off—damn, it's cold in here!" He turned his back to the brothers, bent down, and started moving the wood around the fire pit with the poker, trying to make the fire grow bigger. Without turning around, Malcolm asked, "How many of us can say we met ours the right way?"

The brothers looked at him, smiling and laughing, which gave him the momentum, to ask, "So, brothers? What jumped first? The dick or the brain? And I'ma throw in a little something extra for you too. Have you guys heard the phrase 'she was all that and a bag of chips?'"

The brothers nodded and said a collective "Yah."

"Instead of chips, I wanna know: What type of cake was she? 'Cause when I think about those cakes, I can't help but think about those brown rounds."

Magic laughed at Malcolm and asked, "Brown rounds? Whatchu mean, playa?"

"He means that round booty, dumbass," DK said, laughing. "He's talking about what type of woman she is."

Malcolm stood up and turned around to face the brothers. "Take me, for example. When I met my wife, Tracy, she was definitely a spice cake—just as spicy as she wanted to be, *just sassy*. Yah, when we first met, my dick jumped first, 'cause my baby's body was bangin'—still is. My dick was talking to me, fellas, and I was a listening. Fellas, my big mistake was never bothering to peel away the wrapping to see what type of gift was really underneath all that fine-ass wrapping paper that was making my shit jump. You feelin' me?"

Magic said, "We feelin' you, playa. You should've unwrapped the package and found out what type of woman was really inside that bangin' body—used that brain of yours instead of that magic stick."

"Right," said Malcolm as he sat back down and looked straight through the brothers and out the windows. "Fellas, Tracy was a looker. Nice hair, full lips, perky lil' titties, and a nice round, fat booty. She definitely was a spice cake. Girl had a helluva mouth on her. At the time, I thought it was cute 'cause she would always speak her mind, talk trash. Everybody would tell me, 'Man, check your woman. She's running that mouth of hers.' But like I said, I thought it was cute."

The brothers looked at him as if to say, *Yah, that's what you get.* And Malcolm told them, "I admit it, I went along with it—probably even encouraged it. Maybe I even deserved this 'cause I laughed at all her stunts, all the while saying, 'Get 'em, baby.' But now"—Malcolm hung his head and started shaking it slowly—"she's pulling *that* shit on me, and the shit she's pulling, man, it's starting to get old, real old, and quick."

The Doc picked up his pencil and pad and scribbled something down. "Okay, Malcolm, let's talk this through. Let's talk about, as you put it, 'that shit.' What are some of the things Tracy's done to make you feel the way you're feeling? Start off with the most egregious. Let's see if it's as bad as you may think it is. Maybe we can come to a resolution and get you past these feelings you're having."

"Aiight, Doc. I can give you a whole shitload of examples, but hey, I got one for you: For example, Tracy made dinner one night—which I thought was odd, 'cause she don't really cook. She made this spaghetti dish, with the garlic bread and salad, which was good; and I didn't think anything about her not eating. I was, like, okay, my baby made me some din-din—how sweet. We talked while I ate. Good conversation, and as usual, Tuesdays are my b-ball days; and I had plans on going to play with the fellas after I ate. Well, as I was leaving, she brought out my gym bag, kissed me on the forehead, handed me my bag and keys, and calmly told me, 'When you kissing that bitch, just know that she's tasting my juice.' I looked at her—in a fucked-up kinda way, I suppose—and asked, 'What in the hell is it now? What are you talking about, Trace?' Come to find out, she thought that I was creeping on her, which, I admit, I probably was—who wants to deal with her bullshit? And she told me she had put her period juice in the spaghetti sauce I had just ate, that if the trick was going to have a piece of me, then the trick was going to have a piece of her too. Every time I put my tongue down that other woman's nasty-ass throat, she would be tasting her pussy."

Malcolm had shut the room down. The only words coming from the brothers were a bunch of expletives: "Goddamn," "Shit," and "Fuck."

"Yep. Yep. I remember that," said Mike. "Tracy's a trip. She's my sister-in-law and everything, but I don't know how you put up with her shit most of the time, man. Especially after all you've done to hold down the fort when she was going to grad school: Working two to three shifts back-to-back to make ends meet, and she's still trippin'—or all the times you had to get off from work, pick up the kids, feed 'em and put 'em to bed when she had to work late, and she's still trippin'. Or how about the countless times you had to bail her ass out of a tight jam when she stuck her foot in that there mouth of hers? And she's still trippin'." Mike started laughing, almost choking, trying to get the words out. "Hey! . . . Tell . . . tell the . . . fellas about the time she sent that drag queen up to your job."

Brass couldn't hold it in anymore; he started cracking up. He finally got out, "WHAT? You lying homey! You's got to be lying. No, she didn't do that to our boy!"

DK leaned over Magic's shoulder, trying to help him find some sound bites on his laptop, and shouted, with a little sarcasm, "Yah, Malcolm, tell us about that time, man!"

Malcolm gave Mike a dirty look and told the fellas, "Yah. Then there was the time she had this drag queen come up to my job and humiliate me in front of everybody—my supervisor, line workers, every-fucking-body—talking about she was Ms. Plavana DéMonét, a.k.a. Tracy Cole, and that she was not going to be the other woman. And the outfit the dude had on—man, I was so fucking embarrassed." Malcolm threw his arms out asking, "Fellas, come on now, what woman does that to her man? And don't even get me started on all the other crazy shit she's done. Fellas, don't get me wrong, I love Tracy; but that spice cake . . . man, it's turned into a fucking fruitcake—for real. It's like that movie where the dude says he never knows what he's going to get from the box of chocolates . . . well, hell, I feel the same damn way. I never know what in the hell I'm going to get from day to day; and lately, it's been nothing but nuts and fruit. No cake or anything having to do with any substance. Just a nutcase—a fucking fruit basket. Is that egregious enough for you, Doc?"

The Doc's eyebrows rose almost to the start of his hairline. He puckered up his lips, twisting them from side to side, as he thought about what he was going to say. "Well, I would say that Tracy's methods, not to mention motives, of getting your attention may appear to be somewhat extreme. However, there are always two sides to every story, and I would need to get her side to draw a more accurate picture of the problem—which may stem from something deeper than what's being portrayed here."

"Naw. Naw. I ain't even trying to hear all of that, Doc. It's been one thing after the other. If she ain't calling somebody, she's driving by their house. If she ain't driving by their house, she's hiding in somebody's bushes. If she ain't hiding in the bushes, she's scheming or doing some kind of crazy-ass shit. AND THE LAST STRAW! The last straw was her calling that damn radio station and blasting me on the air."

Magic said, "Hold up! Got that right here." And he started playing the sound bite of when Tracy called up the radio station.

"You mean this call?" asked DK as V, who was filling in for Melissa that day, started talking:

"Welcome back to K103.5. This is your girl, V, standing in for the sweet, sweet Melissa Morgan, who is off on a date somewhere with her boo, Mr. Quentin. Hey, Q! Caller, you are on the line."

"Yeah. Hello. I'm calling to make a dedication."

"Okay. What's your name, caller?"

"My name is Mrs. Cole."

"Mrs. Cole, do you have a first name?"

"Oh, it's not my first name that really matters. Ask your girl DeDe what I mean."

"Ooh! Oh my goodness, DeDe, do you know what this caller is talking about?"

"No, I'm sorry. I don't."

"Oh, now the name doesn't ring a bell? Well, let me say this, Ms. DeDe, I'm Malcolm's wife. You do know Malcolm Crawley, am I right? You did just sleep with him a few days ago, am I right? I'm the woman whose name is on the marriage certificate and on all the birth certificates of his kids. I'm the woman whose mouth you're stealing the food from by living up in that condo he's helping you pay for. And that cheap-ass Benz you're so proud of—I would like to point out how low down on the list you are. Baby girl, that's a C class, okay? I'm pushing the 750. I got handbags that cost more than that bucket you're driving, but woman to woman, I'd like you to break it off. A man is a man. You can't expect but so much out of them, but as a woman, who I'm sure would like to be married one day herself, I hold you to a higher standard. One day, honey, you will find your soul mate; and you will marry him, and you will want him to be faithful to you and your family. And you will hope and pray another woman, such as yourself, won't come and break that family apart. That said, I would like to dedicate Shirley Brown's 'Woman to Woman' to you. I hope it inspires some compassion in you for me. And if not for me, then my children. And if not for my children, then yourself. Good night, ladies."

Brass said, "Yep. Yep. Dat's it. I remember dat homey."

Quentin, who had been quiet for most of the retreat, concurred. "Yah, I remember that too. Melissa couldn't stop talking about it. Hell, all of Dallas was talking about that one, man."

Magic, being the instigator, played a snippet of the chorus from Teddy Pendergrass's "The Whole Town's Laughing at Me," which caused the brothers to say "Noooo!" And they all started cracking up at Malcolm.

Malcolm looked at Magic in a way that made his facial muscles stretch inward toward his eyes—his black pupils were big as acorns—a look that told him, and the rest of the brothers, *I'm pissed*. If Malcolm could spit fire, he probably would have. He would have burned the lodge, with the brothers in it, straight down to the ground. He shook his head at DK and Magic and said, "Y'all wrong for that, my niggas." And then he stood up, taking several swigs from his drink, and held up his hand as if telling the brothers, *Wait a minute*. With his hand up, he swallowed a few more sips and then said angrily, "Brothers! I'm telling you, that shit ain't right. Y'all know it ain't. It don't make no kind of sense, and that shit didn't sit too well with me, fellas—not at all. Tell you the truth, I'm at the end of my rope with Tracy . . . She has one more time to disrespect me—one more fucking time."

"Whatchu gone do, man? Whatchu gone do?" asked Magic, instigating, getting Malcolm all wired up.

"Man, the next stunt she pulls, I'm out. I'm gonna calmly pack my shit up and walk the fuck out the door. I ain't gone say nothing, I ain't gone look at her, I ain't gone even turn around. I'm just gone head to the door, walk out, and be gone. Gone for fucking good."

DK turned to the Doc and whispered, "Hmph. A drunk man's words are a sober man's thoughts—so they say."

The Doc smiled, and, while looking straight at the brothers, said underneath his breath, "So they say. I believe it's about to get real interesting in here, brother DK. Real interesting. I'm just going to let this all play out like it should. Letting the brothers talk and vent like this is probably more useful than anything I could ever say at this drunken moment."

Malcolm asked, "Aiight. I'm done, fellas. Who's next?"

There was an "augh-hum" at the back of the room, and the brothers turned to see where it came from.

"Well, brothers," Pastor Levine began. "I was married, and my stuff jumped when I met my piece of cake too. Lord God, that probably should've been clue number one right there. A clue telling me that she was not what I needed . . . not what I needed 'cause she turned out to be one of the biggest whores in town— and we're in Dallas, my brothers." He turned to DK and asked, "DK? What's the population of the Dallas metro?"

DK did a quick Google and answered, "Looks like it's about 6.4 million."

"Like I said, one of the biggest whores in town. Brothers, I'll never forget that day. I wanted to do something special for my lady, so I took off from work and came home early one day for lunch. I was going to surprise her, take her out to her favorite restaurant; and I'll be doggone if I didn't catch her—how can I say this—pelvically massaging one of my best friends, right there in my house . . . in our bed, I had just got out of not too long before, and I was still paying for. So, brother Malcolm, I guess I had a ho cake. Nothing more than cornmeal and a little bit of water, fried up in bacon grease—just cheap, but I admit, it was damn tasty at the time."

Everybody's mouths dropped wide open. The brothers looked at Pastor Levine as if to exclaim, *What did he just say!* "Don't look so surprised, my brothers.

I wasn't always saved—that, of course, came later; but this was the beginning of my salvation. In my worldly life, I used to be a performer . . . a male dancer, to be exact—"

"YOU MEAN A STRIPPER!" Brass piped up.

"A stripper, brother Brass." Pastor Levine got up, propped himself up behind his chair, and glanced up at the ceiling before saying, "Uh-huh, I can tell you my stuff jumped, first. Yah, fellas, I was married. Married to one of my biggest fans and supporters—onstage, that is."

"Aww man, you gotta tell us da stage name. What did you go by?" asked Brass.

"Tastee-D," replied the pastor. "And I know you know what the *D* was for."

"All right now, tell the truth, shame the devil," said Magic. "Testify, Pastor, TES-TI-FY!" He got up, did a little holy ghost dance, and asked, "What type of fan was she, playa? We want to know about that cheap and tasty ho cake." He started licking his fingers and said, "Mmm hmm! Sounds like this is gonna be finger-licking good."

The pastor's brows knitted as his hands clinched into fists in response to Magic's antics. "Well, I married one of the regulars who always came to check out the show. To make a long story short, three months after we were married, I caught a fellow performer—my best friend at the time—in bed with the woman I thought I loved. Six months after that, we were divorced; and there was a baby on the way. I didn't ask any questions, fellas. I just played the role like she was mine."

"You kiddin' me, right?" asked Mike, leaping out of his chair. "What the fuck? You took care of a kid WHO MAY NOT HAVE BEEN YOURS? Uh-huh, I know that ain't so. Is it?"

The pastor glanced down at the floor, a hurt look on his face, and rubbed his chin. "Yes, brother Michael, I did what I thought was right." He shrugged his shoulders and took a deep breath. "I was scared. I was scared to death to find out the truth . . . That little girl was something I needed in my life at the time—something to live for, something to hold on to when I thought my world was coming to an end. I had already lost my wife; I didn't want to lose her too."

The Doc, who was writing everything down, looked up from his notepad and asked, "Pastor? If you don't mind me asking, how old is your daughter?"

"She'll be twenty soon."

"So you've been single—well, unmarried—for twenty years?"

The pastor, trying to find some humor in the question, attempted a grin, but could only make his lips slightly turn up to the right. "Well, if you put it that way, I guess so. I married when I was nineteen, divorced when I was nineteen; and baby girl came when I was twenty."

"Pastor, I didn't even know you had a daughter," said DK. "Is she in Dallas? I mean, I've never seen her at the church, and no one ever speaks of her. Who is she? What's her name?"

"Yes, brother DK, Chéri—that's her name—is in Dallas; and no, you probably haven't seen her around the church. Our relationship is a bit—how can I put it—strained at the moment." He sucked in a big gulp of air and then slowly let it out, frowning as he did. "All I'm going to say is that the apple didn't fall too far from the tree. That's all I'm going to say, brothers. That's it. No more questions about my daughter and our relationship."

The Doc looked at pastor Levine and then around the room at the brothers, and then said with such eloquence, "Brothers, I've heard some powerful life stories throughout the retreat: Donnell, your confession about yourself; Brass, your powerful discovery about your past; Malcolm, your revelation about your relationship with your wife, and your displaced dream; and, Pastor Levine, your moving testimony about the little girl you claimed as your own, without question. Brothers, we all have something that has chained or bound us for a portion, if not, for most, or all of our lives.

"Silent Sons walking through life—chained, bound, and burdened by life's circumstances; but tomorrow we're going to break those chains that bind us and set ourselves free. We're going to let go and be free of everything that's ever held us back. We're going to start believing in and trusting one another. More importantly, we're going to start trusting—"

"I know where you're going with this, Doc, and you're right," said the pastor. "I haven't been able to trust a woman fully since then. That's why, in my opinion, I have such a special connection with Pat. I've been there . . . stood in her shoes. I know what it's like and what she's going through, what her hurt feels like, because there's nothing worse than loving someone and finding out that their love for you is not as deep or as meaningful as your love for them."

Donnell, who had been cradling his head in his hands, looked up with an evil look on his face. He pointed at the pastor and told him, "Listen, I'm getting sick of you judging me, man. I'ma tell you this for the last time: It was never my intention to hurt Pat, okay?"

The Doc called out Don's name. "Donnell? Breathe, brother, breathe. Just relax."

Donnell threw up his hand and waved it down at the Doc, as if he didn't want to hear anything that was about to come out of the Doc's mouth. "Naw, man, I'm just saying. Sometimes two people get married for the wrong reasons."

"What do you mean, brother Don?" asked the Doc.

"I'm just saying, Doc. Sometimes two people can get married, but while traveling down the same road together, one just outgrows the other—growing apart with each mile traveled. And before you know it, they come to a fork in the road, and a decision has to be made. Do you both go down the same road, head in the same direction; or does the one that's grown the most break off in a different direction? Me and Pat broke off in different directions. May not be right, may not be fair, but that's what happened. I went in a different direction, and Pat stayed at the fork in the road."

Brass said, "Hell, that's life. We all know life ain't fair. Nobody gives a shit about anybody, man. You gotta live for you, homey, 'cause just like my mom's always said, nobody's gonna give a shit if you live it or don't. They gonna judge you, regardless. So you may as well live it and be happy doing it. Do you, homey? Do you?"

There was nothing left to be said. The brothers quietly sat around the fireplace, listening to music and watching the sun set around 10:08 PM. Magic had Lenny Williams's song, "'Cause I Love You" cued up to play and, in no time, had it bellowing from the speakers. The brothers didn't move or make a sound. They just stared at each other. They didn't sing, not even just mouth the words. They just sat, listened, and took in the soulful artistry of Lenny belting out those sweet, melodic words.

In the middle of the song—where Lenny starts rapping, "Have you ever been in love"—out of nowhere, to everyone's shock, Quentin said, "I used to be in love like that. Matter of fact, I played this record over and over and over trying to get through it all."

The brothers perked up, and DK and Malcolm stared at Quentin, who had been silent and shy all throughout the retreat; and with the flip of a switch, they watched him come to life. He sat up and scooted to the edge of his chair and said, "Yah, I used to remember the exact place on the record player to put the needle down. And when I heard Lenny talk, it was as though he felt my pain . . . as though he knew exactly what I was going through."

The Doc asked, "Who was it, Q? What happened? Can you tell us about it?"

Quentin looked at the Doc, and his eyes were watery and bloodshot. DK couldn't tell whether it was from the liquor or from Quentin becoming emotional. Q wiped his eyes with the back of his hands and said, "Doc, I loved this girl like I never loved anyone else. She was my everything. We grew up together, went to high school together, and then to college together. We were inseparable. She was adventurous, kinda crazy, like I like 'em, but not like Malcolm's crazy-behind wife."

Quentin laughed and shook his head. "My baby was cray-a-zee. I remember . . . . it was a couple of weeks before my birthday, and we were out shopping downtown. As we were walking, she asked, 'Q, baby, if you could have anything for your birthday, what would it be?'

"I stopped and told her I didn't know. Well, there we were, standing in front of this neon-lit tattoo parlor with all these skull-and-crossbones posters in the windows. As a joke, I told her, 'Hey, Allison, why don't you get a tat. I think it would look sexy on you.'" Quentin fell back in his chair, shaking his head. "I'll be damn if that girl didn't drag me into that tattoo parlor. I told you she was crazy. So we walked inside. It was a little seedy, kind of dingy looking. I guess she must have sensed my apprehension, because she grabbed me by the arm and pulled me to where this biker guy was getting a snake tattooed on his forearm. The snake was going up his arm; its body was black, its tongue red and forked, its eyes yellow—it definitely stood out. She looked at it and said, 'Oh my god! That's amazing!' And she told the tattoo artist that she wanted one just like it, but bigger. She wanted it to go down the whole left side of her body. And she told me that that was going to be my birthday gift. And on my birthday, after it had all healed up, she did one of her nasty dances for me and played this fresh cut from that new Spike Lee movie—damn, what was the name of that movie? The first, maybe second, movie he did back in the day." He turned to the brothers. "Y'all remember, don't you? It was kinda like a musical at an HBCU." Quentin looked around the room, as though to find someone to help him out. "Damn! What was the name of that movie?"

"That was *School Daze*, playa," Magic told him.

"Yah, that was the movie! And "Perfect Match"—because we were the perfect match—was the song she came out dancing to—making that snake wiggle on that fine, high-yella body of hers. She even did a rattling noise through her teeth. Fellas, that made me hot as hell—sounded just like the rattle from a rattlesnake. Man, she freaked me something good that night. She was perfect for me—intelligent, witty, funny. Hell, I knew her thoughts; and I would say what she was thinking, just by looking at her, before she could say it herself. It made her so damn mad.

Malcolm asked, "Brother? What happened? If it was like that, why aren't you two together?"

Magic started the song up again, but he started it at the part when Lenny began to speak; and tears just started pouring from Quentin's eyes. "Man, I don't know. One day, she was on campus; and the next day, she was gone. I looked for that girl everywhere. Even went home to see her momma, but she didn't know—so she claimed. But I kept looking, though. Soon, it wasn't long before my freshman year turned into my senior year; and I was packing up and moving out of the dorm, leaving college and moving to Dallas. Man, for those four years, I felt a pain like no other. That thang knew it hurt me, man. After that, I wouldn't allow myself to fall like that again—not for anybody. Not even Melissa."

Quentin's story left the brothers speechless; their mouths hung open, and jaws looked as though they were on their way to the floor. The room was quiet . . . motionless . . . everything in it was at a standstill. It was as if they were suspended in time—floating through voided space. Everyone could feel the rawness and hurt in the room and couldn't help but tap into Quentin's pain. It was so bad that every single brother was either broken down by his story or feeling or thinking about their own life's pain, and the only thing you could hear was Lenny singing:

Oh, oh, oh, oh, oh, oh, oh
And I cry, I cry,
Oh, oh, oh, oh, oh, oh, oh, oh, oh, oh, oh, oh, oh, oh, oh
And the tears would fill up in the wells
In the wells of my eyes, aww baby
And then it got so bad, it got so bad
Till one time I thought I'd roll myself up in a big 'ole ball and die

X said, "Man, I've never heard this song before. Or maybe I hadn't paid that much attention to it."

Everybody looked at him and said, "WHAT!"

"What are you talking about, X? Man, this is the *hurt man's national anthem*," said DK. "Just like that 'Superwoman' song, by Karyn White, had black women locked in arms back in the day, singing all that 'Kum Ba Yah' and shit."

"Yah, X," said Quentin, "this song right here will get you through, man. I'm *telling* you."

The Doc asked, "How old are you, X?"

"Thirty-one, man."

"Well, there you go," said the Doc. "You young folks nowadays. I swear."

"Nigga? Don't tell us you ain't never been hurt and ain't never heard this song," said Magic. "Everybody in this here room's been hurt in one way or another—and you don't know Lenny? LENNY! Come on now, X!"

"Naw, can't say that I have. Not like that. And unless Jessie breaks my heart—and I don't think she will—I don't think I'll experience it."

The brothers just sat there and shook their heads in disbelief.

Quentin called out Magic's name and said, "Hey man, I know we're supposed to make a toast—which we haven't been doing—but I'm going to make mine now. And hey, do your boy a favor and play that Lenny Williams one more time—in memory of my girl, for old time's sake."

Magic gave Quentin a wink and a thumbs-up, and Quentin raised his glass and said, "Brothers, I'd like to say that this retreat has really meant a lot to me. It made this silent son open up and talk about something that's been stored deep, deep inside of him for a long, long, time. I haven't talked about it to anyone for years. So here's to you, Doc, for being the great open-upper that you are. And to DK, Magic, and K103.5, for putting this here, all together. And to the Brotherhood—a great group of guys who couldn't be more different and diverse—who share the same plaguing problems we black men face. I salute you, my brothers, I salute you."

The brothers raised a toast, and each one followed suit with their own toast, bravely telling each other what the retreat has meant to them. Magic played the song again; and as Lenny started crooning his emotionally charged hit, the brothers, except DK, started singing, humming, and talking along with him.

DK, who had drifted off in thought, was far, far away in a distant world—a world where he found himself traveling back down that red clay dirt road in Albany, Georgia. He was standing in front of that clapboard house that had caused him so much pain, watching the X on the red flag flap around in the wind, popping with each flap. He walked across the yard, past the beat-up red truck; dodged the barking dog; and ran up the steps to the wooden porch, which let out this loud squeaking noise, announcing his arrival. As he stood on the porch; he crouched over with his hands on his knees, huffing and a-puffing, and took a couple of deep breaths before looking back over his shoulder into the yard. "The truck's gone," he said. "What the fuck?" And the dog, which his moms always told him to never run away from, was gone too. The red clay dirt had turned to black; and chickens and hogs were running wild in it, kicking up clouds of dust. He took a final deep breath and made his way across the porch, where he automatically took out his house key, as though he was standing in front of his mom's house, and stood motionless in front of the door.

Before he could find the courage to put the key in the lock, the door swung open; and his pop's moms was standing there in the doorway, with her large girth filling the doorframe. She had her plump hands on her hips, and her fingers and her right foot were just a-tapping away. She had this makeshift turban—made out of that Confederate flag—wrapped around her head, and she cocked her head to the side and looked down at him, saying, "Lord, look-a-here, if it ain't that stray, *again*. Ain't no need for you to keep coming round here, honey, looking for something that don't want chu. Listen, Dickey ain't here. And I sure as hell don't want or need you round here either. I gots enough problems taking care of my own damn chillen, let alone, somebody else's stray. I beez damn if I needs me another mouf to feed or somebody else to clothe. You hear me? Uh-huh. Now, you go on. GET! Get your black bastard ass off dis here porch. Go on now. I dun told you we ain't taking in no strays."

DK thought about all the relationships he tried to develop over the years but then simply pushed away—to avoid being hurt. It was his defense, his shield; and he knew it. *I got to hurt them before they hurt me*, his subconscious always told him; and with that, he knew what bound him: *the not knowing*. The not knowing who his pops was and the feeling of rejection and hurt it had left him.

As he pushed his pops out his mind, he found himself in another quandary. He knew he had to tell the brothers about the ICON Awards and that all-too-important show with the divas. It seemed he could never find the right time to do it. But the brothers were now in a feel-good moment, which he couldn't break; and he shook his head and told himself, *Damn! I gotta tell them before we make it back to Dallas, but how am I going to pull it off?*

Chapter 14

The Brothers' Retreat
Day 4: Am I My Brother's Keeper?

Friday, June 26, 2009
Angoon, Alaska

The Doc and Magic were the first to meet in the dining room; and as planned, they met with the lodge's staff to ensure that the room was set up for the retreat's last Brotherhood session. While the Doc paced back and forth, going over his notes, Magic helped the staff break down the hefty dining room table, as the Doc insisted he needed it removed for a specific arrangement requiring four smaller round tables, which seated three, for an experiment he had planned for their last session. The Doc's insistence made Magic work hard to ensure that the tables were correctly positioned in the middle of the room and that breakfast was set up buffet-style along the room's wall of windows overlooking the lake. When everything was complete, the two sat at one of the tables, eating, laughing, and discussing the upcoming meeting's strategy; and that was where the brothers found them when they arrived around 7:30 AM.

"Brothers, come on in and have a seat. Sit anywhere," said the Doc as he pushed away from his table and stood up to greet them. "That's right, sit anywhere—it doesn't matter where."

The brothers came in, one by one, and showed some brotherly love to Magic and the Doc. They either grabbed a seat or headed straight to the buffet line. Then they noticed DK walk in and stop dead in his tracks; he hadn't even made his way well into the room before he let out a couple of loud whistles, drawing everyone's attention to himself.

"Brothers, I have something I need to run by you before we begin, and I don't think there's going to be a better place or time to do it." Hitting his thighs with his fists, DK let out a slow and painful grunt before saying, "Okay, brothers, I'm really trying to find a good way to put this."

"Aww, man, just say it. What's on your mind?" asked Malcolm as he continued to load up his plate.

"Well," DK answered, throwing a snide smirk Malcolm's way, "let me start off by regretfully announcing the first casualty of the Brotherhood—the first brother to drop out, that is."

Dumbfounded, everybody turned around and started looking around the room, trying to figure out who it was.

DK looked over at the Doc and then at the brothers and said, "Our boy Magic here, whose intention, I now understand, was only to come up with us and provide support for us brothers, has decided not to participate in the Doc's upcoming experiment, or the Brotherhood going forward. But I do have some good news about our brother: He's not entirely through with us yet. As a matter of fact, he's gonna continue to sit on the sidelines and provide the support, I know, we'll probably need with this here Brotherhood thing—just not as an official brother of the Brotherhood."

DK walked over to Magic and slapped him on the back and grabbed his neck, shaking his head. "Let's give this brother a round of applause for keeping us entertained and in stitches throughout our stay."

DK, the Doc, and all the brothers started clapping and chanting Magic's name for a good minute or so, before the Doc waved them down and told them, "Get ready to pick up your plates, because I'm going to assign you your tables and let you know how we're going to progress from here. But before I do, I believe brother DK has something important he wants to tell us." The Doc looked at DK and started to egg him on, get him to say what he needed to say. "Don't you, brother DK? I believe it has something to do with one of our Sunday-night radio airings back in Dallas—if I'm correct. Right?"

DK cleared his throat and looked over at the Doc. "That's right, fellas," he said, scratching the back of his head. "K103.5 believes it would be a good idea to tackle some of today's relationship issues by putting some realism in our discussions about what black singles and couples face today. To do that, they want you guys to do a show with the divas—"

"THE DIVAS?" asked Brass and Malcolm at the same time.

"Yep," replied DK, "the divas."

"You mean doing a show with Pat?" Donnell asked. "Airing our dirty laundry over the radio to *all* of Dallas? Man, you must have fell and bumped your motherfucking head. You know that shit ain't gonna happen. Nah-ah. Not with me, at least."

All the brothers basically said the same thing Donnell said, and DK was stumped. But with some quick thinking and a little ingenuity, he came up with a quick save. "All I'm saying, brothers, is that the station thinks it would be a good idea to discuss what it's like being single and dating in Dallas—get both points of view in an open forum—as well as discuss the issues black couples face in their relationships today. Just think about it, fellas. . . . I tell you what, since I don't have all the information yet, just do your boy a favor and don't completely count it out until I get all the info. Okay, fellas?" DK clasped his hands, as though he was about to pray, and bowed to the brothers. "Thank you, my brothers—and *please* don't count it out, fellas. Doc? I guess it's on you."

"Thank you, brother DK. All right, brothers. I know you guys are probably worried after that one. I can see it all in your faces. But if I can change course and get you guys to go over and stand in front of the windows, we can get this exercise—or experiment, as I like to call it—started, and we can get out of here and head on back to Dallas."

All the brothers except Magic hesitantly got out of their chairs and slowly walked over to the windows and stood in front of the buffet line. The Doc grabbed his pen and notepad from his table and walked over to stand in line with them.

"Good. Good. Good." he said as he looked down the line. "Now, brothers, if you haven't noticed by now, you're all sitting three to a table. And yah, you probably guessed it—I'm going to put you into groups. So when I call the first brother's name, I want you to just pick a table—don't worry whether it has your food on it—and sit down. When I call the other two brothers' names, just kindly sit down with the first brother. It's as simple as that. So are you ready to get started?"

The brothers answered a weak "I guess."

The Doc, taking it for what it was, clapped his hands and said, "Let's get started, then.

"For our first table, brother Brass, will you pick a table and sit down."

Brass looked down the line at the brothers, shrugged his shoulders, and did as he was asked.

"Good. Good. Thank you, brother Brass. Pastor and Miguel, will you please join brother Brass at his table."

The pastor and Miguel went and got their plates from their tables and sat down with Brass.

"Now, for our second table: Donnell, will you pick a table? Excellent, brother, excellent! Michael and Xavier, please join brother Donnell.

"And now for our last table: Brother Malcolm, will you have a seat. Brothers DK and Quentin, will you please join him."

The two brothers looked at each other and did as they were told, and all the brothers sat at their tables with looks that said, *What's going on?*

Magic, just as he and the Doc had discussed, started working his equipment for the last time and began playing "The Best Man I Can Be," by Ginuwine, Case, Tyrese, and R.L. of Next; and it began to ease, if not, lift some of the tension in the room. The Doc told the brothers to get situated, and they got up and made sure they got their plates and breakfast drinks from the other tables, and then got seconds and drink refills while the Doc walked over to the flip chart that he had asked the lodge's staff to set up for him. He proceeded to write the following:

Group 1	**Group 2**	**Group 3**
Pastor Levine	Michael	DK
Brass	Donnell	Malcolm
Miguel	Xavier	Quentin

"Okay, brothers. These are the groups you'll be working in for the remainder of the Brotherhood. And for your information, this is an ongoing experiment that I conduct with all my groups. It's proven to be successful because as society has shown us, no one is going to help us black brothers other than us helping ourselves. You're in these groups to help each other.

"Now, before I tell you how I came up with the groups, I want to preface everything by letting you know that in the years of working with groups in this way, I typically see at least one group having difficulty, or its members having problems getting along or supporting one another. The turmoil within the group may get so severe that members will either ask to join another group, disband, or drop out and stop coming to the sessions altogether. I anticipate one of these tables will meet this fate."

Xavier asked, "I'm curious, Doc: How did I get placed with Donnell and Mike here?" He looked over at Mike and then at Donnell. "No disrespect, my brothers. I'm just curious."

Mike said, "No disrespect taken." But Donnell looked at him as if he was plum crazy.

The Doc answered, "Remember when DK asked you guys to write down the names of two people on the card by your plate? The two people you trusted the least? It was back on day 1 of our retreat—the first impressions day— although, I'm pretty sure that your mind-sets have changed since then, now that you've gotten to know each other a little better."

All the brothers nodded with quizzical looks on their faces and slowly answered.

"Yes."

"Yah."

"You're right about that, Doc."

"Well," said the Doc, "we're going to talk about the concept of projection in this session. And what I mean by that is that we see in others what sometimes lives in us."

"What?" asked Brass. "What are you talking about, Doc? You gots to break it down in common-folk talk, homey."

The Doc walked over to Brass's table and told Magic to play the song again. "As a matter of fact, brother Magic, if you can just play it over and over until I tell you to stop."

Magic winced at the Doc but did as he was told. And as the song started playing over again, the Doc stood behind Brass and looked around the room to get a good feel from the brothers—see where they were at—and looked down at Brass, making sure they made eye contact. "Often, brother Brass, unbeknownst to you, your distrust or discomfort with a certain brother indicates that there is something about him that is probably a part of you, that you may not know much about, or have addressed yet—"

Brass interrupted, looking up at the Doc, frowning, "Huh? Real talk, Doc. Real talk, man."

The Doc started laughing. "Okay, brother Brass, real talk. Brothers, I put you in these groups for a reason. It's going to feel awkward—if not downright uncomfortable at first—but to get you to that better place, and to understand ourselves, we have to go through a little discomfort. So, getting to the discomfort: At each table, two of you brothers picked the third brother as the brother you trusted the least. The brother that sat down first was that brother."

"Aw shit, FOR REAL!" asked Malcolm. "'Cause, man, I was the first person to sit down at my fucking table."

"So was I," said Donnell. "This is kinda foul, man."

"I was too," added Brass as he looked up at the Doc, all cross-eyed.

"True enough, brothers," said the Doc as he walked around the tables. "You brothers may have been the first to sit down, and noted as the least trusted by the brothers at the time; but listen, you're actually *a special gift* to your group."

"How so?" asked Brass, looking at his table mates with a little hate in his eyes.

"Well, brother Brass, the least trusted brother is really a special gift to the rest of us—especially to the brothers at his table. He's going to be the key to you learning more about yourselves. Brothers, I want you to look closely at the man you least trust in your group. Get to know him well."

DK said, "I don't know, Doc. What can I possibly learn from Malcolm that's going to enrich or enhance my life? Not to down you or anything, Malcolm."

The Doc shook his head. "You'll be surprised, brother DK. Once you get to know each other—which most black men don't do these days for fear of being labeled as something that they're not—you'll be surprised at what you'll be able to learn from one another; but most importantly, you'll be surprised at how much you can help each other. And, brothers, no one's coming to your aide—sometimes not even family, as brother Brass pointed out. Look out the window of any house, in any neighborhood, in any city; and you'll see what I mean. It's going to be up to us to help each other get through those rough times and push each other as we *climb* up that mountain. And from my experience, once you brothers get to know each other, you'll find out how much you really have in common, just by the mere fact that each of you are facing the same societal challenges and dilemmas—just on different levels, depending on your background and circumstances.

"All right, fellas, that's enough of my preaching. Right now, I just want you brothers to listen to the words of this song. Magic? Play it again, from the start."

As the song played again, the brothers listened; and this time, they understood. They got it. And the Doc asked them to go around each table and tell their respective groups, and the entire Brotherhood, what he wanted them to help him accomplish, how they could help him be *the best man he could be.* And for those who didn't know, or didn't want to, he told them it was okay—that they were going to be working together for a long time, and that they would have time to think about it as they got to know each other and came to trust their group mates and every man in the Brotherhood. They would open up when the time was right.

Malcolm, Brass, and Quentin were the first to open up, and were the most vocal; but the Doc already knew their story. He saw DK staring into space, and he jokingly asked, "Brother DK? What's wrong, my brother? You still searching for that something?"

DK shook his head and blew the Doc off, although he knew he was, indeed, still searching and didn't know quite how to let it out or make it happen.

The Doc continued, "All right, brothers, let's give each other some love and get out of here."

The brothers gathered in a circle, and the Doc asked them, "Am I my brothers' keeper?"

They answered, "Yes I am!"

The Doc asked again, "Am I my brothers' keeper?"

The brothers answered, "Yes, I am!"

"One more time: Am I my brothers' keeper?"

And the brothers shouted at the top of their lungs, "YES, I AM!"

The Doc told the brothers he wanted them to make a pledge. He wanted them to pledge that when they finally overcame that something that had chained, bound, and burdened them throughout life, when they finally broke those chains and were set free, they would recognize that they were free, give thanks, and say out loud, *Lord, thank you. I'm finally through with being through. I believe I'm healed.*

"Brothers, I want you to pledge before your fellow brothers and God himself. I want you to repeat these words: 'Lord, thank you. I'm finally through with being through. I believe I'm healed.' Let's all say it together."

The brothers, standing around in the circle with their arms intertwined over each other's shoulders, said in unison, "Lord, thank you. I'm finally through with being through. I believe I'm healed."

Pastor Levine shouted, "Good God, ALMIGHTY!"

And they broke the circle and started giving each other brotherly hugs, firm handgrips, and daps. DK said, "Brothers! Let's get out of here. The 2009 Brotherhood Retreat is finally adjourned. We'll see you guys back in Dallas. And remember, our first airing of *The Brotherhood* is on Sunday, July 5th—less than two weeks away, fellas. Our girl Jessie has already sent you your itineraries. So, fellas, let's pack up. Don't forget to tip and say good-bye to the lodge's staff, and don't forget your fish either. Let's get out of here and head on back to Dallas."

Chapter 15

K103.5: The Brotherhood Goes on Air

(DK's POV)

*A*fter a long two-week wait and a little drama with some of the brothers, Sunday, July 5, 2009, had finally arrived. The debut of *The Brotherhood*. And as we cut the fool and got up in everybody's business while waiting to go on the air, I sat there in the studio in awe. I tell you, man, as I looked around the table, I saw eight brothers that couldn't have been more different, in every way imaginable; but for this brief moment, we were one—nine roads converging together, and they all met here, at *The Love Forum*.

Magic said, "DK, in five . . . four . . . three . . . two . . . one."

And it was on. Teddy Pendergrass with Harold Melvin and the Blue Notes played in the background—Magic sure knew his shit—and slowly but surely, all of us started getting in the mood, swaying back and forth and chiming in one by one. Soon we were all grooving to the song and singing:

The world won't get no better
If we just let it be
The world won't get no better
We gotta change it, yeah
Just you and me

Later, as the song was coming to an end, I jumped the show off by saying, "K103.5, that was the Teddy Bear, Teddy Pendergrass, with Harold Melvin and the Blue Notes, singing 'Wake Up Everybody.' Man, oh man, what a true and powerful song, and it still holds true today. K103.5 family, what better way to ease us into the all-new *Love Forum* than by saying, Wake up, my people!' And, Dallas, it's not going to get any better—unless we change, that is. Change involving you, me, our thoughts, our customs, and our tolerances. That being said, K103.5, this year, we're going to do just that; and the brothas are going to lead the way. It's going to be a forum to remember, y'all: A forum by brothers, for brothers, and for those that love brothers and want to understand us more.

"And to our newest K103.5 listeners, *The Love Forum* was started by the ever-so-sweet Melissa Morgan—damn, we miss you, Lis. Our sweet Melissa Morgan passed away, tragically, earlier this year, leaving behind the forum as her gift and legacy. And in true spirit, we're going to continue on. So what is *The Love Forum* you ask? *The Love Forum* is geared toward discussing and solving our relational issues, keeping that spark in our current relationships, healing from our past relationships, and finding the 'one' for that right relationship. Can I get an 'amen,' Dallas?"

"Amen, brother DK! Amen!" seconded Pastor Levine as he waved his hands in agreement.

I laughed. "That was Pastor Levine, y'all. And, Dallas, this is your boy, DK Love, along with the music maestro himself, Mr. Kirk 'Magic' Wonder. And you know, ma boy Kirk is always throwin' it down and keepin' it right. And speakin' of throwin' it down, K103.5, we're about to get crunk up in here! Crunk, y'all! Magic? Magic, my man, why don't you ease us into this year's *Love Forum*—which we've appropriately retitled *The Brotherhood*, by the way. And, Dallas, listen to me: Ya boy guarantees that this is going to be one helluva show. 'Cause the brothers are going to break it down and let the sistas know what's really on our minds. And I'm sure y'all really want to know what really went down with those relationships on the first *Love Forum*, don't you?" I know you do."

"Yah!" said Mike as he got up and leaned into the microphone. "We definitely got some things to say about that!"

I laughed again. "I hear you, Mike. And, K103.5, if you miss any one of our forums, I gotta tell you that the one coming up on August 9, is the one you don't want to miss. And my boy, Michael Crawley—that would be Mike over here, you know, Jessie's old flame—will be hosting the show with all the fellas and *The Love Forum* divas you grew to love from last season. Yep. We'll all be sitting right here in our brand-new studio telling you, Dallas, what really went down, from both sides. So let me break it down for you. The previous year's *Love Forum* participants, *The Love Forum* divas—"

"Divas!" Brass said angrily. "You gotta be freakin' kiddin' me, man! The only thing dose crazy b-i-t-c-h-e-s did was stir up a whole lot of shit, yo— making da brothas look bad, except for this light-skinned nigga ova here." He pointed at Miguel. "And it's time to put that [beep] to bed." And then he started laughing, hard.

"Damn, Brass, you got issues, yo. Magic? Ease us into another groove, man. Play that Oran Juice Jones cut 'The Rain,' which, K103.5, is one of our theme songs for this year's *Love Forum*." In no time, Magic had the song playing and I moaned out, "Aaahhh . . . yah! That's it, Magic. That's what I'm talking 'bout, boy!"

That groove started bringing back some memories, and I started singing along and rapping with Oran Juice.

"Aiight, DK, blow it out the water, man! You think the ladies will be able to stand the rain?" yelled Magic as he increased the tempo of the song. "Damn! Does this song bring back some memories or what, y'all?" Magic started laughing and cutting up. "What did bruh-man say, DK? 'Don't touch that coat!' The brother handled his business! Got rid of ole trifling homegirl, sent her packing—told her to get to steppin' for her trifling ways; and from what the brothers are saying, ladies, y'all got some trifling ways!"

"Magic, man—and you too, Brass—y'all ain't right, but I guess you keepin' it real. Aiight, K103.5 family, to help us with the show's relationship issues, we've brought in the tough but frank Dr. Franklin Mayweather. The Doc got us started by suggesting we get to know each other and get some of the issues out on the table before we began the official *Love Forum*. So prior to this show, all the brothers got together for a four-day, three-night retreat in the snowcapped mountains of Alaska—yep, as far away from Dallas as possible. In other words, we weren't going anywhere, as there was no packing up and leaving, just confronting the issues head-on. And, Dallas—boy, were there issues! All during this year's *Love Forum, The Brotherhood*, we will be playing bites from the retreat and letting the listeners in on some of the topics discussed, and if I tell you it got heated up at the cabin, then believe me, it got heated up at the cabin—hot and furious at times, even leading up to blows. So, Dallas, it's on. Man is it on, so let's get started by introducing the forum's brothas.

"First, we have Dr. Xavier Houston—we call him X. He's one of those successful black brothers who's not new to the traumas of the emergency room. Brother-man stares death in the face on a daily basis, and I'm not sure if y'all remember Jessie S. Harris, from the first *Love Forum*. Yes, the bangin' sister who's just tight to death on all points—remember that poem, y'all? Let's check him out. Magic, play that bite with Dr. Houston talking to Melissa and our girl Jessie after Jessie wrote that lustful poem about that black coffee—and for all y'all that didn't get the poem and for all our new listeners, Ms. Jessie's poem, "Black Coffee," is a metaphor used for us black brothas. Magic? Are we set? Aiight, Dallas, my man Magic says we're good to go. Let's listen. Here's Melissa Morgan starting us out, with Dr. Xavier Houston and Jessie S. Harris."

> "Okay, well, maybe that man is Dr. Xavier Houston. He's on the line right now, and it seems he was quite taken with those beautiful words you just shared with us, Jessie. Hello, Dr. Houston. What would you like to say to Jessie's hot tail? You might have to watch out for her, Doc!"
>
> "Good evening, Melissa, divas, and especially you, Ms. Harris. My name is Xavier, calling from Gilford Hills. I have to say, I was blown away by the depth and complexity of your words."

"Ooh, Jessie! Dr. Houston knows some big words! Girl, you might want to keep this one around. Quite an improvement from the last couple of scrubs trying to holla!"

"Melissa, girl, you're a mess! Hello, Dr. Houston. Thank you for the compliment. I was just trying to capture my feelings about my ideal mate, intertwined with my feelings about love. Yeah, I know, sounds a little corny."

"Corny? Not at all! You did an excellent job. And as an avid coffee drinker, all I can say is that you have a strong cup of dark roast, café mocha–style, right here at your fingertips, waiting to be sipped."

"All right, damn boy! Hold up, Jessie girl, I might have to take this one for myself. Whew, he came on strong with that one! Now, Dr. Houston, I know you're all dark roasted and café mocha–style, but my girl Jessie likes her coffee dark and bittersweet."

"Dark, yes. Bitter, no. But I definitely can be sweet to the right one, Melissa."

"Well, all right, Doc! Dallas, you got to admit, ma' boy is smooth. And for all y'all wondering what became of Ms. Jessie Harris, bro man, Dr. Houston, has nabbed her—took her straight off the market, brothas, with his smooth-talking-ass."

I had to laugh at that one as I reached across the table to give X a high five and mouthed, *All right, my nigga!* "Well, K103.5, he'll eventually tell us how he got Ms. Harris—soon to be Mrs. Houston, I hear! All I can say is wow and congratulations, my brother!"

"Thanks, DK. Appreciate you, man; and evening, Dallas—and, DK, that name change for Ms. Harris is coming real soon, my brother. Real, real soon."

"I hear you, Doc. Now if Dr. Houston is known for saving lives, and damsels in distress, then the good reverend-doctor Richard Levine is known for saving souls."

Brass hollered, "Weeelll, oh yah! Hallelujah! My god!" And he waved his hands in the air and rocked back and forth in his chair. "Whew! Thank ya! Thank you, Jesus."

"Man, Brass, if you don't stop tripping, man—anyway, Dallas, Pastor Levine comes to us from Greater Antioch, and he's sure to keep us grounded and give us that religious spin on those topics that are sure to be on fire at times. Pastor Levine had to deal with some heated discussions on the retreat, and boy, there were real tense moments where his faith came into question; but on the positive, we got to see where this single man is on the dating scene and how he goes about dating women, especially all the women throwing themselves at him in the church. Well, ladies, hold back, 'cause brother-man has a lady of interest; and if you remember Pat from the first *Love Forum*—

yeah, the sister going through the bitter divorce—well, she is Pastor Levine's lady of interest. Pastor, say hello to the K103.5 listeners; and if you can just give all the single ladies, and fellas, some words of encouragement, 'cause as all of us know, it's rough out there."

"Well, K103.5, this is Pastor Richard Levine, and I bring greetings and blessings from Greater Antioch. Yes, it's rough out there for so many of our sisters and brothers; but I would say, have faith. Remember faith and that mustard seed. Faith will get you through the lowest of lows and take you to the highest of the highs. DK, not too long ago, one of my church members came to me with a wonderful testimony. This lady had been praying and praying and praying for God to bless her with a good man; but no matter how many times she prayed, how hard she prayed, or how long she prayed, it seemed her prayers fell on death ears. She said that with time, she prayed less and less; and soon she stopped praying to God for a man altogether. She figured that her lot in life was to be alone. But one day, I saw the same lady; and she had the biggest smile and was just simply glowing, so I asked her, 'Sister Hattie? Have I missed something? You sure look radiant today.' She raised her hands in praise and said, 'Do you know, Pastor, that last week I became Mrs. Thomas D. White? After seven years of loneliness, God finally answered my prayers.'"

"And let the church say, amen! Wheeewww, I feel the spirit! Hallelujah!" Brass said sarcastically.

"Dallas, that's our boy Brass, acting a fool as usual. Man, I do believe you missed your calling. You should have been a comedian, 'cause, bruh-man, you're in here cracking jokes like they're going out of style. Well, Dallas, your boy Brass's description is all too familiar. One of those single brothers who's no stranger to the dating game, and he lets us know how a playa puts it down to get what he wants. All I can say is that you're a trip, man. And yes, Brass was the man everybody loved to hate on the first *Love Forum*. And if we don't play any bites about this brother, we got to play this one. After this *Love Forum* airing, the lines at the station were ringing off the hook for weeks. Let's listen in as *The Love Forum* divas put our boy in the hot seat."

> "103.5, 103.5, 103.5, this is your girl V, sitting in the pilot's seat tonight while Melissa and Quentin celebrate their, ugh, 'I met you on this day' anniversary. Well, ladies and gentlemen, you know I got my girl's back and have to represent. The Love Forum's got issues tonight. Now, my girl Britt just made up with her boo, Brass, who just returned from a Mexican cruise with another woman. Yes, y'all, and he was living with Britt when he went on the cruise. Chile, I can't talk about it anymore . . . I'm all talked out. My girl has to tell you the rest. I'm just too outdone!"

"You know what, V, you can be outdone, because at the end of the day, this is my life, and Brass is my man. What goes down over at 235 Charles is our business."

"Britt, girl, you ain't never lied. If you like it, I love it! Now, just tell the listeners how it went down. I'll let them call in and set your silly behind straight."

"You and the listeners can kiss my ass. Oh, sorry, D-town. What I should say is that I know there are plenty of women out there who can relate to what I'm going through. And, V, you're right, my man did leave and go on a weeklong cruise while we were living together. But he did not sleep with her! What? What are y'all laughing at? He didn't!"

"And how do you know this, Britt?"

"Y'all are really starting to piss me off! DeDe, I know because he looked into my pretty brown eyes and told me so. He said they didn't [beep], well, do it, and all that slut did—and he called her an ugly [beep]—is suck his [beep]."

"Girl, I don't even know what to say, other than b-i-t-c-h, are you for real? Are you hearing yourself? Do you actually believe that mess? Girl, it couldn't have been me, because just like him, his [beep] would've been on a cruise too, floating, piece by piece, in the Gulf of Mexico. Car, clothes, and every little piece of nothing he had. Yah, that's right, I'm coming for you . . . mmm-huh, Ms. V, said it! Yes, I did. You better hear me, girl. Words for the wise. Jessie? Do you believe this shit?"

"V . . . I know that's right, girl. You better preach."

"Well, why wouldn't I believe him, V? Jessie? I'm not saying Brass is perfect. And I know it was fuc—ooh, excuse me—I know it was messed up how he went on that vacation with that slut, but he is just not the type to lie. I mean, the Negro told me what he was doing before he did it! I knew he was on the cruise because he told me. He was on a business trip!"

At the same time, all the brothers shouted, "A business trip!" Just like the divas had shouted to Britt during their *Love Forum* taping. Damn! I could hardly hold it in, although everybody else was all fucked up from laughing so hard that they were either in tears or damn near it. Dude must be so humiliated. I cleared up the air of humiliation and unpleasantness by saying, "Damn, Brass! Man, you got a lot of explaining to do. One thing is for sure, though: Dallas, you may hate the playa and his game, but bruh-man will definitely keep you in stitches. Hold on, Dallas, don't start calling up here yet—we're going to get to Brass later. He's gotta give us his side of the story. Whew, man." I laughed. "K103.5, we're still laughing up in here about this [beep]."

"Now, our next brotha is Miguel. Miguel is happily engaged to one of our first *Love Forum* beauties. Yes, the former Miss Black Texas, Darlene. And Miguel will give us the 4-1-1 on dating and proposing. And yeah, the brother proposed on *The Love Forum*. He'll let us know why, how, and when he's about to make that turn on Newlywed Drive, and whether he sees making that turn on this new road as enriching his life for the better. Magic, play that bite of Miguel proposing to Darlene."

"No doubt, DK. My boy Miguel started a whole lot of shit for us brothas that day, but ma boy was smooth, though. Here's that smooth operator, and I'm throwing on that "Smooth Operator" by Sade in the background for the full effect. Okay now, DK and Dallas, here's our boy Miguel doing what he does best, with the ever-so-sweet Melissa Morgan and his new fiancée, Darlene."

"Hello? Caller, are you there? This is the ever-so-sweet Melissa Morgan."
"Hello? Yes. Melissa? This is Miguel."
"Miguel? Hey baby! Whatchu doing calling up here?"
"Yeah, Miguel! Whatchu doing calling up here for Darlene?"
"Melissa, this is for my baby, Darlene . Oye bebé, usted es el amor de mi vida."
"What? What did he just say? Darlene, girl, are you going to tell us what he just said? 'Cause you know I do not speak Mexican, girl!"
"Oh my god, Lis. He said, 'Hey, baby, you're the love of my life.'"
"Darlene, baby, I know you've been hurt; and I know you're grappling with our love, but I want to be the one who eases your pain and helps you catch that love. When you feel like you can't go on, I want to be the one who provides the words of encouragement. When you stumble and fall, I want to be the inspiration that picks you up and puts you on solid ground. When your heart is empty, I want to be the fuel that fills you back up. Baby, I know there's baggage—and we all have some—but I'm willing to carry that baggage. And if you let me, I'll show you that it's not too heavy, nor is the load too great. Darlene, let me be your Mr. Too Damn Good. I love you so much, baby. And I want to marry you. I'm calling to ask you to spend the rest of your life with me. I want to make you my wife."

"Go 'head on, bro man, go 'head on. Handle that business!" said Malcolm.

"I know that's right, man. Stand up, y'all. Stand up! Let's give the brother his props. Get them glasses up. Get 'em up, fellas. All right, to my boy Miguel who's showing us brothas how to really lay it down," said Quent.

I laughed. "I know that's right, Q. Now, Donnell is our *almost* divorcée, and I'm sure all of you remember Donnell and Pat from the first *Love Forum*. Bro, all I got to say is, God be with you, 'cause the women on here are ready to tear you up. What you got to say for yourself?"

"DK, I'm ready, yo. All I got to say is that it didn't go down like it was portrayed on the first forum. I'm just glad I now have the chance to tell my side of the story," replied Donnell as he sat sternly in his seat, almost to the edge.

"Ahhh, look at him. K103.5, our brother is ready to pounce. Hold your roll, brotha. Hold your roll." I kinda laughed as I said, "Well, when we get to telling your side, you better come with it, man—that's all I gotta say. Next, we have Malcolm Crawley and Michael Todd Crawley. These two are the brothers who we got to know, very well, on the first *Love Forum*. There was so much interest and controversy surrounding these two playas—one married and the other we just didn't know—that we had to have them on this *Love Forum*, if only just to tell us what happened with them and where they are now with their relationships. And, man, of all the brothas, these two definitely brought the issues out at the retreat. Whew, lawd! Drama and issues.

"Last but definitely not least, as Melissa would always say, is Quentin. Quent was Melissa's beau, and we had to go through fire and brimstone to get him to do the show. He consented, however hesitant, saying he wasn't sure what he would get out of this, other than making good on a promise; but maybe it will be therapeutic, at the very least. And it's a good thing to bond with some brothers. Of course, Quent has gone through his own ordeal with the death of Melissa; the birth of his beautiful daughter, Meli—yeah, short for *Melissa*—and just the strain of dealing with the legal system to get custody of his daughter.

"Welcome, my brothers, and thanks for being a part of *The Brotherhood!*"

Chapter 16

Sweet V's

(DK's POV)

August 8, 2009

*J*essie had this day planned down to a tee, and she spared no expense. She kept reminding us that we were K103.5 celebrities; and for the ICON Awards, we needed to look the part. So she scheduled us, along with the divas, for a pampering and a sprucing up at her friend V's beauty parlor, which she co-owned with her cousin Sweets. Hence, Sweet V's Beauty Shop. We arrived at about one o'clock in the afternoon—in a black stretch limo, I might add—after we picked up our suits and tuxedos from the Armani shop in Saks. And I'm telling you—Saks? In the Galleria? You know my girl spared no expense. And when us brothers got out of the limo and made our way into Sweet V's, it was like walking into a butcher shop where the patrons, who happened to be all women, were eagerly waiting for the butcher to bring out the meat. Guess who was the meat? All eyes were on us as we walked in the door. The women just looked at us, staring us up and down, like vultures looking at road kill, just licking their lips.

After we made it inside, the brothers and I stood at the door, looking around; and all of us had the same expression on our faces: *Wow!* And I said to myself, *Damn! This place is the effin' shit!* If I didn't know we were in V and Sweets' place, I would have sworn we had walked right up into the wrong effin' salon—a white salon, for sure, except for the lady DJ from K103.5, who was all set up in the corner, announcing, "Check this family. The brothers from *The Brotherhood* are hanging out at Sweet V's today. They've just walked in the door. Hmm. Lawd. Lawd. Stop by and check them out, and get your hair and nails done while you're at it. And, ladies, hear me when I tell you this: They're some fine-ass brothers with some big egos—you know I just set this up, don't you? This goes out to the brothers—my dedication to y'all, fine asses. This is Beyoncé, with 'Ego.'"

Guess I'm just used to the hole-in-the-wall barbershops with the pictures of either Martin Luther King Jr. or Jesus hanging crooked on the wall, or posters and banners of the last couple of NBA championship teams; but this place was first class. I mean, floor-to-ceiling windows, distressed brick walls, wooden floors, and everything done up in taupe, black, and chrome—just classy. Kinda reminded me of Chef Luda's place about a half a mile down the road, where we were going for a late lunch afterwards.

Sweets and V were in the back of the salon, and came out from behind this *huge* stainless-steel and slate wall fountain, which took up the whole damn back wall. The air was filled with the sounds of water falling, like a waterfall; but it was nothing compared to Sweets' overbearing mouth: "Hey, y'all. How y'all doing? Welcome to Sweet V's!"

When the two hit the light, you could tell they were related just by looking at their heart-shaped faces and dimpled chins; although the look fit more nicely with V's soft features and perfectly shaped lips. The upper lip was shaped like a heart—plump and kissable.

V let out a low, husky laugh, her smile lighting up her face as she greeted us. "Welcome to Sweet V's Beauty Shop." And she spread out her arms like Vanna White on that TV show *Wheel of Fortune*, after revealing the puzzle of the day.

Sweets slapped her on the shoulder and muttered something under his breath about the bitch always stealing his thunder. I looked at him and smiled. He was wearing some sort of fake fur vest—I heard him tell one of the patrons it was chinchilla—and some pinstriped pants that were tapered at the knees. I could hear the brothers behind me giggling like little girls, saying, "Lord, what in the world?"

Needless to say, with all of the brothers and divas in the place, and about twelve to thirteen of their regular patrons, it was chaotic, if not a circus. V busied herself shuffling people into the empty stylist chairs of black leather and chrome; and when those were all taken up, me and some of the divas, who arrived before us, squished our asses together in an already-tight love seat. I noticed Sweets looking down at X's shoes—X told me they were size 13—and licking his lips. He quickly snatched X up. X didn't look like he had a clue as to what was happening, so he just let himself be pulled by the arm. Sweets pushed him down into one of the stylist chairs and pulled over a gray trolley cart filled with blow dryers, brushes, razors, and other shit I didn't recognize or cared to know about. He pulled out a cloak from the bottom tray and made a big production of tying it around X's neck.

Sweets looked at himself in the mirror and smiled at his reflection. "So," he started while combing his hands over X's trimmed locks, "how would you feel about some highlights?"

X, who you could tell was a bit uncomfortable, chuckled a little at first. Then he scratched his head. "Just a trim and a shave will do, Sweets. It is Sweets, right?"

Sweets made a *tsk* sound as he dipped his hand into the top tray of his trolley and said, "Not too adventurous in the hair department, huh? Don't matter, though. Yes, I'm Sweets, and my hands are going to work pure magic on you. From the looks of it, you need it. Listen here, once I'm done with you, your girl's gonna be all over you. By the way, which one of these heifers in here done snatched you up?"

X said, "That would be Jessie, V's friend. She's not in here."

"OH MY GOODNESS! MS. JESSIE! Boy! That's my soror-sista girl. I do her hair every week. Hmm-huh, show do. Matter of fact, she was in here earlier this morning. She has a busy schedule, you know. Child, my diva is the shit. And let me tell you, I threw down, 'cause her hair is—what?—fierce!" Sweets turned X around in the chair, gave him a look-over, and said, "Hmph! And she ain't never lied. You fine . . . with some big ole feets. I wonder what else is big?" He laughed. "I'm just kidding. You gotta have fun, honey. Now you know I gotta do my girl's boo justice. I'M GONE HOOK YOU UP!" He pulled out a pair of sharp scissors and hooked his thumb and index fingers in the holes as he looked over X's hair.

X was just a laughing. He sounded like he was having the time of his life. "Is that a promise?" he asked.

Sweets' hands moved as though he was a ninja on steroids as he expertly clipped the twists on X's head. "Boy! I'll give you free haircuts for a year if Ms. Jessie don't start ripping those pants off the moment she sees you!" He gave X a wink through the mirror and told him, "V tells me you and Ms. Jessie are getting close to walking down the aisle."

I zoomed in on the conversation, 'cause it was sounding more as though Sweets was just trying to scoop up some gossip rather than make small talk; and as promised, I was trying to be my brother's keeper.

X nodded at Sweets—the smile on his face was so wide it made the skin around his eyes crinkle—and answered, "I'm getting there, I'm getting there. A woman like Jessie—you gotta work for it, Sweets. You know what I mean?"

Sweets nodded robotically, mumbling "Uh-huh," and let him continue.

"I figured her out. With Jessie, you gotta do these *grand* gestures beforehand and just build up to the moment. She's definitely a romantic at heart; so when you get there and finally pop the question, she's going to be feeling very romantic and deeply in love with you that there'd be no other possible answer than a 'Yes, yes, yes.' In fact, her birthday's coming up, on October 31st? Yah, October 31st, and I want to turn it into this grand event. I'm going to invite all her friends, her family, just everyone she loves; and we'll have food, music, lights—the whole nine yards.

"WHEW! Lawd! All that?"

"All that, Sweets. Just to show her how much she means to me."

Sweets's mouth curled up tight; he seemed impressed. "Mmm, aren't we rolling in the dough? I see you aren't playing with yours. Big money. Mr. Big Spender. Ooooh, Daddy," he teased.

X slammed his hand on the armrest and let out another deep chuckle. The soles of those size 13 shoes tapped on the wood floor, as if he was Ray Charles or that tap dancer Gregory Hines. "Naw, just doing everything for my girl," he said, waving his hand in front of his face, still laughing at Sweets's antics. "Hey, Sweets? Do you know a good event planner that can help me put this shindig together? Parties were never my thing. I'm going to need professional help with this one."

Sweets' lips widened, and his eyes grew big as he paused his snipping, so he could put both hands on his hips, looking as though he was going to announce a solution to world hunger or something. "Honey, you're looking at the best event planner this side of fabulous. Just give me a time, date, and a whole lot of cash—I know you got it—and I'll give you an affair Dallas will not soon forget."

The two went on and on, talking about themes, color palettes, beverage selections, and hors d'oeuvres choices. Once Sweets was done tidying up the X's goatee, the twosome exchanged numbers; and X said he would call over the weekend to set up a meeting so they could discuss the party plans further. Sweets promised to come up with a draft presentation by then.

The Doc was next on Sweets' list. Sweets made sure the chair and the floor around it were clean and free of hair, before instructing the psychotherapist to sit down.

"What do you have in mind for today?" Sweets asked, smiling at the Doc in the mirror while tying the cloak behind his neck.

"Just a trim and a shave," the Doc said as he smoothed down the cloak on his lap.

Sweets sighed dramatically, resting the back of his hand against his forehead as if he was a lovelorn Juliet in a Shakespearean production. "All this 'Just trim and shaves'—ooh, it makes me sick. My poor ole heart is just weeping."

Doc Mayweather cocked his head to the side, where some of the patrons and I were sitting. "I'm sure the ladies—maybe even DK over there—will let you experiment with their hair."

Sweets pouted a little. "Let's hope so." And then he let out a big sigh. "I hear you're a love doctor."

The Doc let out a loud sigh—the kind one lets out when one is frustrated with someone—and corrected Sweets. "A psychotherapist, actually—although people do come to me for relationship advice."

"Well, you think you can give me some free psychotherapy today in exchange for a nice cut?" Sweets asked, half in jest.

The Doc spread his arms out with his palms up and halfheartedly smiled at Sweets. "Just talk like we're friends," he said.

As I came to know the Doc, I found that he wasn't the type of brother who turned someone away if he thought they needed it. And looking at the sudden drop in Sweets' energy, it seemed that Sweets really needed it.

Sweets picked up an electric shaver and held it against Dr. Mayweather's scruffy nape, carefully running it up against the bone. "You see, my man—his name is Todd—and I are going through a rough patch. We've been together for a couple of years. At first, I thought he was just shy and a bit of a homebody. It was fun, just staying in and having takeout. Sometimes he'd cook for me, which is really sweet. And then weeks would pass. Disappeared. Gone. Can't get a hold of him, even if I was laying up in somebody's intensive care, clinging to life, with only a few breaths left in me. I mean, I understand that I may not be the most masculine fella, but I need to be me. And, honey, it ain't easy being me." He sighed and put down the shaver, picked up a pair of scissors, and began working on the Doc's sideburns. "It's really starting to get on my nerves. I mean, I care about him; and he makes me feel like I'm the only one in the world—when we're together, that is. But right now, I just feel empty . . . incomplete."

The Doc asked, "And why do you feel that way?"

"Because I know there's another life. He likes women too, but I was hoping that that would just go away in time. Hell, I'd even settle for being number one, knowing that there's a number two, or three or four, just as long as I'm number one." Sweets' face crumpled up; he looked as though he had just eaten something foul. "I'm a goddamn catch. Come on, look at all this!" He pointed toward himself and drew a large *S* in the air. "Sweet and fabulous. The personality maybe a woman's, but the body's all man.

The Doc nodded; and when Sweets finished his performance, he told him, "If you're unsatisfied in your relationship, then why not voice out your concern? Better yet, if you're unhappy, leave. When you do, it will either open the door to a better relationship or close the door to an unhealthy one."

"Uh-huh. Well . . . I don't know about leaving."

"Why are you staying? If you don't mind me asking."

Sweets didn't hesitate, take a breath, or miss a beat. "Two reasons." He looked at the Doc's feet and let out a quiet "Hmph," shook his head, and quietly said to himself, "So sad." Then he told the Doc, "Big feet and a big-ass dick. Hallelujah! That's good enough for me."

The Doc coughed out loud, spewing spit everywhere, which caused everybody to look at him as he sputtered out, "Well, sex is an important part of any relationship." He got himself together and told Sweets, "But it's not the only part. Let's flip the script, shall we?"

Sweets shrugged his shoulders and said, "Okay, I'm listening." He stopped and leaned back against the counter, listening to the Doc, inspecting the back of his head as he did.

"You might want to look at it from a different perspective. I always tell my clients to look at it from the other person's point of view. Step into their shoes. Perhaps it's not that he is ashamed of you."

The Doc paused and twisted his lips to one side, and I could see him mouth, *Although that's probably what it is*. I laughed at his ass as he told Sweets, "Perhaps, it has more to do with how he views himself."

As I thumbed through a magazine, laughing, trying to play it off, I could tell, that what the Doc was saying got Sweets thinking. I looked up at him and noticed that he had even started biting his bottom lip. Hell, he was biting so hard I was scared he was going to bite the whole damn thing off. Kinda amused, I sat there and shook my head as I watched the two. Sweets resumed working on the Doc's hair, but he didn't say anything else. He just cut, trimmed, and shaved, but his eyes told the whole story—he was stewing over everything the Doc had said.

"Sweets, am I done?" the Doc asked after thirty seconds had passed, with Sweets just holding his comb and scissors in midair.

"Oh, sorry about that. Guess I lost my train of thought."

I don't know what happened, but it was as though someone had just snapped their fingers, and boom! Sweets was back to his old jolly, gabbing self. "Well, don't you look handsome!" he said as he turned the Doc around so he could see himself in the mirror.

"All thanks to you," the Doc said. Sweets helped him remove the cloak from around his neck, and he jumped out of the chair. He asked Sweets, "Are we good?"

Sweets nodded and mouthed *Thank you* to him.

The Doc excused himself, mumbling something about making a phone call, and walked outside, where he bumped into this bad-ass piece of tail. When I saw who it was, I said, "Oh, shit." And before Sweets could finish cleaning up his station, Tracy, Malcolm's wife, had slid into his chair without so much as a hello. She was looking at Sweets as though she had something against him, but she always had that expression on her face—at least that was her expression every time I saw her. It was an expression that said, *I'm going to get you. You just don't know it yet.* I'm a pretty brave brother, but Tracy scares the shit out of me—especially after what Malcolm told us.

"Touch up on my roots and the layers around my face," she said sternly, her red-stained lips barely moving.

Sweets didn't even seem to mind her attitude. He clutched his chest and proclaimed, "A woman after my own heart. But before we go there, I gots to give you a piece of my mind, bitch! You're late. You best be glad I'm doing Quita a favor and taking your behind while she's out today. Girl, you best be glad they're paying me extra for you ICON peoples. Believe you me, you would be kicked to the curb, heifer."

Tracy laughed; and after that, they were cool. Sweets tied the cloak around her neck and started talking about everything he had heard from around the streets.

His lips didn't stop moving as he wrapped tin foil on sections of her hair. Then suddenly, he gasped as he remembered some juicy information from his gossip reservoir. "Girl, I hear that DeDe—you know, one of the divas from the last *Love Forum*—is going to be performing at the ICON Awards. And get this, I hear one of the brothers in here is still tipping on his wife and having an affair with her. Ain't that something? And she's supposed to be saved and redeemed. Ain't that the snap to the crackle and pop?"

Tracy raised a perfectly arched eyebrow as she looked up to stare Sweets down. I thought, *Oh shit. Damn, does this nigga even know who this lady is?* I looked down at Malcolm, who was acting as though he didn't even see her, and started to get up to go talk to him, tell him what was up; but then I didn't want to miss anything.

Before I could hear any more of what they were saying, V's beautiful face appeared in front of me, blinding me with that gorgeous smile. She had lost a lot of weight. She was hunched down, with her knees bent, so that we were eye level with each other; and her already-low-cut shirt showed a healthy amount of cleavage. Hey, I'm a man. You flash those things in front of me, and I'm gonna look.

"You're my next, DK," she told me, her melodious voice tickling my ears. She took my hand and began dragging me toward an empty chair that was a spot away from where Sweets and Tracy were still talking.

"What're you planning to do to me, girl? I don't wanna come out here looking like some clown," I teased her as she tied a cloak around my neck.

She just shook her head and laughed a girly laugh. It was sweet; it sounded young and matched her baby face to a tee. "Don't you worry about it. I'm not my cousin." She tilted her head in the direction of Tracy and Sweets, who were still yapping, and let out another laugh.

I listened; it seemed as though they had already jumped courses. Sweets was now entertaining Tracy with tales of his new gig as X's event planner. I shook my head in disbelief, because he still didn't know who he was talking to. I motioned to Malcolm to go check on his woman, but he just brushed me off and continued talking to Brass. So of course, I caught a 'tude and left it, along with his rude ass, alone.

I looked back at Tracy while V was getting her stuff together; and by the look on Tracy's face, I could practically see the wheels turning in her head as she leaned closer to the mirror to inspect the color on her hair. I heard her say to Sweets, "I know a group that sounds just like the Jones Girls, and I can get them dirt cheap too—if you want them. They'll even perform the Jones Girls' signature hit, 'You Gonna Make Me Love Somebody Else.'"

Sweets cackled. "Girl, I love that song. You know what would be funny?"

"What?"

"Girl, wouldn't it be something if his wife dedicated that song to him, or that DeDe, just like she dedicated that Shirley Brown song when the divas did their show? Girl, wouldn't that be a mess?"

I didn't hear Sweets' exact words because my damn phone started ringing just then. Everyone looked at me, all annoyed, as if they'd never had their phones ringing in public. I looked at the caller ID and saw Judge Hoffanstanter's name flashing.

"Aren't you going to answer that?" V asked while she pulled stuff out of her beauty trolley.

I shook my head—as in, hell no, I wasn't going to answer. I just knew the judge was calling to talk about Pat and Donnell's drama, and I didn't want to get anywhere near that. V kept looking at me as the phone kept ringing, not going to voice mail as it should; and I told her, "It's the judge. He's been trying to get a hold of me for days now. Probably has something to do with Donnell and your friend Pat over there. You know they're in the middle of that ugly, if not bitter, divorce."

"Hmm, I know about it. Look at him over there. I can't stand him."

"V? Donnell's my boy. Don't start. I don't want to get in between their mess—with you or the judge, if you know what I'm saying."

I shrugged my shoulders and let out a big whiff of air. I expected V to start wailing about supporting Pat, but she just licked her lips and smirked. "That's fair, but you might wanna put that phone on Vibrate, because it's starting to irritate me."

I laughed at her candor and thought, *V's an all-right girl.* "Yes, ma'am," I said and gave her a mock salute, which earned me a slap on the ear.

She tilted the salon chair back and gently placed my head on the headrest. She then grabbed a razor in one hand and a bottle of aloe vera in the other. The charm bracelets on her wrists made a soothing, jingling sound whenever she moved, and I closed my eyes and thought, *That's nice.*

"Now, this is gonna go real quick," she said. "I'm just gonna clean you up, get rid of that facial hair, and you're good. You're a handsome man, DK. We don't need to do much work on you," she said, giving me a wink. Damn, that twelve-year-old boy of mines would be blushing from head to toe right about now if he heard me say that to you."

Hmm. Is this woman flirting with me? I looked up at V and caught her looking down at me. I smiled. She was flirting with me. "That's some sweet talking you doing, V," I said.

She placed a hot towel around my face and told me to relax as she rubbed my arms, which were resting on the armrest.

"All about customer service, DK, all about customer service. I go after the tips, comprende? I'm after the tips," V drawled before throwing her head back, laughing at her own joke. "Any plans about what you're going to be wearing for the ICON Awards?" she asked as she spread some aloe vera on my neck and started stroking it with the razor.

"I got me a nice Armani suit, courtesy of either K103.5 or one of the ICON sponsors," I told her.

She started humming, and I could feel her breath against my cheek. It smelled as though she had just eaten some sort of strawberry jam.

"Did you get one of those fashion-forward Armani suits? You know, the ones with the pencil-thin ties and skintight trousers?" she asked with a slight lilt in her voice, kinda joshing me.

"Naw, none of that. None of that shit," I said, picturing myself in one of those skinny suits you see the kids wearing today, the kind the models wear in women's magazines.

"Why not? I bet those skintight trousers would look so good with those toned legs of yours."

I smiled as she kept dishing out the compliments and staring me down as she kept stroking my neck with the razor.

"Naw, V. If I wore that, everybody's gonna be looking at me like I lost a screw, especially the brothers. I can hear them ragging on me already." I smacked my lips together as I thought about all the names the brothers would call me if I showed up in the kind of suit V wanted me to wear.

Her face tightened up, her expression growing serious. "Who cares what they think? I had to learn my lesson the hard way. Remember? I was a big girl before I lost all that weight. And, honey, I'm dealing with the same issues skinny as I was when I was big. Lesson learned. So as long as you feel good about yourself, that's all that matters, right?" I did a carefully timed nod yes, in between the strokes of the razor. She didn't say anything else; she just went on cleaning me up. When she was done, she stood behind me and placed her hands on my shoulders as she cranked the chair up so I could see myself in the mirror. All of a sudden, she screamed, "OUCH!"

Which made me jump and cry out. "What!?"

She said, "Put me on a stretcher, and just . . . TAKE ME AWAY! That's my jam!"

I looked at her as if she was crazy, but then I started laughing anyway and asked, "Who is this?"

"Boy! That's Keri Hilson with Ne-Yo and Kanyé West with 'Knock You Down.'" With her hands moving down my chest, she started dancing behind me as she looked at me in the mirror. "By the way, you look good, DK."

Her smile was infectious; it made me feel that everything was right in the world. I told her, "You don't look so bad yourself, V." And I thought about Ms. Doretha, who said the third time was the charm. I didn't know where V was going to fall into the equation, but I was game to find out.

Chapter 17

K103.5 ICON Awards

(DK's POV)

*T*he night of the ICON Awards had finally arrived, and it felt as though it had taken us centuries to get here. I sat in the dressing room with the brothers, just cutting the fool, talking trash, and just effin' around until it was our time to go out and accept the humanitarian award for Melissa. For some reason, I just couldn't keep still; it was if I had AD/HD or something—not that I was taking attention deficit/hyperactivity disorder lightly or anything; I just couldn't keep my ass in that chair. I just had to go out to see what was happening out onstage, and my feet just went to walking. As I neared the stage's entrance, I could hear the announcer say, "ICON, let's welcome, Jessie Simone Harris." I caught a glimpse of Jess disappearing into the lights, and then I could hear her start to address the audience.

"Good evening, ICON Awards, and welcome to the beautifully restored Music Hall at Fair Park. Yes! Just gorgeous, y'all, don't you agree? My name is Jessie S. Harris, and I'm the marketing and program consultant for K103.5, and it is indeed a pleasure to be with you this evening. As you know, Melissa Morgan provided the impetus for what we now know as the ICON Awards of today. From its humble beginnings some six years ago, the awards have definitely grown: Grown from several nominating categories to over twenty— the Humanitarian Award being one of them. Ladies and gentlemen, I'm here tonight to present the K103.5 Humanitarian Award, posthumously, to our very own Melissa Morgan. And I cannot do this alone, y'all. So to help bestow this prestigious honor, I'm excited to introduce the next performer—a true diva in every sense of the word. And we're not just happy, we *are* ecstatic to have her back in our great city of Dallas. So without further ado, please give a warm round of applause for my best, best girlfriend, and gospel music's newest rising star, DeDe Kravitz—better known as DeDe-K.!"

"That's my girl!" I shouted as applause and cheers echoed throughout the auditorium. I stood on side of the stage, hidden behind these huge velvet-like curtains, and watched as Jessie, beautiful as she wanted to be, finished introducing DeDe. Suddenly, just that quick, the stage went black; and a single bright beam

135

of light appeared and illuminated DeDe from above. It was as though my girl was glowing! And I can't lie: I stood there thinking, *Damn! She looks good as shit.* Not soon after, a large screen lit up behind her and began showing images of artists who were no longer with us. And then my girl opened her mouth and began speaking. It was almost as if I was listening to angels sounding horns in heaven—and I was fixated on every word she said, and on her.

"I'm DeDe-K, ladies and gentlemen. Whew! Yes! What a year this has been! Hasn't this been a year, y'all? Yes, lawd, a year of triumphs, as well as a year of losses. And we lost some giants, y'all—one giant in particular, who just happened to be my dear, dear friend. Well, you knew her as the ever-so-sweet Melissa Morgan." DeDe's voice started to crack, and I grew a little worried. I was afraid she was gonna blow it; but my girl paused, adjusted the microphone, and somehow found the strength to tell the audience, "Well, I knew her crazy tail simply as Lis. And as we're sharing our fond memories of Melissa tonight, I have to share this wonderful story with you: It happened a few days ago. I believe it was on a Wednesday. Well, I was sitting down taking one of those mental health breaks—you know, one of those breaks where you have just had enough and need to get away from it all? Yah, y'all know what I'm talking about. Well, as I was taking one of those breaks, an ICON producer walked right up to me and sat himself down, his thigh slightly touching mine—it was that close, y'all—and child, you know, I looked at him like, *Honey, do I know you?*"

The audience and I laughed for a good while at that one. Afterward, as we quieted down, DeDe laughingly said, "Well, that was his response too. He laughed and introduced himself—Christopher Walker, I do believe—and said he had a question to ask me. Well, my eyes went straight down to his ring finger, 'cause y'all know I'm saved and redeemed! Can I get an Amen, ladies! Hmph! I know that's right, y'all. And I thought, *Now I know he's not going to ask me what I think he's going to ask, not with that wedding band on his finger!* But he was genuine and candid and asked me this beautiful but troubling question: If I had to describe Melissa Morgan, how would I describe her? Well, delighted that it was *this* question for one, and after some careful thought, I immediately answered that Melissa was a beautiful, dedicated, strong-minded wonder whose life, although cut way too short, was dedicated to service: service to her god, service to her beloved K103.5, service to Dallas, and service to those on the journey to finding that true fulfillment in life, including that all-too-familiar journey we all face—the journey to finding sweet, sweet love. Remember *The Love Forum*, y'all?

"Yes, Melissa Morgan was L-O-V-E —the epitome of those four letters. And when the K103.5 ICON Awards contacted me concerning performing, I told them, 'Oh my god, I just don't think that's a good idea. I mean, I probably wouldn't be able to make it through the beginning of a song without breaking down and crying my eyes out, let alone have a clue of what song would do justice to honoring my girlfriend.' And, folks, you know how God just intervenes and gives you the answer when you need it most? hallelujah! Whew, Jesus! SHA-SHA-LA-HAMBA-DA! You gotta praise him, y'all. Got me in here speaking in tongues. Well, family, I just happen to be listening to some song bites for my upcoming CD entitled *Sang Girl*—oh, you're clapping, thank you so much—and a song began playing that just took my breath away . . . and, Dallas, I fell in love. I fell in love with this song and knew, at that moment, that God had sent me a sign, and I can only thank Armstead Edwards and James "Budd" Ellison for writing and composing such beautiful words and music. And a special thanks to the ultimate diva herself, Mrs. Patti LaBelle, for not just singing, but, girl, for sangin' this song. Armstead, James, and Patti, thank you for 'You Are My Friend.' ICON, although I've changed the words for this special occasion, I hope I do it justice for you tonight."

For some reason, I couldn't move. I just kept staring out onto the stage at DeDe. There was something about her; she was just—well, hell, stunning!

"She looks good as shit, don't she?" asked Malcolm as he and Mike walked up behind me.

"Yah, man," I replied, a little dry. I tell you, ever since the retreat, he and Mike had been as irritating as two long crooked thorns in my goddamn ass.

"Damn, that DeDe know she's fine. Look at all of that!" Mike said as he jumped into the conversation.

"Why y'all talking about my girl like that? It's disrespectful. And y'all know she's changed. She's saved now."

"Saved? Saved from what, my nigga?" asked Malcolm.

Mike cockily said, "Hell, the only thing she's saved from is my bro's wife, Tracy, coming to tear that ass up for fucking up their marriage. Hell, that's about all she's saved from."

"Don't hate, man. Just know that the girl has changed. Give her that, *damn!*"

Mike came back with, "Changed? Nigga, please. Once a trick always a trick, and believe you me, I know a fucking trick when I see one." He flashed a big-ass conniving grin that said, *Yah, nigga. I said it. What?*

"Mike?" Malcolm said with a little laugh. "You wrong for that, man; but you may be right, 'cause you know I'm still hitting that shit, right?"

"Malcolm! You fucking kidding me. You still hittin' that, yo?"

"I can't be telling you niggas everything. But yeah, hit it yesterday when she got off the plane. Met her at the Four Seasons, where she's staying. Hey, DK, that is where the ICON guests are staying, ain't it? Room 421, to be exact, right? Maybe I should tell your sour ass how the room's decorated, or maybe even describe that good shit for you. Better yet, here"—Malcolm waved his pointer finger in the air—"take a sniff, niggas. That juice is still on my finger, yo."

I pushed his hand out of the way and said, "Yah right, nigga. Get for real. You ain't hittin' shit. Your ass is just salty 'cause you got caught up in your own web of deceit. Now, why would I want to believe you still hittin' that when my girl has so much to lose? Plus, didn't you just hear her? She don't mess around like that no more. My girl keeps telling you fools she's saved and redeemed and not messing round with married niggas no more! The new DeDe is singing for the Lord, and she has her eyes on the prize."

"Yah, and that prize is about nine inches long, four inches wide, with a fat mushroom head laying right here in these Calvins, yo."

Mike and Malcolm kept going on and on until I stopped paying them much attention. All I kept thinking was, *Niggas, get the hell out of here. Shit, you messing up my high!*

They finally realized that I wasn't paying them no mind and threw some crazy looks my way and said the-all-too-familiar phrase: *This nigga's trippin' man, let's go,* and walked off. I didn't care though (nor did I believe their shit), I was too wrapped up in watching DeDe as she entertained the audience with energy you just couldn't put into words. I watched as she grabbed the mic from the microphone stand and walked across the stage (walk baby, walk) as the spot-light followed her every move. I could hear her sweet voice say, "Count? . . . Ladies and gentleman, Reggie Davis, better known as the Count is our wonderful music director working especially hard down there in the orchestra pit (hey sweetie)," laughing, "he's been directing the band all night. Let's give him a wonderful round of applause. Yes! Count, you and the band are playing so beautifully tonight (audience, don't you agree?).

"Well, ICON, here we are. We lost some beautiful people in 2009: A beautiful writer, Mr. E. Lynn Harris; a wonderful singer, Robert Brookins—I just loved his 'Where Is the Love' duet with Stephanie Mills; the King of Pop, Michael Jackson; and yes, our very own Melissa Morgan. Lis, girl, I know you're looking down on us tonight and smiling with that big, beautiful smile. Girl, you are my friend, and I miss you so, so much."

I just stood there and watched the reaction of the audience, who began to stand and cheer as images of Melissa appeared on the screen. This was Jessie's big day, one that would surely make her or break her; and she pulled it off—damn, did this girl pull it off! DeDe cleared her throat and bowed in acknowledgement of the audience's applause and cheers. And as I watched, something took a hold of me; and I thought, *This is the one, out of so many women.* And there had been plenty, most of them either not worthy of mention or just as sneaky and conniving as they wanted to be, thus, still not worthy of mention. However, there was something special about this one—at first glance, that is. And, man, the girl started to sing; and it sent my heart a-racing.

"Whoaaa-oh-oh-oh. The pain, oh, oh, the pain. Family, I lost . . . I lost a dear friend. I never knew how much I loved, and missed them, 'til then. Ohhhh, how the tears want quit falling down, my face. And how, my heart (oh how my heart) aches-ay-e-aches . . . Divas, where are you?" DeDe asked as she turned around in search of the girls. "Jessie, Pat, Britt, V, Darlene? Come on out, divas, come on out. My girlfriends, y'all, you probably know them as *The Love Forum* divas."

DeDe started singing again as each diva walked up and gathered around her, "You were . . . my . . . my friend, I never knew how much I loved, and missed you, 'til then. My friend, Jessie, y'all." DeDe gave Jessie a big hug and blew the rest of the divas a kiss. I could see tears running down her face as she started singing, "Jessie, I feel her love, even, though, she's not here; and Pat, it soothes my soul, knowing, people remember and really care.

"Fellas, where are you? DK, Magic, Michael, Pastor Levine, Malcolm, Quentin, Xavier, Miguel, come on out! Ladies and gentlemen, introducing the brothas from the new, and improved *Love Forum*—better known as *The Brothers Speak*."

DeDe stood there for a second as we made our way to the stage and gathered around as Jessie and the rest of the divas held hands and embraced each other. This was just a powerful moment: The brothers and divas together on one stage, honoring our girl Melissa Morgan. DeDe looked up at the ceiling. She closed her eyes, shook her head, and began humming. Then she broke out singing, "I've been around, and around, and around." I heard someone in the audience say, "SANG, girlfriend!"

And DeDe laughed and said, "Ha! Isn't this beautiful, y'all? Whew! Lawd! Aren't they just some beautiful brothers? Black Coffee, y'all. DK, come here, sexy boy."

Hell, I walked right up to her fine ass and said, "Hey, sexy your damn self!"

The audience laughed and gasped—I guess in shock—at the same time. Oh well, gotta move on; and I looked at the teleprompter and started my speech on cue.

"K103.5 family and ICON audience, it's so good to be here—and in the presence of so many of our good friends too!" I gave DeDe a big hug and stood right by her side and thought about saying, *Girl, the things I would do to you.* But I followed the teleprompter and said, "I tell you, DeDe, I sure am going to miss saying, 'Girl, you know you fine' to Melissa—which was definitely an understatement. But most importantly, I'll miss her presence in our lives. And as we've heard, time and time again, so many Dallasonians will miss her as well."

"That's right, DK," said Magic, on cue, as a row of microphones were lowered down in front of us. "DK, DeDe, brothas, divas, Melissa was involved in so many charities; but she's best known for using the radio as her platform for social commentary."

"That's right, Magic! Our gul Melissa did just dat," said Brass. "She raised awareness about da black community like no other. And with *The Love Forum*, she not only brought dose relationship issues to da front burner, my gul, also burnt a few of us brothers with dose heated *Love Forum* discussions. "

Hell, I couldn't help but laugh as I glanced over at Donnell as the mistress of ceremonies brought over Melissa's award.

"Ain't that right, Donnell?" asked Brass.

"Well, Brass, man, you may be right on the money with that one. But I think my purpose for being here tonight is to let everyone know that Melissa left her legacy for the brothas to tell our side of the story. And we'll be doing just that on the brand-new *Love Forum*, which we affectionately call *The Brothers Speak*. And, folks, it's all happening this Sunday, August 9th; and our very own Michael Crawley, this distinguished bro standing next to me right here will be our host." Donnell let out a sly but hearty chuckle while elbowing Michael. "And, Mike boy, I gotta feeling the K103.5 women are going to rip you apart for breaking our girl Jess's heart. And, Jessie, I have to tell you, you look absolutely stunning, baby girl."

Jessie smiled. "Thank you, Donnell."

Of course, Mike couldn't let that one go. "Well, Donnell, I don't know about breaking Jessie's heart, man—although you may want to concentrate on what went down in your own relationship with your wife, instead of getting in mine."

The expression on everyone's faces said the same thing: *Damn! What the hell was that all about. And what's wrong with you two?*

I could see Jessie, out of the corner of my eye, shaking her head in disbelief. And everyone could feel the love (not!) between Mike and Donnell. After he and Donnell had stared each other down for a brief second, Mike finally got back on track. "But hey, Donnell, man, got much love for you, my brother. I do know that the divas and brothas will be talking hot and heavy about relationships in general. And yes, we'll hit on what went down in our relationships and let the K103.5 listeners weigh in, speak their piece, and get some feedback—if not plain out advice—about their own relationship woes. And to help us out, we'll have some very special—if not distinguished—guests to not only give the brothas some guidance but to help all of the K103.5 family wade through their relational issues. So, brothas, divas, ICON, and our K103.5 listening audience, it's going to be one helluva show tomorrow night. Don't miss it! And, Quentin, I hear everyone's dying for you to clear up some of those commitment issues clouding your name; but more importantly, bro, everyone really wants to hear you talk about the love of your life, and the love of Dallas, Ms. Melissa Morgan."

As the mistress of ceremonies handed Melissa's award to Quentin, the brothers gathered around him for support while the divas slowly moved behind us. When we were all in our designated places, a lady who looked strangely familiar, brought out little Meli and led her over to Quentin; and I kept thinking, *I've seen this chick before, but where?*

Quentin, with little Meli in one arm and the award in the other, cleared his throat and slowly began reading from the teleprompter.

"ICON, on behalf of the brothas and divas standing up here with me tonight, as well as my little daughter, Meli, here in my arms—my Lis would be so proud—I graciously accept this award for the friend, coworker, lover, and mother we all loved and cherished so much. May she live in our hearts and memories forever: And, ICON, may those memories be forever so sweet for the ever-so-sweet Melissa Morgan."

"We love you, sista-girl," cried Britt.

"We love you, Lis," echoed V.

"All right now, that's what I'm talking about. Rest in peace, Lis!" DeDe yelled as she walked over and hugged Quentin and kissed little Meli on the cheeks. "Well, everyone knows you have some pipes, DK—I don't know where you got 'em, but you got some pipes—and WHEW! can you blow. Boy, start us off with the thought of you . . ."

As DeDe handed me the microphone, she was shaking so bad. I smiled, gave her a reassuring nod and wink, and cleared my throat. And as the melody started up again, I began singing, "And I have to tell you, Melissa, that I've been looking around, and around, and you were nowhere to be found. But, God (lord have mercy) told me that you were with us all the time. I've been looking around . . . and looking around, and girl, you were here, with us, all the time."

"Yes, boy, yes! Sang!" DeDe said as she took over; and damn, my girl blew it out the theater. "Divas, you've been around; and, brothas, you've been around. I've been searching everywhere, but all the love and all the understanding is surrounding me right here! 'Cause I've been looking around, and you've been here all the time! My friends, my friends, my wonderful, beautiful friends . . ."

At that point, I was on a mission; and I thought, *Damn, DK. Melissa is gone, and she's still looking out for you, boy.* I was going to have DeDe, and nothing but God himself was going to stand in my way. That was until I went outside, after the show, and walked by Malcolm's car.

Chapter 18

Get Right Church and Let's Go Home
Greater Antioch

August 9, 2009

*T*o tell you the truth, Brass hadn't set foot in a church in over ten years. He just didn't have anything to say, be thankful for, or even give praise for. And as he sat there with the brothers and the divas, watching people run up and down the aisles—he got a kick out of that—he thought, *The more things change, the more they stay the same.* The same ole white uniforms for the ushers and nurses; the same building layout (just a bigger building); the same shouting in the pews and aisles and speaking in tongues; the same sing-a-couple-of-songs, then the welcome, then announcements, then prayer; the same hymns before the pastor comes to deliver the morning word, and the same word about posterity and wealth; the same collection of tithes and offerings with "You Can't Beat God's Giving" playing in the background; the same go-to-eat afterward (that's what they were doing); and the same mentality that church people are better than those still wandering around in the world. And he mumbled under his breath, "If this old bag sitting in front of me, turns around and looks down at me one more time, I'm gonna catch a case up in here."

As he sat there, anxiously bouncing his right leg up and down, ready to leave, he stared straight ahead into space, his mind taking him back to his gram's old white clapboard church on Sunday mornings. He could see his younger self and Margie sitting on the second row, behind the mourners' bench; all the deacons, plain as day, sitting on the right side of the church; and their wives, the deaconesses, facing them on the left side. He could hear their humming and the tapping of their shoes on the scratched-up wood floors. He could see his grams staring at the pulpit, tears in her eyes, occasionally waving her hands and shouting "Hallelujah" as his gramps stood in the pulpit and preached the Word. And as he looked around at this monstrosity of a church, ornately decorated with blue carpet that matched the seat cover of the pews, white walls with heavy woodworking and gold leaf trim, massive gold chandeliers and stained glass windows that seemed to go on and on all the way up to the altar, he tried counting the people, packed from the floor all the way up to the U-shaped balcony that wrapped around to the front of the church. And yet, through all the elaborateness and the hundreds upon hundreds of worshipers, he could still see the same ole deaconesses and deacons in that old white clapboard church on the left and right of him. *Just better dressed and more dignified*, I guess, he said to himself before tuning in to what Pastor Levine was saying.

"Greater Antioch! Raise your hands if you're happy to be alive! Lord God— is he good? I didn't hear you. Is God good?" the pastor asked as he walked back and forth on the raised pulpit, encouraged by the praises, Amens, and singing and shouting of the huge choir—outfitted in white and blue robes—that rang from one end of the pulpit to the other. "You know, it's not Men's Day today. However, my spirit told me that I needed to talk about men today and, most importantly, the state of our black men.

"As most of you know, I recently participated in a retreat, up there in Alaska, with a group of brothers sitting there on my right. Some from the spiritual world and some from the secular world, and my brothers and sisters in Christ, my faith got tested."

You could hear the echoes of "Oh no" and "Lord have mercy" throughout the sanctuary. "Some nonbelievers," he said, looking over at Magic, "even had the audacity—I said 'even had the *audacity*—to say that they didn't go to church or believe in the sanctity of religion. Why? Because they believed most of us ministers, I guess he was talking about me too"—he strutted over to the side where the brothers were sitting—"were living double lives, or hiding something, or may not even be walking in our true light or purpose. Praise God."

"Praise God, Pastor. Praise God," the churchgoers replied.

"I'm here to tell you that all is well here at Greater Antioch, but all is not well with our black men of today."

Magic kicked DK after hearing that and shook his head as he stared the pastor down. Trying not to be obvious, he quietly told DK, "Just listen to him, playa. He ain't right. Just like I said."

DK smiled as Magic continued shaking his head and they both listened to the pastor go deep into his sermon, waiting intently for him to give his own personal tersitmony.

"And, church, as I sat there at that retreat, listening to one of the brothers confront all the hurt, pain, and heartache he has endured on his relatively short life on this earth, and to each brother after him talk about his lot of sad, if not troubling, life trials, I knew that the Lord had put me there for a reason. Church, I'm shaking my head, and my heart cries out, 'cause we're not right. We're not right, and it's definitely not time to go home, as that old spiritual "Get Right Church and Let's Go Home" tells us. And, church, I can tell you, we haven't been right for a long time. And I need to tell you that as of this day, I'm done with the old, and I'm going to tell it like it I-T is. We're about to get right, church. 'Cause when my morning comes, I want to know that I got right, and I want to hear my Lord say, 'Well done, son, well done.'"

DK nodded his head along with everyone else, but his mind was a million miles away. He kept thinking about last night at the ICON Awards, about what he saw in the parking lot after the show: Malcolm lying back in the seat of the car and DeDe's head moving up and down by the steering wheel. He looked at her sitting in the pew in front of him and thought, *Damn, was I wrong about her. Saved my ass.*

Magic couldn't believe that the pastor, after all that went down at the retreat, didn't start off by giving his own testimony, as he said he would. He just shook his head. There was no mention of his past, of his ex-wife, or of his daughter; and he thought, *I don't know how, but everything's gonna come to the light, preacher man, whether you want it to or not.* He folded his arms as he continued to listen to the pastor do his thing.

"And as I sat there, with tears swelling up in my eyes, the only thing that would come into my mind and into my spirit was that song by Kirk Franklin, 'More Than I Can Bear.'" And the pastor began to sing, "Mmmmm . . . Yes! Oh Lordy. Good God almighty! Choir, help me sing:

I've gone through the fire
And I've been through the flood
I've been broken into pieces
Seen lightnin' flash from above
But through it all I remember
That He Loves me
And he cares
And He'll never put more on me
Than I can bear

"HALLELUJAH! I said. Hallelujah, church. Will somebody help me out this morning?"

"Hallelujah, Reverend! Hallelujah!" cried Pat as she sat fanning herself, moving her body from side to side, smiling and laughing.

"Joy-o-eeee (hah!). Joy-o-eeee (hah!). Joy's coming in the morning, my brethren. Yesss! Yesss! Let the church say Amen, 'cause it's coming. Joy's coming in the morning, sister Pat. O Lord!"

The pastor came from behind the podium and started kicking his legs up like a soldier as he came down the stairs of the pulpit and stood in front of the remembrance table. "And as much as our forefathers have endured (hah!), as much as our fathers have endured (hah!), as much as we as men, as black men, have endured (hah!), God (hah!), has not, and will not, put more on us than we can bear. (O Lord, hallelujah! Praise God. Hah!). To my *Love Forum* brothas—Brass, Michael, Miguel, DK, Quentin, Malcolm, Donnell, X, and Magic—trust and believe. Trust in him, my brethren. Trust in him (hah!), men of Greater Antioch. Trust in him (hah!), men of Dallas. Joy is coming to us in the morning. What's at the bottom, (hey-yah!), What's at the bottom, (hey-yah!), What's at the bottom (hah!), shall surely rise to the top. O Lord, my God."

Magic sat there and rolled his eyes. *What a performance.* By the expression on his face, DK, who was looking at him, knew exactly what he was thinking.

"He's getting there, Magic, man. He can't just turn it off cold. If he did, you think all these people would be in here?" Magic just shook his head and grimaced as he looked over at Brass.

Brass just sat there, stoic, as though he was mesmerized. He could see his gramps preaching; and when he looked over at Pat, he saw his grams as she waved her hands and repeated "Hallelujah" over and over. Tears welled up in his eyes; and for some reason—actually, twenty-nine years of them—he got up out of his seat and started to walk past Pat, Donnell, and Quentin. But when he reached the aisle, he couldn't move. It was as though Satan had blocked his way and was holding him back. All of a sudden, he felt a hand on his arm, and when he looked up, he saw Britt.

She smiled and said, "Come on."

But he couldn't. His legs wouldn't move. She nudged him, and as the congregation's eyes fixed on them—some even started clapping, encouraging him and Britt—but it wasn't enough; he grabbed Britt by the waist and turned her around toward the exit. All the guilt, shame, hostility, and the resentment, stored for so many years, surfaced. He saw his mother strung out on crack. He saw his grandpops on his knees, clutching his heart. He saw his head in between his cousin's legs. Every bad thing in his life flashed in front of him, and he just couldn't turn around. He had been in the same aisles before, different places and different times; walked up to be saved; asked for forgiveness; and asked for help. But every time, his prayers fell on deaf ears.

Pastor Levine watched him walk out with Britt, and his heart cried out, "Lord God, that reminds me of the ole Negro spiritual 'Ain't Gonna Let Nobody Turn Me Around.' We gone have to turn around people, including me." He leaned against the table and filled the congregation in on the struggles of the Brotherhood and where he stood in the midst of it all. He told them that he too faced challenges and struggles, and that starting next week, he would be addressing them.

"Let's get out of here, church. Choir? Sing that James Cleveland song 'Get Right Church and Let's Go Home.' And, church, let's go into those closets, get your houses in order. Let's meet that joy in the morning with rightful hearts." Pastor Levine knelt down before the congregation and raised his right arm to heaven. "Lord, we come to you in prayer, asking you to prepare our hearts. Get us right, Father. Get us right."

Chapter 19

The Battle
The Divas vs. the Brothers

(DK's POV)

*I*t was Sunday night, and the hyped-up battle between the divas and the brothers was about to hit the airwaves. It was absolutely nerve-racking waiting, in a sea of bodies, for it all to begin; and the overall mood was tense—really, really tense. Especially with twenty or so bodies crammed inside the studio booth, almost sitting on top of one another. And those conditions made it chaotic, at best. I was nervous as all get-out, especially with all the commotion over the divas' return to the forum; but I put my nervousness in check and tried to appear cool, calm, and collected as I wiped away the small beads of sweat forming above my brows. I motioned to Sharon, who was outside the booth, to turn up the air-conditioning as the room was boiling over with mad, crazy levels of estrogen and testosterone, and it was making me—and everyone else in the room—nervous as hell.

Magic said, "DK, in five . . . four . . . three . . . two . . . one."

And it was on. The moment was here, and I manned up and dived right into it.

"K103.5, this is your boy DK 'Love' Niles, and the *Quiet Storm* is on fire tonight, y'all. For one, we not only have our boy Michael in the pilot's seat— Wassup, Mikey-Mike!—we have five beautiful sisters in the studio with us. Who are they, you ask? Well, we have Ms. Jessie, Mrs. Pat, Ms. V, Ms. Britt, Ms. Darlene, and the beautiful songstress herself, who agreed to break away from her music career and join us all the way from LA, Ms. DeDe-K. You know them better as the *Love Forum* divas."

The divas collectively said, "Hey, DK. And hey, K103.5 family."

"All right, all right," DK said jokingly. "You better recognize the family divas, and K103.5 family, guess what? Yah, yah, I hear you out there, and you got it. For the next couple of hours, we're going to be talking about relationships like you've never heard on the forum before. It's gonna be unscripted, unedited, and uncensored—just effin' raw convo. So, Mike, my man, take it away."

Magic turned Mike's mic on, and Mike jumped in like an old pro. "Thanks, DK. And not only do we have the divas in the house—all looking ever so lovely—we have some special guests in the studio as well. And, family, you might know this *young* lady from the first *Love Forum*."

Someone piped up, "*Young?* I know that's right, Michael. I already like you, honey!"

Mike laughed. "You heard her. We have the one and only Dr. Laura, the Relationship Guru, joining us. Now, we can't leave the brothers uncovered, so to get that male perspective, we also have another relationship doctor in the house—Dr. Franklin Mayweather. Good evening to both of you."

Dr. Laura and Dr. Mayweather said their greetings and nodded at everyone in the room.

"Now, before we begin, because this is going to be the battle of all battles, us brothers, and the divas over here, have prepared our own battle songs to entertain you with. What do you say, guys? Ladies first?"

DeDe didn't wait for an answer. She launched right into the opening of the Honey Cone's "Want Ads," and the rest of the divas joined in; and their voices blended together in perfect harmony.

Jessie cried out, "I know that's right, girls, we need to put it in the *want ads*."

When they were finished, the Divas hollered as DeDe gave the song a tasty but colorful close: "I'm saved and redeemed and that Negro and I are through."

I looked at her. *Yah right, not after what I saw you doing to Malcolm in the car.* But I kept things professional. I rolled my eyes at her before turning away and looked down at my boy Mike.

"That was amazing, ladies—really good, really good. I can tell you ladies worked real hard on that," Michael said, laughing as the women settled down. "But it's all going to be for naught because we're just going to decimate you! Start us up, Magic!"

At Mike's cue, Magic began b-bopping the classic tune of James Brown's "It's a Man's World," and I jumped right on in and started singing and the rest of the brothers joined in.

"Ain't that the truth!" Jessie yelled out in the background, "Sing, DK! SAANNGGG! 'Cause you ain't telling nothing but the truth!"

The other divas started laughing when DeDe backed her up and said, "I know that's right, girl!"

We continued singing as the divas listened appreciatively, snapping their fingers and swaying their heads from side to side. After we sang the last words of the song, the ladies clapped for us politely, giving us our props for, I had to laugh, our entire rendition of the song, and DeDe said, "All right, all right, y'all may have won that one, singing the whole damn song; but that's it!"

Mike nodded and winked at her. "Don't hate. We're going to win all the challenges, and there's three, K103.5. And this is how it's going to go down: The first challenge, which we've already done, was to come up with and perform our fight song. And as you've heard, family, the brothers definitely won that one."

The brothers started barking, and V, who couldn't be outdone, started meowing like a cat and clawing in the air. The rest of the divas followed suit, and Magic said, "Catfight, catfight. I think them puttie cats want to throw down y'all." Which made everybody break out in laughter, easing some of the tension in the room.

Mike piped back in. "Get them putties, Magic. Get them putties. . . . Now, the second challenge is to answer several calls from the listening audience. Dr. Mayweather and Dr. Laura will guide that challenge and judge us on our answers.

"The third challenge is to tackle a male-female relationship issue that one of the divas or a brother is having with someone in the room. I hear y'all out there saying, 'Oh hell.' Well, that's exactly what we said when they told us. So you're asking, how are we going to do it? Well, to give you the rundown, Dr. Laura made the divas and the brothers write down what we wanted to get off our chest and put it in a coffee can. The divas wrote their issues on pink paper. Us brothers wrote ours on blue. Our boy, Dr. Mayweather, had to close his eyes and pick out one of the pieces of paper, and he'll read it out when we get to that point of the show, which I am *not* looking forward to."

You could hear Magic joking around in the background, instigating. "Yah, Doc. You let us down, man. How you gone pick the pink paper? You traitor."

The Doc just smiled. "It's up to you, brothers, to make sure you're on point with your side of the situation. And to make sure we get our listeners involved— get that audience participation going—we're asking the K103.5 family to weigh in on the discussion. So, family, call in and let us know what you think. Let us know if you agree with the brother's point of view or the sister's. After the last phone call, we'll tally up the listeners' responses; and whoever gets the most votes wins the challenge."

I nodded at Mike and the Doc, and took over as Sharon gave me the cue that it was time to go to break. "K103.5, this is your boy DK again, and we have a special sponsor this evening, who's providing you with uninterrupted programming tonight. This evening's episode of *The Brothers Speak*, featuring the lovely divas, is sponsored by none other than Dallas's favorite Cajun restaurant. That would be Bailey's. And I believe Sharon is telling me that we have Ms. Bee from Bailey's on the line."

"Hello? Am I on the air?"

"Bee, this is DK. What's happening over there at Bailey's tonight?"

"Well, DK, we're actually wrapping the night up, but before we did, I wanted to call in and say a warm hello to all the brothers and the divas. I'm inviting all of you down to Bailey's for a special lunch—on us, of course."

Everyone said their thank-yous for the invitation, and Magic asked, "Bee, what kind of lunch do we get?"

"You're going to get our famous—and Dallas's favorite—seafood sampler platter. It'll be waiting for each of you, and a guest, the next time you come down and pay us a visit. And for the K103.5 listeners—I'm not going to leave the family out—for the rest of this month, just come down and mention the code *brotherhood*, and you'll receive 20 percent off our famous seafood sampler platter."

I said, "Girl! I'ma say it like Chef Luda would say it: That sho' does sound good, critter." And I clapped a couple of times, laughing at myself imitating his ole ass.

"DK," Bee said, laughing, "boy, you're a mess. Now you know I can't forget about you. So, just for being one of our favorite and loyal customers"—Bee cleared her throat and softened her voice—"I have a special treat for you. A free sweet dessert of your choice."

I said, "All right now, Bee. You gone make me fall in love with you, girl." I laughed and looked around the room; and my eyes, for some reason, fell straight on V. Where before she was just a-smiling and a-laughing, batting those lashes, now she just had this sour look on her face.

Malcolm said, "Damn! You got women, calling in, offering you all kinds of sweets and goodies. You better go on up there and get that *cake*, man. Just make sure you peel back that layer of frosting. Do that check, brother. Find out what's underneath before you take that bite."

I laughed at Malcolm as I thought about him at the retreat. "Thank you, Bee. There you have it, K103.5—20 percent off a seafood sampler platter just by mentioning the Brotherhood. And, Bee, if you're listening, I'm coming to get my dessert, girl." After I said it, I made sure I looked over at V, who had rolled her eyes; then stuck out her lips and looked down at her nails. I shook my head and asked myself, *Is she jealous?* I looked at Mike and asked, "You ready for our first caller?"

He looked down at me and gave me a thumbs-up before taking over again.

"I believe we're ready, DK." He asked Magic, "My man, is Francine still on the line?"

"She's on line 1, Mike."

"Thanks, Magic. . . . K103.5, we know you've been anxious to hear all about what the divas have been up to, and I believe Francine's question, for the divas, is going to answer that for you. All right, divas, this is the second challenge. Francine? Are you there? What's your question?"

"Hey, Michael, you can just call me Frenchie."

"Okay, your question, Frenchie."

"My question is for all the divas, especially Ms. Jessie. Can you tell us if *The Love Forum* brought you love, or any closer to finding it?"

Mike said, "Hmm. That's a good question, Frenchie."

It was a good question and I chimed in, "Frenchie, that's a damn good question. Ladies? Who wants to go first?"

V leaned into her microphone and cut her eyes at me. She told the listener, "Frenchie—wait a minute, is this the Francine, a.k.a. Frenchie from Arlington, from the last *Love Forum*? If I remember correctly, 'Ms. Granted, I can't deny I wasn't being the best kind of woman; and come on, girl, you know if he ain't getting it in the relationship, he's damn well getting it somewhere else. And hell, why should I deprive myself?'"

"Yes, girl. Okaaayyy! You better ask somebody," Frenchie laughingly replied. "That would be me. And just like I said back then, 'I didn't want him for a husband, and he definitely didn't' want me for a wife; but that big [beep] was good as [beep]. And afterward—after the nasty, that is—he got his [beep] and got the [beep] out, 'cause I had [beep] to do.'"

"Damn, girl!" I said, "we just beeping all through your shi[beep]. Foul mouth behind."

V rolled her eyes at me. "Whatever, DK! Anyway. Girl, we just *love* you! You were one of our favorite callers. It's so good to hear your voice. Anyway, Frenchie, to answer your question: I don't know about it helping me find love, but it did open my eyes to certain things in my life—like my weight and self-esteem issues. You know, I lost a whole lot of weight, girl; and I can say that it also brought me and my son, Jerome—hey baby—closer together."

"I agree," said Britt. "I don't think I was anywhere near finding love myself. It probably helped me to realize, with the help of my girlfriends here, that maybe what I was looking for, or thought I had, wasn't really what it was, and definitely not what I needed in my life. Matter of fact, it cost me big-time—my career, livelihood, and, most of all, my self-worth." She looked over at Brass and then quickly looked down when their eyes met.

DeDe said, "I feel you, girl. I learned a valuable lesson my own darn self, but no love." She turned to Pat. "What about you, Pat?"

Pat sighed heavily. "Well, I remember when we first came on *The Love Forum* and I told Melissa that I was off the market. Now look at me. A year later, back on this damn show, and back on the market. So, Frenchie, no, I didn't find love. Hell, I couldn't even keep it. I just lost it—*twice*, back-to-back. I lost my dear friend Melissa Morgan and my husband, Donnell, who's sitting across from me by the way. And, Frenchie, girl, that last loss was probably for the best."

Everybody looked at Donnell and kind of snickered under their breath. "But I will tell you this, Frenchie: I'm not sure if *The Love Forum* brought any of the divas love. If it was there, it was there; if it wasn't, then it wasn't."

"Amen, girl!" said Britt.

"Girl, you 'bout to have me get up and start shouting up in here. I see the pastor has rubbed off on you," DeDe said as she hummed a few bars of a spiritual hymn. At the end, she said, "Hale-luh . . ."

Pat looked at DeDe cross-eyed. "Girl, you're too much. As I was saying, what *The Love Forum did* do was provide a support mechanism for the divas to get through some of the trying times we were facing. Lord knows those were some trying times. And that support mechanism, coupled with those trying times, opened up some wonderful relationships." Pat looked over at the pastor and smiled. Then she turned to Jessie, who was sitting next to her, and asked, "Don't you agree, Jessie?" She then turned and looked in Michael's direction.

Jessie looked over at Michael too, and then over at X, and then quickly glanced down at Quentin before answering, "I'll have to agree with you on that, Pat. I too lost someone that I thought I loved. Girl, I'm not gone even lie. He broke my heart. But you know, love is a funny thing: *Sometimes you get it right, and sometimes it gets you right.* You know what I'm saying?" She grabbed Pat's hand and looked over at X, smiling. "Frenchie, I think you might have hit the nail dead on the head, girl. I don't think I found love, but I do think it brought me closer to finding it."

X's face squinched up as he looked at Jessie, puzzled; and I could see him looking dead in her mouth as she spat out, "But I believe Darlene may have a different spin on your question."

"YES, DIVAS! Yes! Yes! Yes! Yes! Yes! Frenchie, girl, my love was confirmed on *The Love Forum*, and I LOVE IT! But just like Pat said, if it's there, it's there; if not, it's not. I just happened to have love that was already there, and it was confirmed and consummated by a marriage proposal, by my Miguel right here on the forum."

The divas looked at Darlene with slight grins and softly clapped for her, which let me know that we had some jaded sisters in the room—too jaded to be happy, even for their own friend. I guess what they say is true: You can't be happy for someone else if happiness doesn't reside within you first.

I said, "All right, fellas. We gone let our boy Michael rest those vocal chords of his and go to the phone lines. Our next caller, Tamika, is calling in to get some advice from the fellas. And I hear she's in South Dallas singing that Honey Cone song, and she has her own *want ad* she needs to put out there. She's wanting some advice. Tamika . . . Tamika? Girl, you tearin' it down ova there, aren't you? We hear you. So tell me, Tamika, tell your boy DK what your want ad—on our e-dating service, of course—says that you want in a brotha."

"DK, my ad is all good. Check out that Vulupshus Girl profile—it's spelled v-u-l-u-p-s-h-u-s. But anyway, listen. I thought I found the perfect brother for me, but I have a question for the brothers. Hopefully, y'all can give a sister some insight. So here's the issue: I met a brother, [beep] is his name, a couple of weeks ago in our work complex—I'm in Building 100, and he's in Building 600—and on our first night out after work, it was a casual get-together. Nothing fancy, one of those 'Let's get a bite to eat after work and chill and get to know each other' nights. Well, we finished eating and talking and then went our separate ways, and we would basically text each other after that. And I'm thinking, *Well, damn! Don't I, at least, get to hear your voice sometime?*"

"So no verbal contact, just text messages?" I asked.

"Uh-huh. And you know, at first it was okay—kinda cute, kinda not—and I let it slide. But I'm the type of woman that when I've had enough, I'm going to come out of the box on your behind—"

"Naw, Tamika, you didn't come out the box on our brother?" I asked.

"Who!? Oh yes, I did! Why is it appropriate for him to text me for an hour when he could just dial the number and we can talk, voice to voice? Tell you the truth, I was getting sick . . . of . . . that! And that's not the end! Soon afterward, my woman's intuition started to kick in, and I began to notice a pattern—"

"Oh Lord, what type of pattern were you noticing?" I asked. "Come on, tell the brothas and our listeners."

"Well, DK, for starters, we would always go out, like to the movies or for dessert or something on the weekdays—never on the weekends. Granted, I know that everyone has a different schedule during the week; however, you should be able to at least connect on the weekends. Right? Not!"

"Okay, Tamika, maybe you're just blowing this all out of proportion?" Miguel chimed in.

"Nah-ah. Every time—and I *do* mean every time—the weekend approaches, he disappears. And when I asked him about it . . . I mean, there's always some excuse. Excuse number 1: 'My roommate's birthday is this weekend.' Excuse number 2: 'I have other commitments that I can't get out of.' Excuse number 3—and this is my favorite, by the way: 'I need to get that overtime.'"

"Well, those could be legitimate and excusable if they're not reoccurring frequently," interjected Malcolm.

"Tamika? Did you hear my boy Malcolm?" I asked.

"Malcolm?" There was whispering in the background: "Girl, I know he did not just say Malcolm. Ugh! Girl, there must be some interference coming in from the radio. Turn it down. Did he just say Malcolm? Ain't that the loony who was sneaking around on his wife?"

"Tamika? Tamika?" Brass was laughing. "Hush all that gossip ova dare, girl. Dis your boy Brass."

"Hey, Brass!" She made a high-pitched, shrill noise and then started laughing. "Whatchu doin'? Made it back from that Mexican cruise, ey?"

"Chillin' . . . and you got jokes? Listen here, ma. You just a weekend gul in reverse! You and your situation come a dime a dozen. Tell me this: Have you ever been to homey's place?"

"Well . . . no, I can't say that I have."

"Aiight. So you only get to see him on the weekdays. Right? No weekends? So tell me, Tamika, what does your boy's roommate do?"

Tamika let out one of those long "WHEWS" and laughed a little. "You so noisy, Brass. All I know is that my man lost his job and just got hired where I work. He had to cut his expenses, so he moved in with a friend."

"Your man, huh?" Brass laughed. "Male or female—the roommate, I mean?" asked Brass.

"Well, hell, I assumed the roommate was a male," replied Tamika.

"And what does the roommate do?"

"Brass, I don't know. I guess he works out of town because [bleep] says he has the place to himself on the weekdays; but he works so much trying to get back on his feet that he's rarely ever there."

"Now. Tamika, gul, all the questions I've been asking you—hell, you should have been asking. Ma, you just a *weekend gul* in reverse. Magic? Magic? Hey, homey, play that "Weekend Girl" by the SOS Band, 'cause my gul, Tamika, is being (what?) . . . played. Homey got a gul and she's home on the weekends leaving the weekdays free for him to play."

"Humph! Is that what it is, Brass?" asked Tamika.

"Yap! That's what I see, ma. Next time you get that text—and my boy's texting you because text messages cost less than voice minutes—ask him straight up. Better yet, wait to do it in person. Dat way, you can get the full affect—see dose facial expressions, check out da full body language, ma."

I noticed the divas were dying to put in their two cents, but the Doc wouldn't let them interrupt. I caught Sharon, out of the corner of my eye, pointing to her watch; so I wrapped it up and said, "All right, Tamika, I think you got the Gospel According to Brass. Give us a call and let us know how it went down. Let's see if my boy Brass got some skills."

"Oh, you don't have to worry about that, DK. I'm going to definitely let you know the outcome," replied Tamika.

"All right! That was Tamika from South Dallas, and my girl got man troubles, y'all," I said sarcastically.

Brass laughed out loud. "These are some silly rabbits. Now she's been trick-ed-ded and don't even know it. Silly rabbit, don't you know that tricks are for what?" asked Brass.

"LOL. I know that's right, Brass," I replied. "Now, K103.5 family, I just been notified that we got time for one more caller; and I believe this call is for both the divas and the brothers. Rodney? Rodney? You're on the line with the brothas and the divas. Ask your question."

"Hey, how y'all doin'?" Rodney said on the other end.

Mike quickly answered, "We're doin' good, bruh. What's your question for us?"

"Well, since all of you are there, brothas and divas, I just wanna ask how y'all have been coping with Melissa Morgan's death."

Taken by surprise, they all looked to each other, like they didn't know what to say. Noticing everyone's reluctance to answer, I decided to take the lead: "You know, Rodney, I think we've all experienced the loss in different ways. Lis has always been close and dear to me, and, man, it still hurts thinking that she's no longer with us."

I looked over at Doc Mayweather and thought about the whole *silent son* thing and opened up, hoping that everyone would follow suit. "But what really helps us, I think, is knowing that Melissa wouldn't rest if we didn't move on and live happy lives. Every day I go on trying to fulfill my life in her honor. In fact, she left each one of us letters telling us her wishes and hopes for all of us." I choked up a bit talking about the letters. "In my letter, she actually told me that the love of my life is a breath and touch away, and I know just how much she wants me to look for that love." I looked around the studio and asked, "What about everybody else?"

Magic spoke up next. "She told me that I'm gonna find peace and happiness and be part of a bigger plan which will impact several lives.

"My letter says that my happiness will rely on a female friend. Still looking for that friend, ladies. Who's out there that wanna be friendly with me?" Magic asked. The brothers laughed, and the divas looked at him and rolled their eyes.

"Well, for me, she said that the lesson I've yet to learn will stare me hard in the face, and my song of life will be beautiful and rewarding," DeDe interjected.

V smiled softly and said, "Lis told me that the man of my dreams was in reach all along, and that I'll heal. I will understand and I will find comfort, and most of all . . . peace. I always think of Lis when I feel down and out. Her words give me hope."

Britt shared, "Well, Lis told me that the man of my dreams will surprise me. That he'll be professional on the day tip but a thug on the after-hours tip. She told me, 'Britt, sometimes God moves you when you don't take his heed and don't move as he directs you.'" She sighed deeply and reached across the table for Brass's hand.

Darlene said, "You know what she told me? She told me to trust my heart, and that no marriage or situation is perfect. The rain and storms I'll endure are just like those on God's green earth—the rain and storms, not only clean the surface, but are the nourishment which makes God's creations not only grow but thrive. She wished for my marriage to grow physically and thrive spiritually." Her eyes started to tear up, and rivulets of tears dropped down her cheeks. Miguel reached over and wiped them away, and Darlene knew that Lis's words were real.

Jessie was the next to speak up. She chewed on her bottom lip, wondering if she should even say anything since X was present. "She told me . . . she told me"—Jessie paused and let out a deep sigh—"that I'll find love in the strangest of places, but I shouldn't question it."

Pat spoke up last. "Lis told me to look to God, and said that I'll have to bear ridicule and unpleasant gossip, but I will stand firmly on my ground and by my belief. She said the man I love will love me even more for this." She paused and bit her bottom lip, trying to hold it all in. "Lis always believed in me, so much more than I believed in myself; and when that turmoil comes, I know she'll be there watching over me like an angel."

Donnell, who sat quietly in his chair, leaned back and scoffed. Then he looked at Pat in a malicious way that didn't make any sense. "Maybe you'll avoid all that ridicule and gossip if you just stop acting like the b-i-t-c-h that's always after me and my kids! Why is that Judge Hoffanstanter calling me up at my job?"

Everyone in the room was stunned at Donnell's nasty exclamation, and no one saw it coming. Dr. Mayweather immediately tried to step in and quell the situation. "Brother Donnell, how did you know what was on the paper? But to be so emotional, if not rude about—"

Pat jumped up before Jessie could stop her and lunged across the table, her hand missing Donnell, who pushed his chair back just in time. "Oh! So they're your kids now, is that right, Donnell? When we were married, you barely even saw them! You were too busy screwing that ho of yours, and now they're your kids?" Pat had one hand on her hip, and the other hand she waved back and forth at Donnell. "Yah, yah, you're right. The judge is handling everything. Just admit it, Donnell. You're just fighting me for custody because for some reason that I can't fathom, you just hate me and want to make my life a living hell. I'm not gone let you, though. So don't you sit there and tell me that you care about *my* kids!"

Donnell's face crumpled into an ugly sneer, and he yelled back, "Don't you dare say I don't care about my goddamn kids! And the only reason I had to go out and look for a better woman was because you were frigid, selfish, and don't think I don't know you weren't creeping too!"

Pat started to laugh mockingly, rolling her eyes. "This takes the mother effin' cake. Did everybody hear him? This bastard gone have the nerve to blame me for being a lying and cheating piece of scum. Ooh Lord, give me strength. There's no hope for you, Donnell—no hope." She pointed her finger at him.

"I tell you this, the world would be a much better place if you just got hit by a bus, a car or whateva—just SPLAT!" she drawled, as if to make sure Donnell understood that she meant every word she said.

Donnell was about to stand up as if ready to jump on Pat, but Mike barred him with an arm to his chest. "Pat I think you should sit down, calm yourself," Mike said, coming to Donnell's aid, trying to diffuse the situation.

Jessie gaped at him, her mouth open like a fish. "You've got to be kidding me? You're siding with that chauvinistic pig over there." She raised a long elegant finger and pointed at Donnell. "SERIOUSLY? You should be telling him to shut his trap, *for once*, and grow the [beep] up."

"Jessie, come on, now is not the time or place for one of your feminist speeches," Mike shot back.

X immediately jumped in to Jessie's defense. "Hey man, don't talk to my girl like that. What's wrong with you man? What's wrong with both of you?"

"Awe man, shut the hell up! I was nutting up in all that before you even came on the scene."

X, who I could tell had been caught off guard and taken aback, picked up his glass of water and threw it over at Mike, striking him in the center of his chest. Mike lunged out of his chair and jumped over the table at X, and Don grabbed his legs and pulled him back.

At this point, it was a mess in the studio, and I waved over to Malcolm while signaling him to turn everyone's microphone off. "All of you fools sit down and shut up!" I made a signal to turn only my microphone on. "Everyone, this is your boy, DK 'Love' Niles. Unfortunately, there's very little love in here at this moment; so we're going to take a much-needed break. Magic, play a little something for us. Whatchu got?"

"DK, I can't think of no other song than that Edwin Starr's, 'WAR' to start a much needed triple play to get us all calmed down."

"Cool. *The Brotherhood: The Divas vs. The Brothers*—and that shonuff is what it is—will be back. Enjoy the music, y'all." I waited for the music to start playing before I rounded off on everybody. "We're all supposed to be professionals here. What the hell was that about? Pat?"

Pat stomped her foot. "Why don't you ask him?" She cocked her head toward Donnell. She looked at him with disgust before storming out of the booth. The divas quickly followed her.

Pat, Jessie, Darlene, V, and DeDe were on their way to the ladies' room when they crossed paths with Sweets, who was just coming off the elevator.

"Sweets! What're you doing here?" V greeted her cousin with a kiss on the cheek and then rolled her eyes. "Lord have mercy. Did you hear?"

"Yes, honey. That was some drama—no, comflama—right there, ladies. I was listening to all that mess on my way here." Sweets said as he kissed each girl's cheek. "What in the world happened?"

"My ex-husband's sorry ass happened," Pat said. "Tell me you didn't come, all the way down here just to see us go at each other because, I hate to break it to you, that's not going to happen. I am too much of a lady for all of that."

Sweets shook his head. "Actually, I was coming to see Ms. Jessie here." He looked Jessie straight in the eye and told her, "There's something I need to tell you—something that you need to know."

Jessie looked at him quizzically. She and Sweets had never really been all that close, rarely interacting outside of the salon; and she was just there yesterday, and he didn't say anything. She couldn't think of any reason why he'd want to talk to her, of all people. "Why don't we convene in the ladies' room? Shall we?"

The ladies and Sweets entered the restroom, which was thankfully empty; and Sweets looked at V and then glanced over at the stalls. She took the hint and checked every stall to make sure there was no one inside. They all stood in a circle and waited for Sweets to start talking.

"Well, this is actually the first time I listened to the show since the ones with Melissa Morgan, and hearing about the Brotherhood, and all that testosterone gossip, just didn't pique my interest. But since I knew V was going to be on, I tuned in, much to my surprise. Uhm . . . how am I going to put this?" Sweets took a moment to collect his thoughts and then blurted out, "HELL! There's no good way to put it! Michael Crawley—that is your ex right?" He looked at Jessie pointedly.

Jessie, looking terrified and bewildered at the same time, answered, "Yeah. Why do you ask?"

"Well, I know him too—except he gave me a different name. And, girl, I almost fell out my chair when I recognized his voice. Not that I haven't been listening to it for well over two years now. But I've known him as Todd. Not Michael," Sweets finished cryptically.

V's eyes widened. "You mean—"

"Exactly," Sweets confirmed.

The rest of the divas looked at V and Sweets, wondering what they were talking about—except for V, who already knew; and then it all clicked when V said, "Hmm, hmm, hmm. Lord, first, my husband. Now this."

Sweets said, "Yes, Ms. Jessie. Todd is, well was, my boyfriend."

Jessie shook her head and looked at them as if she was waiting for them to tell her they were playing some sort of joke on her. But the expressions on V's and Sweets's faces told her they were completely serious. Her mouth dropped open in disbelief. "You mean my Michael and your Todd is one and the same?" She didn't really need to ask, but she just had to. "I can't believe this! All this time? How long?"

"Long enough to know that while he was with you he was creeping with me," Sweets said with conviction. "I knew he was creeping with some other heifer, but never in my wildest dreams would I have ever thought it was you. Not my soror-sista girl, V's bestest friend and my bestest client?"

V enveloped Jessie in a tight hug, and soon all the other divas joined in.

"That bastard!" Jessie said between her sobs. Her hands and shoulders were shaking; she was absolutely livid.

Sweets couldn't stand it. Michael—Todd, whatever he was calling himself—had played them both. Well, he would not get away with it. "We're going to get him back, Ms. Jessie. Trust and believe me, soror-sista girl. Trust and believe. You just leave it to me!" Sweets left the ladies in the restroom, as Jessie began going into an emotional meltdown. Once he was alone, he took out his cellphone. He did a quick Google search, and his finger quickly hit the telephone link to *Creepers*. "Hello? Good evening, is this the TV Show *Creepers'* answering service? Yes, I'll hold. . . . Oh, okay, you're back. Listen, I need for someone to get back with me—a-s-a-p. I have someone creeping on me that I need the show to expose . . . get the real scoop . . . set him free. My number . . . okay, are you ready?"

Chapter 20

The Debriefing

(DK's POV)

August 10, 2009

*J*essie and I were called to the office of K103.5 vice president Demetrius Williams; and both of us knew, or at least had a hunch, that this meeting had something to do with last night's divas-versus-brothers debacle, which ended with the divas meeting up in the ladies' room and leaving the station shortly thereafter, abandoning the show and outright refusing to come back on. Jessie herself ran out of the bathroom, crying uncontrollably.

We met at the elevator, and spent the ride up to the fourteenth floor trying to agree on what we would say to Demetrius in our defense. When the doors opened, Jessie grabbed my arm and asked, "You have my back, right?"

I looked at her, as if to ask, *Come on, girl. You know I do.* And she squeezed my arm and rested her head on my shoulder, which caught me off guard; and I asked myself, *Hmm. What's this all about?* This was totally out of character for her.

We headed down the hallway to his office, looking for room 1421. When we arrived, we found Sharon, his wife, sitting at his conference table with her legs crossed, banging a pen against a notepad she had on her lap. Demetrius, a tall, athletic brother—everyone says he kinda favors the Chicago Bulls' Scotty Pippin—had on this sharp, expertly tailored Brooks Brothers suit, with these bad-ass Allen Edmond shoes that said, *I'm the boss,* if not, *You better recognize. You're looking at somebody important.* He was standing at the window in a stoic poise, silently peering out, when Jess and I tiptoed in and made our way over to his conference table. We sat down quietly next to Sharon, looking at her and silently asking, *What's going on?*

But before she could answer, Demetrius turned to us. "Well, suffice to say last night was a complete and total disaster—a travesty for the station and *The Love Forum* on all levels. You guys should really be embarrassed."

Jess and I looked at each other; and Sharon, coming to her own defense, said, "Embarrassed? Embarrassed for what? Why should I be embarrassed?"

"I don't believe I missed any words. Embarrassed because this show is your baby, Sharon. And YOU LET IT IMPLODE ON YOUR ASS!" He looked at us with disgust. "You *know*, you should be embarrassed to have even put something like that together. Whose idea was that anyway?"

Sharon hung her head and coughed into her hand. And like a kid caught with her hand in the cookie jar, she quickly glanced back up at Demetrius and then back down at her notepad. He frowned, nodding his head. Then he grunted. You could tell he was getting angry, as the muscles around his mouth twitched and his brows came together and eyelids scrunched up.

And just as I always did with Melissa, I kicked Jessie underneath the table, letting her know: *Here we go. Get ready.* And sure enough, Demetrius walked over, leaned against the back of a chair, and looked Sharon straight in the eyes. "Sharon, I think you know that this is *not* what I had in mind. Definitely not what I envisioned when I agreed to do another *Love Forum*. Don't you remember the first one?" he asked.

I caught Sharon rolling her eyes. They probably would have fallen out if she had rolled them any harder, but that was it. Although Sharon was a talker and never one to be at a loss for words, she was quiet now. I guess there was nothing to say; she just looked down and started beating her notepad again. Demetrius pulled out a chair and sat down a ways back from the table, never taking his eyes off her. I watched his body language as he bent over, rested his elbows on his thighs, and clasped his hands, twirling his thumbs over and over; and I thought, *This isn't good.* We sat in silence, watching him with disappointment all over his face as he looked from Jessie, to Sharon, to me; and there was nothing we could do or say. He was right. The whole thing was a disaster.

"I don't know what you three have planned for the forum; but I assure you, if it has any resemblance to last night, it needs to—no, it's going to change. *Before* you leave this office."

Sharon tried to explain her vision and the direction of the show, including how everything was drama-driven for high ratings. And she even presented some preliminary numbers to back her up and show how the forum blew all the other station programming out of the water; but unfortunately, Demetrius didn't want to hear it. He held up his hand. "Sharon! Come on now. We've discussed this time and time again. And every time, I keep telling you the same damn thing—that sometimes ratings come second when there's a positive image or message you want to convey. If the programming is good, the ratings will follow."

Sharon said, "I know, but—"

Demetrius got up. "But nothing! I can't believe you sometimes. Do I need to remind you again—"

"No, Demetrius. I really don't think I need to be reminded, again."

"No, I think you do. When you asked me to bring back *The Love Forum*, what did I say?"

"We're going to go through this again."

"Sharon?"

"Okay. Okay. You said that you wanted the brothers to be portrayed in a good light, that you wanted a discussion of the issues that plague black men. You were tired of seeing the black man as the womanizer, abuser, a convict, a drug addict, a thief, and associated with just about every conceivable negative image or stereotype anyone could come up with. You wanted to uplift the brothers and show Dallas the other side of the coin. Show *The Love Forum* and the brothers in a positive light."

"Because?"

Sharon looked at him, all cross-eyed; but the look on his face told her that he didn't care. He just sat there, looking at her, waiting for a response.

"Because," she said, "the brothers always get a bad rap, and there's always two sides to every story. And, Demetrius, that's what we were trying to tell you—both sides of the story."

He let out another one of those husky grunts and said, "Sharon! You're *killing* me. Like I said, I want *The Brotherhood* to mean something, to send a message of hope and give clarity and a voice to our black brothers out there. It's not supposed to be a forum for airing out our dirty laundry. We're not running a circus in here, and we're definitely not producing a soap opera. I tell you, sometimes we black people can be our own worst enemies. Do you think Donnell and—what's his wife's name?"

"Pat," I said as I got up and headed toward the white board.

"Thank you, DK. Do you think Donnell and Pat deserved to have their laundry, dirty as it was, aired out like that?"

"Well, for one, it was already out there," answered Sharon. "We were just trying to help them clean it up, wade through their issues, get to the bottom of their story. And as Melissa always said, we can all learn from somebody else's story. Maybe some of our listeners could have gained some insight from Pat and Donnell's dilemma and used it to solve their own problems."

While Demetrius and Sharon continued their argument, I motioned to Jessie to join me; and I just happened to really check her out as she walked up to the board. She was usually sharp when it came down to her work attire; but today, she was wearing a fitted purple pantsuit that, I have to say, accentuated every curve of her body while still allowing her to maintain a professional appearance. Her face was clear of makeup, save for the light pink gloss on her lips; and her thick hair was pulled back in a tight ponytail. It was clear that either she meant business today, or she was really going through something; either way, she was not a happy camper. And right now, she wasn't looking too good in Demetrius's eyes. Hell, neither of us was, if the truth be told; but I had a plan to change our situation.

I scratched the back of my head and cleared my throat, drawing everyone's attention to the white board. Once I saw that both pairs of eyes were on me and Jess, I started my campaign to turn the situation around. "I know I'm partly at fault. I was supposed to act as the moderator, but I didn't control the conversation as a host should have. I let it get out of hand. And when all hell broke loose, I shoulda done something."

"No, to be fair, I should've stepped in when I saw that things were getting out of hand," Jessie said with resignation.

"I didn't call this meeting so you can point the blame," Demetrius said authoritatively. "However, I must say that I'm proud of both of you for exhibiting accountability and maturity; and that is something I value in the people I work with. And with that, I believe we should move forward and find a solution to ensure last night's episode doesn't repeat itself. I don't want to come back in here next week, or the week after that, discussing the same thing over and over again."

"You're absolutely correct, sir," Jessie interjected. "One thing's for sure: I don't think we can last a full year at this pace and with this amount of discord. Maybe we should cut the forum back down to six months."

We all nodded in complete agreement on this one; and soon, all eyes were on me.

It was all or nothing right now, and I took the chance and dove right in. "Mr. Williams, it would be nice if you would give us a chance to restructure *The Love Forum*, because I think we lost sight of Melissa's original intention for the show. True enough, you want to talk about issues that *plague* black men. And, Sharon, you want the ratings impact from the drama; however, *The Love Forum* was created to bring people together and keep them together through discussions of situations that will keep the spark and fire in a relationship. But now we stand at a crossroads." When I said that, I was reminded of Donnell; and for some reason, I smiled. I got what he was saying: "We're at a crossroads, where some people can move on but others can't even connect. You're always hearing that there are no good men or good women out there. Why?"

Demetrius moaned and asked, "Okay. I hear you, DK, but where are you going with this?"

"Mr. Williams, you paid for us brothers to go to Alaska and spend four days discussing our lives with one of Dallas's, if not the South's, leading psychotherapists . . . why don't we tap into those conversations and the issues raised there, like being silent sons, and share that with the K103.5 family? Maybe we can start there and discuss why black men and women can't connect and have difficulty keeping that relationship going. They say that a lot of black marriages end in divorce—that is, if we even have a chance to get to the altar."

Demetrius moaned again, and Jessie looked at me and pitched in: "Mr. Williams, I think what DK is trying to say is that you can have your forum. Use the Brotherhood's retreat as the platform for bringing forth and discussing real-life issues that plague black men, issues that may prevent them from establishing and maintaining healthy relationships."

Sharon said, "Boring! Where is the drama in that?"

"That's just the point, Sharon. We let controversy be the drama."

"Hmm," said Sharon, "I'm not sold. We need drama on the show. If not, it's going to be another preachy, bland discussion that no one is going to tune in to." She looked at Demetrius and rolled her eyes. "And, Demetrius, you'll be asking me to find something else to replace it with."

Demetrius grinned as though he knew she was right, and she looked back over at me. "Give me an example, DK. Give me something to work with."

I had the perfect example and just waited for Jessie and Sharon's response. Then I told them, "Take this discussion the brothers had at the retreat: We talked about our fathers and if, and how much, they contributed to our lives when we were growing up. Some had fathers, but the majority of us didn't; so who was raising us? Women. And it's been that way since the civil rights era—women heading the household; and I'm proud to say that I came from one of them. So if it's so effin' hard to find a man—a good man at that—why? Wouldn't a woman raise a boy into a man that she would want another woman to have? Or would she raise a boy into a man that would contribute to strengthening the female mind-set of 'I don't need a man,' and 'I can do bad all by myself,' and 'Get what you can get while you can get it'? Have the brothers—the ones that want to share their experiences—join in on the discussion, and have the K103.5 family call in and share their opinion. Then you will have open dialogue that's based on controversy rather than on the brothers' drama-filled lives."

Sharon leaned forward and tapped her index finger against her pursed lips, thinking. We had worked with Sharon long enough to know that she always needed a moment to collect her thoughts. So after a couple of seconds, her face lit up like a lightbulb. "I like it! I really, really like it. What if we throw in some guidelines, though? We all know that *The Love Forum*'s appeal is that it's unscripted and spontaneous, but what about if we throw in some guidelines of general ideas that will be discussed in each episode? That way, every session will have meaning and direction. It won't just go down as a smorgasbord of senseless discussions—which, I'm going to say, has worked up until now."

Jessie muttered, "Hmm. That's right, that's right." She kept nodding her head. "What do you think, DK? Is that doable?" She tilted her head to face me, giving me a wink.

"It was actually the direction I was thinking of," I said as I started writing my ideas on the board. I wrote 'The Plagues of a Black Man' and underlined it. Then I wrote underneath:

Silent sons (Who are they? / When your man doesn't talk to you)
Black male stereotypes (Moral vs. ethical vs. man-made) and the repercussions
Health (Where do we stack up?)
Education and jobs (Opportunity vs. survival)
Parenting (Is a mother raising a black male doing enough?)
Relationships (Are we carrying too much baggage to sustain one?)
Monogamy (Humans aren't even designed to be monogamous, but can we try?)

I said, "See, we talk about issues that are relevant; but now, controversy replaces the drama."

"But we don't want to cut down on all the drama! Some people tune in just for that. I know I would," Sharon said laughingly, looking at Demetrius all the while.

Jessie cocked her head and pointed at Sharon. "I'm with you, girl. You do have a good point. There's a big difference between PBS's *Tavis Smiley* and Bravo's *Real Housewives of Atlanta*. Which one would you rush home to see?"

Demetrius just rolled his eyes. "That's not what the show is about, ladies; but I like DK's idea, although I'm not quite sure about some of the topics on the list. He looked at me quizzically. "Humans aren't designed to be monogamous?" He let out a smug smirk. "An-ee-way, the idea of setting guidelines for every show is good too. I think the combination will allow us to expand the discussion beyond the personal lives of the brothers and focus on the issues that affect the community as a whole. And, Sharon, I'm going to compromise on your drama too. Just find that right balance. *Please*, baby!"

Sharon pulled out her reading glasses and started jotting notes down on her notepad. "Education and jobs—that's a really good discussion piece. I think a lot of our listeners would be able to relate to that. I just need to find the right kind of drama to give it that "Wow!" factor. So people would want to tune in and hear about it."

"What else?" Sharon asked.

"I do have another suggestion, Sharon and Mr. Williams; but it's going to require funding. But I think the payoff will be well worth it."

"What is it, DK?" Demetrius asked.

"Well, we all know that Miguel and Darlene are getting married in Brazil on November 15. I was wondering, what would be better than showing the K103.5 family that true love does exist, and can be found, than by covering their wedding and airing it on the forum?"

Before anyone could say "yay" or "nay," the office phone rang. Demetrius got up to answer it, putting the caller on speaker.

"Hello, Darla. This must be an important phone call?"

"Mr. Williams, you asked me to hold all your calls, but this call is for Mrs. Williams. It's her doctor's office calling. She indicated that it was a call she was waiting for and to call your office should they call."

"That's fine, Darla. She's right here."

Sharon bolted to his desk and picked up the handset. "Yes, Doctor . . . yes . . . yes . . . you're kidding me! Three months? Oh, this is good news—good news, I tell you. Thank you. Thank you. Thank you. A specialist? Uhm . . . is there any reason to be concerned? . . . Hmm . . . yes, I'm here . . . plenty of rest . . . Okay, I can do that, and I'll make that appointment as well. Thank you again. Yes, good-bye now."

Sharon rubbed her tummy and looked at Demetrius, happy but worried. It looked as though the two of them had finally succeeded in conceiving a child; and as she cradled the phone in her bosom, she burst into tears.

Demetrius told us, "Excuse us, please." And he went over to his wife. Jess and I felt an eerie sense of pain inside the room and quietly exited the office.

Outside the door, Jess looked at me and said, "I guess that means we may be on our own with the forum. It appears to be good news, though. I'm happy for them."

I looked at her, worried. "Yah, but now we have the weight of the world back on our shoulders. For some reason, I feel just as bad leaving as I did when we arrived. What are we going to do, Jess? Do you think we can actually pull this off?"

She gave me a look that said, *I got my own effin' problems.* She told me, "Everything is happening as it should, you'll see."

Chapter 21

The Plagues

(DK's POV)

"K103.5, it's 9:24 PM on this Sunday, September 6, and *The Brotherhood* is back and in full effect. We started one hour early, and we're fastly approaching the thirty-minute mark. Once again, this is your boy DK 'Love' Niles with the mad, cool disc jockey Mr. Kirk 'Magic' Wonder; but tonight, my people, it's going to be anything but cool. That was Aaliyah with 'The One I Gave My Heart To,' ending our old-school triple play. And, ladies, from what we're about to discuss, you may not have an opportunity to give your heart to anyone if we keep this course. There may not be any brothers left. The pickings will be real, real slim. But before we get back to it, I *gotta* give a shout-out to Bee, over at Bailey's, for the out-of-this-world vittles she had delivered to us right here in the studio—fried green tomatoes, catfish, and jalapeño hush puppies. Lord have mercy, girl! It shonuff was good. Bee, I keep tellin' you, you gone make me marry you, girl. But on the real, thanks for always looking out for us.

"So, family, now that we're back from an extended triple-play music break—and for those of you who are just joining in, we've had some interesting conversations thus far. To catch you up: The brothers have been talking about what plagues us as black men. Dr. Xavier Houston, better known as X, was telling us about the issues that will not only impact our men but will also have far-reaching implications for our community for generations to come. And, family, our black men are suffering."

"That's right, DK," said X as he adjusted his microphone. "At the beginning of the show, we heard the infomercial, which several of us black physicians put together, concerning our black male teens and young men, how black males from ages fifteen to twenty-four either die from homicide; unintentional injuries, usually motor-vehicle related; or—and this astonished my peers and me—suicide. *Suicide*, man. Our young black men think there's no other option than taking their own lives. This should be our wake-up call, everyone."

Magic began softly playing "Wake Up Everybody" by Harold Melvin & the Blue Notes; and X nodded, winked at him, and continued talking. "And for

167

the brothers that make it past those three, the likelihood of facing HIV and HIV-related deaths rears its ugly head and stares them dead in the face between the ages of thirty-five and forty-four, as HIV-related deaths replace suicide as the third cause of deaths among black men. I refer to these four as 'HUSH'—homicide, unintentional injuries, suicide, and HIV—because nobody's talking about it. NOBODY!"

Brass, bless his crazy self, started mocking X: "*Hush*, boy, we don't talk about dat. *Hush*, boy, black people don't commit suicide. *Hush*, boy, HIV and AIDS is dat nasty man's disease. What y'all need to be doing is stop all dat sinning and getting right with Jesus. Black people address everything except da issue, and then always throw God into da mix to make something right or justify their point. But one thang's for sure, we sho' know how to keep up with the mess—who did this and who did dat and what da Joneses got (and how I need to keep up with their asses) or don't got."

X looked at Brass and smiled at his crazy butt. "So, ladies, as I was saying, you think it's hard to find a good black man now—just wait. Sadly, we're losing a generation of brothers. And, DK, we've only scratched the surface of our problems. We haven't even touched on falling behind in education, high school dropout rates, lack of accessible and affordable health care, and lack of job opportunities. And with the burden of all of this on our black shoulders—which we silently carry around as Dr. Mayweather explained to us earlier, tonight—do you honestly think we can keep up a healthy relationship on top of everything else we're dealing with?"

As X continued to talk, I got everything ready for the first caller. I was feeling really good, if not proud, that all the brothers were back in the studio, sitting around the table in perfect harmony. It was the first Brotherhood session since the meeting with Demetrius; and as I had predicted, Sharon had gone on maternity leave, with no one even knowing if she was coming back. And Jessie, for whatever reason, gave me free rein to run the Brotherhood as I saw fit. She said she needed to concentrate on marketing the show—get it out over the Internet into different cities—and left me with the unattractive task of cleaning up the mess from the last show. And I tell you, I had a lot of fence mending to do.

Before I got all the brothers to consent to come back on, I had to promise them that there would be *no more* effin' drama, as many of them said that they would definitely drop out if there was. And just as Demetrius wanted, I planned an evening—with the help of Dr. Mayweather, X, and a special guest—that would get Dallas thinking, if not talking, about the issues that plagued us black men, with a peek into the future to boot.

"Yah, man," said Brass. "We're da lost generation. Where's our voice? Who's looking out and speaking up for us?" he asked. "Just like my moms said,

'Nobody gives a [beep] about nobody but themselves,' especially when it comes to our black boys and us black men. And don't let money be involved. God help us then."

I had to cut Brass off before he got too deep into his "nobody helps anybody" tirade: "Hold that thought, Brass. I want to go to the phone lines. Brother? Can you hear me?"

"Yes. I can hear you, brother DK."

"Okay, my brother. Who am I speaking with, and where are you calling from?"

"This is Mitchell—Mitch—originally from Mesquite. And it's like we were born to fail, DK."

"How'd you arrive at that notion?" I asked.

"First, let me preface what I'm about to say by pointing out that there are some brothers who make it. I'm one of them, and boy, did I have a hell of a journey. But for the majority of us, the odds are simply stacked too high. Depending on where you live and the support structure you have around you, the odds are stacked so high that the only thing you can do is fail."

"Okay, brother, I hear you talking; but what exactly are you trying to say? Why do we black men have it so bad?" I asked.

"Okay. Let's start off with seven out of ten black children living in single-parent households—that's 70 percent of us—which are typically headed by a female," Mitch cockily told us.

"Yah, man, I've heard this diatribe before: *If we were raised by black women, we should be the epitome of their ideal mate.*"

"Au contraire, my brother. I beg to differ on that point. I don't think we should be blaming our black females raising kids alone. Remember, I'm a by-product of one of those households. Instead, maybe we should change the discussion to, 'what goes on in the house is what comes out of the house.'"

Magic said, "OH SNAP! I can feel the heads rolling every which way off of that one. I can hear the single moms talking 'bout"—he put his hands on his hips and started twitching his body, acting sissified—"'I know he did *not* just say that! I know I did *not* just hear him say that!'"

I laughed. "Brother, you just caused the phone lines to blow *up*. For real, though. Mitch? Hey man, don't you go nowhere. I'm gonna put you on hold and pick up Kari who's on line 2. Kari, this is DK, girrrl. You know I'm instigating. You hear Mitch over there in Mesquite? What do you have to say about his comment?"

"DK, I'm a single mother, and it's hard. I have to juggle work, day care, coming home and cooking, and putting him to bed. And whatever little time I have left, it's dedicated to cleaning and getting ready to do it all over again the next day." She started sniffling. "I don't get any assistance from his daddy. I get

169

fifty dollars a month in child support. If I have to raise him to be self-sufficient and not have to depend on anybody to get what he can get, and use who he can use to survive, so be it." The sniffles turned into all-out crying. "I'm tired, and I'm hurting; and I can't get no help. I don't even know if I'm going to be able to pay the electric bill or put food on the table. Sometimes I go without eating so my son can have . . . and I admit, sometimes I use men to get what I need. We all do."

"WOW! Hmm. Kari? I don't know this brother's side of your story. But DAMN! Fifty dollars? Brothers, we got to do better if we can. Hold on, momma, we gone see if we can get you some help, so you won't at least, set that *using* example for your son to imitate with the females when he grows up."

X told me to patch Mitch back in, and I asked him, "Mitch? So you heard Kari's story—Magic? Are we getting her some help? Good. Okay, Mitch, what I want you to do is bulletpoint why you say we're born to fail. Let's go. I'm going to say 'bullet,' then you answer and take it over from there. Bullet."

"Education. I'm an educator, and I've worked within both primary and secondary education for some twenty years. I'm currently teaching at a Houston HBCU. Yah, I'm catching you guys over the Internet. Do you know that only 52 percent of our black males in Texas graduated last year? Fifty-two percent, man. And we're not even the worst state. Of the ones that graduated and attended college, most were so ill-prepared that they ended up in developmental classes when they arrived, just to get them to a level where they could be successful. And even then, many of them dropped out. So they make it through high school, get into college, and then they drop out. Probably left with a hefty student loan to pay back, putting them farther behind the eight ball.

"Bullet. Dropout rates. You've already lost 48 percent of your young black males to inadequate education, so if Texas had an enrollment of 340,000 black males last year, at 48 percent, then 163,200 didn't graduate. Did you hear me, man? Now multiply that number by ten years. Do you get the picture? So there you go, ladies. The majority of you are graduating high school, going on to college, and getting your degrees. You want the same thing in your mate, but he's hard to find. I wonder why?"

"WOW! That can't be right, Mitch. Are you sure about that?" I asked.

"The best source of power is awareness and educating ourselves. Go to the Schott Foundation for Public Education—www.blackboysreport.org—and look at the state-by-state report on black male education. You'll be surprised, if not shocked, by the numbers.

"Bullet. Jobs. So now you have 163,200 black males looking for jobs without a high school diploma. Hell, it's hard for a black man to get a job *with* a bachelor's degree. Add the brothers who have dropped out of college and are back at home, and you can see why so many of our sisters are having a hard time finding a good man. Hell, the half that are left behind, end up in that HUSH cycle for black males that the brother on the panel talked about, or in prison."

I told him that the brother's name was X and then said, "I know that's right, Mitch. Go 'head, boy! Mitch? Hold on for a second. We got our boy Quentin over here, who happens to be a human resources staffing manager for a major staffing company. So, Q, what do you have to say about Mitch's comment, especially about jobs?"

"He's on point, DK. Although I mainly staff managers and senior-level executives—who, by the way, have their own set of problems with being mistreated and disrespected by their non-black counterparts, as well as by our very own people—when I did staff non-exempt labor, or hourly workers, it was pretty dismal for our black brothers. Just to give you some insight as to what we're up against, I just came from a conference, where we highlighted the plight of black male employment. And yes, the high unemployment rate for black males is well documented, but not well covered by the media; but perhaps what's alarming, DK and brother Mitch, is that many corporations hire black females over black males as they get the double-whammy effect of two minorities for the price of one: female and black. And truth be told, they buy into the perception that black females are less intimidating than black males."

"Damn! So you're saying that even if we do, do what's right, we still have an uphill battle?"

"Sad but true, DK." Quentin threw his hand up. "And another thing: I don't know if you caught this, but there was a show—I forget the name—where they had a black male and a white male apply for the same position. Similar credentials, but the white male had a long criminal history and the black male had no criminal record. Guess who got the job?"

"Damn, man. They would rather hire a criminal over a good brother."

"Just some things we see in the business, man. I tell my clients, when they encounter this, to keep their chin up and move on. It probably wasn't a place where they would want to work, or where they would have a chance of being successful anyway.

"So, bullet," Q said, mocking Mitch. "The ideal that black males will be the financial pillars of and providers for the family may not be accurate for the twenty-first century. How can we be?"

"Yah! How can we be, homey? Black women think dat they're going to find da perfect man, the man of their dreams, and build dis fairy-tale life and live happily ever after. Hell, the world ain't even happy!" yelled Brass, getting all tensed up, if not hot and bothered, by the conversation.

"Q, this is sounding bleaker and bleaker by the moment."

"I agree, DK. You know, back in the day, when we were growing up, the older folks always stressed that education was our way out of darkness." Q started laughing and beating the table, which made everybody look down at him. "Man, every time I heard it, I pictured the statue of Booker T. Washington, *Lifting the Veil of Ignorance*, and my grandpops always reminding me of this famous quote by Booker T."

I sat there thinking. Just like at the retreat, it was those quiet ones who had the most profound, if not prolific, things to say; and just like his story about his girl back in the day, which shocked us all, Q didn't disappoint. I asked him, "Q? What did he say? What was the quote? Do you remember?"

He threw his head back and started wringing his hands, trying to remember. "Yah. Yah. Mr. Washington said, 'A race, just like an individual, lifts itself up by lifting others up.' I don't think we're going to see anything accomplished anytime soon until we start lifting ourselves up."

"Just like I've been telling you, brothers," said Doc Mayweather, nodding in agreement.

"Yah. You're right," Q said, nodding back at the Doc. "You hear that, sisters? You can say you don't need a man all you want, but your bitterness tells the true story. But hey, now you know that there's a lot going on with us brothers; and until we're happy, we can't make you happy."

Magic cried out, "OH NO, YOU DIDN'T GO THERE!"

"I'm telling the truth, man. And we can't look for a handout, because it's not there. It's not out there, and it's not going to be there—*ever!* We and we alone let this happen. History repeats itself when we ignore what has passed. And with these statistics, how long do you think it will take before the oppressed will overtake the oppressor, before the have-nots will take from the haves?"

I sat there and thought, *DAMN! This brother went deep. Hell, we can end the show right here with that alone.* By this time, I noticed that Demetrius was at the window talking to Jessie. He was looking in and nodding his head in what looked to be approval. Jessie tapped at the watch on her wrist and pointed to the studio's wall clock, telling me to watch my time. I wanted to get back to relationships and how our plight might play a huge role in why so many black men and women were finding it very hard to come together, but I was short on time and needed to get to our special guest. Before I knew what was happening, Malcolm had thrown out a bunch of questions.

"So, X, Q and DK, what do we do? I mean, it's like a vicious cycle. We're not getting the education promised to us. We're not getting jobs to support ourselves and our families. What do we do, man? What can we do?"

There were a whole bunch of eyebrows raised, but no answers; so I said, "Family, we may not be able to answer these questions today, and we may not know what the future holds for the black males out there in our audience; but maybe we can predict the future for the ones here in the studio. When we come back, we'll be joined by a very special guest. One who's no stranger to K103.5 or *The Love Forum*. Magic? Take us out with that "Wake Up Everybody." Again, family, *we'll* be back."

We all sat and pondered on what we just heard; and before I knew it, it was time to go back on air as I heard Magic say, "DK, in five . . . four . . . three . . . two . . . one."

"Family, welcome back. And as promised, I have a very special young lady here in the studio." You could hear snickering in the background.

"I don't know about young, DK."

I smiled. "You're as young as you feel, Ms. Doretha. Family, joining us for some much-needed insight into our future is Ms. Doretha."

"It's my pleasure, dear," she returned with a graceful bow of her head. "I've wanted to talk with everyone for a while. I've been listening to your show all this time. Lord, there has been so much negativity. So I felt it was my duty to come down here and perhaps share some insight into your futures. Bring some light into the darkness." She smiled down at Q, a look of approval and pride written all over her face.

"That's definitely something we want to hear," I said. "So how does this work, Ms. Doretha? We're going to ask you the questions? Or . . ." I left the sentence hanging and waited for a response.

"You can ask me the questions, dear. What do you want to know, DK? What can Ms. Doretha do for you this evening?"

I played with the stubble on my chin. I woke up rather late and failed to shave, but that's another story for another day. "Why don't we start with the brothers that want to get their readings. Then if we have time, we can take a couple of calls from our audience."

"Yes. I like that idea, dear." Ms. Doretha looked at me. "I have a feeling you'll be contacting me later."

And I thought, *Huh?*

Then she looked around the room and asked, "Who would like to go first?"

Donnell was the first to raise his hand; and I don't know why, but I looked at him kinda funny. Probably because he was the last person I thought would raise his hand, especially after what happened on the last forum. I guess I wasn't the only one taken by surprise, 'cause I caught Jessie looking at him through the window with a worried look on her face. I thought, *Oh shit, here we go with this divorce, and I'm gone get my kids' bullshit.*

"Your date of birth?" Ms. Doretha asked.

"April 7 [beep]."

Ms. Doretha hummed and closed her eyes, as if channeling the entities around her. She held out her hands over the table, slowly touching it, and then slowly began to raise them, before stopping and letting them hover in midair. She looked like a woman possessed. "Dear, it has been a long and difficult journey for you—one with many decisions. You keep questioning yourself, asking yourself if you're making the right choices; and you're torn." Ms. Doretha paused, dropped her hands, and started tapping the table with her fingernails. "Because of your personal wants and goals, you have caused much pain to those you love and, in one case, have loved. Follow your heart, dear. The right answer lies there. You'll see it soon enough, but not before a series of events, which will be devastating to you, will force you to see what you don't want to see. But it's nothing you won't overcome. Is there anything else, dear?"

Donnell looked at Ms. Doretha as though she had shot him through the heart. He said no. Ms. Doretha said, "Very well, then, dear. Who's next?"

Mike coughed, and Ms. Doretha looked down the table at him. "Your spirit is strangely familiar to me. Your name?"

"Michael Crawley."

Ms. Doretha had an astonished look on her face and turned to the window, where Jessie was standing. She didn't ask him his birthday, and without missing a beat, she said, without taking her eyes off Jessie, "A storm is brewing." She turned back to look down at him; and before she spoke, she closed her eyes. "A storm is brewing, but you've already received a heads-up and have turned the situation around." Ms. Doretha opened her eyes and hummed, smiling at Mike. "Hmm. That's right, dear. Keep thinking that way. I love that old proverbial saying too: 'Let no weapon formed against me, prosper. And for the ones against you, it will not.'"

Mike looked at her with a puzzled look on his face, but he didn't ask her what she was talking about. "You don't need to ask; nor do you want to. You're going to be safe." Mike didn't say another word. He thanked Ms. Doretha and asked, "Who's next? I believe I'm good."

X held up his hand. "I guess I'll be the brave one, Ms. Doretha. My name is Xavier Houston. I was born on December 9."

Again, Ms. Doretha looked out the window at Jessie. She let out a long sigh and picked up a deck of cards and pushed back her chair and walked down to X. She told him to shuffle the cards. "Now pick one, dear."

X picked out a card, and Ms. Doretha laid out several cards in front of him. "Look, dear. You have wonderful cards. And look, the Two of Cups. Shuffle again and pick out a card."

X shuffled his cards again and picked out the same Two of Cups. "You have entered, or will enter, into a fulfilling relationship."

I asked Ms. Doretha, "What kinda card is that?"

"Dear, the Two of Cups is the card where you have a man facing a woman, both of them staring into each other's eyes. It typically signifies a deep understanding between the two—an understanding or feeling that's not felt by many others. This is a union based on passion and strength. It's a relationship that all of us seek or wish to have in our lifetime. Nothing will ever come close to a relationship such as this."

X had this big cheesy grin on his face and looked out the window at Jessie, who was sporting a half-ass smile; and I looked at her too, puzzled because I didn't see happy or ecstatic behind it. But she had been acting funny lately anyway—strange, ever since the last forum.

"Hmm," hummed Ms. Doretha as she laid out more cards. I just wanted to make sure, dear; and it's confirmed. There's a dark cloud surrounding you, too. Have you ever been hurt before?"

X laughed out loud. "No, Ms. Doretha, I've never been hurt. What's with this hurt business with all you guys?"

"Are you sure?" she asked.

"No, and with the news that you just gave me, I don't think that I will. I've found the woman for me, and we're face-to-face."

Ms. Doretha hummed once more. "Hold on to your heart, dear. You too have a storm brewing."

Magic blurted out, "Niggas, y'all got some foul fortunes up in here. Nah-ah! Pass me by, Ms. Doretha. Nope. Don't want to go there. This here bull[beep] . . . the fortunes being told up in here . . . ain't nothing but bad news. Bad news, playas." Magic started sounding off like a sheep. "BAAAAD! Just like the bad news that's been predicted for the rest of the black men out there."

All the other brothers were nodding their heads, as if they were thinking the same damn thing. It was written all over their faces. And to lighten up the doom and gloom, I said, "Magic, let's go to the phone lines. Do we have a caller?"

"Line 1, DK. It's our girl Frenchie again."

"Hello? Frenchie? You're on the line with *The Brotherhood*. Say hello to Ms. Doretha and ask your question. Go 'head, girl. Talk to us."

Frenchie had this flirty yet melodious voice, which echoed around the room. "Hey, Ms. Doretha. Hey fellas! I just want to know one thing, Ms. Doretha."

"What is it, dear?"

"Will I ever find the man for me? I've been searching, and searching, and searching, to no avail. Girl! I'm 'bout to give up. And from what I've heard tonight, it doesn't look so promising."

Ms. Doretha let out a slight giggle. "Dear, I can tell you're a mess. You're definitely a handful. Hold on. I'm walking back to my seat. Your birthday?"

"September 13."

"Hmm. Good date. And great news, dear. I do see a man—a very well-to-do man at that. A doctor."

"A DOCTOR! Come on, Ms. Doretha, are you for real? Girl, don't be teasing me."

"Yes, dear, a doctor. However, both of you will have to complete the journeys you're presently on, first. For one of you, the journey will be short. For the other, the journey will take time to finish. There will be great healing needed. Hmm."

"What is it, Ms. Doretha?"

"Are you looking for a job, dear?"

"No . . . not really."

"Are you, maybe, going to school for something? Maybe to better yourself?"

"Yes! Oh my god, I'm going to get my masters in nursing."

"Yes, because I don't see you doing the same thing. When you become director of nursing and he becomes an administrator for a rival hospital, the two of you will meet at a conference of similar minds."

My girl didn't even ask about the job. You could tell where her priorities were. The only thing Frenchie was concerned about was the man. She asked, "Ms. Doretha? How long will that take?"

"Not too far from the present and not too far in the distant future, dear."

"Did she answer your question, Frenchie?" I asked.

"Oh yes! Thank you so much for your time, DK and Ms. Doretha."

I laughed out loud. "Okay, girl, don't you call up here no more."

"Well, at least not anymore tonight, DK. I got the answer I need; and boy, I'm going to sleep good tonight. And I don't even have to reach inside my nightstand drawer."

We all laughed at Frenchie, and the forum went on from there. Ms. Doretha took in a couple more calls from the listeners and then said her good-byes and left. *The Brotherhood* continued, jumping across various topics, with each topic bringing a new insight and opinion to the table. We discussed prison and the justice system. Magic told me that the judge was holding, but I decided not to use him and didn't patch him through. We also found ourselves discussing fatherhood, but there was a silent argument—Donnell and Pat's custody issue. Dr. Houston led the discussion on health care. He even entertained some callers who had medical questions, but he made sure to tell them that the best thing to do was to go to their physicians, as no matter how good a doctor was, there was no way he could make an accurate diagnosis over the phone. At the end of the show, I felt as if *The Brotherhood* had accomplished Demetrius's vision and had reached a major turning point; and as I looked around the table, I thought, *Maybe this is what Melissa had in mind when she wanted the brothers to do* The Love Forum.

Chapter 22

Brass to Gold

October 29, 2009

Ever since childhood, Brass had never liked the dark. He could stand it if he was left with no other choice; but if it was all left up to him, every single light, *everywhere*, would always be on. Not one to thrive on fear, the first thing he did once his feet hit his apartment's torn linoleum floor was to turn on the light switch to the left of the door. He kicked off his shoes and walked over to his coffee table, where he dropped his keys inside a small fishbowl. A gift Britt gave him on his birthday, because he always misplaced things. He stood there and emptied his pockets into the bowl, dropping his cellphone, wallet, and a few coins into it, before walking into his tiny kitchenette. He reached for the refrigerator's metal door handle and gave it a couple of light tugs before finally getting it to open. Peering inside, he grimaced as he stared at white walls and a lot of empty wire shelves. A carton of milk, a couple of eggs, a few slices of bologna, and the front and back ends of a loaf of bread were all he had. Money was kind of tight, as he was putting everything he earned into the party he was planning.

"For the Love of Money," his favorite ringtone, blared from the living room; and he shut the refrigerator door and walked back to see who was calling. He picked up the phone and glanced down at the time: 2:30 AM. "Damn! Who's dis?" He frowned at the unidentified number scrolling across the screen. He was always careful about giving out his personal number, so he knew it was too early—and against the law—for a bill collector to be calling, especially to collect some money, which he didn't have; but something tugged at him to answer and not let the call go to voice mail. He flipped the phone open and exhaled a rough "Hello" through his nose.

He could hear labored breathing on the other end, which caused him to pull at his shirt collar nervously, as he didn't know what to expect. "Who the hell is dis?" he asked gruffly, the annoyance coming through in his voice.

"It's me."

Brass breathed a sigh of relief.

"Britt?" he asked, although he knew who it was. He could recognize her soft, smoky voice anywhere; and he was glad to hear it now. Over the years, it had become a source of comfort for him, although he never let her know it. Just hearing her voice relaxed his muscles and calmed his usually restless nerves. "Baby, why you gotta scare me like that?" he asked with a hint of humor as he licked the sweat off his lips.

There was a sharp, strangled gasp before an outburst of sobs. Brass tried to understand what she was saying, but she wasn't making any sense. He struggled to make sense of the few words he could figure out. And he just pictured her sitting alone somewhere, probably with a cigarette in her hand, crying hysterically, with her shoulders just a-shaking and mascara-stained tears running down her face.

He had been with Britt, on and off, for over four years now, and he could tell the difference between each one of her cries: Between the one when she's happy and the one when she was pissed off at him; he even recognized the one when she was just plain sad. But this one here made his heart drop under the heels of his shoes. Any feeling of relief he'd felt earlier, when he first heard her voice, had now evaporated. "Britt, talk to me. What's wrong?" he asked, almost pleadingly. "You all right? What's going on, baby?"

"I don't know, Brass. I don't know," she mumbled. She must've said it seven or eight times before trying to get anything else out. "I was just getting off from work, back from a late-night flight from Charlotte to Atlanta." She sucked in a long puff from her cigarette and watched the lit end of it blaze down to almost nothing, the smoke making her voice raspy. "I had pulled out of the parking lot where us stewardesses usually park and . . . and . . . oh God, I was so scared, Brass." She started crying again; and again, he struggled to understand the words she said.

He sat down on the couch and rested his head against his hand. He shut his eyes and tried to calm himself. He knew exactly what she was about to say, because the same thing happened to him a couple of days ago. "Baby, just breathe, okay? Breathe."

His heart was racing, and he could hear her taking deep breaths, trying to calm herself. It took a minute or so for Britt to calm down to where she could talk and he could understand her. He asked, "Tell me, what's going on? Where are you now?" he asked calmly, trying to soothe her with his voice.

"I'm sitting in front of some fire station . . . somewhere off the highway." Britt said she was going to run in, but didn't know what kind of danger she was in, or if her mind was getting the best of her. She also didn't know what kind of trouble he was in and didn't want to do anything to get him in more trouble than he probably was already in. She started whimpering. "I'm . . . I'm . . . so scared, Brass. God! I need to get out of *here*."

"Whatchu mean?"

"I'm getting out of here!" she yelled. Then she caught herself and tried to calm down. "I'm supposed to fly out to Dallas for Jessie's birthday party tomorrow. I'm thinking about staying with her for a while. Hopefully, my job will let me fly out of Dallas rather than Atlanta. What do you think? I mean, I'm all by myself here in Atlanta. You think it's a good idea?"

"Yah, maybe," he answered. Scared himself, he waited a minute before asking, "You okay now? You want to tell me what happened?"

Britt took a deep breath and exhaled slowly. "I was driving . . . on my way home . . ." Brass noticed her voice was steadier this time around, although there were still some soft sniffles here and there; but at least she could now get through a sentence without breaking down. "I noticed this black car on the side of the road at the exit of the airport. When I passed it, its headlights came on; and it pulled off behind me. I was like, okay, because I thought it was odd at first and really didn't think it was anything; but when I looked back in the rearview mirror, it seemed like it was following me. And when I got to the highway, whoever was in the car started brighting me, baby—flashing their headlights like they wanted me to pull over."

"Aww shit, for real?" he said as he covered his mouth with a clinched fist. "What did you do?"

"I got the hell out of there! As fast as that lil' Fiat would take my black ass. Boy, I was zooming in and out of traffic like a crazy woman. I zoomed right to the first exit I could get to. Oh my god, Brass, it must've been by his grace and mercy that this fire station was right off the exit. And when I looked back in the rearview mirror, they had turned off too. I don't know if they saw me parked here or not, but they drove right by me."

Brass gripped the phone tighter. He felt a heaviness in his lungs, making him gasp for air. He began to stutter. "D-d-do you think . . . you think it has anything to do with me?" he asked, his voice laced with guilt.

Britt kept muttering, "I don't know." But deep down inside, they both knew. She just didn't have the heart to tell him. She couldn't give him a straight yes. And all the things that she went through because of him started flashing in her mind: The last was when she lost her longtime job at American Airlines. She cried for weeks when she had to leave her beloved Dallas and move to Atlanta, to start all over from scratch with Delta. But she always put him first. She always did things to make him feel better, regardless of the consequences for her; and she wondered why she couldn't shake him. What was it about him that kept her coming back? She loved a thug, but was this just too much?

Brass fell back against the sofa and rolled his eyes toward the ceiling. The mere thought of all the pain Britt had gone through, and was still going through because of him, made him cringe. He was thankful that the brothers' battle with the divas had brought them back together after their awful breakup. *But this thing here*, he thought, *may just split us up for good.* "Damn," he said quietly to himself. He sure didn't want that to happen. Out of everybody walking out of his life, he couldn't stomach Britt abandoning him too.

"It won't be long, Britt," he said earnestly. "I'm gonna get us out of dis life. I'm gonna go straight, and soon you're not gonna have to worry about shit like dis no more." This was a promise he intended to keep.

In between her wheezing and sniffles, Britt coldly said, "Whateva, Brass." She didn't want to doubt him, but she'd heard all these promises before; and the same shit just kept on happening. Sometimes, it would feel as though he was doing good by her; but then a couple of weeks into it, he would just go back to doing the same damn things—scheming on somebody, trying to get over on them to get their money.

"This Brotherhood thang is good, Britt. I got a strong feeling about dis here. I know I can do it this time, and I'm gone do it for you," he said to her. "I feel different now, Britt. When I hear da brothers talk about what they've accomplished, I think I wanna get dere. I wanna be able to stand on my own two feet, da right way like they're doing. They're changing me, baby. They're giving me da hope and strength dat I've always needed. And maybe . . . maybe now I got it."

Britt didn't say anything, but he knew she was nodding her head; he could tell by the sound of her hair brushing against the shoulders of her flight attendant's jacket—a sound he was all too familiar with.

"I hope so, Brass," she said.

"Hey? You got money?"

Britt rolled her eyes. *No, he just didn't.* "Hmm, why?"

"You go back to da airport and get a hotel room. Stay dere until it's time for you to fly out. You'll be safe at da airport."

"Uh-huh, that's what I was thinking too," she said, perking up. "I'm going to take my scared black ass right back to the airport. I don't need to go home to get anything. I got everything I need in my travel case."

"Okay. Pull on off. Keep talking to me until you get back to the airport. You got enough minutes and battery?"

"Yah," she answered.

"Okay. Good. Pull on off then."

Britt looked around before slowly pulling out of the fire station's parking lot. "And, Brass?"

"Yah, baby."

"I'm glad to hear you talk about how good the show is for you. Melissa told me in a letter that it would be good for you. She was right, I guess; and I'm glad . . . And, Brass?"

"Yah, Britt?"

"You can always count on me, you remember that. But I'm at the end of my rope. I can't keep living like this."

"I know, Britt. I know. And I promise you, baby, it's gonna be different dis time. I'm gone make dis shit right."

◆　◆　◆

By the time Brass and Britt had hung up, Britt had just walked into her hotel room at the airport. She promised to text him right before she boarded the plane so he would know she had boarded all right. Brass closed his eyes and fell asleep right there where he was. He was awakened a few hours later by his cell phone, which he was still clutching in his hand. It was DK.

"Hey man, you still coming?"

"Yah. Yah. I'm on my way, man. Give me a few minutes," Brass replied.

He flipped the radio on and then ran to the bathroom to wash up and brush his teeth. He threw on a fresh shirt and reached over to turn off the radio. But then he stood there with his finger hovering over the radio's power button and listened as Magic said, "K103.5, if you have to be at work before 9:00 AM, you got seven minutes, or guess what? Your slow behind's gonna be late. This is your boy Mr. Kirk 'Magic' Wonder on this dreary Friday morning, and our boy DK is playing hooky today, y'all.

"And for all of you that's about to leave the house, it's a brisk forty-eight degrees outside; and most of the metro area is experiencing light showers."

Brass turned the radio off, grabbed a jacket, and headed out the door to meet DK for coffee and to finish planning Miguel's bachelor party. As promised, the two came up with a plan for a party that the brothers would never forget.

Twenty minutes after hanging up with DK, Brass walked into the restaurant and was greeted by "Hello! Welcome to the Waffle Shack." He spotted DK at a booth, already enjoying some waffles and a cup of coffee.

"Yo, bro, how's it going?" DK had a wide shit-eating grin on his face.

Brass gave him some dap and scooted into the booth, settling on the couch opposite him. "It's been good, man," he replied, the lie coming out of his mouth just as quickly and easily.

"Hmm. That didn't sound too convincing, bruh-man. What time you got to be at the car wash?"

"Got to be at work at noon. And it's been kinda a bad mornin', man," Brass said as he moved the silverware out of the way.

A waitress came over to take his order just then. "I'm good," Brass said. "Thanks, baby gul. Well, maybe a glass of water."

The waitress looked at Brass and turned up her mouth and muttered something under her breath. Brass just shrugged and mouthed "crazy woman" to DK.

DK nodded in agreement and stuffed a piece of waffle in his mouth before telling him, "Aww, man, I gotcha. Tell the lady what you want."

"Some eggs, bacon, toast, and a glass of orange juice," he told the waitress, who took the order down. "Okay, thanks. It'll be up in a few," she said dryly.

"Damn! She got issues, man," Brass said, rolling his eyes at the woman as she was walking away.

"I know, man," DK said, watching her. "Let's see how she treats everybody else. Maybe it's just us, or you," he said, laughing. "Anyway, man, back to business. So what do you have planned for Miguel's bachelor party?"

Brass threw his head back and started laughing. "What do I *not* have planned for him?" he said, winking at DK as if to say, *You know what's up.*

DK took another bite of waffle and blissfully hummed as the butter melted on his tongue. "Are we all set with the entertainment and the hotel?" he asked around a mouthful.

"Didn't your mama teach you some manners? Close your mouth," Brass scolded jokingly. DK just threw a sugar cube at his head and smiled as Brass told him, "I talked to Quentin, and one of his girls is helping with the entertainment."

DK shook his head and laughed. "It's always those quiet ones that have the freakiest side to 'em, ain't it?" He asked jokingly, "Don't tell me Q's still kicking it with that female from the ICON Awards? The one that was handing out the awards—I think she even brought lil' Meli out."

Brass nodded. "Yep. That's the one. And I hear she's stripping down there at Club Onyx."

"What?"

"Yep. Now your boy ain't one to gossip, so you ain't heard this from me. But da word is, she's a freak and gets down with the get down." Brass kicked DK under the table, nodding his head. "You know what I mean?"

"You're stupid, man. I ain't messing with you. What about the hotel, you got that squared away?" DK asked.

"Yep. We're at da Broulàis. The owners are some peeps I did business with before."

"Yah right, Brass," DK said, giving Brass a puzzled look. "The *owners?* You? Doing business with the owners of that fine-ass, five-star hotel? Yah right, Brass. What kind of business, man?" he asked suspiciously.

"Nigga. Some work. DAMN! It's all legal," Brass said defensively. "Anyway, man, I called dem da other day and told them one of my boys is 'bout to get married . . . tie da knot . . . 'bout to get put on *lockdown.*"

"You're crazy, man," DK said as he sipped his coffee. "They're gonna hook us up, right?"

"They're hooking us up, man. Got a banquet room for da casino party and a suite for da real shit. And Q said that his girl Cherí—I think her stage name is Cherry Bomb—got some of da baddest, and I mean da baddest, ladies lined up for da party. Y'all niggas gotta make sure y'all make it rain too, 'cause they all about da money; and they gone be in da house making that cherry pop." Brass started making a popping sound and gave DK a mischievous smirk. "You down?"

DK shook his head. "I'm down, man." A devious smile spread across his face, too.

"Aww, nigga, you down for anything," Brass kidded. The two shared a raucous laughter between them, which earned them some not-so-pleasant looks from the other patrons in the Shack.

The waitress came back with Brass's orange juice, bacon, eggs, and toast. She glanced over at the table, her eyes alternating between Brass and DK, as if she expected them to stiff her on her tip money or run out without paying. She put the last plate down. "Enjoy," she said before turning around and leaving in a huff.

"Man, why black people got to always treat their own like shit? Look at her over there talking to them white people like they gone leave her the fattest tip and we ain't gone leave her shit." DK's expression turned serious as he sipped his bitter coffee, as if its taste had a direct effect on his mood. "Anyway, man, when you asked me to meet you here, you said you had something important to tell me. By the sound of it, I kinda figured we weren't just meeting about Miguel's bachelor party. We're not, are we now?"

Brass sighed as he scraped up a couple of big heapings of eggs with his toast and scarfed them down, as if he hadn't eaten in days. He looked at DK, without a clue as to why he called. No, that wasn't true. Of all the brothers, DK was the one brother he trusted the most. The others were either too caught up in their own drama to care about anything else, or didn't seem as if they would understand. "Am I really that easy to read?" he asked with a nervous chuckle.

DK scoffed. "Naw, my girl Lis must've rubbed off on me, I guess—when it comes to reading people, that is."

Brass cracked a smile and jokingly flipped him off. "All right, man, since I can't seem to get nothing past you. The truth is, I've been having some problems for a while; and I'm in some deep shit."

DK raised an eyebrow and dropped his coffee cup down on its saucer. He waved off the waitress coming toward them and asked quietly, "What kind of problems?"

Brass gulped audibly. His Adam's apple bobbed up and down his throat, and his hands were growing cold and clammy, as it had always been hard for him to own up to shit he did, especially shit he wasn't proud of; and he hated the feeling of letting down those people who had trusted him. "I'm in a bad situation, man," he said under his breath. "Now I think I done dragged Britt into it too."

DK ran his hand down his face, his mouth gaping open like that of a hooked fish. He looked everywhere but at Brass as he tapped his fingernails on the table, thinking, *Damn! What's this dude 'bout to lay on me?* He asked, "What kind of problems, man? What you done dragged Britt into?"

Brass wrapped his hands around his shaved head, as if trying to cocoon himself in a safe place. There was this vague feeling of shame in admitting his wrongdoings to someone who had placed an inherent trust in him. But he knew that in the long run, this was better than DK finding out some other way. "The truth shall set you free," he remembered his gramps always preaching to him, and Brass guessed his admission would tell him if his gramps was right. He would soon find out how legit this Brotherhood thing really was.

He told DK everything. He came straight out with it, not leaving anything unsaid, any stone unturned. When he finished, DK didn't say a word. Seconds turned into minutes as DK sat there, still in shock.

Brass asked, "Whatchu thinking 'bout, playa?"

"Mexican account?" DK asked. "Check cashing scam? FBI?"

Brass could see in DKs eyes that his friend was still trying to absorb the bombshell that he had just dropped on him. Then DK asked the one thing no one had ever asked Brass. "Why, man?"

Brass dropped his fork beside a few bites of scrambled eggs left on his plate and rested his hands on his thighs as if trying to get some leverage before launching into his explanation. "You know my moms is over there at Shady Grove, right?"

"Your moms is *alive*! Man, I thought—I mean, you sure made it sound as if she was dead."

"Naw. But the lifestyle she was living took its toll—HIV . . . cancer . . . now Alzheimer's." Brass shook his head and took a minute to get himself together. You could see him fighting back the tears, "Yah. She's over there in a double room at Shady Grove. Some of my peeps helped me get her in there—Medicare, Medicaid, all that stuff—but I still got to cover some of the expenses."

"That nursing home over there by the hospital?" asked DK.

"Yep. Not much, but I gots to take care of Moms." Brass's voice sounded as though there was a golf ball lodged in his throat.

DK looked at him, really looked at him, trying to see whether Brass was trying to get one over on him—run some type of scam as Jessie said he always ran on his girl, Britt—but he didn't see it. Either Brass was a really good conman, or he was coming from a whole new place. "I'm not one to judge, Brass. I think I woulda done the same thing—hell, anything for my moms," he said without blinking. "But I know you're telling me all this because you need help." He held out his hand for Brass to take. "I got some connections—a favor to cash in from a judge, as a matter of fact. And I promise you, all of the Brotherhood will be there to help you through this. I'll definitely see to that."

Brass reached out to shake DK's hand; and for the first time in many years, he felt that things might just be looking up for him.

Chapter 23

Miguel's Bachelor Party

October 30, 2009
The Broulåis Hotel

"Oh shit, Jacki-O's in the house!" yelled Brass as Magic started testing his equipment, filling the room with the nasty grind-house music of Jacki-O's "Pussy (Real Good)."

"Hey, Brass?" said Magic. "You so nasty, nigga. Gone have these girls coming out to some freaky, nasty shit like this, yo."

"Naw, homey, it ain't me. I swear!" He started laughing out loud, twisting his body to the left, then to the right, doing his own stripper dance. He dropped it like it was hot, "Hey! How they gone be doing it, man?" he asked as he started bouncing up and down off the floor, which got DK and Magic laughing too. "Let me stop playing around before I make y'all niggas hot for real," he said as he bounced back up. "Naw, our boy Quentin said dat, dat Chéri chick needed her girls to come out to dis jam, 'cause they're gonna give Miguel a show he ain't never gonna forget. And, niggas, I can't wait to see it."

"All right now," DK said, a little concerned. "We want Miguel to get married, not have Darlene dropping his ass before he walks down the aisle over some stupid shit. My boy only has sixteen more days left before he walks, *now.*"

"I know that's right, man," said Magic. "Aiight, playas, I'm done on my end. Place looks good too: Gots the streamers going on, gots the liquor, gots the food, gots the music and those freaky videos cued up. Now all we need are the rest of the fellas and dem cherry-poppers to roll through."

DK looked at his watch. "Nine o'clock, fellas. Let's head on downstairs." And the three grabbed their suit jackets for the semiformal affair and headed down to the Majestic Ballroom, where they found quite a few partygoers and some of the brothers already gambling and getting their food and drink on. DK spotted the Doc at the blackjack table and made his way over to him.

"Doc Mayweather. How's it going, man? I'm glad you could make it. You winning anything?" he asked.

"Naw, brother DK. I guess I'm a little rusty." The Doc looked around the room. "This is really nice, DK. First class, my brother, first class. You got the blackjack and poker tables, keno and slot machines, even bingo." A waitress was making her way around the room with a tray full of champagne, compliments of the hotel; and he grabbed a flute as she passed by them. "Thank you, young lady."

"Yah, it is nice. Can't take all the credit, though. The hotel throws these Casino Royale parties for their hotel guests all the time. We just lucked out and caught the tail end of one for Miguel's bachelor party. All thanks to our boy Brass." And they said in unison, "Who always has the hookup." And they laughed, because in just that short time, they knew him so well.

"What y'all laughing at?" asked Brass as he came over and grabbed a seat, motioning for the dealer to hit him with some cards.

The Doc revealed another losing hand to the dealer and then asked, "Brass, you ready to lead the *Brotherhood* discussion on Sunday? You only have two days left to get everything together."

"Doc, I got dis. DK's helping me out with the format, and Magic has all the music lined up for my *Top Ten All-time Favorite Slow Jams* countdown."

"And the topic? You're still keeping it?"

"Yep. Nothing stirs up more controversy than people talking about *creeping* on each other."

DK butted into the conversation: "It's what the K103.5 audience said they wanted to talk about in our last poll. Doc, you just make sure you're at the studio on time, 'cause . . . I have a feeling we're probably gonna need your advice."

The Doc laughed and patted DK on the shoulder. "I'll be there, my brother." He looked at Brass as he took a sip of his champagne, looking at him over the rim of the glass. "Brass? I hear Britt flew in for Jessie's birthday bash tomorrow. Is she staying with you or with one of her girlfriends?"

Brass didn't mind the Doc getting personal with him. As far as he was concerned, the Doc was like the family he never had—a big brother to guide him through life's obstacle courses. "Yah, she's staying with Jessie, Doc. Picked her up from the airport and drove her ova dare earlier today." He looked at the Doc, who was still looking at him from over the rim of the champagne glass. "Don't give me that look, either. I'm gone do right by her this time around, Doc. I swear."

The Doc said, "You better." And one by one, the brothers started showing up and gathered around the blackjack table.

"Who's bringing Miguel?" asked X as he noted that Donnell, Quentin, Miguel, and the pastor were M-I-A. "And where's everybody else at?"

"Donnell's here," said Mike. "He went around the corner to the Q-T to get some cash and to get me some dollars for the freak show."

"Well, damn, speak of the devil. And look who he's walking in with," said Malcolm as Donnell and the pastor walked in together.

Although the pastor and Donnell had their differences, it did appear that they were at least trying to get along. They walked up to the group, and everybody gave each other some brotherly love. "Q and Miguel just drove up. They're right behind us," said the pastor. "I just wanted to come and show my support for my brother Miguel, but I won't be able to stay long."

"We know the deal," DK said as he shook the pastor's hand. "Miguel will appreciate you coming, though. Hey, I hear you're a big karaoke fan. You're in luck. There's a competition going on. Plus, it'll keep you out of any trouble. You got time to play a couple of rounds with your boy?"

The pastor said yes, and time quickly passed as the brothers gambled, ate, and drank. DK and the pastor spent the night crooning out old gospel and R&B tunes, trying desperately to outdo each other and win the online video competition that was being broadcast on an oversized LCD screen above the stage. Soon, Brass and Magic rolled out a big three-tier paper cake, and Brass yelled out, "Gather round, fellas. The festivities are about to begin."

DK, keeping the pastor out of trouble, pointed to the door and ushered the pastor out to a little sitting area in the hallway, where they found Doc Mayweather sitting down on one of the three settees, licking his wounds from an embarrassing loss at the blackjack table. DK shivered as a blast of cold air hit his right side and turned to find the automatic doors wide open and a couple of the dancers straggling in from the parking deck. They asked him if he was with the bachelor party and if he knew someone by the name of Quentin. "We're sorry. We forgot the room number we're supposed to go up to."

"Hey, ladies," he answered. "You're heading in the right direction. Take the elevators at the end of the hall there—only two of the three are working—and go up to room 1107. Knock on the door. Your boy Quentin should be up there getting things ready for you guys."

They said their thank-yous and told him, "We have one more coming. She's trying to find a parking space."

"Okay, ladies," DK said and then turned to the Doc, who was putting on his coat. "You getting ready to go, Doc? You sure you want to miss all this?" he asked as he turned back to look inside the ballroom.

Both he and the Doc laughed as they watched all the brothers whooping and a-hollering, especially when Brass gave Miguel one of those lighted sabers and told him to cut the cake. When he touched it, it gave off a bright spark and a loud boom, filling the area with smoke. The cake's top flew off, and a plump elderly woman jumped out, shaking and gyrating. Everybody started laughing their asses off, especially when Brass told Miguel, "This is what you're going to eventually end up with, homey; but don't worry about all dat tonight. We got da real deal waiting for you upstairs."

DK noticed that Mike and Donnell were standing next to each other, laughing and cutting up with everybody. He scratched his head. "Doc, I gotta ask," he said as he helped the doc adjust the collar on his coat. "It's amazing how some of the brothers are bonding, especially Mike and Donnell over there. I'm curious, man. Why did you put those two in a group together?"

The Doc rolled his eyes and shook his head. "Well, Donnell was the brother Mike and X trusted the least. Mike wasn't too far behind, and X—let's just say with two self-centered brothers in his group, I thought if anyone could ground Mike and Donnell, a doctor definitely could." The two looked back into the room at the two brothers, who were still carrying on; and the Doc said, "They can learn something from a man that gives of himself and cares for others, a man with good bedside manners, so to speak."

The pastor nodded. "I agree, Doc." And he sat down on a settee arm and stared around the room, his eyes finally fixing on Donnell.

They watched all the brothers, who were still gathered around the cake, and overheard Brass tell them, "Aiight, homeys, throw dose fake-ass chips in—I know y'all wish they were real—and get dose ones, fives, and twenties ready, 'cause we're headed upstairs to get this freak party started. Room 1107, fellas."

And as if a bomb had exploded or someone had set the room on fire, a wave of bodies quickly rushed through the room's double doors, cramming into the hallway and quickly navigating down to the elevator lobby. Seeing the crowd at the elevators, Donnell, Mike, Miguel, and Brass joined DK, Pastor Levine, and the Doc, and waited for the crowd to thin out.

As they stood and waited, they started shooting the breeze and felt a cold snap of air rush in from the sliding glass doors of the garage. The brothers shivered, crossing their arms, and turned to see who was bringing in all the cold air. They watched as a young lady in a well-fitted trench coat that was tightly tied around the waist, walked in, rolling a small travel case behind her down the hall.

Brass said, "Damn! Fineness in motion, fellas."

The Doc chuckled. "I guess that's the other performer they were talking about—the one parking the car."

As she approached them, the expression on her face immediately changed. *Unhappy* was written all over it when she looked down the hall and noticed the crowd at the elevators. She stopped in front of the brothers and pointed down to the crowd. "You gotta be fucking kidding me. Are the elevators not working?" she asked, with a hint of disgust.

Pastor Levine did a double take and yelled out, "WHAT! Chéri?" He hopped up from the settee, a look of distraught plastered all over his face.

"Oh God, *not* you, man. Whatchu doing here?" she asked, jokingly. "You here to get your freak on too?" She was making fun of him.

"Watch your mouth," he told her firmly. "What are you doing here, Chéri?" he asked as he looked her up and down.

The pastor knew something was up; he had been in *the industry* long enough to know when someone was working, and the worry lines ran deep across his forehead. He had been trying to turn Chéri's life around for the longest time. He frowned as he took in everything: Her painted face and her hair, which was gathered up and secured by a long hairpin (a prop she was probably going to use in something she was up to); her heavy perfume; and the white fishnet stockings and black pumps. Her continued taunting and disrespect sent him into a rage; and he reached for her trench coat, causing her to lean back, and he grabbed the coat's lapels with both hands, yanking it open so all the brothers could see the white-laced, two-piece teddy underneath.

Chéri's jaw dropped. She couldn't believe he just did that. She bucked up to him as she told him, "No you didn't just put your hands on me!" And she turned her head, looking at him angrily. It was as though she had zoomed out and everybody around her disappeared. There was only her and Pastor Levine. And she thought, *If it's a show he wants, then goddamnit, it's a show he's going to get.* And she started bouncing her body up and down, making everything gyrate. "Like you don't know. You know what I'm doing. I'm 'bout it, 'bout it. I'm making that money. That's right. Making that money. Making *that* money!" She pointed at the pastor's head with one hand and then with the other in a rhythmic motion.

Brass zoomed in on Chéri's breasts, watching them jiggle. Then he looked at the pastor, and then back at Chéri. "Good God Almighty, there is a god. Hallelujah! And?" He elbowed DK, who noticed the same thing.

"Praise God," DK said.

The Doc and Miguel shook their heads at the two and stayed where they stood, quiet, not quite sure of what to do, or what was really going on. They didn't even have any idea who this girl was.

"Chéri?" the pastor said calmly, trying to diffuse the escalating situation. "You know the Bible says—"

"DADDY! Take that Bible talk and go on somewhere, NOW!"

Donnell and Mike looked at each other funny. Mike mouthed *Daddy?* to Donnell and grabbed his arm, pulling him close. "You need to record this, man," he whispered.

Donnell, thinking about what his lawyers had told him earlier in the week—that he didn't have a good chance with the custody battle—reached for his phone and started recording just as Chéri stepped out of her coat, turned around, and started backing it up on the pastor, making that booty clap.

"This is what makes that money, Daddy," she said, laughing as she performed a little stripper dance in front of him. And although she was a-ways away from him, from Donnell's perspective, it looked as though she was right there, backing it up on his crotch.

"DONNELL!" DK yelled, slapping the phone out of Donnell's hand. "What are you doing, man!"

"Donnell jumped on DK and told Mike, "Get my phone, man." And he started shoving DK, pushing him up against the arm of the settee, where he fell over, Donnell landing on top of him. The two began duking it out on the settee, and the brothers at the elevator ran down to see the fight. Miguel and Brass tried to break them up; and as they tried, the Doc did his best to calm everything down between the pastor and his daughter.

Chéri knocked away the Doc's helping hand and picked her coat off the floor, grabbed her travel case, and pushed the pastor out of the way as she headed to the elevators in her white teddy for all to see. The pastor, teary-eyed, watched as she walked away and got on the elevator, the doors immediately closing as soon as she was inside. He shook his head and turned his attention to the drama still unfolding between DK and Donnell.

"Don't do nothing you'll regret, man," said DK.

"Fuck you, man," Donnell told him as he grabbed his phone from Mike's hand.

"Karma's a bitch, man," DK said, lunging forward, pointing at Donnell. "Karma's a bitch, man! Remember that, jigga."

Donnell threw up his hands at DK and said, "Whateva, nigga."

As everything started to calm down and Donnell and Mike went outside and DK and the Doc went into the ballroom to talk, Brass looked at Miguel and jokingly told him, "Nigga, don't look so sour. Hell, we promised you fireworks and a night you'll never forget. And trust me"—he laughed—"you ain't ever gonna forget this shit." He threw his arm around Miguel's shoulder, who quickly told him in his native tongue, "Era algún lío, hombre. No?"

"What does that mean?" asked Brass.

Miguel repeated himself in his heavy accent, "That was some mess, man, wasn't it?"

"I know," Brass told him, laughing. "My boys were going at it! They'll be all right, though. Let's go upstairs, man. You're getting married in a few days. Remember? We need to get this marriage started right, homey."

Chapter 24

Jessie's Birthday
You Gonna Make Me Love Somebody Else

Saturday, October 31, 2009
Halloween

"*H*ello?" Jessie answered groggily, fumbling with her cell phone after having been awakened from a deep sleep.

"Dang, girl, what's going on over there? What's all that noise?"

"DeDe?" she asked faintly.

"The one and only. Hey, momma, were you asleep?"

"Uh-huh. Me and Meli were taking a nap. The operative word being *were*, girl."

"WHATEVA! Wake your tired behind up. It's supposed to be beautiful in Dallas today, and you're in bed? Girl, what are you doing asleep this late in the afternoon? And where are you, by the way?"

"Over at Quentin's house babysitting," Jessie said, yawning. "He's at some job fair today. What's going on?"

"I missed my nine o'clock flight fooling around in the studio trying to finish that crazy CD. I'm finally about to board and head on over to Dallas for your four-months-removed birthday bash. Halleluh, girl. Halleluh to your man, that is. Girl, he worked it out, got me on a later flight. He even hooked me up and had me upgraded to first class. Woohoo! Praise God."

Jessie, still groggy, asked, "What time is it, De?"

"Almost two o'clock, your time. And the word is, X is going all out for your birthday tonight. . . . I mean, all out."

"Yah, that's great, Dee. But you know my birthday is not on some damn Halloween. My birthday was months ago. I don't even know where he got that shit from. It's like I kept telling him, and telling him. Girl, I think I done told him 51 million times that my birthday's in June; and yet, here we are at the end of October. I could just scream! But I got a trick or two for his behind. It really will be a trick-or-treat night—more like a night of horrors—once I'm done performing."

"All right, hateful bitch. . . . But, Jessie, he went through a lot of trouble for—"

"Girl, hush. He needs to be taught to listen when I tell him something. And what better way for him to learn than to find out the hard way, after all the work and money he's put into it? Hmph! I'll betcha he'll remember then."

"The evil monster is rearing its ugly head, I see. Can the church say 'Amen'?"

"Whatever, DeDe. And I know you're not trying to call somebody out—not with that sordid past of yours."

"OH, GIRL! No, you didn't come for me. Don't blame me and X for your issues with Michael. Hmph! And you're over there . . . secretly yearning for and laying up in the man's house that you really want to be with, but can't. Girl, I'm too through with you." DeDe started laughing at the situation. "Well, at least act surprised, girl. You know you're not supposed to know about this party. And whatever evilness you've hatched up, I hope it doesn't backfire on your black ass. And that's all I got to say. Halleluh, and good-bye!"

◆　◆　◆

X put his Jaguar into overdrive and put the pedal to the metal as he raced against air, wind, and time. Still wearing the scrubs from his sixteen-hour shift, which he hurriedly departed from a little early, he glanced down at his watch and breathed a heavy sigh of relief when he saw that he still had twenty minutes before his three o'clock appointment. As he raced to meet Sweets, he thought about the last time he was late: Just a mere ten minutes, and Sweets, being the grand diva that he was, walked straight by him, waving a hand in the air as he headed for the door, calling over his shoulder, "Talk to the hand, 'cause the diva is leaving the building."

When X grabbed his arm, Sweets went off on him like a sailor talking big-time trash in a Chinese ("me love you long time") whorehouse. It was so bad and went on and on that X just wanted the ground to open up and swallow him whole. He had definitely learned his lesson.

As he approached Bailey's, he noticed that the area's square was spookily decorated. He giddily pumped his fist after spotting a front-row parking space just across from the restaurant. Before anyone could get the spot, he sped up, swerved into the lot, and whipped into the parking stall. He hurriedly grabbed his jacket from the backseat, threw it over his scrubs, and got out. He looked down at his watch. "Five minutes, thank the Lord." He wiped his brow and ran over to the pay box. Then he ran into Bailey's and up to the maître d's stand, where a middle-aged gentleman greeted him with a friendly nod. The maître d and X got to know each other quite well, as he and Sweets had been down at Bailey's almost every day for the past several weeks, planning Jessie's surprise party; and X always made sure he spoke and acknowledged the brother.

"How's it going?" he asked with a wide smile, extending his hand.

"Everything's going all right, Doc," he replied, shaking X's hand. "Tonight's the night, huh?"

"Yep," X answered, nodding enthusiastically. A picture of Jessie, with her beautiful wide smile, was flashing in his mind.

"I'm hearing she's one lucky girl. Everybody's talking about this here. No one has ever seen anything like this, Doc. You're going all out, aren't you?"

X shook his head, the tips of his ears feeling hot. "Naw. Naw. Not as all out as I should. And to tell you the truth, I'm the lucky one." He jingled the keys in his pocket. "I gotta head inside. The crazy guy I'm usually with is waiting for me, and he'll throw a bitch fit if I'm a second late. Have you seen him?"

The maître d shuddered at the mention of the little dude with all the attitude, who was built quite well for a man of small stature. He knew Sweets, and he definitely remembered the exact time he went off on the doc and pointed to the main dining area. "He's over there at the bar."

X thanked him and made his way down the steps and over to the bar. Sweets was nothing but visible with his newly highlighted Mohawk hair and electric blue fitted blazer. He was cradling a clipboard in one arm and dramatically gesturing with the other as he talked; and the moment X walked up, Sweets gave him the look of death and a lot of 'tude. "You're late!" he said.

"I ain't late. Don't even try it. I walked right through those doors at two minutes before three. You can go ask the maître d'," X teased with a little lilt in his voice.

"Whateva. Come on, handsome, walk with me. And I'm only forgiving you because I have no time to dillydally around." Sweets rolled his eyes and looked down at his clipboard, checking off items on the first page. "Flowers and decorations have arrived. Check. Lights and music are being set up as we speak. Check. Bee is in the kitchen supervising the food. Check. Entertainment will be here in four hours' time. Check. And all that's left for you to do is deliver the birthday girl here at precisely seven o'clock. You think that you can handle that, mister?"

X rubbed the back of his neck and sucked his bottom lip in. Then, in a somewhat calculating manner, he said, "I've already told her we're going out for dinner. Something fancy." He made it seem as if he had just come up with some genius plan. "So I know she's gonna primp herself up something good for this night."

"How original," Sweets said with a blank look on his face.

X, a little annoyed, threw up his hands and said sarcastically, "Who cares about originality as long as it works."

Sweets just looked at him sideways and then sighed exasperatedly. "I guess." Then he swung open the doors to the party room. "So how does it look?"

X walked in, and his mouth dropped open. He looked around and knew he had definitely made the right choice in using Sweets, despite his being very temperamental at times. The room looked like something straight out of one of those architectural or home-and-garden magazines: ornate flower arrangements—a combination of white orchids and yellow calla lilies—and tables draped in fancy silk linen were strategically placed around the room to form a dance floor, which was modestly decorated with purple and gold confetti and weighted balloons. There was a makeshift stage set up at the far end of the room, which could be seen as soon as one walked in the door. Right above the stage was a large banner, also in purple and gold, that said, "Happy Birthday, Jessie!" Right beside it was a life-size picture of Jessie looking simply gorgeous with little makeup on and her hair pulled back in a French coif.

X remembered taking that picture on their way back from a colleague's dinner party. He remembered thinking how beautiful she looked with her hair pulled back, showing off those high cheekbones and that luscious pout. He remembered how once they got home, he had grabbed a camera and asked her to smile.

"It looks good, Sweets. Damn good. Man, you did an *outstanding* job. I'm . . . I almost don't know what to say. I'm impressed, man. You do have skills."

Hearing this, Sweets' downturned mouth turned up into a happy smile that seemingly brought him to life. "I'm glad you like it. But, honey, we're not finished yet. Next, Bee's gonna let us taste some hors d'oeuvres, see what we like best so they'll make more; and maybe she'll take pity on our poor souls and serve us some lunch too. But before all of that, let's walk on over to the square, where the real festivities will be held; and then we can come back and go over some of the last-minute details for your sit-down dinner celebration that you so insisted on having."

X and Sweets ran across the street to the square, which was nothing more than a small park with a few ornamental trees, stone benches, and a large white Victorian gazebo that sat smack-dab in the middle of the square. Sweets, who had convinced the neighborhood association to let him hold the event there if he would make it a Halloween festival for the neighborhood, had turned the square into a morbid cemetery, with the gazebo as the crematorium surrounded by tombstones, coffins, and figurines of ghosts, witches, and goblins everywhere. Sweets knew the look wouldn't be complete without lighted jack-o'-lanterns, slimy red blood, and tons and tons of spiderwebs strewn all over the place. He motioned to one of the special-effects guys to come over and asked him, "Okay, can you do a test run? This is Dr. Houston, the one throwing this shindig. Can you show him the fog machine and the strobe lights in action?"

As the fog filled the square and the strobe lights pierced the sky, marking the event's location, Sweets climbed up the gazebo steps and went to each of the three mics, "Testing one, two, three . . . testing one, two, three . . . testing one, two, three. I guess they're all working. So, does this meet with your approval as well?"

X shook his head and smiled at Sweets. "You're the man, Sweets. You're the man. Three microphones? Who's going to be performing other than DeDe, who should be arriving within the next hour or so?"

Sweets looked at him proudly and then spoke as if he was about to make an announcement that would affect many lives. "I've booked one of Dallas's favorite girl groups. They call themselves Savoir Faire, and boy, they sound just like the Jones Girls. And they will be covering all of the Jones Girls' signature hits too."

"What hits? Anything I've ever heard of?"

Sweets rolled his eyes and sighed. "Oh God, must I? Must I really?"

X knitted his brows. "Listen, man, I need for this night to be perfect. It has to be the night she'll always remember. All I'm saying is that I've never heard of the Jones Girls before."

Sweets threw up his hands. He cocked his head to the side and looked up at the gazebo's ceiling, rolling his eyes. Then he blurted out, "Nights over Egypt"? "Who Can I Run To"? "You Gonna Make Me Love Somebody Else"? He looked at X, who had this blank look on his face, and shook his head. "Hmph! Hmph! Umph! So sad. . . .Well, don't fret. They'll be singing all the old-time favorites from groups you probably should know—groups like the Emotions, Sister Sledge, Rose Royce, and the list goes on, and on."

"Where did you find them?" X asked as they walked down the gazebo's steps.

"A client of Quita's—damn, I can't even remember the sister's name right now—put me in contact with them. And don't look at me like that. They're all that and a bowl of chips, trust. I assure you, they're not going to disappoint. They're going to make your night, a night everyone will not soon forget—just like you said you wanted. Now, if you're ready, let's head back over to Baileys and see if Bee has those hors d'oeuvres ready."

♦ ♦ ♦

A short, fat man wiped the beads of sweat off his forehead as he angled a video camera under his table to get a better focus on X and Sweets talking and eating hors d'oeuvres in a secluded corner of the party room. The static on the earpiece stung his hearing, and then the voice of another man came through. "Got anything juicy, Jay?"

The man shook his head even if his partner couldn't see him. "They're just eating and talking. I don't think there's anything here. You sure we could trust that Crawley dude?" he asked, eyes still fixed on X and Sweets.

"Just keep at it. There's gotta be something. He sounded real sure."

"It don't look like it. I don't know, man. This is like a lawsuit waiting to happen," Jay said as he watched Sweets scrunch up his face after swallowing something that didn't look like it agreed with him. "We'll follow them for a few more days; but if there's nothing, let's just drop this."

"Come on, Jay, Crawley's mah man. He ain't lying. You got to trust me, dude."

"Aiight. Aiight. I gotta shut up. People are starting to look at me funny sitting here talking to myself and all," Jay said, moving his mouth self-consciously before biting into a chicken wing.

"Hey, I'm sure we're gonna get something tomorrow, dude."

Jay snorted, his eyebrows meeting above his nose. "We better, 'cause we've wasted a whole lotta time and money on this shit already."

◆ ◆ ◆

X knocked on the white door three or four times before his hand went back to fixing his tie. He could hear Jessie scurrying around inside and leaned over and peeked through the window to find her running around looking for things to put in a tiny gold clutch before stopping in front of a mirror, doing a last-minute check on her face. A full minute passed before the locks clicked and she stood in the doorway, looking like a supermodel in a fitted red bandage dress that clung in all the right places. Her hair was pulled back in a bun, showing off her graceful long neck; and X gawked, as if it was the first time he ever laid eyes on her.

"Well, don't you look dashing," she greeted him, lips pursed, eyes scanning him from head to toe.

"I needed to make sure I looked acceptable beside your gorgeous self," he said before leaning down to place a chaste kiss on her red-painted lips. "Happy birthday, sweetheart," he whispered against her ear.

Jessie turned her head and pulled away, but she thanked him with a brief hug. "You said we had reservations at seven, didn't you?"

X nodded as he interlaced his fingers with hers. He closed the door and gave her a gentle tug, urging her to walk along with him. "Yeah, got us the best seats at Bailey's," he said, looking behind him to watch the reaction on her face. A soft frown told him she didn't seem too keen on the idea. "Anything wrong?"

Jessie shook her head and quickly adjusted the look on her face into a happier expression. While she did love the cuisine at Bailey's—she'd give up an ovary for their bourbon chicken wings, and she ate lunch there two to three times a week—this inept afterthought of a birthday celebration just fueled the mean-spirited thoughts blazing through her head. She had pictured them going somewhere more posh or possibly out of town, just somewhere that would feel more special, especially for a birthday missed. *So much for that*, she thought. But never did she imagine a night at Bailey's, and her mouth twitched as X opened the car door and neatly ushered her inside. She didn't know if she would be able to make it to Bailey's without going off, and she sat frowning as she thought about how it seemed as though her boyfriend, who was forgetful and appeared thoughtless, thought dinner at Bailey's counted as a birthday celebration.

The streets were bustling with activity as they approached Baileys. Biscayne Street, even Bayou Street, were filled with pedestrians and lined up with cars. "Seems like tonight's a busy night for the area," Jessie said as she peered out the window. "And look . . . what's going on over there in the square? Look at that place . . . and the music. Hey! Ain't that "Who Can I Run To?" And she started snapping her fingers and singing the chorus. "Oh my god, X, will you look at all the little ghosts, goblins, and trick-or-treaters! They're so cute."

"Yah. Yah. Look at all that. It's a perfect night for it too. Not a cloud in the sky, and it's a crisp sixty-nine degrees—not too hot, not too cold." X pulled into a parking spot and started letting the convertible's top up

Jessie asked again, "You don't know what's going on?"

"I don't know," X said snidely. "You want to check it out?"

"Well . . . no, we probably should just head on over to Baileys. I don't want to lose our reservation."

X assured Jessie that they were fine with the reservation and coaxed her into going over and checking out the happenings in the square. Once they got there, they were bombarded by a gang of trick-or-treaters and were chased up to the gazebo by one of the live witches Sweets had hired. X dragged Jessie up the stairs and then bent over, hands on his knees, pretending to catch his breath. Suddenly, a spotlight illuminated Jessie's face, and her eyes widened when she saw the crowd in front of her: They were holding posters and banners that said 'Happy Birthday,' and she immediately picked out the faces of her beloved divas and the *Love Forum* brothers in the sea of fifty or so smiling and cheering faces. Her mouth hung open as her eyes wandered among the crowd. Confetti started raining down on her, and a bright disco ball was lowered. It glittered above her and X.

"Surprise!" hollered X.

Jessie clutched her heart, trying to hold herself back from screaming, but it didn't work. "Oh my lord, my lord, my lord!" she exclaimed as her lips stretched into a grin.

"Happy birthday Jessie!" the crowd shouted.

X was by her side holding a bouquet of orchids and calla lilies and looking thoroughly pleased with himself. He did good—he definitely did good, and she slapped his arm before drawing him into an embrace. "Oh my god, you did this! You sneaky, sneaky man!" And she forgot about any wrongdoing she had planned and said to herself, *Even though you're four months late.*

X laughed, throwing his head back before returning her hug. "Guilty as charged!" he admitted readily. "Happy birthday, Jessie," he whispered in her ear. "I love you, baby." He grabbed one of the mics and held Jessie by the hand.

"I'd like to thank everyone for coming and helping celebrate my baby's birthday today, which we're celebrating a little later than usual. But there's always a rhyme and reason for everything."

Jessie had a bewildered look on her face, and what X said next took her breath away. "You see, Halloween has a special meaning in my family. From my great-great-grandfather, to my great-grandpops, to my grandpops, to my dad— all of us Houston men proposed to our women on this very day, and went on to have fruitful, happy, lifelong relationships. The same kind I want to have with this woman standing right here."

You could hear the gasps in the audience as X dropped down on one knee and pulled out a lavender box from the inside pocket of his blazer. "Jessie S. Harris, the love of my world, I fell in love with you the first time I saw you at the K103.5 pajama party; and as I pursued you, wooed you"—X turned to the audience and blushed—"made love to you, I could never have found a more perfect woman to share my life with. Jessie? As you hold my hand"—X opened the box and took out a two-carat ruby engagement ring with eight accent diamonds set in platinum, and placed it on her ring finger—"will you be my wife?" he asked.

Jessie was overwhelmed. "Oh my god, oh my god, oh my god, XAVIER!" This was definitely not what she had in mind, and she looked out at the crowd, searching for Quentin's face. She spotted him holding Meli, nodding his head up and down in approval. She looked at him, waiting for him to do something, come to her aid; but he just continued nodding his head and clapped with everyone else. Jessie smiled at him, shrugged her shoulders, and answered X, "Yes! Yes! Yes!"

And as X bounced up off his knee, DeDe came onstage and started singing "You Are So Beautiful" by Joe Cocker. And then he lifted her up off the Gazebo floor and passionately kissed her as the crowd cheered them on.

The two walked hand in hand down the steps and into the embraces of her beloved divas. She kissed each of them, and they hugged all the brothers and thanked them for coming to their special day. Jessie went around the crowd, thanking everyone for coming. She caught up with some people she hadn't seen in quite a while, like Harriet James, her old boss from DataComm International.

Harriet was in her mid to late fifties and was a well-respected name in the marketing world. Jessie learned that since leaving her old office, Harriet had indeed resigned and was making a big move to New York to take on the role of marketing consultant for a well-known multinational corporation. It wasn't a difficult decision: She didn't have roots in Dallas; and she had no husband, children, or family. And as they caught up with one another, Harriet had a somber smile on her face when she told Jessie, "Maybe some magic will happen for me in New York. You know, you're lucky, Jessie," Harriet said as she tipped her champagne glass back, every movement showing class and pedigree. "For women in my time, it always felt like you had to choose between your career and a family. And when you chose a career, you had to work twice as hard to get half the recognition you deserved . . . just because you're a woman. I'm glad times are changing, and it's great to see young women like you get the chance to have the best of both worlds." Harriet nodded her head toward Dr. Houston, who was on the other side of the square talking with Malcolm and DK.

Jessie felt a blush crawl up her cheeks. "You said it yourself, Harriet. Times are changing. You can still have both," she said encouragingly, squeezing the arm of the woman whom she now considered her mentor.

The executive gave her a demure smile. "I don't know. I haven't had too much luck in Dallas; but hopefully, I'm not too old. Maybe something will happen in New York," she said, winking at Jessie before breaking out in a high-pitched laughter. "Just in case it doesn't for me, I want you to promise that you'll keep on climbing that corporate ladder and make sure you never let that man of yours go."

Jessie threw her head back and laughed. "As long as you promise me you won't give up on the dream! I know it's hard to find a good man out of the lot we have nowadays. Lord, do I know all about that; but, Harriett, don't give up on love. After the career is gone and you've closed your last deal, what will you have left?"

"I don't know, Jessie. This may be the new reality for so many of us sisters." She took another sip of her champagne and swallowed hard. Then her eyes began to well up with tears. "We'll look up one day, and time will have passed by so quickly. We'll seem to have it all—house, clothes, shoes, and cars—but inside, we're just dying." The tears fell from her eyes, but she smiled at Jessie. "I'm so happy for you, Jessie. You found the career and a good man to go along with it."

Jessie thanked her, and then they kissed each other on the cheek and vowed to stay in touch.

◆ ◆ ◆

The celebration had moved over to Bailey's, and the party room was jumping. Some of the patrons from the restaurant couldn't resist popping in and participating in the festivities. The dance floor was filled with partygoers doing the Electric Slide. The champagne was flowing from bottles to glasses.

The hors d'oeuvres made their way around the party room on the arms of the beautiful wait staff in black tuxedos. Bee had artistically decorated the hen and sausage gumbo being served as the entrée—which was the rave of the party. And as the partygoers ate, drank, and danced, various people made their way to the stage to say thoughtful and encouraging words to the new couple. Harriet had just finished giving a heartfelt tribute when the lights were turned down low and the music from the speakers came to a halt. The lights came on onstage, just as Sweets went up and pulled out one of the mics from the microphone stand and addressed the crowd, "Is everyone having a great time?"

A loud chorus of cheers was his answer. His energy was bouncing off the walls, infecting everyone inside.

"Well, we have a little musical treat for you. Thanks to my new friend, Tracy." He paused and clapped his hands toward where Tracy stood a few steps behind Malcolm. "Come on up here, Tracy girl. While she's making her way down, I have to tell you that we found this gem of a group of girls—"

As Sweets entertained the crowd with his colorful story of finding Savoir Faire, Tracy slinked her way down the crowded dance floor, shaking hands with all the patrons who were giving her props for finding Savoir Faire, all the while eyeing her scum of a husband who, in her eyes, appeared to be appreciating every piece of ass he could see. She scoffed. *He'll get his before the night is over,* she said to herself. And as she approached him, she couldn't help but notice those broad shoulders she loved, once upon a time. Now she was just sick of them. Seeing them reminded her of the nail scratches she would find running down his back, and those definitely weren't hers.

She let her deft fingers crawl up the back of his arm. Malcolm looked behind him; and the moment their eyes met, she could detect the resentment in his eyes, no matter how hard he tried to hide it.

"Enjoying yourself, hubby?" she asked, her voice dripping with sarcasm.

He cleared his throat and took a chug of his beer. "Yah, you?"

"Uhm, I will be."

Tracy gave Malcolm a cryptic smirk and made her way to the stage. She ran up to Sweets; and the two of them hugged, giving each other smooches. "Hey, diva. Girl, you are made up to nothing but fierceness. Look at you."

Tracy said, smiling from ear to ear, "Thank you, baby. And don't you look dashing yourself. That blue tux . . ." She looked at the crowd and leaned into one of the mics. "I see the skinny cut is in, y'all. It's fitting him, ain't it?"

Sweets rolled his eyes. "Hmm-huh, and you know this."

The two laughed, and Sweets grabbed her by the waist and pulled her to him. "Girl, are you ready to introduce this group, officially?"

"I am. And, boy, let me pull away from you. You're 'bout to get me all hot up in here." The audience started laughing, and Tracy looked over at Jessie and started waving. "And to my soror-sista Jessie (skee-wee) and her fiancé, Dr. Xavier Houston, I wish you nothing but the best. You see, I started off deeply in love, just like you two. I found and married a wonderful man . . . Malcolm? Malcolm, honey, where are you?"

"Malcolm? You mean *The Brotherhood*'s Malcolm? That Malcolm over there?" Sweets asked, pointing.

"Yes, and thank you, Sweets. You're so crazy. You know that's my husband. Audience, ain't he crazy? Anyway, can somebody shine a light on the gentleman standing by Jessie and Xavier's table?" Tracy directed the spotlight right on Malcolm's face. "Yes, that's him. Everybody give him a round of applause. That's right, Jessie girl. You and Xavier have a happy life together, but just make sure you don't hit the point where you have to question that love, like I'm doing right now."

Sweets looked at her and said under his breath, "Whatchu doing, bitch?"

Tracy ignored him and clapped her hands, "Ladies and gentlemen, please welcome Savoir Fairrrrrrre! Singing a song I want to dedicate to my husband, Mr. Malcolm Crawley."

Three young ladies walked onstage, wearing matching gold loose shift dresses that stretched down to their midthighs, with matching oversized gold hoop earrings. A familiar bass beat started, and Tracy's smirk widened as she watched the horrified expression on Malcolm's face, as if a train wreck was unfolding before his eyes. Savoir Faire began to perform:

"Come on, everybody, GET UP! I know you know this. GET UP!

"If you have a love that's been treatin' you bad, we want you to *wave* your hands in the air. That's right! Wave those hands y'all. Let 'em know that if they keep doing what they're doing, treatin' you the way they do, they gone drive you to love somebody else."

Tracy waved her hands triumphantly and allowed herself a moment to just enjoy the music for what it was—music, and great music at that. Savoir Faire was an amazing group after all; in fact, they were all that and a bowl of chips, just as she said they were. But their performance was overshadowed by a room filled with giggles, some straight-out laughter, and vicious whispers of gossip. Jessie and Xavier looked at each other, grimacing and shaking their heads at each other. Then they turned to watch an embarrassed Malcolm just stand there, light shining on his face, in complete and utter disbelief. He was just, through.

Tracy, basking in her triumphant glory, trained her sights on her husband once more and was completely satisfied as she reveled in his embarrassment. But her satisfaction was only momentary as she noticed something else taking over Malcolm's face. Yes, he was embarrassed; but more than that, he was just plain hurt. Tracy fought to keep the vengeful smirk glued to her face even if her armor was being chipped away at the edges. Malcolm looked at her straight on, and shook his head before moving out of the spotlight and walking out of the room. Tracy watched him go, not doing anything. But her heart tugged at her, and she wondered if she had gone too far.

The crowd tried to focus on the performance and not so much on Tracy and Malcolm's silent war; but they noticed that shortly after Malcolm walked out, Tracy excused herself and made a beeline for the door. By this time, Doc Mayweather was getting all the brothers together.

Savoir Faire was thankfully oblivious to the drama going on offstage and went on with their set, sending the crowd into a frenzy. As they wrapped their set up, Sweets came back onstage, looking a bit flustered.

"Lord, you black people can't just ever go nowhere and have a good time without cutting up and acting a plum fool." He looked over his shoulder at Savoir Faire. "But that was awesome, ladies!" He conjured up some applause for them. He heaped up some more praise on them and led the crowd into another round of applause. "Now, this is the time I would call Dr. Xavier Houston up, but . . ." Sweets held his hand over his eyes, squinting, "I see he's on his way out with the cavalry." He purred like a hungry cat and told the audience. "And what a *wonderful calvary* it is." He yelled out, "Y'all need a horse?"

And the audience turned around to see the Brotherhood leaving the room and started laughing at his joke. "Guess not. Moving along. So, while we give the girls time for another wardrobe change"—he turned to the band—"can you guys play some upbeat old-school stepper's set jams?" He turned around and peered out into the crowd. "Where our steppers at? Where you at? Oooooh, that's it, band. This is for you, steppers. Get to steppin', y'all. And, Ms. Jessie, I know your future husband has left the room, so I'm on my way over to your table, girl. We gone show 'em how it's really done."

♦　♦　♦

The brothers and Dr. Mayweather tracked Malcolm down and found him sitting on one of the stone benches in the square. The Doc, surrounded by the brothers, approached him and asked, "Are you all right?"

There was no response.

He asked him again, "Brother Malcolm? Are you all right?"

Still no answer.

The Doc tried one more time. "Brother Malcolm, do you remember our pledge? Are you through?"

Malcolm held his head down, holding back tears. After a while, he looked up at the Doc and replied, "Doc, I believe I am. *I'm definitely through with being through. I know I need to be healed, man.*"

"Do you know what you need to do?" asked the Doc as he reached out and pulled Malcolm up off the bench.

"I think it's time for me to let this go, man. It's time for me to leave Tracy. This just confirms what we both knew all along—we're just faking the funk. I'm miserable, and she's got to be miserable too."

"Are you sure about this, brother Malcolm? This decision will have a huge impact on your relationship going forward. You know that, right?"

Malcolm looked at all the brothers and said, "I know. I just want to feel the way I felt at the retreat. That was me, man—not this person that everyone wants me to be. I love Tracy as the mother of my kids, and I definitely love my babies; but I got to love me too, right?"

All the brothers gathered around Malcolm and lifted him up in a group hug, showering him with encouraging words. He was in the midst of a storm, and he was the first to be healed. He asked DK to drive him home, where he quickly packed a couple of bags. DK didn't ask him where he was staying or going, or what his plans were; he just drove Malcolm to his house. He left him there and headed back to an emptying Bailey's where he found Bee clearing the tables in the party room.

"Hey girl. I see there's just a few stragglers at the buffet table fixing some to-go plates." He laughed and tried to make a joke. "Ain't they ghetto?"

"Okay!" she answered. "I know that's right, but hey, we'll just throw it in the trash anyway."

"How did everything go tonight?"

"Boy! Before or after all the drama!?"

"Yah. What a mess, huh?"

"I know. It was like watching a soap opera," she said with a laugh. "Aren't you going home yet?"

DK shook his head. "I actually left and came back . . . for you," he said bashfully, rubbing the back of his neck.

Bee looked up at him with those wide brown eyes, her mouth curling into a pout. "I'm going to have to stay here and clean all of this up, and then I still have to clean up in the main dining room."

He tried to hide his disappointment at her obvious rebuff. "Oh. Okay. Yeah, I get it."

Bee immediately shook her head. "No, no, that's not what I meant."

DK puffed out his chest, feeling a bit stupid for jumping to conclusions. It sounded as though Bee was willing to give him a chance after all; and the chemistry, heat, and sexual tension between the two of them was intense. And somehow, during the course of the night, he found his body pressed against hers; and their lips were locked in a passionate kiss, his tongue teasingly at play with hers. Bee could feel his hardness press against her thigh, and she moved her leg, pressing it harder against his dick to get a good feel of the length and width of it.

DK backed Bee up against the wall, passionately kissing her mouth, her nose, her eyes, and her ears. Eventually, he had to pull himself back, like he did back in the day when he was a teenager, slow-grind dancing with a girl in the basement with the blue light on and having to stick his butt out 'cause he was either embarrassed by the raging hard-on he had and absolutely did not want her to know, or was on the verge of exploding, big-time, in his pants.

"I think I probably should be going," he said, as he could feel his wet boxer briefs sticking to his leg from all his precum. He knew that if Bee moved her leg up and down one more time, she was going to make him cream in his pants.

"Yah," Bee said, blushing, "that's probably a good idea."

"Can I call you later tonight?" he asked, taking out his cell phone. "What's your number?"

"Give me that," Bee said jokingly, plucking the phone out of his hand. "Oh, wait, I think you have a call coming through." She started laughing. "Hmm. And what's this all about?" She started reading the message: "'Do not answer. It's—'"

DK grabbed the phone from Bee's hand, and he watched the screen flash the judge's name. *Why is the judge calling me at this hour?* He was really getting irritated by the judge's relentlessness. He was now calling two to three times a day, writing letters, which DK tore up and threw in the trash without reading. He even had messengers stop by the station; luckily, DK's assistant was smart enough to make up a story and send them away.

"Maybe it's something really important?" Bee suggested.

DK shrugged. "Whatever it is, it can wait 'til later. Now, where were we? Program your number in. What time should I call you tonight?"

"I should be home by 2:00 AM. You can give me a call after that."

"I will," he said as he gently held Bee's chin and guided her lips up to his.

"Whew! Mr. DK Niles, what am I going to do with you?"

DK smiled and kissed her lips again. "Mmm. I bet we can come up with something." He laughed. "Let me get out of here before we get ourselves into some trouble."

Bee laughed, "Okay, hon. I'll be waiting for my call."

DK pimped out of the room, turned around, and struck a pose. "I gotcha, girl. Hold on, let me take a picture of your beautiful smile so I'll have something to look at while I'm talking to you."

As DK drove home, he kept looking at Bee's picture. When he got home, he found Malcolm asleep in the living room with the TV on. He turned the TV off, got a blanket, and covered him. He looked at the clock and gave Bee a few minutes before calling. The two had so much in common. They talked and talked and talked until the sunrise started casting light into their bedroom windows. DK asked Bee to join him for breakfast at a local Waffle Shack; he just didn't want to stop talking to her.

And as they each got ready to meet, they were thinking, *This is going to be a good day.*

Chapter 25

Creep, Creep, Creep

November 1, 2009

*F*or a bunch of self-proclaimed creepers, these guys, JJ and Max, certainly sucked at creeping. It took a couple of days before Sweets finally confirmed his suspicion, *Are they following me?* he asked himself for the umpteenth time, because he'd been spotting these two, with their cameras and little unmarked white van, since day one. And this was the day when his suspicion was getting the best of him.

Sitting down at a little café across the street from Sweet V's, minding himself and his chocolate-filled croissant, he fanned himself furiously, as his suspicion was getting him all hot and bothered, worked up in the worst kind of way. "This is working on my last nerve," he said as he kept looking across the street at the van, unable to take his eyes off it. Finally, he decided he'd had enough. He dropped his croissant and told the waitress, "I'll be right back, sweetie." And with theatrics only he was capable of displaying, he stomped toward the van and started banging on the sides before going around to the back.

"Hello? Hello? WHO THE HELL IS IN THERE?" he yelled as he looked through the back window. "You got thirty seconds to open up this damn door, before I call the police and tell them that TX00Q123 is the tag number of a white box truck, with a man in a hoodie inside, following my black ass around. And look"—he held his cell phone up to the window—"911 is on the screen; and I got my finger on the call button. Uh-huh, I see you. You better come on out if you know what's good for ya'. I ain't playing around neither."

Not soon after he uttered his last words, the door flew open; and Sweets glared up at a short plump white man. A high-pitched "Who!" came out of his mouth, and he thought, *I know this can't be the stalker. Not out of shape like this.* And although he wanted to laugh, he couldn't. He just stared the man down, deep frown lines running across his forehead, especially when his eyes caught the name *Creepers* on the chest pocket of the man's shirt. "*Creepers?*" he asked as the stalker, with a dumb look on his face, acknowledged the question with a slow nod of the head. "Yah, I'm with *Creepers.*"

206

Sweets just threw up his hands. "Well, I be damned." He shook his head in disbelief. "If this ain't 'bout a bitch. OH MY GOD, I CAN'T BELIEVE THIS SHIT. A bunch of dumbasses! Why the hell are y'all following me?" he asked as the man jumped down from the van's tailgate.

"Aren't y'all supposed to be following Todd?" he asked angrily, pointing a finger in the man's face. "Get to talking, 'cause I'm in no mood for bullshit today."

"Look, man, this is my first case; and I'm just doing my fucking job!" he answered. Sweat had collected on his forehead and the sweat stains in his armpits seemed to have spread down his sleeves.

Sweets didn't know what to think or say as the guy just went off and started talking, apparently to himself, answering himself. This caught Sweets off guard, and he muttered under his breath, "What is this fool doing?"

Now livid, Sweets put both hands on his forehead and slowly slid them down his face, grunting the whole time. He stood there and watched the man talk to himself. Sweets clasped his hands over his nose and mouth, shaking his head. "I don't believe this shit—dumb *and* crazy." But upon closer inspection, he noticed a tiny Bluetooth headset in the creeper's left ear. This sent him over the edge. He reached over and ripped it off and held it against his own. "Who the fuck is this?" he yelled into the earpiece

He heard only static at first. Then a voice answered, "Who the fuck is this?"

He noticed a tall thin man running toward them from the café. He had the same shirt on, and Sweets thought, *Oh shit, you done done it now, boy.*

"Look, we don't want no trouble!" the guy said through the earpiece as he approached the van with both palms raised, to signal that he didn't want to cause trouble.

"Peace, my ass. You need to tell me why you two have been following me instead of Todd!" Sweets said in a tone that left no room for arguments.

JJ and Max looked at each other and started whispering, nodding in agreement. The thin one looked back at Sweets and started talking. "I'm Max, and this here is JJ."

Sweets rolled his eyes. "And?"

"Look, dude, like I said, we don't want no trouble. We just got a lead about you and a guy named Dr. Houston. We're just doing our job, man," Max explained.

"ME AND DR. HOUSTON!? What the hell are you talking 'bout? Y'all are some real dumbasses. Y'all are supposed to be following someone else—not me!" Sweets said, bucking up to JJ as if he was about to do something. "Who authorized this?"

Max slipped his hands in his jeans and began bouncing on the balls of his feet. He wanted to say "Call the station," but he knew the station didn't know anything about all of this, because he had canceled Sweets's investigation and was just doing Michael a favor. "Listen, if I show you who arranged this, who canceled your investigation and turned the shit around on you, you got to promise to forget all about this here. Okay?"

Sweets's eyes widened. He was stunned by what Max had told him and just nodded his head—"Yes, yes, of course"—because he was desperate to find out who did this to him, spoiling his vengeful plans.

Max reached in his pocket, took out his cell phone, and started scrolling through a list of names and numbers. "This gone be the end of this, right, man?"

Sweets nodded as he waited for Max to turn the cell phone around. "It's actually a friend of mine, not a friend-friend, but I know him well enough. He's good people. Told me that some nut—I guess that's you—was trying to do him in."

When Sweets saw the name on the cell phone screen, his nostrils widened, and his brows furrowed—all of which said, *I'm pissed!* "Is that fucking so!" he exclaimed as he pushed the phone away. "The nerve. The fucking nerve! Even trying to bring Dr. Houston into this." He folded his arms across his chest and sighed deeply, shaking his head. "We're good. I'm gone forget this like I promised. I'm definitely a man of my words. But don't get it twisted. If I even think I see a white van following me around, let me tell you—you, JJ here, and everybody up at that fucking *Creepers* will be speaking to my motherfucking lawyers. Capice?"

Max and JJ nodded as Sweets mouthed, "I'm gone get him. I'm gone get him. I'm gone get him."

◆ ◆ ◆

"K103.5, K103.5, K103.5. It's da end of da weekend. Booooo! Yah, I know; but we're starting da week off right with da freshest radio programming to hit da airwaves. Yah, you got it. Da Brotherhood's back in da house, and we're in full effect tonight. Nobody's missing. Haha! Family, its Sunday, November 8, ten o'clock, a sultry sixty-nine degrees outside with a nice southeasterly wind blowing through the D-Town. And yes, this is your boy Brass in da pilot's seat tonight.

"So, say hello to my boys DK (sitting ova here with his legs all up, acting like he has da night off), Miguel (eight more days, man), Michael (wassup, Mikey-Mike), Donnell (with his bad [beep]), Xavier (da other doc in da house), Quentin (our proud single dad; wassup, lil' Me-laaay!), Pastor Levine (gettin' his church on from Greater Antioch), Malcolm (da great American chef-to-be), Doc Mayweather (who'll be keeping it real up in here with me), and our boy Magic (who's gonna help me out by counting down the best love songs by my favorite male artists—Brass's *Top Ten All-Time Favorite Slow Jams*).

"Now dat dat's out of the way, we're gonna get right down to it. Starting the countdown, coming in at number 10 is Barry White with 'Can't Get Enough of Your Love.' And, family, dem blue lights in dem basements and on dem dare porches were glowing something strong when dis jam came out. Callers, call in if you know what I'm talkin' 'bout."

As the music played, Brass briefed the brothers on the night's topic; and the phone lines started blowing up about Barry White and those blue-light in the basement nights. Magic prepped the first caller; and as the music came to an end, he announced who was on the line.

"Brass, I have Shirley on the line with a comment."

"Ms. Shirley, whatchu know 'bout dis here music, gul? Hey, this ain't da Shirley Brown that sang that song . . . what is it, y'all?"

DK said, "'Woman to Woman,' man."

"Yah, that's it."

Shirley cleared her throat and answered, "No, but I've had to call one or two skeezas about my man."

"Haha! Look here, Shirley, it's strange as [beep] dat you called up here when you did. I'm gone use you as a seque to announce da discussion for tonight." Brass laughed and then asked, "So, Ms. Shirley, tell us why you had to call some sistas up about your man."

"Lord, I was calling to talk about Barry White, 'cause I haven't heard that song, or his music, in soooo long. Thank you, Brass. It's so good to hear his voice again. But to answer your question, *no*, I didn't just call her out. I checked both of them. I put him in check for cheating and let her know that he had a woman: First call, shame on you. Second call, shame on me. Third call, bi[beep], I'm gone kick your motha[beeeeeeep]."

"Shirley, you ain't right. Bye, gul. Now, our number 9 song is by a Motown legend; and we're playing it to get y'all in the mood for our topic tonight: 'Why Black Folk Always Creep.' We gone continue the countdown with a song from 1973. Here's the legendary Marvin Gaye, family, singing my number 9 all-time favorite jam—'Let's Get It On.' 'Cause that's exactly what we're doing—according to some reports out there—getting it on."

"There goes them morals again, man—spiritually adept, but morally corrupt."

Brass laughed. "That's our boy Magic, y'all. Hold that thought, man. Family, when we come back, we gone have Doc Mayweather give us the scientific reason why men and women cheat. And yah, I said women, 'cause y'all women cheat *too*. Y'all just don't get caught. I bet a couple of us brothers up here in the studio can testify to that."

Malcolm said, "Yes, lawd."

Brass yelled out "HALLELUJAH!" and started tapping his shoes on the studio floor, making it sound as if he was shouting. "Get ready, Doc. We fixin' to blow this [beep] out da water, man. Controversy, controversy, controversy. We'll be back, family . . . Awe, shucks now. Sing it, Marvin. Sing that song, man."

When *The Brotherhood* came back on the air, Brass reiterated to the listeners that the leader of the night's session had the option of letting the brothers talk about anything or use their wild card to steer the discussion in whatever direction he chose. For tonight, Brass indicated that he chose to let the K103.5 listeners choose the topic. "Okay, family, on da *DK and Magic Morning Show*, beginning last Monday, we asked you to pick a topic dat you wanted to hear da brothers talk about; and folks, creepin' had da most votes and won out as da topic you wanted *The Brotherhood* to talk about. So, Doc? Our girl Jessie—who's right outside da booth, family—said dat there was some scientific information you'd like to share with da family and get their opinion on. So, what's the information?"

The whole studio was quiet as the Doc leaned into his microphone; cleared his throat; and, without missing a beat, had the phone lines lighting up when he told the listeners, "So, in the grand scheme of things, not too many animals— and we're a part of the earth's animal kingdom—mate for life. The BBC, British Broadcasting Corporation, had an interesting article in their Science and Technology section which the journal *Science* published sometime ago."

"The BBC?" asked DK.

"Yah," said Xavier, grabbing his mic. "Most American journalists won't publish articles that deal with information that may be too far to the left of conventional thinking."

Brass told him, "Go 'head, Doc. Bring it home, man." He hushed DK and X with a gesture of his hand, causing them to look at him crazy.

"Thank you, brother Brass," the Doc said, laughing a little. "As I was saying, only about 3 percent of the earth's mammals are monogamous, and we're not one of them."

"What!"

"That's right, brother Brass. Animals that fool around, according to the journal, do so because of a biological urge. In a monogamous relationship, an animal, including us humans, are either biologically monogamous or socially monogamous. Although there are exceptions to every rule, most humans are socially monogamous."

"Socially monogamous? What does that mean, Doc?" asked Brass.

"You learned the behavior. Whether you learned it from Momma, Daddy, Big Momma, Auntie Pearl, school, church, wherever."

Brass and the other brothers kept saying, "WHAT?"

"That's right, brothers. You eat because of what?"

"I guess to survive, aye, Doc?" said Malcolm as he gave everybody the sign that he had to use the bathroom. Mike got up and joined him.

"Yelp, and if you put it into perspective, most people cheat because we're just naturally wired to do so—according to the scientific journals, that is. When it comes to me, I look; but because of my love for my wife—and I've been taught that it's wrong to cheat—I don't touch."

Brass said, "Family, there you go. I see the lights are telling us that the phone lines are be-be-be-bee-zee. Oh my god, it's like Christmas up in here with all dese red lights blinking. Let's take a few calls, but I wanna flip the script before we do. So, family, the Doc has given us the 4-1-1, but what are some of the other reasons you think men and women creep? Caller, you're on da air. Can you hear me?"

"Uh-huh, I'm here. Listen, I heard Ms. Jessie likes tea? Well, baby, have I got some tea for her—and oh, I'm 'bout to spill it. I'm gone spill this tea, honey."

"Dude? You mean Jessie, as in Jessie Harris? From the *Love Forum* divas? Our program director?" Brass clarified as he waved for her to come into the studio.

"Uh-huh."

"Yo, man, who is this?" DK asked.

"DK, you know who this is. Don't play. And some of you other people in there know who I am too. Okay! I'm just calling to let you know the other reason why men creep."

"Why's that?" asked DK.

"'Cause they be sleeping with other men's honey."

"Sweets?" asked DK as he put his hand over the mic. "Hold up, Brass, let's go to break. Matter of fact, what's the number 8 song in Brass's all-time-favorites collection?"

Brass was caught off guard. He was just a shaking. It was apparent that Sweets was pissed, and Brass looked at DK with a blank—*What do I do?*—expression on his face.

"The family can't hear you, Brass. What's the number 8 song, man?" asked DK again. "And give us the number 7 song too, while you're at it."

Brass looked down at his list. "Uhm . . . DK . . . uhm . . . uhm . . . number 8 . . . dat . . . 1992 love song by . . . uhm . . . the ultimate crooner . . . uhm . . . Brian McKnight with 'One Last Cry,' followed by a tie at number 7—Eric Benét with his 2005 hit, 'I Wanna Be Loved,' and Maxwell's 2009 jam, 'Pretty Wings.'"

"Cool. Cool," DK told him. "Magic? Take us away, man. I believe it's about to get crunk up in here. Family, we're going to break and handle some business—*off* the air! So here's an extended stint of Brian McKnight, Eric Benét, and Maxwell.

DK looked around the room, giving all the brothers a puzzled look before asking, "Okay, Sweets, what's going on? And where's V?"

"This ain't about Ms. V," he said, distaste unmistakable in his voice. "It's about Ms. Jessie."

Jessie asked, "Hey, Sweets, boy, what's going on with you?" And she started to laugh, trying to downplay everything, hoping he wasn't about to do what she thought he was going to do. And with an uneasy feeling, she decided not to take any chances. She asked, "Hey, Sweets, does this have to do with what we discussed in the ladies' room a couple of months ago?"

"Yes, ma'am," he answered. "And I'm thoroughly pissed right about now."

"Sweets, I know you're upset; and so am I, but—"

"Girl, you don't know the half of it. I want you to listen to this, 'cause this is just 'bout a bitch." There was some fumbling in the background and some static, and then Sweets said, "JJ and Max, I know I gave you my word; but right about now, my word ain't about shit. Payback's a bitch." And you could hear a somewhat-grainy recording with cars passing by with horns blaring, and people on the street talking, and then Sweets's voice coming on loud and clear: "Hello? Hello? Who the *hell* is in there?" You could also hear a whole lot of banging against a door or wall going on in the background.

Sweets said, "This is what I recorded earlier today."

He let it play, and X couldn't believe it. "What? Is this for real, man?" he asked in a hurt voice. "Are you talking about me?"

"Hmm-huh," said Sweets. "And I called Todd on it too. I sure did. And when I played it for him, do you know what he told me?"

It was as though death had taken over the studio. Nobody really wanted to say anything, but Sweets told them anyway. "He told me that I was a messy, vindictive queen—worse than a woman, and hell, he might as well be with one if he had to go through this shit. As a matter of fact, that's exactly what he was going to do 'cause that's what everybody expected of him anyway."

Jessie was stunned—so shaken up she had to sit down, causing X to get up and run over to her; trying to comfort her and make sure she was okay. "Oh my god, Sweets! Oh my god," she kept on telling him.

It didn't take much for the brothers to put two and two together; and when the door to the studio opened, the scene got really tense.

"Hey, what's going on?" Mike asked as he and Malcolm walked back in and he recognized Sweets's voice on the line.

"And if you're listening right now, Mr. Todd, I only got one thing to say to you." Sweets paused, and a deep exhalation of breath could be heard over the line. "Take care, and I wish you well. Whatever you decide, I guess you know what's best for you."

Mike didn't know what to think. He went off the deep end, yelling for someone to tell him what the hell was going on and punching holes in the studio walls. Donnell jumped up and pushed him and Malcolm out of the room to explain to them what just went down. Everybody watched them through the studio's windows, and DK didn't even say thank you or good-bye to Sweets. He just dropped the call.

Donnell opened the door, and all eyes were on him. He didn't have time to make it past the door's threshold because DK cornered him and asked, "And?"

Donnell didn't look at anyone in particular and just said that Mike was outta there. "Mike said that there's too much fucking drama going on with the Brotherhood, and that, what just went down wasn't right—that we entertained this freakin' nigga."

Malcolm came in behind him after walking Mike to the elevator, to make sure he was all right, and said the same thing: "Man, that wasn't right. How y'all gone destroy a good man like that?" he asked, somewhat angry and hurt.

There was no explanation offered. The atmosphere inside the studio was nothing but dark and gloomy. Everyone was preoccupied with the scandal that had just happened, and it was especially hard on Malcolm and Jessie. Although Jessie was saddened and felt Sweets's pain, she was able to breathe a sigh of relief that things didn't spiral out of control and wreak permanent damage in people's lives. Malcolm, on the other hand, sat stunned. He didn't know what to think or believe.

As everyone settled in for a peaceful night's rest, DK pressed the button for his mic to come on as Jessie signaled that they were on air. "Good evening, ladies and gentlemen, and welcome back to *The Brotherhood*. Now to pull y'all in on what just went down, let's just say that the last caller had an interesting take on why men and women cheat—this caller said one reason is not being able to live their lives because of society's expectations or whatnot. So whatever people can't do in the light—guess what? They do it in the dark."

Magic piped up. "Didn't Jill Scott sing something about what comes to the light—"

"Yah, she did, Magic, but in a different context. And quit interrupting, man. But on a more somber note, family, I might as well get this out of the way. One of our brothers, Mikey-Mike, has just left the building." DK paused. "Brother, I hope you're doing fine, wherever you may be right now. And I'm dedicating this song, "Perfectless" by Tevin Campbell, to him, family. I think it speaks volumes about what just went down in here . . . 'cause we need to be able to live in harmony, y'all—let people be who they are and live their own song. 'Cause in the end, if what I do doesn't hurt you or nobody else, who gives an effin' bleep."

As the night went on, the K103.5 listeners, clueless to what happened earlier, continued with the heated debate on creepin'. And as midnight approached, Brass began to do a recap for the Best Love Songs According to Brass. "And that's da gospel," he said as he looked down at his paper and began to read:

"Number 10, family, is Barry White's 'Can't Get Enough of Your Love.'

"Coming in at number 9 is Marvin Gaye's 'Let's Get It On.'

"Brian McKnight came in strong with 'One Last Cry' at number 8.

"Number 7, 6, and 5 were all ties. Number 7 was a tie between Eric Benét's 'I Wanna Be Loved' and Maxwell's 'Pretty Wings.' Our second tie of the night was a battle for da number 6 spot; and our boys Anthony Hamilton, with his 2008 jam 'The Point of It All,' and Musiq, with his Y2K signature hit, 'Love,' took this spot. Our last tie for da night, coming in at number 5, is 'With You' by dat redheaded boy Tony Terry, and 'Giving My All to You' by our boy Johnny Gill, who made all the ladies swoon.

"Number 4 was da Teddy Bear himself, Mr. Teddy Pendergrass, with 'Come Go with Me.'

"And coming in at number 3 is da master of love himself, Mr. Luther Vandross, with his 1983 hit, 'Superstar/Until You Come Back to Me (That's What I'm Gonna Do)'

"Donny Hathaway, who you just heard, took da number 2 spot with his 1971 classic, 'A Song for You.'

"And my number 1 all-time favorite slow jam—Magic, can I have a drumroll please?" Brass asked, motioning to Magic. The drumroll ended with a whole lot of cheering. "Ladies and gentlemen, da number 1 song in da Best Love Songs According to Brass—and that's da gospel, peeps—is the ultimate seventies jam. Family, da number 1 song can only be *da hurt man's national anthem*—"'Cause I Love You,' by our boy Lenny Williams."

Brass folded up his list and winked over at DK. "Ladies, you say black men don't know nothing or understand anything about love. Well, I beg to differ. And your boy just gave you ten reasons why. DK, it's on you, man. And, brothers . . . hey, homeys, keep doing what you do—putting it down with da ladies."

Suddenly, Jessie was jumping up and down, signaling to him and DK through the window. All the brothers turned to see what all the commotion was about, and Brass frowned when he saw the two officers appear behind her. "Good night, family. Same time, same place next week," he said as he pressed his mic's Off button and ripped his headset away from his ears. "Jess, what's going on?" he yelled through the glass.

The two officers stormed inside the booth and headed toward Brass, who looked on nervously at the armed police officers as they reached for him and cuffed his hands behind his back. "Brasselton Minyard, you are hereby placed under arrest." One of the officers started to read him his rights.

"What the fuck is going on here!" DK yelled, feeling protective of his brother. He had always thought of Brass as his little protégé.

The officer read out a long list of charges and then calmly explained, "You can come down to the station with all your questions; but for now, we have a warrant to bring you in."

DK held his hands up. He and the rest of the brothers knew it would be of no use to argue. They might only end up with more trouble than what they started with. As they dragged Brass away, DK called out his name. Brass slowly looked back at them, a desperate look on his face.

"We're going to take care of this, Brass. Don't you worry, man," DK promised.

Brass didn't look as though he put much stock in DK's words, but he nodded nonetheless.

Chapter 26

Something's Got a Hold of Me

"**Y**ou dirty son of a bitch! You son of a bitch! Haven't you done enough?" Pat yelled into the phone, her hands shaking with anger. She should have killed him when she had the chance; but now, she just wished she could reach into the phone's speaker and strangle the hell out of Donnell with her bare hands. She'd do it too and not feel a bit sorry. "Nasty motherfucker!" she kept saying as she stared with bloodshot eyes at an e-mail on her bedroom computer. Unable to tear her eyes away from the video clip playing in one corner of the screen, she watched the scene play out as Pastor Levine was engaged in some sort of heated argument with a scantily clad woman she had never seen or heard of before. She stood horrified, shaking her head, thinking, *What was he thinking about?* But the shocker came next: "OH MY GOD!" she screamed as she stared at the scantily clad woman, who looked to be backing it up on the pastor. Pat grabbed at her neck and swallowed as she watched the pastor grab the woman's waist. And then the video went black.

Donnell laughed mockingly on the other end, reveling in the distress and heartache he was causing. "Why are you mad at me, Pat? You should channel all that anger toward that despicable lover of yours. You never can keep a good man, can you? You just drive them to do nasty things," he taunted. "Pastor, my ass. Getting a lap dance from that nasty, dirty tramp of a daughter—"

"DAUGHTER!?" she asked.

"That's right. His *daughter*—that's just *sick*. And I heard she gets down with the get down too. Just disgusting . . . And him, acting so self-righteous all the time, talking about saving souls. Hell, he needs to work on his own damn soul, and that nasty daughter of his too, with his pompous ass. What a hypocrite. What would the church and those good ole Christian folk think about all this? Huh?"

"Oooooh! You make me *sick*! You'll never be half the man that he is!" Pat retorted, gritting her teeth. "How could I have ever married you?"

"Whatever, Pat. *Nasty things*, remember that. You just drive us to keep things from your ass—like me with Val, and now the pastor with that Chéri, his freaky-ass daughter. And what do we eventually do?" He started laughing and clapping his hands. "We leave," he said, taunting her.

"I would be hurt, except I wouldn't expect more from a sexist lowly piece of filth like you. I pity Val. She got stuck with a pig like you," Pat said.

Donnell just cackled, knowing that he had the upper hand in the situation. Earlier in the week, his lawyers told him that things were looking bleak for him, as mothers typically got custody of the children; and with the pastor—a good, upstanding citizen—in the picture, it made the forecast much bleaker for him. "Like I care about what you think of me, Pat? That's just precious. You listen here, and you listen good: If you don't want me to expose the pastor for what he really is—a hack—you better start thinking about dropping everything. If you don't, I'm gonna expose him for what he really is. It's up to you, Pat. You choose."

The phone's *click* signaled the end of the call. Pat dropped it to the wooden floor of her apartment with a thud. Her shoulders curled inward as her body was racked with sobs.

"Pat, what's wrong?"

She whipped her head around to discover Pastor Levine standing right behind her, fresh out of the shower with a towel wrapped around him. His eyes zeroed in on the video playing on the computer and he saw the e-mail that told him it came from Donnell. It didn't take a genius to put two and two together.

"I'm so sorry!" Pat cried out as she wrapped her arms around Pastor Levine's middle, her tears pouring onto his bare chest.

He wrapped his arms around her and kissed the top of her head, smelling the sweet scent of her hair. "Shhh, it's not your fault. You didn't do anything," he assured her.

"Oh, Richard, what are we going to do?" she asked desperately.

The pastor cupped her face in his hands and forced her to look into his eyes. For a moment, he was awed by this woman's face—this woman who had suffered so much pain. From cancer to the emotional torture and abuse at the hands of Donnell, who was still causing her pain. It was a testament to the strength of her heart that she could still look at him with such kind eyes; and although his heart said no, he mustered up enough strength to tell her, "You're going to keep fighting for your kids. I won't let you lose them on my account. I'm not going to let that happen."

Pat's heart ached with what the pastor was telling her, but she didn't protest. She loved Richard, and he had done so much for her; but her children were her life. "What's going to happen now?" she asked.

"I guess we'll need to distance ourselves from each other," he said, gathering up his clothes. "Donnell may not have done it with the best of intentions, God knows that, but you know, Pat"—he took a deep breath, his eyes downcast and his lower lip quivering—"he's right. I've been hiding this secret for a long, long time. The embarrassment was just too much, and I've tainted my own morals trying to hide it . . . and my past." The pastor stopped and stood in front of Pat, motioning to her, with the move of his head, to sit down on the bed. "One of the brothers said that the most profound testimonies comes from true life experiences. I believe the congregation has a right to know about my past, this secret I've been keeping, and what kind of man has been leading them."

Pat felt compelled to get up and wrap him in a tight embrace. "You're a good man, Richard. A good man."

The pastor smiled as he hugged her. "I'm no saint now. I got to pay my dues like everyone else." He kissed her ear and rubbed her back. "We'll get through this, Pat. And if it's God's will, we'll find our way back to each other."

Pat left the bedroom in tears, and the pastor gathered up the rest of his clothes and belongings and walked out of her apartment, and out of her life. He got in his car and just sat there, not knowing what to do or whom to trust. His heart was heavy and burdened. He couldn't trust anyone in the church: While they had good intentions and meant well, they nevertheless had a gossiping nature; and he didn't need their good intentions right now. He started fumbling around in the car's center console for a CD—*any* CD, he thought—to help him get through this. He grabbed a CD case, opened it, and saw Doc Mayweather's card, but no CD. He shook his head, smiled up at the car ceiling, and took this as a sign. Before he knew what he was doing, he was dialing the number to the Doc's office. A few minutes later, he was explaining everything to him.

"Well, everyone did sign a confidentiality statement, so there shouldn't be an issue there," the Doc said. "However, if this comes down to a legal proceeding, we may have an issue or two. Let's see if we can get somebody from K103.5 on the line to shed some light on this from their end."

The pastor could hear fumbling and some rustling of papers in the background before the Doc came back on the line. "I think I have DK's number around here somewhere. Hold on again, Pastor . . . Okay, I got it. I'm calling him now. As he sat and waited for DK to pick up, the pastor closed his eyes and quietly said to himself, *"I'm through with being through. Lord, God, the change is going to start right here."*

When DK picked up, they explained the situation; and he calmly assured the pastor that he had a plan. He was meeting with the judge later this week, and he would run everything by him when they met. The pastor just needed to sit tight. He told the Doc, "We'll call you if we need to, but I don't believe we will. What we're about to do shouldn't involve you. If Donnell wants to go there, we're gonna go there too."

When DK hung up the phone, he thought, *Damn! Two favors I have to ask of the judge. I hope his shady ass won't make me have to choose between Donnell, the pastor, or Brass.*

◆ ◆ ◆

It had been almost a week since Brass found himself in jail. DK, Malcolm, Quentin, Miguel, X, and the pastor had gone to see him. He had even gotten some letters from fans of the show, who offered their prayers and support; and DK brought them along, thinking it would make Brass feel better. The brothers had never set foot inside a jail, and they were a little let down when they learned they could not see Brass face-to-face. Instead, they gave the letters to the jail attendant; and then they were led to a small room with several booths.

"Booth number 9, gentlemen," the attendant told them.

There was one phone, a chair, and a small video screen in the booth. DK shrugged his shoulders and picked up the phone. He noticed the clock on the screen had started to tick down from 15:00 to 14:59 and kept counting down with each passing second. Each brother said their hellos and shared encouraging words; and before their time ran out, DK told Brass to stay strong, and that he was meeting with the judge later on and would add Brass's case to the list for the judge to work on. Brass said, "Okay," but he was worried about his job, and making sure that his moms was taken care of.

"Hey man," DK told him, "don't worry 'bout nothing. We're going to pull all the strings we can, and I'm gonna cash in all my favors to make sure you get your life back, man. And we got your moms covered too." But before hanging up and leaving, DK, with the brothers backing him up, also made Brass promise that he would turn his life around when he got out.

Brass, recognizing that there was really no one but the Brotherhood to help him, agreed in a heartbeat.

◆ ◆ ◆

Pat had been on edge the last few days since Donnell's threatening e-mail. She couldn't go another day without talking to someone. She didn't let anyone know, not even Jessie or the rest of the divas. She couldn't sleep; she had been up all night praying and praying, but she couldn't find any solace in prayer. When morning arrived, she sat in bed with her arms folded across her chest, crying. She opened one of the drawers of her nightstand to take out her Bible, hoping to find some scripture that would get her through the day at the office; but when she picked it up, Melissa's letter fell out of it into the drawer. And although she had read it hundreds of times, if not a thousand by now, she opened it and read it again. It didn't click the many times she read it before; but this time, her eyes went straight to the judge's name, and she began to read and to understand what Melissa was telling her:

Pat, girlfriend, things will look rough, but there's a rhyme and a reason why me and DK recommended you for the job with Judge Hoffanstanter, seize the moment when it comes girlfriend (you'll know when) and everything will work itself out.

And as Pat made it through another day at work, she carried Melissa's letter around with her for strength. She would read it when she got discouraged and when the work dwindled down as the clock ticked closer to five in the afternoon. She prepped herself for an impromptu meeting with the judge. She smoothed down the wrinkles on her skirt and made sure all her buttons were in place. She gave her reflection on the small compact mirror on her desk a once-over to make sure she looked clean and polished. Then she left her cubicle and walked over to the closed office door at the end of the hall. She peered through the glass window to the judge's office, to make sure he wasn't on the phone, and then knocked before slowly opening the door. She poked her head through and asked, "Judge? Excuse me."

The judge looked up from a manila folder that lay open on his lap. "Yes, Pat?" he asked.

"Judge Hoffanstanter, may I have a moment of your time?" she asked as she stepped inside but stayed at the door, one hand still on the handle.

The judge adjusted the glasses on his nose and sighed. He probably thought she was going to nag him again about some office policies or the lack of work supplies. Not that she blamed him. Pat had always been a hard worker and prided herself on her dedication and efficiency in the workplace. She also made sure everyone worked as hard as she did, including her boss. She had been especially obsessive about work during her stint at the judge's office. She couldn't help herself. Work became her getaway, the only place where she could escape her problems at home; but the look on her face told the judge that this wasn't the case.

"Take a seat, Ms. Carter." He motioned for her to come in and sit down in front of his desk.

Pat primly sat down, her ankles crossed. She fisted her hands against her skirt.

"What is this about, Pat?"

Pat took out Melissa's letter from the side pocket of her skirt and gripped it hard. She raised the letter to her mouth, kissed it, and took a deep breath and sighed as the judge watched her with a worried look on his face. Pat closed her eyes and licked her lips. "I'm sorry, Judge. I don't want you to think that all this is about anything in the office." She turned her head to the side, coughed with her hand to her mouth, and said softly, "It's personal."

The judge's gray eyebrows furrowed. "Go on," he urged her, more worried than ever.

"I know you've heard about my problems at home," she started. "My separation with my ex-husband hasn't been running as smoothly as I had hoped. We are still fighting each other for custody of the children. This time, though . . . this time he crossed the line." She had to fight back the tears of anger that threatened to spill. "He's bringing in people that shouldn't be involved."

The judge frowned, concern written on his face. He leaned forward and placed his elbows on his desk, cradling his chin in his hands. "Okay, let's talk about it. What happened?"

"Pastor Levine and I had been involved recently, something that Donnell knows. A week ago, during a party they threw for a friend of theirs, he caught the pastor in a rather compromising discussion with his daughter, on video."

"Wait, are we talking about Pastor Richard Levine of Greater Antioch? I've known Richard for years. I happen to be on the church's legal counsel board. I don't recall hearing Richard has a daughter. Are you sure about this, Pat?"

"I don't want to go into details, but it's something that could threaten the pastor's good standing in our congregation."

"Okay, so what's the down and dirty?" he asked.

"Donnell says that if I don't give up all rights to the kids, he'll expose the pastor to the congregation and, basically, end his career." Pat was breathing heavily by the end of her story. Her skirt was now wrinkled from her twisting at it.

The judge nodded slowly, calmly absorbing the information. "Is the pastor aware of all of this?"

Pat nodded. "Yes. And we had a long discussion about all of this already. Basically, we decided to end things between the two of us. He's also going to just knock the air out of that ole air bag Donnell, come clean to the church. But it's not fair that he would have to give up everything for something my heartless and shameless ex-husband has schemed up!" Pat had worked herself up to a point where she was about to jump out of her chair, but the judge stared her down with a look that forced her back in place.

"Pat? Listen to me. I know you're upset and probably want to kick Donnell's black ass this very minute. But let's walk through this. First, to be honest, I think coming clean is a smart move by the pastor. With him coming forward and telling his side of the story, whatever Donnell's original intentions are, they're thwarted. He'll have to come up with a second game plan. What we need to do is make sure that he doesn't."

Pat's facial expression changed from angry to quizzical as she nodded, listening intently to the judge.

"Do you still have the video that Donnell is blackmailing you with? Because that's what it is, essentially—blackmail," the judge said gravely, leaning back in his chair, waiting for an answer.

"I sure do. He sent me an e-mail with the video and his demands, talking 'bout how I should stop trying to get my children back. Does that work?"

The judge nodded. "You do realize that what he's doing is blackmail and extortion, which is a federal offense. You could take him down, possibly have him put in jail for this. Or you could turn this on him and use it to make sure he never bothers you again."

Pat's eyes widened at the realization. She didn't want Donnell to go to jail—the kids did need their father—but she definitely wanted him to leave her alone. And with the pastor coming clean to the congregation, he would be safe, with nothing to hide; and Donnell would not have anything to use against them. She smiled at the possibilities. They could turn the tables around on Donnell and give him the short end of the stick, for once. She jumped up from her chair and ran around the judge's desk, almost knocking him back against his credenza as she bombarded him with a big hug and an equally big kiss on the forehead.

"Oh my god, thank you. Thank you, Judge Hoffanstanter," she cried out excitedly. "And don't be trying to say that I've been in here trying to molest or sexually harass you either." And she found herself laughing through her tears of happiness. She couldn't believe that, for once, she had gotten the upper hand, that the judge had resolved *all* her problems in one sitting.

"You're welcome, Pat. Now here's to hoping you'll be a lot nicer to me in the office from time to time," he teased.

She laughed good-naturedly and promised to give him a break every now and then, to not be such a hard ass, from time to time, that is.

◆ ◆ ◆

Friday had finally arrived, and DK was eager to meet with the judge. Unbeknownst to him, the judge, after so many attempts to contact him, was excited to finally sit down and discuss a few things himself. Having cleared his schedule for a two-hour lunch break, he sat amid quiet stares and gossip about last week's *Love Forum* among the patrons, who appeared to have more of an appetite for gossip than for food.

The judge had asked to meet at Bailey's, and DK didn't question it. He figured he could drag Bee out for a quick coffee break afterward. DK and Bee horsed around, and she noticed he was a little nervous. She brought a drink over, wrapped in napkins so no one would notice, and told him, "Looks like you need something to calm your nerves." *And she was right*, he thought. He took the screwdriver to calm his nerves, and he felt a bit wretched about meeting the judge because he had his own motives for agreeing to meet with him. For one, he needed some help for Brass's case and knew that the judge's influence would be beneficial for them. And, two, he needed to discuss the pastor's issue.

DK kept watching the entrance to the dining room and perked up when he saw the judge making his way through the maze of tables, texting as he walked. He huffed as he took a seat across from DK, grabbing the glass of water in front of him and gulping down half its contents before acknowledging him.

"DK 'Love' Niles. How you doing? Man, it's a good thing I finally got a hold of you. You're one tough man to track down," the judge said in his gravelly voice, trying to recover from his apparent rush to get there.

DK squirmed in his chair. He knew that he was the sole reason for the holdup. He didn't know what could have been so important for the judge to need to talk to him, but he wanted to get his business out of the way before the judge went into his spiel. "So, Judge, remember that favor me and Melissa talked to you about?" DK scratched his head. "Man, I think it was after you got elected, and it was the grand opening of Bailey's. Well . . . I kinda need to cash that favor in, if you don't mind," he said.

"What are you talking about, Love Niles?" the judge asked as he continued texting.

"I need to talk to you about my boy Brass and Pastor Levine, if you don't mind."

"If you talking about that issue Pastor Levine and Pat are going through with Donnell and that video he sent them, I've already taken care of that. And I already know about Brass being in jail from Doc Mayweather. You just e-mail me all the information, and I'll see if I can take care of it."

DK looked across the table at the judge with a look that said, *Okay!* "That was easier than I thought it was going to be. So you gonna tell me what this meeting's about?" he asked. "Why have you been trying to get me to meet with you for"—DK looked up at the ceiling, counting—"almost the last five months?"

"In a second. I'm just waiting for our third companion," the judge said.

DK eyed him curiously. He thought it was just the two of them. Bee came up to the table just then. "Hi, Judge," she said, grabbing her order pad from her apron pocket. "What can I get you to drink, hon?"

The judge kept on texting and said without looking up, "Bee, I think I'll have some of that good ole sweet tea of yawls."

At that moment, Chef Luda appeared at the judge's side; and Bee said, "Okay, hon." She patted Chef Luda on the shoulder before heading off to the bar.

"Sit on down, Luda," the judge said, patting the seat of the chair next to him. DK didn't know what to make of all of this. First, he thought it was about that apprenticeship stuff, but he hadn't made up his mind about letting them know about Malcolm yet. And he and Bee didn't tell anyone about them dating, so he knew that wasn't it either. So it came as a shock when he came to the table and sat down between Judge Hoffanstanter and himself.

"What's going on here?" DK asked, suddenly getting a nervous knot in the pit of his stomach.

"DK, I am aware that you and Chef Luda have met before," the judge started.

The two men nodded to confirm the judge's assumptions.

"Over a year ago, my frat brother here asked me to help him find someone that would make his transition much more peaceful and complete."

"Transition?" asked DK.

"Yah, DK, I'm not faring so well. I don't know how much time I have left in dis here world, so I started getting my affairs in order. I needed to set some things straight in my life, and I needed to right some wrongs."

DK looked at Chef Luda and then at the judge, as if to say, *What the fuck are y'all talking about?*

Then the judge said something that threw his world in a tailspin: "DK, it took me a while, but I've compiled all the data." He reached inside his coat pocket and took out a brown envelope and handed it to DK. "The lost young boy that Luda asked me to search for turned out to be you, DK 'Love' Niles."

"What?" DK asked, shaking his head, looking at the two men as if he had just been hit in the face with a bat.

"DK, I don't know what to say. I guess I needed to find my way. And that didn't include being tied down with a child at that time. Time passed by, and memories faded; but after Momma passed away, I remembered how she always used to ask me, 'Dickey, whateva happen to that stray?' *Stray* was a word she used to call other people's kids. I knew I had to find you. But after you and your mother moved away from Albany, I had no way to contact you. Through the years, I tried to search for y'all through some of the old relatives I knew of; but that never amounted to anything—almost like they didn't want me to know." Chef Luda reached across the table for DK's hand, but DK instinctively pulled it back.

Chef Luda let that pass. "Well . . . I went to the judge here, hoping he could help me search as I knew he would have more access to things, like records."

DK felt as though a train wreck was unfolding before his eyes, hoping it wouldn't hit but remaining powerless to stop it. His hands shook as the realization came to him; he knew it before the judge said it.

"After much searching through old records, I was finally able to locate your son, Chef Luda." Judge Hoffanstantet turned to DK. "DK, meet your father."

Suddenly, there was a thunderous crash as a tray with sweet tea and a screwdriver crashed to the floor, followed by the high-pitched, shrill "No!" coming out of a shocked Bee's mouth.

The three men looked up and saw a horrified Bee break down, crying "No!" over and over, tears streaming down her face. DK saw the pain on Bee's face as she dropped down beside the table and knelt down by her father's side, holding on to his thighs.

"It can't be! IT CAN'T BE! DK can't be your son!" she said, her eyes begging for the judge's words to be nothing but cruel lies. "He's the one . . . he's the one," she cried out.

Chef Luda clutched his chest as his eyes widened in horror. "He was the man? The one you wanted me to meet?"

Bee didn't need to say anything; her eyes said it all.

They never heard what Chef Luda had to say as his eyes rolled to the back of his head, and then he fell to the floor.

Chapter 27

The Love Forum: A Special Edition
Chile! Whatchu Talkin' 'Bout?
(DK's POV)

Saturday, November 7, 2009

*I*t had been one hell of a tumultuous week for the Brotherhood, especially for me. And just like Jessie, I found myself walking down Ms. Doretha's driveway. Melissa said that I would know when to see her—about me, that is. And after this thing with Chef Luda and Bee, just like what happened with Jessie, Ms. Doretha's name kept popping up in my mind. And although I hate to admit it, I was hurting; and I guess I needed some answers that good ole Doc Mayweather wouldn't be able to give me.

I hadn't seen Ms. Doretha since the "Plagues" episode of *The Brotherhood*; and just as she said I would, there I was, standing right at her doorstep with a heavy heart and my finger on the intercom button. Before I could even press it, "Hello, dear" came through the intercom. "I've been expecting your arrival," she said.

The lock clicked, and the door swung open; and there stood Ms. Doretha. "Come on in, dear. I've made us some tea," she said as she took my hand and guided me to the kitchen.

I didn't know what to say, and I guess she sensed it as she pulled out a chair that had a deck of cards in front of it and a nice cup and saucer. Nice china. Ms. Doretha had some class. She patted me on the shoulder as I sat down. "Sugar or honey with your tea?" she asked.

"Sugar please," I replied, and she poured the tea in the cup and placed a bowl of sugar down in front of me.

"Well, dear," she said as she pulled up a chair beside me and cradled her head in her hand, "you must know who your father is—true?"

"Yes, ma'am," I said.

"I guess the next question you must answer is, what are you going to do with this newfound information . . . with the relationship? Are you going to walk away, or forgive and embrace him and your new family?" She poured herself a cup of tea and added a little honey in it. Then she giggled and looked over at me. "Lord, boy, you're a mess." She picked up the cards and told me to pick one. I did, and she asked, "What is it?"

I looked deep in her eyes as I showed her what I had picked.

"The Judgment Card, dear. This is a hard card to read sometimes, but I'm all too familiar with your journey. Your past has met the present, and you must choose which direction you want to take so that you can move on with your future."

I shook my head as I gave her a puzzled look. "Okay, what are you saying, Ms. Doretha? Come at me straight. I can take it."

She hummed and smiled at me. Then she looked me in the eyes—for a long time. "Dear, you've dug up the grave, and the coffin is open. What you've sought all your life, the answer to your prayers, is now staring you dead in the face. Nothing's buried anymore. You're going to have to face what you're going to have to face—no matter how long you put it off. Once you face it, you'll put it to rest; and you'll be able to move on. This card, for you, is about healing and renewing yourself, making a decision, forgiving, and moving on."

◆ ◆ ◆

Sunday, November 8, 2009. K103.5's *The Brotherhood.* After last week's disastrous show, every one of us was looking over our shoulders, making damn well sure we weren't being creeped ourselves. And I'd be straight-out lying if last week's *Creepers* mess didn't make for some real tense situations among the brothers. Hell, it was so intense, and emotions were running so high that we were either yelling and hanging up on each other, blasting each other on *other* radio and TV programs—'cause everybody was calling us up, wanting a piece of the action—or avoiding one another as if a deadly plague was spreading through the group, knocking us off one by one. Come to think about it, that's exactly how it was going down.

Donnell had outright quit. The fiasco involving Pastor Levine and Pat didn't go down too well, and boy, were we all pissed at him over that. But despite him being underhanded—what with all that conniving shit he did to keep his kids, whom he eventually lost anyway—we broke down and begged him to come back to *The Brotherhood,* thinking we could help him turn everything around; but no one could convince him to do the right thing by the pastor and Pat: that was to apologize and just come back on the show. In all honesty, though, most of us were thinking that it probably was a good thing he was gone for good. You can't change or fix somebody who doesn't want to be changed or fixed.

And as for our boy Mike, he wouldn't even return our phone calls. It was as though he had fallen off the face of the earth. Or maybe we were just dead to him. Even his own brother, Malcolm, had a hard time contacting him; and when he did, there was nothing Malcolm could say or do to persuade him to come back, or even just to talk to us. All Malcolm would tell us was that Mike was leaving, something about him pursuing a job offer out of state or something like that, and that he didn't have any plans of returning. And although I hurt for Donnell, the pastor, and Mike, again, I found myself in another effin' quandary: *how to turn this shit back around.*

As for my girl Jessie, she was going through her own issues—boy, was she going through them—and wasn't faring much better at coming up with a sound plan on what to do with *The Brotherhood*; and I really didn't think she cared. So she was no help. And I don't know why, but I had a flashback and remembered what the Doc told us back at the retreat—that some brothers would drop out and try to make it on their own. I guess he was right, and I was thinking, *Who's gonna be next?* And with that thought and the realization that not one brother, not one, wanted to come back on the show this week, I knew I had to improvise and come up with something. And I'll be damned. It was as though fate had stepped in and opened a window and poured in a blessing. I got an interesting, if not emotionally charged, phone call from V and Sweets.

Sweets said he had a whole lot of shit that he needed to get off his chest, and V followed up and pointed out that considering last week's show, and her own life experience, if we were going to continue doing a show about black men, we couldn't do one without having a discussion about a voice that had been silent within the black community for a long, long time. And I won't lie, I hesitated on this one. I really didn't know what to say when they called to ask me if they could come on. I was a little uncomfortable at first, but I was always a champion for the underdog; and when they drilled home their point, especially with V's story—and damn, what a shocker—I couldn't help but agree.

So after a good many phone calls to *Creepers* (poor Max and JJ), and with Demetrius's blessing—a very broken-down Jessie was the only one not feeling it—K103.5 was going to pierce the taboo ceiling and talk about what the black community keeps sweeping under the rug, to its detriment. And I looked at Jessie as she mouthed and counted down with her fingers: *five . . . four . . . three . . . two . . . one.*

"K103.5, K103.5, K103.5. I wanna welcome you to this special edition of *The Brotherhood*. And I'm here to tell you, this will be an interesting forum tonight, y'all. Your boy is flying solo. Yes, I'm doing a special edition of *The Brotherhood* without the brothers; but our boy Magic is in the house—as always, without fail—to help us out. Wassup, man?"

"Hey playa, it's kinda empty in here, ain't it." Magic started laughing, pointing at all the empty chairs. "What we got in store for *The Brotherhood* this week, playa?"

I looked at him sideways. He was always stirring up some mess. "Man, we're going to put the black community on blast tonight."

"WHAT!" he said as he played one of those "dun, dun, dun, dun" sound-bites. "Aiight. I guess I need to be white tonight, yo. Maybe Chinese or Mexican, 'cause I ain't in the mood to be a blasted mofo."

I laughed at Magic, throwing my hands up and flipping him off. "All right, man, you got jokes. But anyway, family, in weeks past, we've heard all about the Brotherhood—our lives, our thoughts, our hearts. And I can honestly tell you, so many things have happened since that infamous Alaskan retreat over four months ago. Some of our brothers, unfortunately, left the Brotherhood to find their own way. Good luck, Donnell and Mikey-Mike. Some of the brothas, with the help of the Brotherhood, have sought out a different direction in life. Go, Malcolm. That's my dog. And some . . . well, they continue to be battered by stormy weather. Keep your chin up, Brass and Pastor. It's as if life won't give them a break. But all of us, regardless of our journey, have opened our eyes—if not by force, as y'all saw last week—and have started changing. Changing for the better.

"And to answer Magic's question, tonight, we're gonna see if our community can take a couple of steps—small ones if need be—in the right direction. And to help us out, I've invited two special people in my life to help discuss what our community just keeps sweeping under the rug. We just won't let it go, y'all; and that rug's getting lumpy with all the damaged lives it's smothering.

"Our guests will, hopefully, shed some light on what's been considered to be taboo by many in our community." I worked my way through my spiel, making sure to keep my voice suave and steady, 'cause I was nervous about this topic. I took a sip of water, wetting my lips, before continuing with the introductions. "Our first guest is someone I'm sure our family is all too familiar with. She's one-half of the duo behind the best beauty shop in downtown Dallas, if not the entire city, and one of the divas who kept the family in stitches from *The Love Forum* with Ms. Jessie and our departed Melissa Morgan. Family, give it up for the lovely and vivacious Ms. V!"

I raised my hands and waved at Magic to play the applause sound-bite. "Come on, K103.5, show my girl some love!"

V laughed as Magic indulged me. She adjusted her headset as she leaned into the microphone. "How's everybody doing?" she asked. And on cue, Magic pumped in some hooting and cheering sound effects that exploded big-time in the background to help V out and liven things up.

"Sounds like everybody's doing real, real good, I hear," I said, laughing. "Now, our second guest is a rather controversial figure around the K103.5 studio, especially after last week's *Brotherhood*, which featured a visit—kinda, sorta—from the notorious television program *Creepers*. Hey, Magic, play the *Creepers* theme music."

Magic had it playing in no time. "Yah, yah, that's it," I said approvingly. "Now, this guest right here is not just gonna talk about why he did what he did, but maybe he will give us some insight into his personal life—what makes him tick, and oh Lord, that all-too-controversial lifestyle he leads."

Magic started up the Motown Better Days mix, of Carl Bean's "I Was Born This Way." And when that thumping beat came on, everybody started bobbing their heads, clapping their hands, and tapping their feet.

"Yah, family, this is a Motown classic too. Surprised? Hell, I was. And Lady Gaga ain't got nothing on this jam. Please give a crazy, if not illified, K103.5 welcome to our boy, Sweets! Who, if you don't know, is the other half of that fantastic business duo from Sweet V's Beauty Shop."

"Work, diva, WORK!" Pat said as Sweets started dancing to the music. "You betta vogue, soror-sista gurl! VOGUE, bit[beep]!" And she got up and started vogueing with him, clapping and laughing, encouraging Sweets on. In the middle of one of his dance steps, Sweets leaned into the microphone and let out a huge "HEY, Y'ALL! I know that's right, Ms. V, with your crazy self." Then he turned around and dipped down to the floor in a pose. We all laughed, 'cause Sweets was mad, crazy funny.

I told him, "Calm down, Sweets! Damn, boy, you tearing it down up in here, aren't you?"

Sweets twirled around and nodded his head to the beat and gave me a wink and a nod, and whispered, "Uh-huh, and you know this."

As the music faded out, Sweets sat down, wiped his brow, and started wringing his hands as though he was nervous or something. And to be honest, V and I were a little worried too, because Sweets was having second thoughts about being here; and I was on pins and needles 'cause I didn't need for anything to go effin' wrong.

Sweets wasn't sure if coming down here was a good idea or in his best interest—what with his and V's business and everything. But having had seven whole days to think about last week's airing, he had some misgivings about what happened and needed to make a public confession, get everything off his chest—tell everyone about how he did everything out of spite and anger, and felt he had sacrificed some of his integrity. But he was really sorry that he hurt someone he really, truly cared about. He was in love; and sometimes love makes you do strange, if not hurtful, and crazy things—especially if you think that the person you love has hurt you too.

"So why don't we get this show on the road," I said, slapping Sweets on the back. "Let's talk about this thing right here, Sweets. And, K103.5 family, I could've had Pastor Levine, from Greater Antioch, come in and give us the religious spin on our discussion; but we already know how that discussion is gonna go down. Or I could've had Judge Hoffanstanter come in and share his ideas from a political and legal perspective, but I didn't want to muddy the waters with all that judgmental mumbo jumbo. I want to talk about this from a human perspective without the craziness and hate.

"So, Sweets, I'm going to ask you the million-dollar question, everyone's been dying to know, and we might as well get it out of the way. So, what was that whole *Creepers* thing about? What were you trying to do?"

I wasn't pulling any punches, and everyone inside and outside the studio looked at Sweets, their eyes glued to him, bursting with hungry anticipation for his answer. Sweets cleared his throat and took a moment before drawing his lips tightly together and leaning toward the microphone.

"I was angry, and I wanted to teach that S-O-B a lesson," he said in one breath. "When I found out all the details about his relationship with Ms. Jessie, and that he had been lying to me, I was hurt, for one, and mad as hell on the flip side of things. But I'm over it. It was just one more pothole I crashed into on my road to finding love. It just left some damages this time. But trust, I'm all too familiar with these kinds of bumps in the road. And I haven't found love yet."

"What did you do when you found out what was really going on?" I asked.

"DK, boy, what *didn't* I do. When I found out that Todd, I mean [beep], had turned the tables on me and contacted *Creepers* himself—having me followed— boy, I lost it! And since me and Dr. Houston was planning Jessie's birthday bash, spending a lot of time together planning it, *Creepers* made it seem like Dr. Houston and I were the ones having a relationship. Ain't that 'bout a [beep]."

"[Bleep] NO!" I shouted, unable to hold back the expletive. "Now, I didn't know that," I said, shaking my head in disbelief. I never pictured my boy [beep] doing something so deliberate and vindictive, although Sweets was just as wrong as two left feet himself.

"It's true, though," V interjected. "I saw those creepers creeping around— no pun intended—the shop, especially around the times Dr. Houston would come around, when him and Sweets were planning Jessie's birthday bash. And then Sweets confronted them and got the truth straight from the horse's mouth."

"Max?" I asked.

"You know him?" V asked.

"He's a friend of ours."

"Uh-huh, and that JJ," she added.

"Well, that definitely gives us a bit more clarity as to why Sweets acted the way he did. I'm not saying I'm siding with anyone here, but definitely, I'm seeing things in a different light now," I said as I turned to Sweets once more. "One question, though, Sweets. Are you satisfied?"

Sweets shook his head. "No, I'm not, DK. I'm really not." He let out a heavy sigh that echoed around the studio. "I'm only human, and I was very angry and emotional at the time—especially after the meeting with V's divas in the ladies' room. I wanted to hurt Todd the way he had hurt me and was going to hurt Dr. Houston; but what I did, I feel as if I'd failed a lot of people, especially those that choose to keep their life private, for whatever reason. Coming out is a personal and difficult process, and it shouldn't be used to humiliate and punish someone. What I did was help perpetuate the belief, especially in our community, that there's something wrong with being who I am, something that I should be embarrassed about; but that's not the message I wanted to send to any of the listeners."

I had a newfound respect for Sweets upon hearing those words. I had never really given the hairdresser much thought, but Sweets' conviction was something that he should be looked up to for. "What would you have done different?" I asked.

"I wouldn't have done that show. That's it. I hate that I did it."

"Is that the reason you agreed to come on today?"

"In a way, yes. I don't know how to make things right with Todd. I don't think he trusts me anymore, and I don't blame him. But at least I can talk about it here, about people going through these things like me and him. I know what it's like to be in his shoes. I'm out and proud and basically happy. But once upon a time, I had felt that confusion; and it was an especially difficult time in my life—I think because I was who I was and grappling with who society said I should be. And, baby, it ain't easy being me, but I can't see me being anybody else. I had to grow some tough skin to live like this; but some people can't do it, they won't do it, or they just simply can't do it because of the backlash, condemnation, and repercussions. Who wants to be ostracized, if not, humiliated for who they are? Would any one of us want to be treated differently because we're black? And when we are, how does it feel? That's probably one of the reasons so many black men are on the DL. They get married and conform, because they're not allowed to live freely and do what they need to do on the low, low. We—our community that is—created the problem, and we encourage it."

"Well put, Sweets. And thank you for the insight into what it's like on your side of the road. V?" I called, waving at her. "Now that we've opened the door to the DL brother thing, let me ask you: How did it affect your life? You wanna tell your story?"

V covered her face with her hands and shook her head. Then she let out a loud sigh. "Well, DK, you know I was married—seven years, to be exact—and I was head-over-heels in love. Lord, did I love that man. And we had a beautiful son [beep] together. Oh, okay, I'll just call them Senior and Junior."

"So how did you find out that he was down?" I asked.

V laughed out loud. "I can laugh about it now. Hell, we laugh about it together. We're really becoming good friends. Well, to make a long story short, he went over to my girl DeDe's house to fix some sort of leak she had in her bathroom. And lo and behold! She came home from work, to make sure he was all right, and found him in her bed laying the pipe in some man instead of fixing the one in her bathroom—piping down a twenty-dollar crack ho at that."

V started laughing again. "Sometimes I have to laugh to keep myself from crying." She closed her eyes and shook her head. She opened her eyes again only when Sweets grabbed her hand. "Lord that was an awful time . . . it was a mess."

"So how did you handle it?" I asked.

"I hated him. And I asked myself, *How could I have not known?* But now I know there are a lot of us women in the same predicament. Sometimes were blind; but usually, it's obvious to everyone else. Tell you the truth, I don't know how I handled it. I just did."

"What about your son, V? How's he doing?"

"He's doing good. He now has a relationship with his father, and I'm encouraging it."

"WHAT!"

"Yes, don't act so surprised, DK. And you too, Magic—I see you over there. And I know what you're thinking. No, he was a good father before all the drama, and he's still a good father after the drama. It took me a while; and I admit, I was so mad and hurt that I couldn't see past all the bitterness I carried inside of me. I was going to do everything I knew how to do to get him, make him suffer like I was suffering. And if I saw a gay person, I let them have it too—right, Sweets?"

"I know that's right, girl. You were evil as [beep]."

"But somehow, someway, I got through all of this, 'cause you never know where your blessings may lie or who can help you achieve them."

"You mean, Sweet V's?" I asked.

"Yes. Don't get me wrong, it wasn't instantaneous. I'm still growing, forgiving, and understanding; but what really helped me was when Sweets suggested that I watch this movie . . . uhm, *Far from Heaven*, with that black guy who always does the Allstate Insurance commercials—who is he, Sweets?"

"Dennis Haysbert," he answered. "It's a 2002 movie about life in the 1950s. It also has Dennis Quaid and Julianne Moore in it."

"Yah, that's right. Did you watch it, DK?"

I wanted to lie, but I did; and it was good. Right up there with some of my all-time favorites like *Imitation of Life*, and *The Ten Commandments*, my favorite movies with the classic underdog characters that you wanted to succeed and overcome societal ills. V gave it to me to watch when she was trying to convince me to do the show, and it did open up my eyes as to how people bring or cause misery to other people when they're not allowed to live freely. "Yah," I said, "I saw it. And you're right—it does make you think in a totally different way. I guess if someone told me that I couldn't be a DJ because I was black, or couldn't live in a certain area, or couldn't date a particular girl because she was light, dark, or another race, I would probably be miserable too."

"That's all we're saying," said Sweets. "And you know," Sweets said, pointing at me, "black men aren't the only ones on the D-L. Black women are on the D-L too. You *just* don't hear about it now, do you?" He tapped his fingers on the table and waited for somebody to answer. "I didn't think so. That's because black men don't talk about stuff like that, not like black women do."

"Silent sons, huh, Sweets?"

"Silent sons, DK. Black D-L sistas cause just as much pain and heartache as a D-L brother. You can't keep blaming us black brothers for all of the black community's ills. It's a two-way street, you know. Everybody has some ownership in how we as a community fare."

"Wow . . . I mean, WOW! I never really thought about it like that. You've really put this in a new perspective for me. I've been living in a real shallow world—a real shallow world. I guess our community is really doing ourselves an injustice, huh?"

"A community that's deeply rooted in man-made religion and just as morally and socially corrupt as they want to be," V said. "They need to walk as Jesus did, in love."

I grimaced and thought, *Where have I heard this before?* Then I looked over at Magic, who was just nodding his head at V.

Sweets looked at V, and then at me, and rolled his eyes up to the ceiling. "I guess, Ms. V. It's like my big momma always told me: 'Careful what you plant, 'cause you're gonna have to eventually reap what you've sown. And that harvest may not be what ya had in mind.'"

"That's right!" said V. "Big Momma never lied, and I'm living proof of that."

"Walk like Jesus, Ms. V. Walk like Jesus—in understanding, peace, and love."

I laughed at Sweets and finally realized that the break music was playing. I looked over at my boy Magic, who, I guess, had been trying to get my attention for a while. I looked over at Jessie through the window and noticed she was holding her hands up in the air, looking at me crazy, as if to say, *What are you doing?*

But this shit was deep. "All right, family," I said. "We've just got an earful—WHEW!—and my boy Magic, and Ms. Jessie over here, is telling me that we have to go to break. When we come back, were going to open up the phone lines—they're all lit up too. We gone get this discussion started."

And Magic started up Carl Bean's "I Was Born This Way" again, and we went to break on this feel-good groove.

Chapter 28

A Sunday Kinda Love

(DK's POV)

"*K*103.5, good evening, this is your boy DK 'Love' Niles, and *love* is definitely the word for today. It's all in the air. It's November 15, and again, we're back on a *Love Forum* Sunday. Its 11:30 AM, Dallas time, but 2:30 PM here in the beautiful country of Brazil, where we're broadcasting live and celebrating the wedding of Miguel de Souza and Ms. Darlene Brookes. Not only is this day very special because of this wedding, but today is also a Brazilian national holiday—the anniversary of the declaration of Brazil's republic. And today, Miguel and Darlene are celebrating their own declaration—the declaration of their love for one another. And, K103.5, it's gonna be a Sunday kind of love.' And to get you in the mood, we're going to get you started with a little Etta James song that just oozes with sensuality, love, and beautiful emotions—a song that talks about finding someone to care about you. More than love at first sight, y'all. A song that talks about journeying on a long road to finding that perfect one, and that beautiful song is Ms. James's 'A Sunday Kind of Love.' And yes, Dallas divas and fellas, we all know that you want—and are searching for—this kinda love. So to our happy couple, Mr. and Mrs. Miguel de Souza, here's wishing you a sincere and beautiful nuptials. Well-wishes from the K103.5 family: Happy Declaration Day to our Sunday lovers Miguel and Darlene. You've found that Sunday kind of love!"

Miguel and Darlene had opted for a small quiet wedding with immediate family and a few close friends at a secluded beachfront resort. Quentin, Xavier, and I flew up for Miguel. Jessie, DeDe, V, and Britt—who got us all on a Delta Buddy Pass—flew up for Darlene. For most of the morning, Darlene was driving us crazy, because thunderstorms had rolled in early in the morning, although it soon turned into light rain, clearing just in time for the wedding, which took place on one of Brazil's secluded beaches just forty-three miles from Sao Paulo.

I laughed because I remembered what Magic told me when I had to call him earlier in the morning to figure out how to get some of the equipment to work. "Gloomy," was what he said. "That's all I gotta say, playa. You just bring rain, man; or maybe that god of yours keeps crying for the Brotherhood, or maybe for brothers everywhere. 'Cause everywhere y'all go, there's rain." Ha! That boy. Anyway, it was seventy-seven degrees and humid as hell, but Darlene looked good as hell in a strapless gown with a midnight blue sash tied around the waist; and our boy Miguel was quite dapper in his dark blue tux.

It wasn't anything fancy, but the backdrop was out of this world. You had the white sands of the beach, cradled by the blue waters of the ocean, on one side; and on the other, mountains that started right there on the beach, covered in green vegetation that led up to the rain forest. A simple wedding canopy, draped in white and blue sheer draping, Jessie's suggestion, faced the ocean; and there was a walkway made out of white and blue flower petals outlined by white candlelit beach lanterns.

"So, Miguel," I said, "tell the K103.5 family how it feels to be married, my brotha."

He answered in his heavy accent, "DK, man, it's a great feeling. I just can't even put it into words."

"I'll bet," I replied, laughing at his English. "Aiight, man of few words, what about you, Mrs. de Souza?"

"DK, I'm the happiest woman in the world. So many of us ladies are looking for that Mr. Right; and not only did I find him, he whisked me off my feet and placed me on a ground filled with love."

"Well, K103.5, you heard it firsthand. This is your boy DK 'Love' Niles signing off. I'm about to get my groove and eat on, y'all. I wish each and every one of you your own Sunday kind of love."

Not soon after we wrapped up, my phone started vibrating. It was Bee.

"Hon, I'm sorry, I'm calling you from my brother's phone. Just wanted to let you know that we're here at the hospital, and Momma wanted me to call. We thought you should know that Daddy's taken a turn for the worse."

"Aww, man, I'm sorry to hear that, Bee." Those are the words I typically say when I hear sad news, and it spilled out of my mouth as though it was nothing. Although in my mind and heart, I was thinking, *I really don't care. What does he have to do with me?* "Well, I'm in Brazil right now," I told her, "for Darlene and Miguel's wedding; but as soon as I'm back in Dallas, maybe I can stop by and pay Chef Luda a visit."

"Oh yah, the wedding! I can't wait to hear all about it tonight. Tell them congratulations. And it would be good if you could stop by once you get back. I think he'll like that. He's been asking about you *everyday*. So that would be *real* good."

"Okay. I'll do that. How's everything else going?" I asked. I knew I had to say something 'cause it was kind of awkward, knowing that she was my half sister and all.

"Well, despite everything going on with Daddy, all is good. Oh, wait! We do want to thank you for recommending Malcolm for the apprenticeship. Oh my god, everyone's saying that he's one of the best apprentices they've ever had the opportunity to work with. And he's doing great working with our new chef too." Bee laughed a little. "I think he may be a chef sooner than we all think. He definitely has the skills, and we're all happy that he has just enrolled at the Culinary School at the Art Institute of Dallas too."

"Good, good," I said. And as the realization of Chef Luda being in the hospital and probably dying settled with me, a sense of sadness overtook me; and I quickly told Bee I had to go, and hung up the phone.

"You all right, DK?" V asked.

"Yah, girl. Where's everybody going?"

"We're heading back up to the hotel for the reception. You coming?"

"Yah. I'll be there in a few. Just let me finish packing up the gear. I'll catch up with you, guys." I continued packing up as V walked off, ass just a-bouncing; and something told me to look back up to get a second look. That was when I caught up to V as she was walking up the path to the hotel. Then she stopped and turned around, and caught me looking at her. We looked at each other. She did one of those little-girl waves, and I chuckled under my breath. *She's on the prowl.*

I yelled out, "Hey, V? You betta save me a dance, girl."

She laughed out loud, put one hand on the back of her head and the other on her hip, and then wiggled that ass a little as she rolled her body, turning around while dancing in place. "You got it. And hurry up. I'm saving the first one just for you."

◆　◆　◆

As I danced and serenaded V—she looked so beautiful—I looked over at my boy Quentin and noticed that he had asked Jessie to dance. My face tightened up as I watched them, and I instinctively mouthed, *Oh shit.* I don't know. For some reason, my gut was telling me that it was a little bit more than just a friendly dance. I stared at them, really looked at my boy—the way he held her, the way his hand caressed her body, the way he held her close in his arms. I twirled V around to see if I could find where Xavier was and saw him laughing it up and dancing with DeDe, not even aware of what was going down with his girl and Quentin. I shook my head and thought, *Jessie? What the hell are you doing?* But I could tell she was wrapped up in the moment, just effin' clueless as to how it all looked.

Hell, I don't know. Maybe my mind was playing tricks on me. Naw. Naw. A man knows the game, especially when he's checking someone out or is feeling those strong feelings for someone; and there were definitely some strong feelings going on in that dance. I couldn't take it anymore. I swung V around so I wouldn't have to watch. The less I saw and knew, the better. But V—we're so much alike—zeroed in and saw what I saw. I could see her staring from the corner of my eye. She looked at them long and hard before her expression went from glowingly happy to horrified. I could feel her body tense up, and that confirmed what I already knew. This was not going to turn out pretty.

◆ ◆ ◆

During the weeks Brass sat in jail, all he could think about was God taking his wrong and making it right, as that song by Brian Courtney Wilson, "All I Need," played in his head day and night. Judge Hoffanstanter had come through and made good on his promise to pay back the favor he owed and got Brass released from jail, using his influence to work everything out. He even said he was working on getting Brass's record expunged. And for me, I knew I was changing, because I didn't expect anything from Brass in return. Not that he was in any position to give me anything anyway. I just knew—it was as though there was a burning fire within me—that I'd get my blessing in the end.

Brass knew he was given a second chance and was truly grateful for everything that the judge and the Brotherhood had done for him. Always a man of his word, he found himself making a trip he never thought he would make. But a promise was a promise—God did get him out of his predicament. And as he sat in Greater Antioch, his legs wouldn't keep still. He thought, *I've heard this before, and nothing's changed. Everything's still the same. I know I promised God, but—*

Until he heard the pastor tell the congregation, "Flock—my God, my Lord, help me—before I call the church to worship, my soul told me that I need to give my own testimony this morning. No singing, no music, please. I need to give a testimony on where I've been, how far I've traveled, how far I've come, and how far I have yet to go. Good God Almighty. Can I get an 'Amen' from somebody?"

The church erupted in applause, and the sanctuary filled with a chorus of "Thank you, Jesus"; "Thank you, God"; and a whole lot of "Testify, Pastor."

The pastor grabbed a glass of water off the podium and took a giant gulp before he began to tell his story. "Now, you may see some images or videos that may be quite shocking to you, but they are not what they appear to be. I'm no saint, but I am not the man this individual is portraying me to be. So I stand before you, taking the wind from beneath his wings, for he shall not destroy me." Pastor Levine wiped the sweat of his brow with his handkerchief and bounced up and down on his toes. "And Pat Carter will claim her victory."

The pastor went on to talk about his past, about his daughter, and how he got to that point in his life. Not long after, a different number of choruses filled the place:

"No!"

"What?"

"Say it ain't so!"

Some people even collected their things and walked out.

As more and more people got up and left, a lone voice in the choir started to sing the old Deitrick Haddon song "God Didn't Give Up on Me."

The pastor looked up to the young man and told him, "Thank you, son. And I want to give all the honor, praise, and glory to my Lord and Savior, Jesus Christ. Because there comes a time in your life when you're just through with being through. You know a change has to be made 'cause the same things keep happening to you, or you just can't get out of that rut. Church, I know some people will not want a pastor who's led the life I've led, someone who has turned his back on his own daughter, someone who's been living one life but representing another. For the ones that will stay and charge up that rough side of the mountain with me, yes, I'm in a rut; *but I'm* finally *through with being through.* After today, me helping you and you helping me, we'll both be on our way to being healed. Can I get an 'Amen'?"

Pat, with tears falling onto her white pressed dress suit, waved her hands and answered, "Amen, Pastor. AMEN!"

But as the pastor called the church to worship, no one came. No one moved. The aisles were empty. But something stirred inside of Brass as the choir began to sing the song that had been playing in his head for days. And as the choir sang "All I Need," he closed his eyes and smiled as he thought about the Brotherhood and what the pastor just said; and he prayed, *Lord, thank you. I'm finally through with being through. I believe I'm healed.* And he stepped out into the aisle. He stood there as Pastor Levine held out his arms, calling out to all souls present. Like before, he couldn't move. Pat turned around, to see what all the commotion was, who was coming; and she jumped up when she saw Brass and ran to help him make that walk to God. But Brass didn't see Pat. He saw only the grandmother who had, so many times in her life, walked so many lost souls up to the altar. And amid all the hoopla and cheering, with Pat guiding him, he moved. They slowly made their way down the aisle and up to the altar, where Pastor Levine met him; and Brass fell into his arms. But Brass didn't see the pastor either. He saw his gramps instead, and his knees just fell out from underneath him.

Pastor Levine lifted him up and said, "I am my brother's keeper. I'm going to hold you up and carry you, my brother, until the day comes when you can carry yourself." The church got to its feet as Pat and Pastor Levine surrounded and embraced Brass, as if shielding him from the world; and the clapping, the cheering, and the crying overwhelmed the sanctuary and drowned out the choir singing "All I Need."

◆ ◆ ◆

As I sat in the plane on the flight back to Dallas, with V's head resting on my shoulder as she quietly slept, I jotted down all the information from the day for *The Brotherhood* later that night. I smiled and nodded. Pastor Levine had confronted his past and his present. And as Brass was walking down the aisle to the Lord, on one side of the world, Darlene was walking down the aisle to Miguel on the other. And it verified for me that God could take away the hurt, pain, heartache, loneliness, despair, and whatever physical or mental ailments one has endured in one's life. Darlene, who, as we found out in the first forum, had suffered abuse at the hands of the men in her life, had just married a man who, she finally realized, was her Mr. Too Damn Good. Brass, who had been struggling to survive the best way he knew how, despite his past weighing him down, fell in love again with the man he turned his back on so many decades ago—God. And Pastor Levine had doused his enemies' fire and given a moving testimony of where he was, the road he had taken to get to where he was, and the many more miles he had to go to get to where he wanted to be, not only in his life, but in the lives of the people he loved. I wrote down, "November 15 was a day of *declaration* indeed, a true Sunday kind of love."

Chapter 29

A New Year's Resolution

(DK's POV)

*I*t was January 3, 2010. Ole Father Time had allowed another new year to roll in, and with it, all the crazy self-improvement resolutions that hardly anyone ever kept. Regardless, I decided to ring in the New Year with a resolution as well. I had resolved to be the best man I could be in 2010. What I was thinking about or what crazy ideas were running through my head when I made that resolution, I honestly can't tell you. I was just hoping that 2010 would be a better year for doing it, way better than 2009 had been; but for some reason, I was feeling jittery. I didn't feel that that was going to be the case—not today, at least. As I sat in Bailey's fooling around with Bee and Malcolm, making small talk and laughing and joking around, something made me remember that it had almost been two months since that "A Sunday Kinda Love" broadcast in Brazil—Miguel and Darlene's wedding day—and I don't know why, but my mind went straight to Chef Luda. I had promised myself every day since I learned that he had been hospitalized that I would go see him; but I couldn't make myself do it—not even with Bee and her family constantly asking and pleading. I either found shit that needed to be done at the station, with the brothers, or around the house, or just—hell, anything but going down to that damn hospital. And I tell you, I didn't feel an iota of guilt about it. I just thought, *Serves him effin' right*.

I had tuned Bee and Malcolm out and forgot all about the luncheon planned by Jessie to discuss tonight's airing of the final *Brotherhood* with Dr. Mayweather. She was late as usual. I didn't know why, but I started reflecting on my life and how the Brotherhood had forever changed it. How I'd grown not only as an individual but also as a human being, more importantly, as a man—a transformed man. Not only was I transformed, but all of the *Love Forum* brothers, the ones who were left, went through some amazing transformations as well. I tell you, not one of us could have ever imagined in a million years that all our transformations were even possible. And if you had told me some six months ago, while I sat around a table with nine other brothers in Juneau, Alaska, that I would be where I am today, I probably would have slapped the taste right out of your mouth and shoved it right back in for spite.

Since that November 15 wedding, and the infamous *Love Forum* debacle that preceded it, all of us had done some serious soul-searching. Mine was coming to terms with and forgiving the man whom I had damned to hell hundreds of thousands of times. Forgiving the man who had popped back into my life just as easily as he had walked out of it. Forgiving the man who had left me to fend for myself without a thought or care about my well-being, my needs, or any outright concern. Yep! Luda Bailey, a.k.a. Chef Luda. He had popped back into my life with an effin' bang; and damn, what an effin' bang it was. Not only did I find out that the man I'd been joking around with; eating and drinking with; and asking, if not pleading, for a favor for one of the brothers was my deadbeat dad. But never in my life could I have imagined, or even come close to imagining, that his daughter—the one I was growing very fond of and deep-throating and grinding on, on the regular—was my effin' sister. I still can't get over that shit! Serious soul-searching, I tell you—serious soul searching. I can't recall how many nights I lay in bed just thinking about that shit, wondering how many other brothers were or had actually been in my shoes and had gone all the way without knowing that they were lying in bed with someone no one was supposed to know about and they were never supposed to encounter? Serious soul-searching, I tell you—serious soul searching.

So there I was, thirty-five years old and dealing with a man whom I hadn't heard from or seen in over twenty-five years. His family expecting me to just walk into his arms as if twenty-five years meant nothing and everything was effin' all right. That everything could easily be forgiven. That time just healed all wounds and his dire condition would correct all the wrong. Maybe I was just effin' jaded beyond help, but I guess this was where that New Year's resolution would definitely need to come into play, 'cause Lord knows, there was nothing inside of me for this man—nothing at all. And I had tried. I had tried finding something inside of me to feed off of, if only a damn crumb. Something to help me to come to terms with him, his effin' mother, and the twenty-five years of nothing for this here "stray dog," as his mother called me. Something to help me let him know that *hey, everything's all right. All is forgiven. You can journey on and find the peace you need. I forgive you, man.* But there was nothing. Like I said, Lord knows I tried, but I was empty. There was not a drop of anything in my glass, not a crumb on my plate. I just couldn't get past it; I could neither let go nor move on. And I had this funny feeling. Just like the feeling I had that Saturday morning in March of last year, when all of this Brotherhood stuff began. I could feel that something was about to happen, and I knew it didn't have anything to do with me meeting Jessie and Dr. Mayweather for lunch. My gut feeling kept telling me that it was going to be around the call Bee had just answered 'cause she looked at me and Malcolm and immediately put the phone call on speaker. Leaving Malcolm and me to sit at the table, like effin' dummies, and listen in; and whoever was on the other line was distraught.

"Momma? What's going on? Why are you crying?"

"I'm at the hospital. They called me and told me to come down and prepare the family. You need to get down here, Bee. It's time. I've already called your brother."

"Oh God! Don't cry, Momma." Bee started tearing up and choking up. "You're going to make me start crying."

"I'm sorry, baby. It just hurts. I'm hurting. Oh God! Hurry, Bee. Hurry if you can. I don't know how long he's going to be alert. He's talking right now. Asking where everyone is . . . and, Bee?"

"Yes, Momma."

"Do you know how to get in contact with Dickey?"

"DK's right here, Momma. He's here for a lunch date to discuss his radio show."

"Tell him his daddy is asking about him. Plead with him to come down. Plead with him, Bee. Ask him to do it for me. I'll give him whatever he wants. Please don't let your daddy leave this earth without DK making peace with him. Please! Please get him to come. Hold on . . . oh, okay. The doctors and nurses just left the room. They want to talk to me. I gotta go. I'll see you when you get here. Be careful out there, baby."

"Okay, Momma. Bye."

I didn't know what to say. I looked at Bee, who looked at me with those big, dark eyes. Malcolm elbowed me. "Do the right thang, brutha. You owe him at least that for getting me in here. Don't let me and Bee down on this one, man."

What could I effin' do? I was beyond finding an excuse to hang out at the station (Jessie and Dr. Mayweather were on their way) or with the brothers (Malcolm was right here) or—hell, anywhere but that damn hospital. But I was stuck. And I'd be damned, guess who came running up to the effin' table to make things worse? JESSIE!

"Hey, y'all. WHEW! I'm out of breath. Sorry, I'm late, DK. My goodness, look at y'all. Why all the gloom?"

Bee looked as though she was about to lose it and walked off. Malcolm cleared his throat and got up from the table to give Jessie a hug. "It's Chef Luda, Jessie. Bee just got a call from the hospital. It's time."

Jessie dropped everything and sat down. "Oh God! DK, are you all right? Why aren't you guys on your way out the door? What's going on?"

I was about to answer when Bee came back with car keys in her hand and asked Malcolm to drive her to the hospital. She didn't even look at me. She just said, "DK, I can't make you do what you don't want to. I just know that he would like you there. It's up to you to come or not. You heard the phone call. You know how everyone feels. Dallas Memorial . . . fourteenth floor if you decide to come." She touched my shoulder as she walked by. Then she grabbed Malcolm's hand, and they headed toward the door.

I had already seen the look on Jessie's face. That look my moms had on when she wanted to let me know, *I don't even know the whole story, but I know you're going to do what's right.* Dr. Mayweather walked up, and Jessie filled him in on what was going on. As they talked, I walked over to the bar and had the bartender fix me a screwdriver, double hard on the vodka. After downing two of them, I walked back over and asked Jessie if she would drive me to the hospital. Dr. Mayweather said he would work on tonight's *Brotherhood* and for me not to worry, because they would do a general format and wing it. "Don't worry now. You go take care of your daddy. The show's going to be fine. I have a feeling it may be the best one, if not the most positive, of all of them."

◆ ◆ ◆

We pulled into the hospital parking lot. Jessie winced, and I asked, "Are you okay?"

"Yah, boy, I'm fine. It's just that the last time I was here, well, it was when Melissa passed." She sighed heavily. "Yah, I'm okay. Although I believe the question should be, are *you* okay?"

I didn't say anything. We parked the car, got out, and walked to the hospital in silence. I must have been giving off some strange vibes because Jessie stopped me when we went inside and told me to just stand there and catch my breath.

"DK, you're sure you're all right? Do you need to sit down for a while?"

I just shook my head as if to let her know that I wasn't all right. I was a little hesitant, if not scared. "I'm good. Let's just get this over with," I said.

Jessie grabbed my hand, and we walked over to the elevator and waited for the door to open.

"Jessie?"

"Yes, DK."

"What do I say to him?"

She smiled, gave me a big hug, and told me, "Say what's in your heart. But remember, whatever you say will be with you for the rest of your life and what you'll leave him to go to eternity with. And I'll tell you, like my big momma always told me—and you take it as you will—what goes around comes around. So think about what you're going to say before you say it."

The elevator door opened, and we walked in. I thought about what she had just said. She was right. I needed to let my father know what I thought about him. He needed to think about what he had put me through for all eternity.

244

Jessie and I were quiet throughout the ride, and I watched the elevator floor indicator announce the floors; and I began to get nervous and feel hot. I started to sweat a little as the indicator flashed and announced *5, 6, 7, 8, 9, 10, 11, 12,* and stopped at *14.* The doors opened, and Jessie and I walked out and asked the floor nurse what room Luda Bailey was in.

"OH MY GOD! I know you. You're DK Niles from K103.5. And, Lord, look-a-here, is this Ms. Jessie? Girl, you are fierce! And I love your hair. Is that Remy?"

Jessie nodded a quick yes, her expression saying, *I know you did not just ask me that.* I looked at her, thinking, *Heifer, do we know you?* Although I was taken aback by her brashness—she definitely has some spunk in her—I couldn't get past how beautiful she was. She was breathtaking. I mean breathtaking—*fine as hell.* She was definitely giving Jessie some competition in the looks and body department, if not beating her out. I looked down at her name tag, which was attached to some va-va-voom breasts, which made me think, *Damn!* I read her name out loud: "Francine?" And exclaimed, "Naw! Not Frenchie from the K103.5 call-in line."

She flashed a big-ass smile and giggled. "The one and only. Okay! Now, who are you here to see again, sugar?"

I started laughing and said, "That's right, you are a nurse, with your feisty ass."

Francine laughed too and told me and Jessie, "I'm just playing with you, guys. I love to horse around, as you can tell. Okay, I'm going into professional mode now. Hello. My name is Francine, and how are you two doing?"

Jessie walked up to her, shook her hand, and gave her a big hug. "Girl, you are a trip on our shows. We just *love* you! We're here to see Chef Luda. I'm sorry . . . Luda Bailey."

When Francine told us room 1421, my heart dropped straight to the floor. Ms. Doretha had told me that the numbers *421* would be my sign throughout life, that those numbers would signify that something significant was about to happen—something with life-changing significance. I asked Jessie, "Do you think he's already dead?"

"No! Why would you ask that?" she asked, squinting at me, annoyed. "No! Don't even think that. Matter of fact, he's probably hanging on until all the family is there. That includes you too—you're family."

I slowly sank into a dark place as we said good-bye to Francine, not wanting to go. But Jess and I went on our way and walked into room 1421. I have to admit, I was kind of hoping he was gone; then I wouldn't have to go through anything uncomfortable—just offer my condolences to his family and then leave. I opened the door and saw that everyone was there. It was mad creepy. Momma Bailey was sitting by his side, and she looked at me and said, "Luda? Guess who just walked in? It's lil' Dickey."

He said, "Lawd, have mercy. Come on ova here, boy. Janey, let lil' Dickey sit down." She patted the bed for me to come over and sit by his side.

I walked over to him, sat down, and grabbed and held his hand, which was shaking. I could tell he was scared. I don't know if he was scared of dying or scared of what was going to happen between him and me, and I walked in with every intention of letting him have it. But then I looked at him, and the sight of him shocked the hell out of me. It threw me back. He had lost so much weight. Damn! He didn't even look the same. Not the Chef Luda I knew. He was so frail. I could see every bone in his body. It was like looking at a skeleton with skin pulled over it. Skin that was white with ash. He kept licking his lips, and I asked if he wanted something to drink, some water. He said yes, and Momma Bailey poured me a glass and gave me a straw and patted me on the back. It took everything I had, but I wanted to do what was right—be the best man I could be, I guess. So I put the straw in his mouth and held the glass up so he could take a couple of swallows. I started a small conversation 'cause I didn't really know what to say, and I could feel everyone—Momma Bailey, Bee, Malcolm, Junior, Jessie—looking at me, at us.

"Hey, you're shaking. You all right?" I asked.

He shook his head and answered, "Yes, lil' critter. I'm all right. Da Lord works in mysterious ways, don't he? Yes, he do. The Lord really came through. He answered my prayers, lil' Dickey. Well, at least two of the three that I've been praying for; and even if he didn't answer but one, I would still say thank you for the one prayer he answered."

I asked him, "What prayers were those?"

He struggled to lift his other arm to bring it across his body, so I helped him. He clasped my hand with what little strength he had left. He took another sip of water and then let the straw fall out of his mouth, and I wiped away the dribble with my shirtsleeve.

"I've been praying that I would find you and have all my family together when this moment came. I should have been dead a long time ago, but he has kept me alive this long probably for this reason. And I'm grateful . . . so grateful."

He squeezed my hand a little harder, and his eyes were kind of glazing over. Chills ran through my body, and I just pursed my lips tight 'cause I knew what was coming. My moms had always told me you could tell when somebody was ready to go to the other side because their eyes would look like glass, and his did. Tears started to form in the corner of his eyes and roll down his face. His voice started to weaken as he struggled to say, "The other prayer was to know that you would find it in your heart to forgive me." He closed his eyes and slowly let go of his grip. "I know that may be asking a lot, Dickey. I've made some mistakes in my life. Lord knows I've made a lot of mistakes when it came to you.

But there wasn't a day that I didn't wonder about you, wonder how you were doing, although I knew you were well, 'cause your family made sure of that. I wondered how your life turned out. I know I made a mistake. I just didn't know how to correct it, make things right; and the years just kept passing by."

He opened his eyes and stared at me for a while, and I couldn't do anything but look down at him—a broken and scared man. And at that moment, my heart opened up. What was aching was now filled with something I couldn't even begin to describe. I said to myself, thinking about the Brotherhood as I did, *Lord, thank you. I'm finally through with being through. I believe I'm healed.* And I told him, "I forgive you . . . I forgive you, man." I shook my head, took a deep breath, and exhaled, letting everything go. I laid the side of my head on top of his and whispered in his ear, "I forgive you, Daddy. I forgive you, and I love you, man. And yah, God does work in mysterious ways, don't he?"

I could hear Momma Bailey in the background say, "Thank you, Jesus!" And I heard Bee cry out, "Daddy? Daddy? Can you hear me, Daddy? It's me, Bee."

I was about to get up and let her get closer to the bed, but Daddy pulled me back and wouldn't let go of my hand. He looked at Bee standing next to Malcolm, with her head on his shoulder, her body trembling, crying as she asked, "Daddy, what was the unanswered prayer? Maybe we can help."

His breathing started to get fainter and fainter. It was like you could hear him take a breath, but it took ages for him to exhale and take another one. He smiled; and in between his breathing, he struggled to get a word out. It seemed as though it took him forever to say one sentence—thirty small one-syllable words. Everyone was on pins and needles. We listened to each breath, followed by one word, which grew fainter and fainter and harder to hear with each breath he took.

"Bee . . . I . . . asked . . . God . . . 'fore . . . I . . . took . . . my . . . last . . . breath . . . that . . . I . . . would . . . get . . . to . . . see . . . you . . . with . . . the . . . man . . . that . . . you . . . would . . . spend . . . the . . . rest . . . of . . . your . . . life . . . with."

He took another deep breath and wheezed a little. And we waited. But he didn't exhale. Momma Bailey cried out and fell to the floor. Junior ran over to the bed and fell on top of him. Bee collapsed in Malcolm's arms, and Jessie hurriedly walked over and sat down next to me, wrapping her arms around me for support.

After saying his last word, *my daddy* took one final breath and passed away. He passed a forgiven man, with his family around him. His eyes fixed on Bee and Malcolm, which made me turn around and look at them too. Malcolm was consoling Bee like I would do if she was my girl; and I said to myself, *Daddy, I believe he did. I believe God did grant all three of your wishes.*

Chapter 30

The Final Brotherhood
Being the Best Men We Can Be

"K103.5, K103.5, K103.5. This is your boy DK 'Love' Niles, along with the music maestro himself, Mr. Kirk 'Magic' Wonder. Well, family, I have some sad news to tell you. What is it, you ask? Well, tonight, you'll be listening to the Brotherhood talk about life, love, and our pursuit of happiness for the very last time. Yes, family, it's our last show; but don't get it twisted. Although this may be the final show, we're going to lay it down, on this first Sunday of the New Year, like this joint is happening for the very first time. We're pulling out all the stops and leaving nothing to the imagination. That's right! We're coming atcha with all the effin' bells and whistles, like a breakout show should. So get ready for the show of shows. It's about to be on, family. And like that old saying—'All good things must come to an end'—goes, well, K103.5, we've come to the end of the road, baby. But how sweet it's going to be. Family, welcome to the final episode of *The Brotherhood*. Magic?"

Magic laughed. "I know that's right, DK. Dallas, you got your boy Magic here; and, ladies, I'll be playing nothing but *magical* hits for y'all tonight—'cause it's gonna be a *magical* night, ladies. Make sure you make a wish." He sounded off a kiss and said, "Love ya, ladies. Now, fellas, for us playas, it's a brand-new year, a brand-new gig, and a new direction in life, not only for all the brothas sitting 'round this here table but also for all the brothas out there in our audience. Gotta give all my dawgs a big shoutout. Hey-a-yah-eee! Receive it, my brothas. Now for the radio station business: It's January third, two thousand and ten, and it's a bone-chilling thirty-six degrees—it's shivering weather, y'all. Expect our morning lows to be at or near freezing, if not dipping below. So find that special someone; grab those blankets and pillows, or whatever makes you happy; and snuggle down tight. It may be cold outside, but it's gonna get pretty hot up in here tonight. And to start those temperatures rising, I'm going to play something special; and, family, I had to go way back in the vault to bring out this motherfu[beep] classic. Yah, I cursed. What?"

"All right, Magic! Please tell me you didn't go way, way, waaayyy back in the vault, my brother? Did you?"

"Not way back, playa. Just a few years. DK, man, I had to find something definitely befitting the theme for our last show. I had to find a song that would say what we've been talking about since day one—brothas coming together, y'all. We got to come together, fellas. You feel me? And, Dallas, that's what the Brotherhood will be doing tonight. So here's my dedication to the black coffee of the world, regardless of whatever flava you may be. Here's a song, sung by brothers, for us brothers. Let's try to be the best men we can be, fellas. Here's Ginuwine, Case, Tyrese, and R.L. Oh, and when we come back, we're going to introduce you to the newest addition to the K103.5 family. That's right! K103.5 has a new disc jockey, and he'll be taking over the pilot's seat during the nightly *Quiet Storm* from 10:00 PM to 2:00 AM. So listen in. I'm telling you, the brother's bad. No copiloting needed for this brother. He's coming in to fly solo with his bad ass. And, callers, if you know who it is, call in. The first caller to guess correctly will win two tickets to a dinner at Bailey's, courtesy of K103.5. So call in, and let's see if y'all know something about what's going on down here at the mothership. Aiight, y'all, 'nuff said about that. Here's Ginuwine, Case, Tyrese, and R.L. with 'The Best Man I Can Be.'"

The brothers were back in the booth, and what was left of the Brotherhood—DK, Brass, Malcolm, Pastor Levine, X, and Quentin—quietly sat around the table, with Miguel waiting patiently on speakerphone. Magic had the first caller waiting on the line, and the new DJ sat ready to let Dallas know who he was and to give them a little taste of his disc-jockeying skills. Dr. Mayweather was outside the booth talking to Jessie, who had a strange look on her face but was nodding in agreement. The song was not too far from winding down, and Dr. Mayweather motioned to DK to join them outside.

When he stepped outside, Dr. Mayweather asked, "DK? What do you think about this idea?" He went on to explain the game plan he and Jessie had just hatched up, and DK listened. Although he was noticeably uneasy about it, he didn't say a word.

"Well, what do you think, DK?" asked Jessie.

"I don't know. You sure you want to tell all the brothers' business like that?"

Jessie thought about it and then looked to Dr. Mayweather for some support. She said, "Why don't we give it a try? If it works, fine. If it doesn't, we'll switch gears and find something that will. One thing is for sure: This will be reality radio at its best. The ratings will probably hit the roof, if not crash straight through it."

DK let out a heavy sigh and hit his forehead with his palm a couple of times before saying, "Okay." He looked at the two of them, turned up his lips, and went back in the studio. Dr. Mayweather and Jessie looked at each other with pursed lips and followed DK inside. As the three sat down, "The Best Man I Can Be" faded out.

"Caller, you got your boy Magic doing what he does. You think you know who the new DJ on the block is?"

"Hmm-huh, I sure do. I know who it is, and I know I'm going to be eating real good up in Bailey's once I pick up those tickets. And I know that's right. You don't know?"

Magic laughed and said, "Lord, what do we have on the other end of this line? Aiight, caller, I like a woman who's sure of herself. Who do we have on the line?"

"This is Regina."

"Regina, where you calling from?"

"Plano, baby. Plano's in the house!"

"Okay, we got a live one on the line. So, what's your answer?"

"You, Magic?"

"Me? Girl, I'm already a DJ at K103.5. Whatchu talking 'bout? We said a new DJ."

"No, you didn't. You didn't say that. What you said was a new DJ for the *Quiet Storm*."

"Girl, how you gone argue with your boy? Never mind, Regina. I ain't got time for you. I got a consolation prize for you, though, just for being a good sport and playing."

"Oh, really! What is it?"

"It starts with a *g* and ends with a sound."

"I don't know, Magic. What is it?"

"You ready, girl?"

"Yah! What is it?"

"Regina, your prize is a 'good-bye' and . . . *CLICK!*" Magic started laughing, and everybody in the studio hit the floor laughing and cutting the fool. "Okay, callers. Let me set the record straight. This is a new—one more time, a new—DJ on the scene. If you've been following *The Brotherhood*, then you already know who it is. He gave us one of the best *Brotherhood* segments when he filled in as a guest DJ. Put the next caller through. Caller number 2, are you there?"

"Yes. Hey! Am I on the radio? Did I get through?"

"Yah, you're on the radio, and you're talking to Magic. What's your name? And what's your answer?"

"This is Connie from Carrollton. Is it . . . well, is it Brass?"

"Baby gul, you got it!" said Brass. "This is your new pilot for your flight through the *Quiet Storm*, but it ain't hardly gone be quiet. We gone be making all kinds of noises up in that camp."

"Yes! Yes! Yes! I knew it was you, Brass. I knew it was you, with your fine ass!"

"Gul! Quiet down over there. Thank you for the compliment, though; but I gotta do my job and tell you what you won. Now, Connie, I'm holding up two tickets to one of the hottest restaurants in town. Hold on, baby gul, I think I heard somebody in the studio say—who is it?"

Everybody yelled out, "Bailey's!"

And Brass came back with, "I know that's effin' right! Say it one more time."

Again, everybody yelled out, "Bailey's!"

Brass said, "Music to my ears. Connie, I got tickets for dinner for two. Bring whoever you want now to Bailey's. We gone start you off right with cocktails, if you want 'em. Then you get your choice of appetizer; and then you get to choose from a wide selection of entrées. And after that, if you still have room in that tummy of yours for more, choose from a smorgasbord of after-dinner desserts or dessert coffees. I recommend that black coffee, gul. It can burn off some of those calories you just ate and put your behind to sleep afterward. Listen to me, fellas. I'm talking dirty to her, and she don't even know it."

"Oh! Thank you, Brass! Thank you. And I definitely need to try me some of that black coffee. Humph! Sho' does sound delicious—if it's anything like you."

Brass laughed. "No problem, baby gul. I believe we have another satisfied flyer, y'all. This is your boy Brass coming to you on that real tip—that *Quiet Storm* tip. And starting tomorrow, we'll be taking a trip on Eros Airlines. I gotta warn you, though, it's gonna be a bumpy and dangerous flight. Don't be scared, though. I guarantee you that you'll be in good hands, 'cause I'll be your pilot—Captain Brass, that is—and we're going to embark on an incredible journey. A journey filled with R&B classics infused with some light jazz, a little soulful hip-hop, and some really sensual funk. So, after a hard day's work, we want you to sit back, relax, and just enjoy the ride. Connie, don't go nowhere. We need to get some information from you; and while we do, we're going to play some Prince.

"Let's start this jig off right with 'International Lover,' 'cause our first destination will be scandalous, y'all. We're flying into that 'Erotic City' and get all up in those purple walls, ladies. And just to let you know, Prince's 'Erotic City' will always be the destination for the new *Quiet Storm* with Brass. It'll always be the last song played. The flight is four hours, and I'll be playing everything those aching, lonely, and lusting hearts of yours will desire, and need, to get you through the night. By the end of the show, I'm gonna make you wanna touch yourself."

Brass played a sound-bite of a female moaning erotically and then laughed out loud. All the brothers started clapping and barking, saying, "That's our boy! Throw it down, Brass. Throw it down, man!" Brass started singing along with Prince, "Awwwww-oooooh, can you feel it? Can you feel it, K103.5? Awwwww-Oooooh. WHEW!"

Jessie said, "Well, well. And a WHEW to you too, boy. Hmph! I do say. Now, Brass—Lord, I need to recover after that! WHEW! Lord." Jessie got a hold of herself and asked, "Can you tell the K103.5 audience how this came to be? How did you come to be the new DJ for K103.5, and the DJ for the *Quiet Storm* at that?"

"Hey gul, check dis out. I gotta give credit where credit is due. I owe it all to dis here Brothahood. I mean, without these cats, I probably would be on da streets doing da same 'ole thang. Living a life that was just about to come to an end—I mean literally, Dallas. Me and my girl were wrapped up—if not trapped—in a vicious cycle. But the brothas stepped in, helped out where they could, and eventually helped fix things and got us out of all that mess. Me and my girl are good now, real good." Brass started to chuckle and then clapped his hands a few times.

"I'm sorry, y'all. I'm just thinking about when we first started the Brothahood, and da Doc—Dr. Mayweather over here—challenged all the brothers to be each other's keepers. Let's just say I got kept like a b-i-t-c-h, but it was all good. I'm living proof. Look at the results."

Brass talked, if not testified, for a good five minutes; and all the brothers, Jessie, and Dr. Mayweather were nodding their heads and encouraging him. A few minutes before a commercial break, DK held out his hand and motioned for Brass to wrap it up.

"Dallas, my man DK is telling me I gotta wrap this [beep] up; but before I go, I wanna answer my gul Jessie's question about how I got started with K103.5. I'm telling you, family. Talk 'bout brothas helping brothas. That's just what my man DK did. He helped a brotha out, and it all came about during one of our sessions with Dr. Mayweather. DK found out that I used to be a DJ at a radio station back in da day, and he took a chance on me. He set me up for an audition at the station; and, Jess, when I stepped back into the studio and got behind the controls again, it was like putting on an old comfortable pair of shoes. I just walked right back into it. And after da audition . . . and test, after test, after test, they brought your boy on."

Pastor Levine yelled out, "THAT'S ALL RIGHT!"

DK said, "That's right, y'all. And, family, our boy here is a natural, don't y'all agree?"

The Doc started clapping and cheering, and everyone else joined in. He stood up and motioned for the brothers and Jessie to stand up as well, and he started to chant, "Am I my brother's keeper?"

And the brothers shouted, "YES, I AM!" This lasted for a good while, until DK broke the vibe.

"It's a feel-good vibe in here tonight. I'm telling you, the vibe is all good. Brothers, Jessie, Doc, and K103.5 family, we'll be back after this commercial break. When we do, we'll have the Doc give us his spin on the Brotherhood and tell us what he's concluded about the brothers and our journey with one another. I'm DK 'Love' Niles, and we're heading into that final hour of *The Brotherhood*. Family, Big Jim wants to know, are you hungry? Well, if you are, and you're willing to brave the cold tonight, the drive-through at Big Jim's Rib Shack is still open. We're going to let Big Jim tell you how you can get your eat on; and when we come back, we'll get to the nitty-gritty with Dr. Mayweather and the rest of the brothers."

All the brothers sat around quietly thinking during the commercial break. Magic kept thinking about *The Love Forum* and how the divas ended their show with the Supremes' "Someday We'll Be Together," and all the drama that followed, and didn't know what to expect with the final farewell of *The Brotherhood*. He thought, *Damn! I sure hope this shit ain't gone be full of bitch drama.*

DK waited for the commercial to end and said to himself, *A week ago, I didn't even know if we could pull off another* Brotherhood; *but my girl Jessie worked miracles and brought the brothers back together.* Miguel was absent physically, but he was on the phone and was feeling really good about his experience. Michael and Donnell were nowhere to be found. They wouldn't even respond to the dozen or so phone calls from DK, Jessie, and Doc Mayweather, who pleaded for them to give *The Brotherhood* another go-around. The only brother left from their group was X, and DK already knew how his story was going to end. So in essence, the brothers that stuck together were triumphant on so many levels. As for the brothers who chose to walk the road alone, they didn't fare so well. X, unfortunately, was going to be the last brother to stumble and fall. DK, knowing X's fate, worried about him and found it hard to even look him in the eye. He knew what the future held for him; and at that moment, he wished he had never heard the name *Ms. Doretha*. His heart ached for his brother, and he hoped, with all his hurting heart, that her prediction wouldn't come true for him.

"K103.5, we're back, and we have Dr. Franklin Mayweather on the mic. Doc, you good tonight?"

"I'm doing good, DK."

"So, Doc, you and Jessie put this show together, right?"

"That's right."

"Can you tell our listeners what your game plan was for the final *Brotherhood*?"

"Well, DK, let me get my thoughts together here. Jessie and I wanted the K103.5 listeners to catch up on where the brothers were in their lives. It's been almost two months since our last show, and we thought it would be appropriate to let our listeners know how the brothers, that they've been following for the last past six months, have been doing in their lives."

"Okay, that sounds good, Doc. I think our listeners will enjoy that; but I'm fielding questions from our call-in line, and Curtis from Mesquite wants to know: What, if anything, did you discover while working with the brothers?"

"That's a good question. And, Curtis, it's been an interesting journey. I was fortunate to work with a diverse group of men with diverse problems. If you recall, we had three groups of brothers—three brothers in each group. Group 1 had Michael, Donnell, and Xavier. That group didn't fair too well, and only one of the three brothers is with us tonight. How you doing over there, X?"

"I'm good, Doc. Guess I had to be on the losing team, huh?"

Doc Mayweather gave X one of those *I guess so* looks, and then continued answering Curtis's question. "Then we had group 2 with DK, Miguel, and Brass. That group lost a brother, who got married and moved away to Brazil; but their group had the most significant accomplishments. One brother, by the help of the other two, rose triumphantly after having fallen. He was cleared of some legal issues plaguing him and soon found himself on top of the world—living the life he always dreamed about. Ain't that right, brother Brass?"

"Yep, Doc. You ain't tellin' nothin' but the truth."

Doc Mayweather smiled at Brass and then looked over at DK. "Now, I'm looking at another brother of this group who was elevated to a position that he always wanted for himself but didn't know how to obtain. Nor was he confident enough to think he could be successful doing it. DK is now the new programming director for K103.5. He started with his new career January first. Congratulations, my brother."

Everyone started clapping for DK, and he waved everybody down, telling them to stop. He told the brothers, "Nope. Can't take the credit for this. This would have never happened if it hadn't been for Melissa Morgan (rest in peace, baby girl), Sharon Wisely (hey, new mommy-to-be, stay off your feet, girl), and my girl Jessie over here—I owe you big time for not only believing in me, but also for steering me in the right direction. And as I've told everyone on *The DK and Magic Morning Show*, the show is now carrying a new name. Starting tomorrow morning, Dallas, you'll be waking up to *Magic Mornings*. Yep! The music maestro himself, Mr. Kirk 'Magic' Wonder, will be holding down *The DK and Magic Morning Show* all by himself."

Magic said, "Hey-a-yah-eee! Come check me out, Dallas."

Which prompted all the brothers and Jessie to say out loud, "Oh lord."

Doc Mayweather laughed and looked at DK across the table and gave him a thumbs-up, shaking his head in pride. He asked Miguel if he was still on the line, and whether he would like to share what the Brotherhood had meant to him.

"He encontrado a algunos amigos verdaderos en la Hermandad. That means that I've found some true friends in the Brotherhood. I'm not one of those men who have a lot of friends, and one thing the Brotherhood did for me is bring me closer to a group of brothers. The one I grew closest to was my best man in my wedding. It's been good helping the brothers; and in turn, they've helped me as well. Oh, and, DK, how is the maid of honor? Uhm, what's her name?"

"V, Miguel. Her name is V."

"Yah, V. You guys got any closer?"

"Man, you blasting all my business on the radio. What's wrong with you? Yah, man. As a matter of fact, me and Vanessa are real close. She's an incredible lady, man. She has my back one hundred percent, and I have hers. I definitely can trust my V, man. Family, y'all go on down and check her out at Sweet V's Beauty Shop."

"Hey! Then I know it's going good for you if you said that."

Everybody started laughing, and Doc Mayweather said, "Thanks, Miguel. I know I got to wrap it up before the next commercial break. So, finally, there was group 3 with Quentin, Pastor Levine, and Malcolm."

Malcolm said, "Doc, why you trippin'? You know this was the best group."

"I don't disagree with you, Malcolm. This group did experience some significant life-changing revelations and movement out of the three groups. No doubt about that. One brother, who we just heard from, left his wife—he filed for divorce due to irreconcilable differences—and followed his passion by beginning a new career in the culinary arts. You can taste his culinary creations at one of the best restaurants in Dallas. He's at Bailey's, family."

Malcolm leaned into the microphone and said, "Doc, best decisions I ever made. I'm good now. Real good. And I want to thank DK for hooking a brother up with the apprenticeship at Bailey's and letting me bunk down at his crib while I get things straight." He reached over and gave DK some dap. "That's right, my nigga."

"Malcolm, we're going to have to work on you about using that N-word."

"What, Doc? What?"

"Moving along, Malcolm. I'm moving along. Now, another brother, with the help of the Brotherhood, changed directions when it came to how he delivered his craft; and his ministry has grown as a result. He's also deepened his relationship with a particular woman—all by doing what was right, if not protecting the woman he loved. Pastor, do you have anything to say?"

"Doc, just know that I'm a changed man. When it comes to my ministry, just know that I'm walking by faith and not by that all-too-familiar and common sight. Family, if you want to know what the good Doc and I are talking about, plan to make a trip down to Greater Antioch one Sunday. You'll be able to see, firsthand, what the power of walking right can do."

Jessie said, "All right now."

"Well, Brotherhood, I'm down to the last brother—our brother Quentin. Q is raising his little daughter, Meli, with the help of this young lady sitting right here at the table. Hey, god-momma, Jessie."

Jessie smiled and said, "Hey, Meli. Night, night."

"I believe we're pressed for time, and DK has some questions from our listeners. Is that right, DK?"

"That's right, Doc."

"Okay, I'm wrapping it up, brother. I'm wrapping it up. I just want to share this bit of advice I gave our brother Quentin when we first began the Brotherhood: K103.5 family, unless you confront what's holding you back, your life is going to go around in circles, and you're going to continue to make the same ole mistakes. Confront those demons, brothers and sisters. You'll be able to move on with your life once you do."

"Amen, Doc. Amen," said DK as he nudged Quentin on the side. "We got a question from Cheryl from Rowlett. Doc? Cheryl wants to know how you arranged the groups. Did you pick out names from a hat? Did you ask the brothers to pair up? How did you choose the groups?"

"WOW! The callers are really asking some good questions, DK. Cheryl, to answer your question, the groups were arranged by the men participating in an exercise and choosing the brothers they distrusted the most. If they ended up in a group together, that meant that for some reason, they didn't trust the brothers in that group."

"So, Franklin—" Jessie stopped and quickly corrected herself. "Dr. Mayweather? What was the purpose of this?"

"Another good question. The purpose, or goal, was for the brothers to work together and gain each other's trust. In my years of experience doing this, the brothers that didn't bond usually left their group and joined another or withdrew from the experience altogether. Which we saw with Michael, Donnell, and Xavier's group."

"One last question for you, if I may."

"Go ahead, Jessie."

"What would cause one to leave their group or the experience altogether?"

"Could be an array of things. However, two things always knock on the door of truth afterward. One is that a person is harboring a secret he or she doesn't want anyone to know, and the other is just plain old fear. It's usually the fear of someone finding out one's imperfections."

As Dr. Mayweather continued his explanation, Jessie decided that she needed to know where Quentin was in his life. She knew she cared about him, but she didn't really know if it was mutual. Every time something appeared to be happening, something always got in the way. She decided to take a chance and interrupted Dr. Mayweather.

"I'm sorry, Dr. Mayweather, but I think the K103.5 listeners would like to know more about how Quentin fared with the Brotherhood. What did he gain from the experience? How did he grow from it, and how has his life changed? Quentin, can you tell us how your life has changed?"

Quentin looked at all the brothers and thought something had to be wrong. Did he miss something? Was he supposed to do something and didn't, and thus missed his opportunity to better himself, be happy, become the best man he could be? How was he supposed to confront his demon when he couldn't even find *her*? Embarrassed, he cut his eyes around the room and answered, "My life is the same. Nothing dramatic has happened. I'm just raising my daughter and hoping my birthday—which is March twentieth, by the way—will be much happier than the last."

Jessie asked, "And why is that?"

Quentin, surprised by the question, clenched his jaw and stared at Jessie, hard. Everyone saw it too, and the studio went dead silent. All eyes were on him. He drummed up a short beat on the table with his knuckles and groaned. "Well, Jess, as you already know, last year, *I lost the love of my life* a week before my birthday."

"Oh my god, I totally forgot! I'm so sorry . . . I just . . . oh, God. I failed to connect the two. Quentin, I'm so—"

"Yah." He looked at Jess as if to say, *How could you not remember?* "Melissa— that's Melissa Morgan, family—passed away on March 13, 2009. It was bad. It was a difficult time, Jess, you know that. Wasn't a good time at all, for obvious reasons." Quentin threw his head back and covered it with his hands and moaned, "It wasn't a good birthday, man. Not at all."

Jessie swallowed. It went down the wrong way, and she started coughing. She didn't even think about Melissa passing away and was equally disappointed by what he had just said about the love of his life; but she understood. Brass, in tune to what was happening, noticed the moment was spiraling down, fast, and intervened.

"Brothas, we got to make sure our boy has a slamming birthday. We got a little over two months to plan the shi[beep] right. K103.5, we're going to be taking your suggestions all week long on the *Quiet Storm* on how we can make Quentin's—brother, how old you gone be?"

"Thirty-three."

"On how we gone make Q's thirty-third one of the best birthdays he's ever had." Brass got up and started doing the cabbage patch and said, "Club Onyx, baby! Club Onyx!"

Magic joined in the dancing and yelled out, "Hey-a-yah-eee!" And started chanting, "Nookie real good!"

Quentin threw up his hand and made a screeching noise, gesturing for Magic to stop, laughing. "Naw, brother, I definitely got to bring that plan to a screeching halt. That's okay, Brass. Good looking out, but I remember the last party you planned. I think I'll pass, man."

"Quent? What you saying? Don't be trying to throw salt in the game. We got you, my man. We got you on this. Let us do dis for ya."

Quentin was shaking his head. "Naw. Naw. That's okay, Brass. I think I'm just going to take it easy. Reflect on some things. And my girl has something planned anyway. She's been hinting about it ever since we rang in the New Year." A smile broke out across Quentin's face, and he shook his head. "She's saying that this is going to be a good year for us. We're moving to the next level in our relationship. She keeps telling me to 'wait 'til your birthday,' talking about, 'you'll see.'"

Jessie tried to smile but couldn't pull off even a halfway attempt. She thought, *Lord, were Melissa and Ms. Doretha right? All the brothers have gained something and moved on in their lives. I know it takes him a while to do things and come around, procrastinating, but will this ever happen between us? And, God, when?* She looked at Quentin and saw that he seemed perplexed, in deep thought. But little did she know that he was thinking the same thing.

Chapter 31

Quentin's Birthday

March 20, 2010

The big double three had crept up on Quentin, and today he had made plans to celebrate his thirty-third with Chéri, who had planned a very special evening. She told him to be at her place at eight and left the details on a simple white card with a picture of an antique key and the words "The Key to Your Fantasies" printed at the bottom. On the inside, there were these three simple instructions:

Use your key to open the door.
Put the gift (one of the Twister Magnums) on the coffee table on, and bring in the box.
Open the bedroom door (don't turn on the light) and lay facedown on the bed.

When he arrived, Quentin used his key to open the door, stripped butt naked, put his gift on on the table, and slowly opened the door to Chéri's bedroom. The room was pitch-black, except for the slither of light coming in from the living room; and he used it to guide him over to the bed. As instructed, he lay facedown. Across from the bed was a large bay window, which he was all too familiar with; but today, there was something extra. There were floor-to-ceiling theater curtains, which slowly began to open, letting in a flood of white light that etched the soft silhouette of a perfectly shaped body. He heard the sound of a hand clap, and Prince's "Erotic City" began to play. And that body started to dance—moving, shaking, and wiggling, all nasty as only a true freak could do.

A loud smack filled the room, and Quentin yelled out, "Shit! Damn, girl!" He felt a sharp pain across his back and ass as Chéri assaulted his backside with several blows of a cat-o'-nine-tail whip. She said, "A little bit of pain before the pleasure, baby. Get ready for the ride of your life, birthday boy." And she purred like a cat as she ran the cat o' nine tails up and down his back, stopping at the crack of his ass. She walked around to the head of the bed and stood in front of him, bent down, and licked the side of his face up and down with her tongue. She then put her foot on his head and ran the cat o' nine tails up and down her leg. "Come kiss this kitty. It's waiting for you, daddy. Don't you want this kitty? Tell momma how you want this kitty." She purred again and said, "Don't you hear it calling for you? Ooooh, daaaddy. I know you want it."

Quentin spun around and positioned himself between her legs and kissed that wet spot, making Chéri moan out loud in pleasure. She pushed his head up between her legs. "I got a surprise for you."

Quentin came down for air and mumbled, "Oh yah? What's the surprise?"

Chéri did a short, high-pitched cat call and told Quentin to watch the bathroom door. As the music pumped through the room, somebody slowly walked out of the darkness of the bathroom, one foot in front of the other, like a model on the catwalk, slowly making their way into God's night light. Chéri stood above Quentin's head and danced, throwing her hair from side to side and motioning for the person of mystery to come over. She said, "Girl, do your thang. Come over here and show my boy how we do it."

The moonlight hit the sister's perfect body as she shook, rolled, and bounced around in a tight black teddy that was accented with a multistrand pearl necklace belt around her waist. Quentin checked her out, starting with the Mardi Gras eye mask she was wearing, with these huge red feathers on each side. He slowly worked his way down to her breasts, which were peeking through holes cut out of the teddy, and moved down to her flat stomach, moving down to the perfect *V* that pointed to that goody box. Her hips flared out from her waist, and her legs and thighs said, *I'm going to wrap these mothas around your black ass tight tonight.* And Quentin thought, DAMN! *Nice. She's tight and right! Just the way I like 'em.* His heart started racing and almost jumped out of his chest, as he didn't know what to expect; and the anticipation, coupled with the unknown, was killing him.

He asked himself, *Who is she? What does she look like? What kind of freaky shit do these two freaks have planned for me tonight?* The mysterious woman slowly danced her way over to the entertainment center, and Quentin watched as the moonlight highlighted her body in all the right places. Quentin couldn't believe how tight and right she was—she was even better than Chéri. She did a quick and sexy spiral down to the floor, tapped the Play button on the CD tower, and slowly started coming back up, making one ass cheek rise higher than the other before "Erotic City" came to an end and the new jam "Perfect Match," from the *School Daze* soundtrack, filled the room.

As he was kissing Chéri's thighs, he lustfully watched the sister; and in a low voice, he told Chéri, "Damn, this is nice. It's bringing back some good ole memories, girl. Thank you, momma." Quentin quickly turned his attention back to the sister as she made her way to the bed, doing her nasty, freakish grind to the music. Quentin reached up and started to finger Chéri, watching as this hellified fine-ass sista did her dance-hall grind. His shit was hard as fuck, and he reached down and started stroking it. Chéri reached down, rolled the condom up, and flipped it off Quentin's dick. She touched the head, as it leaked a glob of precum; wiped it off; and slowly licked his juice from her fingers. She kissed Quentin, with it still on her tongue; and he laughed and said, "You's a freak."

"Uh-huh, you know you love it," Chéri said.

Quentin laughed out loud and said, "Yah! You know I do, girl."

"All right, then . . . don't play. You ready for your surprise, baby? Is the birthday boy ready?"

"Hell yah! Bring that shit on, baby. What kinda freaky shit you got for daddy?"

Chéri squatted her pantiless ass down on Quentin's face, jiggled it around a little, moaned, and said, "I hope it tastes good to you, baby. Well, birthday boy, I'd like you to meet someone special—my better half, that is.

"What you mean your better half?" Quentin asked.

"Oh boy, don't play like you didn't know. I'm a sista that has to have the best of both worlds. I'm not just strictly dickly, you know. When I need something big, hard, and stiff, that's where you come in; but when I need something salty and sweet, my girl is the one I call on. For tonight, you can just call her Ms. Pussylicious, 'cause her shit be tasting so, so good. Now, don't get it twisted. This is a onetime deal. She's not really into dudes. My girl just wants to make this a special night for you, and to please me. You good with everything?"

Quentin—wanting to get his groove on—wasn't even fazed by what Chéri had just said. He had told himself over and over that Chéri was nice, and they had a good time together (when they were together); but he definitely couldn't see himself in a committed long-term relationship with her. He looked on as Pussylicious turned around, squatted, and started to shake that ass, making it pop and clap to the beat; and he answered, "Yah, I'm good."

Things were heating up something awful. The bedroom was filled with the smell of pure sex. It was an oven, and Pussylicious had turned up the temperature another two hundred degrees. Quentin lay across the bed on his back, perched up on his elbows, and happily dangled his feet over the edge. He watched Chéri dance above him and then turned his attention to Pussylicious as she did her thang.

"Hey girl, you better work that shit! Work that shit, girl!" Quentin yelled as he grabbed his shit and stroked it.

Even though Quentin was mesmerized by Chéri's better half, for some reason, he kept squinting, trying to get a good look at Pussylicious's face; but that mask, with those big-ass feathers, concealed it. Pussylicious kept dancing, ass just a-pounding. She pulled down the teddy's shoulder straps and pulled the teddy down right below her titties. Her nipples were standing at attention. Beautiful brown nipples—hard, pointing straight at Quentin, who opened his mouth, jokingly, to catch them.

"Come on over here, girl. Come talk to daddy with your fine ass," he said as he began to move his ass around on the bed.

Chéri echoed Quentin's request: "Come on, baby. Let's show this nigga how it's done."

Pussylicious started to dance over to the bed. Her nicely defined legs were killing that dance as she nailed every beat of "Perfect Match," just like Quentin's girl used to do back in the day. She slowly made her way to the bed and grabbed Quentin's foot. She massaged it as she slowly raised it to her mouth and started sucking on his big toe. He moaned, and she slowly took his toe and guided it down her body, stopping below her breast, where she slowly used it to pull her teddy the rest of the way down. All Quentin kept thinking of was how hot she was—from her head all the way down to her feet; and he knew it, because precum was oozing from his dick like never before. He anxiously kept tugging at the tight teddy with his toe—slowly but surely pulling it down. He kept watching her and watching her, all the while getting this strange feeling about something: It was as though something—something he couldn't put his finger on—was coming back to him. Everything just seemed familiar—too damn familiar. He felt that he had been here before; this was déjà vu.

He left Chéri dancing at the edge of the bed and scooted to the other side and just stared. He stared so hard that it threw him off, and he not only lost his train of thought, but his raging hard-ass dick also went limp. He stared, as the mystery woman continued to use his toe to make her teddy go down lower and lower on her body. As he felt Chéri crawl across the bed and lick and kiss his back, his mouth dropped dead open. What was once all too familiar to him, what he could never forget or put out of his mind suddenly came to light: *A tattoo of a black rattlesnake with yellow eyes and a red forked tongue* emerged as Pussylicious's teddy dropped to the floor. She started making a rattling noise, like the rattle from a rattlesnake's tail; and Quentin winced and said, "Huh?" *Did I just see what I thought I just saw? Did she just make a rattling noise like my girl used to? Naw . . . can't be.*

He yelled, "Wait, wait, wait! Wait a goddamn minute. What the fuck!" He pushed Chéri off of him, jumped up, and ran over to the bedroom door and hit the lights.

"Allison? Alli-Mae Rayford? SHIT! Is that you, girl?" Quentin asked with a puzzled, if not distraught, look on his face. He couldn't believe it; and he kept waving his arms and hands up and down and saying "Shit, shit, shit" over and over.

"Naw. Naw. Can't be. Please tell me that's not you, Alli-Mae. Please tell me it's not you," he said.

Chéri quickly jumped up off the bed and said, "Oh shit! What's going on, Quentin?" She turned off the music and stood in the middle of the floor, with both hands on her hips, staring Allison down, as if to say, *Bitch, what the fuck?* Dumbfounded, she shook her head and said, "Is this some shit or what? Uh-huh, girl, where's the camera? 'Cause the shit going down up in here can't be real. Can't be." She jokingly started looking around the room. "Girl, who you done got to pull a prank on me? This is a joke, right?" The room was silent; no one said a word. "Allison? Allison? Do you hear me, baby? What's going on? Do you know Quentin?"

Allison threw her head back; let out a long, heavy sigh; and slowly shook her head. "Yes, Chéri. Yes. I know Quentin." She grabbed her head as sweat started to bead up on her forehead and run down her face. She started coughing and coughing and wiping away the sweat. In between her coughing, which worsened, she got the words out that she felt lightheaded. Chéri told her to sit down. Allison stumbled over to the bed, plopped herself down, and put her head in her lap and just kept shaking it in anguish. Before anyone could say another word, she started hacking, wheezing, and holding her chest, trying to breathe.

Chéri said, "Oh Lord. Girl, not now!" She ran into the bathroom and came back with an inhaler, which she gave to Allison at once, repeatedly telling her to take a couple of deep puffs. Allison did as told. Chéri sat on the bed, put her arms around Allison, and stroked her hair as she waited for her symptoms to lessen and eventually go away.

"Still have the asthma, huh?" Quentin asked as he made his way over to the bed and sat down on the other side of Allison.

After a few minutes, Allison started breathing better. "Yah," she answered Quentin. "It's gotten better over the years." And she started to calm down and pull herself together. "Remember when it used to take me thirty minutes, even a couple of hours, to come down from a bout? And, Lord, if I was sick with a cold, forget it. It could take days, even weeks, to get over it."

Quentin answered, "Yah, I remember." And he hunched over, clasped his hands, as if in prayer, and looked over at the two women, who were cuddled up. "I remember I would hold you so tight just like that. I probably was more scared than you were, but I tried to make you feel that I had you anyway . . . that everything would be all right."

Quentin looked at Chéri holding Allison just like he used to hold her and couldn't help thinking, *A fucking lesbian. All these years, I've been pining for this woman. Can't fucking move on with my life, and she's been a fucking lesbo all the time. I be damned.*

"Allison? What's going on?" Chéri asked again. "Baby, how do you know Quentin?"

Allison leaned over and laid her head on Chéri's shoulder. "We used to be close back in the day—boyfriend and girlfriend . . . Madison high school . . . remember, Quentin?"

Quentin grimaced and nodded his head. "Yah, I remember."

Allison looked at Quentin and noticed the painful look on his face and diverted her eyes. "Matter of fact, we were voted homecoming king and queen;

and everyone just knew we were going to get married and be that power couple everybody envied and hated." She looked back at Quentin and said, "Wow. That's been over thirteen years ago. How time flies." She sighed. "Long story short, our relationship went on well beyond high school and into our first year in college—"

"And," Chéri interrupted, "how did y'all get to this point? How did we get to this point, sitting here, looking at each other stupid."

Allison shook her head and took a couple of deep breaths. "God! I don't know how we got here. I thought I was finished with this years ago. I didn't let it get to the point of marriage. There wasn't going to be any power couple, or being envied or hated. I walked away. I thought it would be better just to leave and not tell anyone—no questions to be asked, no questions to be answered. My god . . . it feels almost like it was yesterday when I packed my stuff, headed over to the college registrar's office, and withdrew without a second thought in my mind. I drove home and left that lie, and the life I used to live, behind. I knew I couldn't live it anymore."

Allison placed her hand on Quentin's back and said in a reassuring voice, "And, Quentin, no words can express the sorrow I had in my heart for leaving you that way. But I just couldn't be the woman you wanted me to be." She put her head back in her lap and said, "I loved you, but I knew I wasn't in love with you—if that makes any sense. I'm so, so sorry." She sighed and turned her head to look at Chéri. "My heart just wasn't in it. Not like it is right here."

Quentin sat up and looked at Allison with a needing-and-wanting-to-know look on his face. "Why didn't you just tell me? Why did you leave me wondering what was going on? What happened with us? What did I do or didn't do? Hell, where were you, and how could you just vanish off the face of the earth? I looked for you everywhere. I even drove down to your mom's house and asked all around town. Mrs. Mamey told me that she didn't know where you were, but I got the feeling she was lying to me."

"Momma probably didn't know, Quentin. After I told her, she threw me out, said that she didn't want to see me no more." Allison shook her head. "Yah. The good Christian woman threw me out, and I haven't seen or spoken to her since. I don't know if she's still alive or what. But I still have love for her, and I don't love her any less for what she did, although I should."

"Allison! Oh my god. You told me that your mother was dead. Have you told me anything about your life that was true?" Chéri asked.

"I didn't lie, Chéri. She is dead! She's dead to me, and I'm dead to her right now." Allison fell back on the bed and covered her face with her hands. "Oh, God. I've been running from my past for so, so long; and now it has come and smacked my ass. Crashed into my life, like a thousand-pound MAC truck smashing into a concrete wall—with all the pieces flying up everywhere. I guess that's my life right now. I'm now finding all the pieces, picking 'em up. Guess I deserve it, though. And, Quentin, I guess, at the very least, I owe you an explanation—if not a hell of an apology. And I know I do."

"Naw," said Quentin, "you've said all that needs to be said. You don't owe me anything. We tried the game of love, and we all know that game has no rules or promises, no expectations or guarantees—just a blank page to be filled out as you go along. Sometimes the story has a happy ending; sometimes it doesn't. Just so happens our story didn't have a happy ending. That's the way it goes, I imagine. Love, I mean"

Allison sat back up and grabbed the necklace hanging around her neck. "Well, at least let me give this back to you." She looked down at the necklace and smiled. "I kept it all these years."

"Give back what?" Quentin asked, looking at the necklace. "Oh snap! No! You ain't still wearing . . . is that my engagement ring?"

Allison unhooked the clasp and slid the ring off. "Here. I kept it as a reminder of how my life used to be. I gotta feeling that maybe you need it more than me . . . for closure, I suppose . . . move on with your life. And I mean, you did pay for it." She gave Quentin a small hug and told him, "So you can stop all the worrying . . . worrying about what happened to me, and all the woulda-coulda-shouldas that went along with it. I'm fine, Quentin, and happy as my life will let me be."

Quentin took the ring, got up, and walked to the bathroom and closed the door. When he reappeared, he had washed away, if not scrubbed off, all of the chaos of the night. He walked over to the bedroom door and leaned against the wall and started banging his head against it, all the while thinking, *I still can't believe this shit. She's been on the D-L.* He pushed away from the wall and started to head out of the bedroom, but stopped when he heard Chéri's voice.

"Quentin? Quentin? Where are you going?" she asked.

Quentin stood in the doorway, contemplating what to do, and then turned around. "You know, that's a good question. Where am I going? Where is this, right here, going?" Realizing that there was a good woman right inside his house, he scratched his head and asked in a low voice, "You know, that's the million-dollar question right now. Why am I here?"

"Oh, you don't know?" asked Chéri, sounding a bit condescending. "You're the one standing there, mothafucka. Why are you here? Huh?"

Quentin looked at the two women holding each other, lifted one corner of his mouth, and replied, "My thoughts exactly." He tossed the ring in the air and then caught it. "Thanks, Allison." And he walked out of the bedroom and didn't look back. He scooped up his clothes, put on what he needed to not get arrested for indecent exposure, and walked right out of Allison and Chéri's apartment and out of their lives for good.

As he was leaving, he muttered his thanks and praises for being delivered from his burden and smiled as he thought about that crazy pledge he and the brothers had made. He said out loud, *"Lord, thank you. I'm finally through with being through. I believe I'm healed."* He ran out of the apartment building and drove home like a junkie trying to get to his next fix. He drove like a madman, not caring about any traffic lights, road signs, or the police. The only thing on his mind was making it home—quickly. Making it home to the lady in his house; and when he arrived, he didn't even bother to make it up the driveway. Quentin ran his car up on the curb, got out, sprinted to the house, bum-rushed the door, and called out, "Jessie? . . . Jessie? Where are you? Jess?"

Chapter 32

Drama at the House

*J*essie, in the midst of tidying up the kitchen, walked out with a puzzled look, trying to avoid looking at him through hurt eyes, and asked, "So how was your night? I didn't expect you home so early. Matter of fact, I told Xavier that I thought I would be spending the night alone with Meli, until I got your call."

After he didn't respond, Jessie finally looked at his face. Her puzzled look suddenly changed to fear, and she asked hesitantly, "Quentin, are you—" Before she could get the words out of her mouth, Quentin rushed over, picked her up by the waist, and then slowly let her down, his soft lips finding hers, thinking, *Hey baby, I'm here.*

Quentin whispered, "Jess, I don't know what I was thinking about all these months, but now I know—I know I love you." He whisked Jessie up in his arms, and she wrapped her legs around his waist. Quentin slowly straddle-walked Jessie up the stairs and into the bedroom all while kissing her passionately on the neck, cheeks, ears, and lips. Jessie was so taken aback by what was happening that she forgot that she had called Xavier to come pick her up. And as Jessie and Quentin made their way to the bedroom, Musiq Soulchild's "Who Knows" was playing in the background. Quentin gently laid her down on the bed, and she caressed his head as he kissed her neck and found her mouth—his tongue passionately caressing and playing with hers. Jessie held Quentin's head with an intensity she didn't know she had; and in that moment, she wanted to let him know that she didn't want him to stop.

"Quentin?"

"Shh. Don't talk, Jess. Just follow your heart . . . I'm here, baby. I'm here. Where I should've been all along. I can't believe it, Jess. God works in mysterious ways, girl. 'Cause tonight . . . tonight, it all came together for me; and it was crystal clear. I finally realized it. I realized that I don't want to lose you, Jess. I need and want you in my life. I need you to be my joy, my inspiration, my one and only. Jessie, baby." He kissed Jessie's forehead, eyelids, nose, cheeks, and mouth. He repeated the words "I love you, I love you, I love you." And he finally said, "I need you in my life, Jessie. Will you be my wife?"

The effect of the words Jessie had longed to hear from Quentin was heightened by the passion she had only dreamt of as Quentin laid his warm body beside hers—every part of him touching her, loving her. She felt his large hands slowly open her blouse and unhook her bra; and she grew moist as he blew softly on her neck, breast, and nipples, gently kissing them. Jessie heard the music in the background and closed her eyes and held Quentin with all her might and softly but passionately returned his love.

The moonlight illuminated them as they lay in a tight embrace, and in her mind, Jessie said, *Thank you, God.* She held him and felt his hard body move down hers, and all she could do was revel in him; and she heard her inner voice say, *God, thank you! I've been in so much pain for so, so long, but now I'm free. I'm free, God. You heard my prayers . . . answered them . . . and you set me free!*

As tears rolled down her face, she felt Quentin move up her body, and she quivered as he slowly licked them away. And as time drifted—like a balloon floating away from the hand of a small child, floating up, up, up, and away—the two lovers reveled in their new moment. Until the doorbell rang.

Jessie yelled, "Oh my god, I forgot! Quentin, it's Xavier." She pushed Quentin aside.

"Xavier?" asked, Quentin.

"Yes!" Jessie answered as she fought off Quentin's hugs and kisses. "I was so upset with you that I called him after you called and told him you were on your way home. Oh my god, Quentin! I can't let him see us like this!"

"So what are you going to do? Jessie, I just poured my heart out to you. I said I wanted to make you my wife. What are you saying to me with this here? Let's make this right and tell him. You're going to stay with me, right?"

Jessie didn't answer and looked at Quentin with a face written all over with fright. She rushed to get up and stumbled around the room searching for her clothes, desperately trying to find each and every piece that Quentin had peeled off of her, and quickly put them on. She ran out of the bedroom and down the stairs and, in a last attempt, tried to adjust her clothes before opening the front door. Still a little disheveled, Jessie opened the door and grabbed Xavier by the arm. "Hey you! You got here fast."

"What are you talking about? You said be quick about it. I thought you didn't want to be around after he got home?"

"I know. I know," Jessie said as Quentin knowingly came downstairs with his shirt wide open, buttoning the top button on his jeans and zipping them up, a semihard dick still evident through the fabric. At that moment, Xavier knew something was up. *I don't believe this shit!*

"I'm feeling real uncomfortable right about now. What the fuck is going on, Jess? Quent? Hell . . . somebody!"

"Xavier, what are you talking about?" asked Jessie.

"Yah, X, what you trying to say? I'm just waking up, man."

"Nigga, what are you talking about? You just got home! Hell, I ain't stupid. What the fuck you talking about sleep for?"

"X, quit trippin', man. I came home a little tipsy—that's why my fucking car is on the curb, nigga." Man, I can't believe you trippin' like this, X. Nothing's going on. Trust me, yo."

"Yah. Yah. Right, man. Jessie? You ready to go?"

"Yes, baby, hold on . . . let me check on Meli and get my purse."

As Jessie went upstairs to check on Meli and get her purse, Xavier and Quentin stood in silence, neither of them looking at each other. Jessie came back downstairs and gave Quentin a hug. "Okay, Quentin. Meli should be good for the rest of the night. Her clothes are in the dryer. Just turn it back on and get the wrinkles out before folding them up. Call me if you need me."

Quentin gave Jessie a tight hug and, as if nothing happened, attempted to give X some brotherly love.

"Naw, that's okay, man," Xavier said as he slapped Quentin's arms down. "Me and Jess need to get the hell out of here before something real, real bad goes down with you."

Quentin held his hands out, as if to say, *Wassup with you?* He asked, "X, man, why does it have to be this way?"

"Nigga, are you freakin' kidding me? Jess? You got your shit, right?"

"Yes, Xavier, I have everything."

"Let's get the fuck out of here. And watch your back, nigga." Xavier grabbed Jessie's arm and pulled her toward the door. Before his foot hit the threshold, he turned around and looked Quentin up and down—a look that would kill if it could—and said, "You really know the meaning of 'am I my brother's keeper,' man. Fake-ass nigga. Like I said, watch your back. 'Cause one fuckup, and I'm going to be all over it. And I swear. Nigga, I swear my hand before God himself: If you even breathe lightly on Jessie, let alone touch her, you gone need an army to keep me off your ass. You got me? Sleep with one eye open, nigga."

Chapter 33

The Drive Home

Something was about to happen, or maybe it was destiny; and Quentin, Jessie, and Xavier knew it—when, how, and where it would happen was the question running through everyone's mind. Two would wish that that something would come sooner, rather than later; and one was hoping it would stay far, far away. Unfortunately, for that one, sooner was now the reality; and that reality was unfolding right outside of Quentin's house.

The house—lit up by landscape lighting and glowing like a Broadway stage—was the perfect backdrop for the night's performance; and the performance and clowning began with Quentin's front door swinging open and smashing against the outside of the house.

Quentin yelled, "What the fuck's your problem, X?" He grabbed X by the coat collar, pulling him backward. Without saying a word, Xavier elbowed Quentin in the chest, knocking him back, and shoved Jessie out of the door and down the driveway. His actions were definitely out of character, not the gentleman-like behavior everyone associated with the name of Dr. Xavier Houston. And although Xavier always found pleasure in opening the car door for Jessie like a true gentleman and tucking her neatly inside, making sure she was well taken care of, the thought of performing the kind act didn't even cross his mind. He just shoved her in the direction of the passenger's side and told her, "Get your ass in the car, Jess!"

He unlocked the driver's door, got in, and flipped the lock for Jessie to let herself in. "Oh, it's like that now?" asked Jessie as she fastened the seat belt and opened the glove compartment to put her purse inside, but her words didn't even register with him. Even if they did, he still would not have responded. Xavier could only see Quentin in his mind, coming down the stairs with his shirt open, zipping up his pants, which could not hide a semihard dick; and he grew more enraged as he looked up at the house, only to see Quentin talking on his cell phone and peering through the window.

"Jess, I'm only going to ask this once. Only once. Is there anything you need to tell me?"

Jessie answered, "Huh? What are you talking about, Xavier?"

"Come on, Jess, don't try to play me. For some reason"—he shook his head, clutched the steering wheel, and stared straight through the windshield—"my soul ain't sitting right with this shit tonight. I just got this hunch. Something just doesn't feel right. Shit just ain't adding up, Jess. And why is this nigga standing in the window looking at us?"

Jessie, who had started to get worried, turned to look at Xavier, who wouldn't meet her gaze, and put her hand on Xavier's arm and calmly said, "Xavier, for the umpteenth time, there's nothing going on. I don't know how to make you understand or believe me when I tell you that there's nothing. Baby, you don't have anything to worry about. There's nothing going on, and there's nothing I need to tell you. Please, Xavier, please. Please, drop this."

Xavier put the car in reverse and turned to look at Jessie dead in her eyes and said, "Okay, then. Enough said. But I think I need to put my foot down on this shit here."

"Oh my god. What now! What are you talking about?" Jessie asked as she turned to look at Xavier and threw her hands up.

Xavier backed the car up and told her, "When you need to keep Meli, I want you to keep her at our place. I don't want you coming back over here. That's all I'm going to say."

"Xavier, I'm not even going there with you. Meli is my goddaughter, and she needs me."

"She can need you at home. I'm done talking about it. Done! And I mean it."

Jessie had never seen Xavier like this, and she quickly let it go, telling herself, *Girl, he's mad at you.* She turned to look outside her window and then turned back to look at Xavier one more time before shifting her attention back to the world outside, thinking, *God, I wish I was out there instead of in here.*

Xavier drove in silence and kept his eyes on the road, but his mind kept replaying what had just happened; and he asked himself, *Did I just get punked? Did I let that nigga punk me? Should I have kicked his fucking ass? Is this bitch telling me the truth? Hell! Am I playing myself? Does she love that nigga?*

Xavier already knew the answer to that last question, and he wanted to see how long it was going to take her to realize it herself; and although he knew in his heart that she was lying, he was going to see how long she was going to play this game, keep up this damn charade. Tired of trying to come up with ways of holding on to what he knew he couldn't, Xavier just cleared his mind and turned on the radio.

"Oh my god, Xavier! Listen to him." Jessie thought this would be the perfect time to warm up the frigid air between her and Xavier, with an attempt at some niceties. "Who would have thought that our Brass would have turned his life around like this—and we're actually listening to him on the radio."

Jessie was still met with silence. Not knowing what to do or say, she retreated into her own little world and stared out the window and watched the world pass by and listened to Brass spin out one love song after another. Brass had the

Quiet Storm loaded with baby-making music, and it was not helping Jessie one bit. First, he played Luther and Dionne with "How Many Times Can We Say Goodbye." Then Stephanie and Teddy with "Feel the Fire." Next was Pebbles and Babyface with "Love Makes Things Happen." And now R.L. and Deborah Cox were driving it home with "We Can't Be Friends."

Jessie wanted to reach over and turn the radio off as images of Quentin filled her mind: his muscles, lips, butt, his thick dick pressed against her thigh. She could smell him on her lips, and she could still taste him. She listened to each song and felt each and every beat and heard every word, moan, and the hum of each lyric. As she listened, something overtook her—an epiphany of sorts. It was as though God was sending her a sign through the music. She sat frozen, glued to her seat, paralyzed; and the only thing she could feel were the tears that streamed down her face. Not knowing what to do, or even how to do it, she opened her mouth; but the words she wanted to speak wouldn't come out. Until she heard Brass's voice.

"This is your boy Brass coming to you on this lovely, star-filled night. And it's gotta be a full moon 'cause it's been proposal central up in here, y'all. See what that Brazilian brother by the name of Miguel de Souza done started? And the brothas are gettin' down with the get down. Go 'head, pimps! Now, we just heard 'He Proposed to Me' by the lovely Kelly Price, going out to Yolanda from William. Congratulations, you two, from all of us at K103.5. Wishing our pimp and pimpette the very, very best." He laughed.

"Yep, peeps. All kinda [beep] is happening in here tonight. Can somebody call in and tell a brotha what the [beep] is going on out there?" More laughter. "Jackie—that's our intern, y'all—said the brothas are finally steppin' up to the plate. Wait. Wait. Jackie is telling us that we have another caller with a proposal from the request line.

"Jackie? What's the request? Huh? What did you say? Oh, okay, folks. The next request comes from a caller requesting one helluva classic. Get ready, y'all. We're gonna put on that Willie Hutch singing 'I Choose You,' for . . . Jackie? Who's this for?"

Jackie ran into the booth and whispered in Brass's ear, which made him laugh. "You kidding me, right?"

Jackie joined in the laughter. "That's what he told me. I think he got played, and his voice sounded so familiar. It's like I've heard it before. I could have sworn it was . . . well, never mind."

"Stay right here, Jackie. Don't you go nowhere. K103.5, my girl Jackie has informed me that the caller wants to remain anonymous but says that he proposed tonight and . . . well, he didn't get no answer. Wassup with that? Y'all women keep crying for a good man; and then when one comes along and tries to do right by y'all, you get all quiet. What's that about? What's really going on,

K103.5? Dallas? My black peoples? I'ma leave y'all to think on that while we play Willie's song. So, without further ado, this goes out to that special lady that didn't say yes. Jackie? You mean she didn't say nothing?"

Jackie started laughing again. "That's what I heard, Brass. Nothing."

"Hold up. Before we put Willie on, let me go Natalie Cole on y'all a[beep]ses 'cause *I just need to talk to the ladies*, especially Ms. Don't Know How to Say Yes; and I hope you're listening. Gul! Don't you know how many sistas out there would kick some ass, including yours, to be in your shoes? So whoever you are, wherever you are, this man just wants you to know dat you're the one, and that he chooses you to be his wife. So listen to Willie, gul. If he can't change your mind, I don't know who or what can."

Jessie heard all of this and, embarrassed, slouched down in her seat, folded her arms, and stared straight ahead, thinking, *Oh my god, is he talking about Quentin? What am I going to do? Oh, God, please don't say my name—or Quentin's, for that matter. God, I hope Xavier doesn't put all this together.* Each second seemed like an hour, and Jessie couldn't wait to get out of the car. She was teetering on losing it, falling completely apart. And a few blocks away from the house, she did. She kept sniffling and sniffling; and soon, she was outright bawling when she heard Jazmine Sullivan's "In Love with Another Man" blare from the speakers.

She sobbed uncontrollably and, with a face covered with black mascara lines, reached into the glove compartment for her purse and blurted out, "Oh my god! Xavier, I'm so sorry. I'm so, so sorry." Talking and apologizing in between her sobbing, sniffling, and choking up, Jessie kept on saying, "I'll understand if you hate me. Really, I would. I'll understand, Xavier. And I know *sorry* is just a word, but I don't know what else to say. I'm in love, and it pains me because it's not with you."

Only blocks away from the house, Xavier was about to lose it himself. So he pulled over. Without saying a word, he reached across the armrest and pulled Jessie to him. He gave her a hug and then pulled back, looking her straight in the eye, and kindly wiped away the fresh tears falling down her face. He reached for and gently caressed her chin and then pulled her to him again, kissing her softly on the lips. He gave Jessie a small peck on the forehead and told her to drive home. He would walk. He just needed to breathe in some fresh air and clear his head. He opened the door and got out.

"Xavier?"

"Naw, Jessie. That's all right. No need to say anything. We all knew this was coming," said Xavier in a hurt voice as he leaned against the car and peered at Jessie, who looked confused. He turned to look at the oncoming traffic and said, "I just didn't think it would get here so fast."

Xavier closed the car door, looked back inside, and told Jessie to drive safe. He stood and watched Jessie crawl over the console, get herself situated, and pull off. He stood there, with his hands in his pockets, rocking back and forth, and watched Jessie head down the road until the car lights faded away in the distance. As she disappeared, it all hit him at once. She was gone, and it was hurting him, if not killing him, down to his core. He pulled out his cell phone and scrolled through the numbers, stopping at Brass's name. He hesitated for a while, and then finally called the number.

"Hello. X, is this you? Yo number's showing up on the caller ID, playa."

"Hey, Brass, man. Yah, it's X. How you doing, man? You on the air?"

"Nigga, you know I'm on the air." He laughed. "What's going on, man?"

"I just called you up to check on things. See what's going on with you."

"Yo, man . . . what's wrong with you? I can hear it all in your voice. Wassup, X?"

"I'm good, man. Hey, do your boy a favor."

"Now come on, X. You know me. That's gonna depend on the favor, homey. Wait! Hold on, X. Jackie's tellin' me Quentin and DK are on the other line. Jackie! Hey gul, put them through."

Brass got the 4-1-1 from Quentin and DK and felt a sharp pain in his gut. He felt the pain for his boy X and felt that he, at the very least, owed it to X to let him know what was going down at Baileys in the next hour or so; and he filled X in on every detail.

X said, "Damn. That's kinda fucked up, man. Real fucked up. But thanks for telling me."

"X? Sorry about that, man. What about that favor, yo? You still need it?"

Xavier said, "Yah, man. Can you play that song for me? You know the one." I need to hear it, man, because I'm thinking about doing something really stupid, man. But it's the right thing to do for some shit like this. I know it is, and I need to squash this."

"You not talking 'bout—"

"Yah, man, you know the song."

"Aw, shit. Naw! No, man. It's not like that, is it?"

"I'm afraid so, Brass. It's like that, man."

Brass said, "Damn, X. What are you thinking about doing, man? Hey! Listen to me. Don't do anything stupid, man!"

"Don't worry. I'm good. I just need to handle some business. About the favor: Play that song for me, man."

"Aiight, homey. Damn, I hate this for you, man. Really, I do. I got you on that favor, though. I'll put it on next—and hey, keep your head up, playa."

"I'm trying, man. I'm trying."

Xavier hung up the phone without saying good-bye and walked down the road a shattered and broken man. The woman he had held dear, put on a pedestal, thought was perfect for him, and himself for her, had left. She had left him in a world of hurt, and he knew that there was no getting her back.

She was gone; and Quentin was the brother who had caused it. As tears welled up in his eyes, rage swelled up in his mind; and he brought up K103.5's app on his smartphone; and Brass's voice spewed from the speakers and filled the nighttime air around him.

"K103.5, your boy Brass is coming to you in full effect tonight, y'all; and what a night it has been. Damn, Dallas, has it been a night! Peeps, I gotta let you know dat your boy just got two phone calls: One surprisingly good, and . . . well, hell, the other, a real, real bad one, y'all. With that being said, I need to put the remainder of our scheduled *Quiet Storm* program on pause. Yep! It's on the back burner 'cause I'll be bringing to you, *live*, a very special airing. Trust your boy on dis here, Dallas. Don't y'all go nowhere. Girls, call your girlfriends. Fellas, call your boys. This will be a *Quiet Storm* Dallas will not soon forget.

"First, though, I need to play this song and send it out to all the brothers— and you too, sisters—going through some pain tonight, especially for one of my homeboys. Dallas, my boy is in some real pain tonight, y'all. And what I'm about to say . . . this [beep] right here . . . it comes straight from the heart. So, wherever you are man, remember, it *will* get better. We all go through this type of hurt and pain, and who better to let us know and get us through than our man Lenny Williams. So check dis out, K103.5 listeners—and my boy. At the end of the song, what happens? You got it. Lenny belts out some beautiful and encouraging notes and words at the end. A new love comes into his life, and that love helps him to heal and get through the disappointment, loneliness, and hurt. Brothas and sistas, it may hurt like hell now; but always remember, love— the type dat will stay and never leave—will eventually come, if you let it. And trust—'cause I can testify to dis—when it comes, it will be oh so sweet."

Jessie listened to Brass as she drove and drove and drove—sometimes in circles. She just couldn't bring herself to drive to Xavier's place, let alone deal with their relationship woes when he eventually made it home; so she decided to just drive around, work things out, clear her head. As she listened to Brass's impromptu programming change, she wondered what in the world was going on and was about to call the station when she heard Brass dedicate Lenny Williams's "'Cause I Love You" to one of his boys. She knew it was for Xavier, and it pushed her to the breaking point; and she broke down completely. Tears streamed down her face as they never did before—not even for Melissa when she died. She didn't know if she could take any more. There was so much pain in her heart that she couldn't bear to listen to Brass or Lenny's velvety voice croon that classic song about hurt and love. It just made her heart sink even more; and it made her think about all the loves in her life who had disappointed her, left her, or did wrong by her and caused her so much grief and pain. She thought about her past loves: Marvin, Vince, and Gary; and she thought about Michael and how he had turned her world upside down. Now she was doing the same thing to Xavier. She began to cry uncontrollably, knowing she was the reason that someone else was going through the same kind of hurt and pain she all too often had to experience in her pursuit of finding sweet—if not true—love.

Not soon after those thoughts ran through her mind, her cell phone rang. Jessie looked down at the console, saw the number, and then anxiously answered the call. "Jessie speaking . . . hey you—" Before she could utter another word, the person on the other end of the line interrupted her, and her heart just about dropped to the floor. She screamed, "Oh my god! What! Lord, what's going on!"

Chapter 34

Say You Love Me

*J*essie hung up the car phone and sped down the road as though a thousand and one man-eating bats were inches away from the car's bumper. She kept dialing Quentin's number, over and over; but each call went unanswered. Frustrated, she cried out, "What's going on, dammit? Why isn't he picking up? Shit! Shit! Shit! Lord, Jesus, please help me!" In between her cursing, she cried; in between her crying, she prayed. She was going out of her mind—thinking all kinds of horrible, crazy thoughts. She kept wondering, *Has Xavier gone off the deep end? Oh my god, has he done something awful?* Jessie couldn't get Quentin's phone call out of her head; she carefully dissected every word of their conversation.

She remembered that he called out of the blue around 11:21 PM and said, "Jessie?" She had begun to answer, but before she could get out another word, Quentin blurted out, "Can you get down here? I'm at Bailey's. I think I'm in a real bad situation, Jess. I need you to—" Then there was a loud crash—it sounded like the phone hitting the floor or something—and the line went dead. No callback. No "Get here as soon as you can." No explanation of any kind. Nothing! Just a loud crash, followed by the dial-tone.

Completely out of her mind, Jessie pressed down on the gas pedal, damn near pressing it down to the floor, and sped through the streets of Dallas— trying her damnedest to get to Bailey's the soonest she could. She just didn't know what to think, and she asked herself, *Is it Xavier? DK? Malcolm? Oh my god, did Tracy do something to Malcolm? Naw . . . that crazy bitch wouldn't go that far. Is Magic all right? Wait. Why is Quentin down at Bailey's anyway? And where is Meli?* She wiped the tears from her eyes, hit the steering wheel, and yelled out, "Oh God! What in the world is going on? Lord, Jesus, please let everybody be all right."

As she approached Bailey's, her eyes grew big as plums, and her mouth dropped wide open, and stayed that way, as she turned onto a nearly deserted Bayou Street. She knew something was wrong because for a Saturday night outside of Bailey's, it wasn't the usual hustle and bustle she was accustomed to. There were no cars and no people; and the building was dark, almost pitch-black, which made her more concerned as she swerved into the parking lot and slammed on the brakes. She didn't think twice; she bolted out of the car and ran straight to Bailey's, not giving much thought to any danger that might be lurking behind its green doors.

When she got to the building, she noticed that one of the doors was partially open. She grabbed the handle, pulled it back just a little, and then quietly stood in the opening to see if she could make out or hear anything happening inside. When she couldn't, she closed her eyes, inhaled a lungful of air and then slowly exhaled, contemplating, *What on earth am I going to do now?* Her brain was processing thoughts a mile a minute; and images of Quentin lying on the floor, helpless and moaning in pain kept flashing in her mind. She was worried beyond belief and knew she couldn't stomach the sight of her baby lying hurt or lifeless somewhere. She mustered enough strength to pull the door open wide enough for her to stick her head inside and peer in. Her eyes went straight to a cell phone lying in a sliver of light, just a few feet away from the door. She pulled the door all the way open, expecting the worst scenario, and eased her way in. *What? Empty? He's not in here. Where is he?*

She began shaking something awful and then hesitantly bent down and picked up the phone. Nervously, she went through the call log to see whose phone it was. "No! No! No! No!" She threw her head back and put her hand to her heart in anguish. "Oh my god . . . it's Quentin's phone. Oh God, what's going on?" Her hand shook violently as she scrolled through the call log and noticed that she was the last person he had called. Then she saw that right before he had called her, there was an incoming call from Xavier.

Scared but determined to find the man she loved, she slowly, carefully, inched her way down the hall. It was dark, and she could barely make out anything in front of her. The hallway grew darker as she got farther. She turned on Quentin's cell phone to use as a flashlight; at the same time, she typed in *911* just in case she needed to hit Send to call for help. She wanted so badly to call out Quentin's name but knew that that probably wouldn't be a good idea, because for one, she wasn't sure if he was okay, and two, there was the scary possibility that something bad had happened, or was still going on.

Functioning on pure adrenaline, Jessie summoned the strength she needed and told herself that she was going to find the man she finally realized she loved and wanted. As she approached the dining room, she forgot about the four steps leading down to the dining area and tumbled straight down to the floor, landing flat on her behind. Before she could get up, let alone get her bearings, she heard footsteps heading her way; soon she felt the presence of someone standing over her. She started crawling backward, backing away from whoever it was. Then she felt a strong hand grab her underneath her arm. Then . . . she heard laughter.

"You okay, baby?" asked Quentin as he helped her up.

"Oh my god, Quentin! Are you all right? I mean . . . the phone call . . . it sounded so urgent, and then the phone . . . well, it went dead, and I couldn't reach you!"

"You found my phone? Got to admit—that was pretty clever, huh?"

Jessie didn't even realize what he had just said; she kept going on and on. "Boy, I was so worried. I couldn't reach you; and after that, I kept calling and calling and calling. Is everything okay?" She couldn't seem to stop running off at the mouth.

"Jess. Jess? Jessie!? Everything's okay. Calm down. Damn, girl."

Jessie paused, and then started up again, "Oh lord. I mean, I was going out of my mind trying to figure out what was going on. Why were you calling? Why did I need to come down to Bailey's? Were you okay? Are you sure you're—"

Quentin placed his index finger on Jessie's lips, and it was as though everything was orchestrated to start with him doing so. The lights came on, and the music began flowing from the speakers. Quentin pulled Jessie into his arms in a tight embrace. Jessie melted into him and quivered as his forehead softly met and rested against hers. She thought, *Oh my god, this man . . . this man.* And she moved her head down to nestle it in his chest, momentarily forgetting about what had led her to him in the first place.

He kissed the top of her head, and she looked up with a strange look on her face when she heard a familiar voice come through the speakers. Jessie looked at Quentin as if to ask, *What's going on?* He turned and pointed her to the stage, where Pat—with a big grin on her face—was standing with her arms outstretched, motioning for Jessie to come down, singing DeBarge's "Life Begins with You." Jessie's jaw dropped. She couldn't believe it. If she wasn't all cried out, she would have started boohooing again.

The stage was dimly lit, and Pat stood dead center, in a beautiful sequined black gown that sparkled underneath a gazillion tiny starry lights. And when she opened her mouth, two spotlights came on behind her and illuminated Sweets and V, who were also decked out in black and were just a-singing and tearing that song up in the background. Jessie was floored. She started jumping up and down. The "oh my god" look on her face said it all.

Pat said, "K103.5 *Quiet Storm* listeners, I'd like to invite you to a special and unforgettable event this evening—and it's happening right now. I'm here to celebrate a very special night, family. A night my dear, dear girlfriend will surely never forget. I'm standing here in a beautifully decorated Bailey's, and this song is dedicated to a special lady—my friend Jessie S. Harris. Come on down here, girlfriend! This is for you, Jessie, from Mr. Quentin Blakely. He told me to say it that way, girl, 'cause you know that ain't even me." Pat laughed, took a deep breath, and started singing:

> *You gave me joy and showed me just what love was all about,*
> *yes I found out.*
> *That I need, you near, to fill that empty space inside of me,*

it's very plain to see, that I need your love,
my life, begins, with you.

"Oh my god, Quentin, it's Pat . . . and V . . . and Sweets. Singing? With a band?"

Jessie watched and listened while Quentin stood behind her and firmly pressed his body against hers, his arms tightly wrapped around her waist. He nestled the side of his face against hers, closed his eyes, and said, "You feel good, baby." And he held her as tightly as he could. They stood there dancing in place and let Pat, V, and Sweets serenade them.

Quentin, keeping up with the beat, straddle-walked Jess to their decorated table in front of the stage, looking up into three smiling and singing faces. Jessie couldn't believe all this was happening, at least not to her, and thought, *Oh my god, this is so beautiful.* Only minutes before, she had felt as though she was at hell's doors; now, it was as though she was at heaven's gates. She touched her face in amazement as she looked down at a table decorated with a simple black tablecloth, with white-and-black-patterned china and pink rose petals strewn everywhere—even on the floor.

Quentin pulled out a chair, which was draped in a white chair cover with a black bow tied around the back; and Jessie quickly noticed a single-stemmed pink rose on the seat. She picked it up, closed her eyes, and took a big whiff and let out an equally big sigh. She felt a soft kiss on her cheek, opened her eyes, and screamed, "DK? WHAT ARE YOU DOING HERE, BABY BOY!?"

DK gave Jessie a big wink and gave Quentin some brotherly love, and then whispered in his ear, "Good luck, brother. We're all pulling for you." He walked up onstage, sat down on a stool surrounded by all kinds of equipment, and started talking into the mic.

"This is your boy, DK 'Love' Niles, and I'm bringing you some l-o-v-e tonight, from the restaurant definitely built on those four letters. We're here at Bailey's, y'all. A big shoutout to Malcolm and Bee, who"—he laughed, shaking his head—"emptied out the restaurant with admirable speed and efficiency. They made sure that this thing right here—this night of new beginnings—was gonna go down without a glitch for our lovely couple, Quentin Blakely and Jessie Harris. And what a lovely night it's going to be! A big thanks to all the patrons who graciously ended their dining experience early. Hope y'all enjoyed the free meal tonight; and next time, we also gotcha covered, compliments of K103.5 and Bailey's. Don't lose those rain checks, y'all. Brass? Man, can you hear me?"

"You're coming in loud and clear, DK. And welcome back to da *Quiet Storm.* It's been a while since you've been in da DJ's seat, ain't it, homey?"

"Yah, man, it has." DK let out a brief but hearty chuckle. "I tell you, man, being the new program director for K103.5 has kept your boy on lockdown, for real. But it's been an incredible journey, and it feels real good to be back in the DJ's seat for this one last time. And, K103.5, as the new program director, I'll be bringing you inspirational and real-world programming. Good times, y'all. And what a time it's going to be tonight, I assure you. You're going to love this one. And if this ain't reality radio at its best, I don't know what in the hell is."

"DK, who was that dat just finished singing? Sounded like our girl, Pat."

"Brass, man, you got it. That beautiful rendition of DeBarge's 'Life Begins with You' was sung by Ms. Pat Riley, formerly Pat Carter—the divorce is final, K103.5. She went back to her maiden name; and yes, Pastor Levine is right here by her side. Sorry, fellas. If you hear clapping, Brass, that's Pat clapping up a storm and giving her props to her sultry backup singers, Ms. V and Mr. Sweets. That's right, the infamous cousin duo from Sweet V's Beauty Shop—and they tore that song up, didn't they?

"And, Dallas, if you haven't figured it out by now, we're down here at Bailey's, where our boy Quentin Blakely, from the Brotherhood, is laying it all out for one of the divas from our first *Love Forum*. Yes, y'all, the diva is none other than our Jessie Harris. And some of y'all are probably saying, WHAT! *What happened to Dr. Houston?* Well, Ms. Harris and Dr. Houston are no longer an item." DK paused and sighed as he thought about X. And then he quickly picked up where he left off. "I think what you're about to hear—only on K103.5 here tonight—is the reason why. I'll be your host this evening, and what better way to bring love to our Dallas listeners than to bring it in full force. *Live*, that is, during this very special edition of K103.5's *Quiet Storm* with our man Brass."

As DK talked, Jessie listened and looked around and tried to piece everything together, even asking herself, *How did he pull all this together? Was this already planned? Naw, couldn't have been. Was he making the calls when he stood in the window at the house? What about the call from Xavier, what was that all about?* But Jessie wasn't in the right frame of mind to even come close to any answers. She was so overwhelmed with happy emotions that tears of joy eventually made their way out and flowed down her face. She couldn't help but wear a smile that was damn near as big as Texas.

The microphone let out a loud screeching noise, and DK said, "K103.5 family, sorry about that. Next we have a poem written by Quentin for Jessie, to be read by the infamous cousin duo, Ms. V and Sweets."

Sweets and V walked up to the microphone. "Okay, I believe we're ready, DK," V said. She looked up at the ceiling and let out a big "WHEW!" Then she looked down at Jessie and said, "Melissa told me, in my letter, that this day would come; and to tell you the truth, I had a hard time dealing with it. But now I see, thanks to my pumpkin, DK, that when you find love—whenever, wherever, and however it comes—it's really all that matters. And who wants to grow old alone? So I'm here—after midnight, I might add, girl—to help you celebrate this special day and read a poem written by Quentin, who you're all wrapped up with. I'm scared of you!" V started laughing. "And I have my beautiful cousin Sweets here to help me read this heartwarming poem entitled, 'When You Find Love, It's All That Matters.'"

V waved her hand in the air and snapped her fingers, as if to say, *Hello! I know that's right. Okay!* She reached for Sweets's hand and held it tight. She held it so tight Sweets yelled out, "Ms. V! Girl, if you don't loosen your grip on my hand—"

V laughed at Sweets, loosening her grip, and smiled down at Jessie. She began to read:

> *L-O-V-E, love. I finally found love, and my heart does wonderful and crazy things every time I think of it and think of you—and baby, it's a beautiful thing.*
>
> *Because of it, and because of you, I see the world through different eyes—and, baby, the world is a beautiful place.*
>
> *Not only can I see the beauty, but I can hear it too.*
>
> *Can you see the beauty, Jessie? Can you hear it? I can . . . simply because I'm in love.*
>
> *I'm in love, and nothing else matters.*

Sweets stepped up to the microphone and read his part:

> *Eternal whispers ring in my ear as I hear your soothing voice*
> *It comforts me, and I find joy in every word you speak.*

He hugged V, and together, they read,

> *L-O-V-E, love.*
> *Now that I found it, it's all I need*
> *And it's all that matters.*

"I hear you, Sweets," said V. And she continued:

> *"Love." It's a word filled with so many emotions and meanings.*
>
> *It's a word that so many of us want to feel, hear, and breathe with every fiber of our being, every fiber of our soul.*
>
> *And when we find it—when it's true love, that is—nothing else will matter.*
>
> *No one thing or no one, can touch or destroy it.*
>
> *It's real and beyond comprehension or explanation.*
>
> *And when it happens, the heart will know—like mine does at this very moment.*

And, girl, in my heart, I know this love, our love, has been divinely blessed and kissed with the breath of God.

Sweets looked at V, covered up the microphone, and said, "All right, bitch. That was *snatched!*" He let go of the microphone and fanned himself while looking at Quentin. "Whew, lawd! Go 'head, Mr. Quentin. Go 'head. I'm feelin' you on that! Lawd, that makes me wanna shonuff find some good love my own damn self—and I said good love. Hmph! Hmph! Hmph!" He looked down at his paper and began to read:

L-O-V-E, love. It's a word I've been avoiding for way too long.
Its four letters that can't even describe the way I feel at this moment.
The way I feel about this woman.
The woman who showed me love when I lost love.
The woman who stepped in and helped me
wade through life's confusing mess when no one else would.
Love. I found it in you, Jessie Harris
And with you in my world, nothing else matters.
My love, will you say you love me? Will you say you'll marry me?

Quentin turned to Jessie, looked deep into her eyes, and asked, "Jessie Harris, will you? Will you do me the honor? Will you be my wife?"

Jessie looked at Quentin, and tears welled up in her eyes. Her mouth started quivering, and her body was just a-shaking. She tried to speak but couldn't find the words; they wouldn't come out. Quentin held her head in his hands, wiped away her tears, and looked her deep in the eyes just as Pat began to sing an old Jennifer Holiday song—"Say You Love Me" —that was just right for the moment. Pat sang the song with a determination that would make anybody say "I love you," and Sweets and V backed her up with a power that not only confirmed that but also overwhelmed and shook the room with an intensity that sent chills down everyone's spine. Quentin stood up and lifted Jessie to her feet; grabbed her waist, pulling her to him; and planted kisses all over her face.

"All I want to hear—the only word I want to hear you say is *yes*. Show me how much you love me, baby. Jessie? Say yes."

Jessie looked around the room and thought, *wow! This man, after so many years of not being able to commit, is asking me to marry him—in front of God and all of our friends. And he pulled it all together with the help of the brothas. Now, how special is that?* She saw what brothers helping brothers could do and proudly looked around the room. She smiled as she looked at Malcolm and Bee behind the bar giving her the thumbs-up. She turned and saw Pastor Levine standing at Pat's side onstage, holding his hands out as if to ask, *So what's the answer?* Close by was V, standing behind DK, massaging his head; and both of them were looking at her as if to say, *Will you just say yes, girl.*

And although love was in the air and all around her, she wasn't quite sure what to say. Jessie was about to open her mouth and say, *Quentin, I just don't know.* But her voice fell silent, and her eyes went blank. She couldn't see or speak. It was as though she was having an out-of-body experience. Everything just disappeared in that flash of a moment; and all she could hear was a soft distant voice calling her name repeatedly: *Jessie . . . Jessie . . . Jessie.* It was a voice she hadn't heard in a long, long time. It was a voice she missed so, so much. It was Melissa.

Jessie could vaguely see her, but she felt her presence; and that voice, loud and obnoxious as usual, was coming in crystal clear. Melissa told her, "Say yes, sista girl. It's all right. I'm okay with it. It's all right, and I'm all right. He's the one. He's the one, Jessie. He's the one." Jessie, after hearing this, almost collapsed in Quentin's arms. As Melissa's presence faded away, Jessie could see Quentin looking at her, waiting for an answer. She could still hear Melissa's voice, although faint: "I'm all right. . . . I'm all right. . . . I'm all right."

And Jessie knew this was her sign. Her girlfriend had shown her the path to love, in every sense of the word; and she grabbed Quentin's face, kissed him, and whispered, "YES!"

"K103.5, I think all the cheering and clapping means a yes. DK, my man, did she say yes?"

"Brass, you heard right. It's official. Jessie Harris is now the future Mrs. Quentin Blakely."

"Oh snap! That's what I'm talking about. Hold up. Oh sh[beep]. All the station's phone lines are—what? Lit up, glowing bright red all ova da place. Dallas, y'all are definitely blowing 'em up!" Brass started laughing and coughing out loud. "Damn, Dallas! I mean, y'all are blowing dem up for real! DK? Man, you think we got time to take a couple of calls?"

DK looked at Jessie and Quentin and asked, "You guys down for taking a couple of calls from the K103.5 family?"

Quentin and Jessie looked at DK as if to say, *We don't think so.* But DK started gesturing to them to say yes.

Quentin said, "Well, okay, DK." And he looked at Jessie and asked, "That all right with you, baby?"

Jessie rolled her eyes and hesitantly answered, "Yah, I guess so."

"All right, then," said DK. "Brass? Man, who do we have first?"

"Ah, shucks now. We got Francine, a.k.a. Frenchie, on the line. Wassup, Frenchie? Shush! Before you even start, gul, what you got to say to our newly engaged couple?"

"Hey, Brass! Boy, you know you wrong for shushing me—what's that all about? Huh? Anyway, listen here. Now that Ms. Jessie—Mrs.-Quentin-Blakely-to-be now—is done with that fine-ass Dr. Houston, how about hooking a sista up with the doc's digits? Remember what Ms. Doretha said? She said I would marry a successful doctor. Who knows? Could be him. Oh, and I don't want to be rude—and your girl's no hater—so, hey, Jessie and Quentin, congratulations to both of you. Wishing you much joy and happiness."

Brass laughed out loud. "'Nuff said, Frenchie. The doc's number? Gul, you ain't even given my boy a chance to recover. We're hanging up with you, Frenchie."

"But wait, Brass!"

"Bye, Frenchie, we're on to da next caller. Okay, DK. I got a long-distance phone call waiting. Hello? Caller? You're on the air with your man Brass during this special edition of the *Quiet Storm*. What's your name, and where you calling from?"

"Hey, Brass. Boy, how you doing? Oh my god, I miss you guys so much."

"Darlene? Gul, how could I not recognize that sexy voice? How you doing, and how's Miguel?"

"We're here in Brazil listening to you crazy guys on the Internet. Where's my diva Jessie?"

Jessie ran up to the stage and stood behind DK, leaning against his back, and began talking into the mic.

"DARLENE! Girl, how are you? It's been weeks since we last talked. Girl, I'm so lonely without you here in Dallas. Hey, Miguel!"

"We're doing good. Marriage is good, his family is good; but this country—girl, Brazil is no joke. We'll talk about that later. Jessie, I'm so happy for you and Quentin. My goodness! Melissa said in my letter that this would happen, but I was like, *no way*. And look. Here we are."

In the background, everyone could hear Miguel telling Darlene in Spanish, "Darlene! Dile a Quentin y Jessie, felicitaciones y buena suerte en su viaje juntos."

"Girl, I hear Miguel in the background. What did he just say?" asked Jessie.

"He wanted me to tell you and Quentin, congratulations and good luck on your new journey together."

Jessie said, "Awwww! Thank you, Miguel." And she motioned to Quentin to come up onstage.

"Now, Jess, you must not know how we roll in Brazil. When we do something, girl, we do it grand. Grandé. I got you on the party line, diva. Hey girls, are you there?"

All of a sudden, a voice started singing: "Today, is the first day, of the rest of your life . . . 'cause you said yes (oh yes), I'll be your wife."

"Oh my god! DeDe? Girl, is that you?" asked Jessie.

"Congratulations, momma."

Jessie started laughing. "DeDe, girl, what are you doing?"

"Well, Britt called me saying something was about to go down at Bailey's. She heard it from Brass—girl, you know he can't hold water—and that it was going to be on the radio; so I tuned in on the Internet, conferenced her in, and called Darlene. We're so happy for you, momma. Hey, Quentin! You're mighty quiet, baby. Cat got your tongue?"

Quentin cleared his throat and said, "Naw. I'm just keeping mine in my mouth. You know. A man of few words, but thanks for calling in and wishing us well. It really means a lot."

"Oooh, no, you didn't go there with me. But, honey, I'm saved and redeemed. Halleluh! Your words cannot destroy me—they just make me stronger. Love you anyway, boo."

Everybody laughed at DeDe, including Malcolm; and they said in unison, "Halleluh!"

"Jessie? Can you hear me?"

"Britt? Girl, what are you doing?"

"Laying up here eating. You know, I never thought that I would be eating for two; but here I am, laying up here listening to all this comflama on the radio, girl."

"How is the little bundle of joy?" asked Jessie.

"Girl! Just moving around, kicking and causing all kinds of hell, just like his daddy. Lord, three more months to go."

Darlene spoke. "Well, we have to get off of this phone. You know, these international rates can kill a girl's cell phone minutes. DeDe and Britt, clap off, bi[beep]es. Hey, Pat, V, DK, Sweets, and Malcolm, love you, guys. Bye now."

Everyone said a collective "bye," and Brass came back on the air with the last caller.

"K103.5 family, this is your boy Brass bringing to the waves our last caller for the night. Yah, I know, I know, y'all want to know: What happened to Dr. Houston? And how did they break up? And so on, and so on; but y'all gone be surprised as to who our next caller is. Get ready, y'all. After the break, that is."

Jessie, after hearing Frenchie and Brass mention X's name, looked at Quentin and asked, "Quentin? On your phone . . . I was so worried, that I went through the call log, and I saw Xavier had called you. What was that all about? Is he all right?"

Quentin looked at Jessie, kissed her lips, and smiled as he nodded his head. "Yah. He's all right. That phone call shocked the shit out of me too. He said Brass told him what was going down at Bailey's, and that he called to do the right thing. He knew you loved me, and that it wasn't going to work between the two of you, so he said he was being his brother's keeper . . . being the best man he could be. He had my back and told me congratulations and wished you and me the best of luck. That was it. Shocked the hell out of me."

Hearing this made things worse for Jessie. She knew that Xavier was an all-around good man and that any woman would be lucky to have him; and for a brief moment, she looked at Quentin and thought to herself, *Am I truly drinking the right cup of black coffee?* Before she could take those thoughts any farther, she heard Brass come back with the next caller.

"Aiight, family. We're back in da house. Get ready, 'cause here we go." Brass started laughing and let out a loud "Whew-hoo!" Then he said, "Young lady, how are you doing this early Sunday morning?"

"Hello, dear. I'm blessed and highly favored this morning."

"MS. DORETHA!" shouted Jessie.

"Yes, dear. It's so good to hear your voice; and I'm so proud of you, Jessie. And you too, Mr. DK Niles. Dear, I'm just calling to say congratulations to you and Quentin. This is really joyous news to hear. Wonderful music to my ears."

In unison, Quentin and Jessie said, "Thank you, Ms. Doretha."

"And I want to share this with you, my children: With my congratulations, I want to let all of you know that with the announcement of this union, my work is complete. And most importantly, our Melissa has finally journeyed home. Yes, children, my sweet, sweet Melissa is finally at rest; and all of you—the divas and the brothas—are on the right path in life. And what a joyful life all of you have in front of you."

Pastor Levine looked at Pat with loving eyes and said, "Yes, indeed, Ms. Doretha. Yes, indeed."

Everyone said their thank-yous and good-byes to Ms. Doretha, and Pastor Levine told Pat that somebody needed to bless Quentin and Jessie's union. He walked up to DK's mic and hugged Jessie and Quentin. Then he cleared his throat. "Good evening, everyone. DK, Brass, divas, and brothers, and to our K103.5 listening audience, this is Pastor Richard Levine; and what a joyous occasion we have just had the privilege of witnessing. Hasn't it been joyous, y'all?"

You could hear Pat in the background answering, "Yes, Pastor. Just joyous. PREACH!" She motioned for the band to start playing softly, and then she started singing backup to "Say You Love Me." Sweets and V joined in.

"Quentin, and you too, Jessie: This comes from my heart—not only as a man of God but as a brother from the Brotherhood. And what a journey the Brotherhood has been on. Folks, I wish only the best for our new couple, and all the new couples here in Bailey's tonight. May God bestow love, joy, and happiness on each of our houses, especially on the house of Quentin Blakely and Jessie S. Harris."

As the music faded into just the sound of clapping and well-wishes, Brass's voice could be faintly heard in the background. "Well, well, what a joyous occasion indeed, Pastor. Indeed, man. Well, K103.5, it's time to get out of here; but before I do, I gotta play one last song. Dis goes out to everyone who's lost a love. To all my brothas, especially my boy X . . . wherever you are, man, I feel your pain. And to all my divas out dare, dis is my girl Whitney Houston singing 'Exhale.' That's that shoop, shoop song. And I gotta say, family, I want you to listen to the first four verses of this song. These are some powerful words to live by, y'all.

"And if you're wallowing in those relationship woes tonight, just *exhale*, family. Well, that's it for me, peeps. Have a good night, and here's wishing you peace and blessings from your boy, Brass. And again, congrats to Q (dats my boy Quentin) and Jessie (you go, go, go, baby gul). Britt, momma, your man's on his way home."

— The End —